HER LAST BREATH

An absolutely gripping crime thriller with a massive twist

CHARLIE GALLAGHER

JOFFE
BOOKS

Published 2018 by Joffe Books, London.

www.joffebooks.com

© Charlie Gallagher

ISBN-13: 978-1-78931-027-6

Author's Note

I am inspired by what I do and see in my day job as a
front-line police detective, though my books are entirely
fictional. I am aware that the police officers in my novels
are not always shown positively. They are human and they
make mistakes. This is sometimes the case in real life too,
but the vast majority of officers are honest and do a good
job in trying circumstances. From what I see on a daily
basis, the men and women who wear the uniform are
among the very finest, and I am proud to be part of one of
the best police forces in the world.

Charlie Gallagher

Chapter 1

Detective Inspector George Elms walked the corridor of Belmarsh Prison with a sense of trepidation. Visiting these places was always a strange experience and not just because he was responsible for condemning his fair share of men to a miserable existence in its grey-walled, ten-by-six-foot cells. The atmosphere was one of pent-up frustration. It hung heavily in the air, mingled with the visible, moving dust and the claustrophobic heat. You could taste it in the air. It got worse the deeper you got, the closer to the Category A prisoners — the 'lifers.' These men were in the high-security wing, destined never again to see the sun as free men. Some would hardly see another soul. It was one of these men that George was here to see today.

The last of the twelve security doors was the thickest of all. He offered his fingerprint. The panel beeped and flashed green. The door pushed open, but with some effort. Neither of the guards who had accompanied him this far offered him any assistance. Now he could see some cells on the other side. His presence seemed to attract movement that was just visible through the tiniest of peepholes, those that weren't covered over. It reminded him of beasts on the outside of a bull ring pushed up against the bars, snorting their disdain, running their hooves through the sand. Desperate to join the fight.

George was led away from the cells and down another long corridor. Numerous rooms were accessible off it with similar dimensions and layouts. The guards led him into the corner room, the last one before the corridor turned sharp right.

'You can wait here,' one said. He moved to leave. They were the first words George could recall from either of them.

'Don't suppose I could have a drink, could I?'

'Yeah,' the man grunted. 'I'll go get him one.'

It seemed he was the talkative one of the two. The remaining guard stood over him, too close for comfort. George could smell his sweat. He sat at the table like he had been told. He took in his surroundings. The walls were brick, painted in a two-tone, smooth grey. The floor was worn wood with rubber repairs where the damage was worse. The radiator was a solid loop of thick steel that pinged and groaned as it worked. It must have been a hundred degrees in there. There were a few magazines. The most recent was from the middle of last year — *Top Gear* magazine. George flicked through it idly. He had long since accepted the limitations of his police officer wage. A Porsche 911 was definitely outside of that. It was nearly fifteen minutes before his attention was drawn to noises at the door.

Henry Roberts was bigger than George was expecting, despite the brief listing his alias as 'The Bull.' As he stooped through the door, his hair fell over his face. He was dressed in a grey tracksuit and was perspiring heavily. His face ran with moisture, his grey, standard-issue track top had a darker stained crescent across the chest. Inmates could wear their own clothes if they wanted to — almost all did. Roberts would be more comfortable in some shorts maybe, a T-shirt certainly. His prison-issue black plimsolls were misshapen where his feet looked to be pushing out of them. He was a slimmer build than his description — the illness must have seen to that — but he still had broad shoulders and hands like shovels. His face was largely concealed by an unkempt beard. His hair too had grown long. It covered his ears and would also be covering the numerous tattoos George had read about that were on the top of his head and part of his neck. He was handcuffed, his hands hanging down in front of him. George had seen plenty of inmates when walking through the prison but Roberts was the first he had seen wearing cuffs. His face was gaunt, his cheeks looked sucked in behind the beard, and his eyes were ringed and deep in their sockets. George had only had a brief opportunity to look through the notes on Roberts, but his understanding was that he was not long for this world. When he moved to the seat in front of George, it looked like an effort. He coughed weakly and then grimaced as though it hurt. He covered his mouth with his hands. When he moved them to rest on the table the cuffs clunked. He looked at George. He looked unimpressed.

'You're the man they sent? The police *Malakh*?' Roberts's voice was deep, like it rumbled up from inside him. The prison guard reappeared with two plastic cups. He put them down on the table and backed away.

'I believe my rank is more commonly known as inspector.'

'A *Malakh* is a messenger sent from God. An angel, to use the more modern expression.'

'No god sent me. Sometimes chief inspectors can—'

'You are to be *my* messenger!' That voice now carried a strength that belied Roberts's fragile frame, a brief flashback to what he once was. He fell to coughing and took a while to recover.

'You might have the wrong end of the stick, mate. I got told to come because apparently you want to talk to

3

the police now. I can't think what we might need to hear from someone like you, but I'm here.'

'Mate?' Roberts grinned widely, showing uneven and yellowing teeth.

'Turn of phrase. Don't be expecting a Christmas card.'

'Someone like me?' Roberts sniffed. 'You know who I am then?'

'I know what you are.'

'And what is that?'

'What version do you want? The media, they generally call you a *monster*. Your defence team would have us believe you are mentally unwell with delusions of being some sort of god. The police profiler reckons you're an impotent virgin who probably had a thing for your own mother—'

'And what about you? What do you think I am?' Roberts leant forward just a little so the cuffs scraped the table. He tilted his head. His eyes were dark and intense.

'Well, we just met, so I can't talk about the impotency. I have to go on the facts that I know. You killed four people and it would have been five had your last victim not been stronger than you expected. So you're a murderer. You've offered no reason for the killings and you've no links to any of your victims. So I guess the media are on the right lines.'

'A monster then?' Roberts leant back and pressed his eyes shut. 'Do you believe in God, Inspector Elms?'

'I believe in hell. The way I read it, you might have a couple of weeks until you get to experience it first-hand.'

'So you do believe in God. You can't believe in hell without the existence of heaven also, right? So you will know that He will punish those who do not know God and do not obey His gospel. I know God, Inspector. I obey His words as they are written in the Bible. When my day comes, I will have nothing to fear.'

'I'm sure there's something in that bible of yours about how He'd get the hump if you killed someone. Am I right? I'm not sure I got the wording right there, but . . .'

'Murder? He would never approve of murder. But the Bible talks of mercy. He is the most merciful one. He sent His son to set people free. In some people the constraints can be less obvious.'

'That's what you did, was it? You set those girls free?'

'You cannot hope to understand. You have much to learn first.'

'Did you have something to tell me? I was told you needed to talk to someone and that you had something to say that might benefit the people whose lives you destroyed. That's the only reason I agreed to sit here and listen to your shit. If you have nothing to say then I have nothing to sit and listen to.'

'I have much to say, Inspector.'

George took a swig of the water. It was lukewarm and had a strange taste. Who knew where the guard had got it from. He finished it, though. The dusty air and the searing heat of the room had conspired to dry out his throat, and the sweat ran freely down his back. 'You get five more minutes of my time. And that's only if the next thing that comes out of your mouth is relevant.'

'I will tell you where the other two are.'

George fixed a stare back at those dark eyes. He tried to hide his reaction. 'The other two?' George didn't want to give Henry Roberts an inch. He didn't know much about him, not as much as he would normally have liked. He hadn't been given much notice. His chief inspector, John Whittaker, had called him late the day before and told him that he needed to visit a prisoner at a Category A prison in South East London. George had recognised the name *Henry Roberts* immediately, the subject of a well-publicised case from a few years back. But it had all taken place a long way from George's patch. The case had been handled by Herefordshire Police working closely with the

South Wales force. George's brief retold how young women had been disappearing on the English–Welsh border. The second of them was found in a shallow grave in the Forest of Dean. Her boyfriend became the third victim, found stabbed to death behind the wheel of his car, which was parked up in the confines of the forest. His girlfriend was assumed to have been snatched from the seat next to him and a manhunt ensued. From what George could tell, there had been little to go on. It was only when a potential fifth victim, a mountain biker separated from her party while fixing a puncture on a fire road in the forest, was approached by Roberts, that the police got their break. He had offered his assistance at first but, when she declined, he turned instantly angry, grabbed hold of her and dragged her towards his van. She was fit, athletic and determined. She got free and found help. Roberts had disappeared but she knew enough: details of his van, his distinctive build and booming voice, his hair shaved close to his scalp and the distinctive tattoo on the top of his head. Angel's Wings — the description that gave the suspect a name. The media gave him a name too: The Bull. She had done well to get away from a man 'built like a bull.'

Roberts was found and charged with the murder of four people and the attempted murder of a fifth. More than three years had passed since those charges were read in court and two of the bodies were still out there somewhere. Roberts had never made any confession nor issued so much as a word to law enforcement save a couple of rambling statements concocted by his legal team. George Elms was the first. Lucky him!

'There are two who still elude you, are there not? Detective Inspector Emma Rowe . . . a good detective . . . a pure soul. She spent a lot of time trying to convince me that I should talk to her about where their mortal remains were. But her position was always a moral one, that I should help the families find *closure*. That was her mistake.

The family should be delighted. Their daughters are with God now. I sent them to him.'

'So what position should she have taken?'

'She didn't have one at that time. That was her problem. There's no way you people could ever understand a man like me. You live in a world of black and white, right and wrong. Life is many different shades. There was nothing she could offer me.'

'And now there is?'

'I am dying, Inspector. You mentioned it already. My day of judgement is coming. When it arrives I wish to be looking out to sea.'

George laughed; he couldn't help it. 'And what? You think you stand a chance of a nice view in exchange for telling us what you did with those women? You really are wasting my time.'

'Black and white, right and wrong. Let me fill in the colour for you, Inspector. You should not be so quick to make your judgements.'

'You have a minute left.'

'You may know that I am a rich man. Old money, I suppose they call it. There's certainly a long history of land ownership in my family history. A family chosen by God. My father has been dead five years. My mother died a few weeks into my trial. The pressures were just too much — it was never fair, the way she was treated. I am the only heir. My estate is considerable — even by modern standards with those ghastly Russian oligarchs buying up much of our capital city.'

'And you think money makes a difference? It didn't count for much when you hired your legal team. Why would it now?'

'We now have a proposal for you — grounded in law and backed up by the European Commission of Human Rights — whereby I be allowed to die at a secure unit situated on the cliffs of Langthorne on the southernmost tip of the country. A prison transfer. It happens all of the time across the country.'

George was baffled. He had lived and worked in Langthorne for fifteen years. He had no knowledge of a secure unit, certainly nothing that could hold Category A prisoners. What was Roberts babbling about?

'There is no secure unit in Langthorne.'

'There is. I've built it.'

'You've wha—'

'Don't feel bad, Inspector. There is no way you could have known. My initial diagnosis came as part of my entrance into the penal system three years ago — that very first medical. The cancer was in the bowel at that point. Surgery removed it and I was told to expect a long and happy future.' Roberts raised his palms at his surroundings and smiled grimly. 'But I always knew that God wanted me by his side. He had summoned me. I endured their treatment — the chemotherapy. They said they had killed off any trace of cancer cells but I knew it would come back. There is nothing manmade that can stand up to the will of God. I instructed work to begin at Langthorne immediately. It is a large property on top of the cliffs looking out to sea. We used to holiday in the area when I was a child. As you know, Inspector, the view is nothing short of spectacular.'

'And you think you deserve to choose your view? To choose where you die? Did you give those people a choice? The ones who died at your hands? They say one of the girls was found in a stinking hole, being picked at by the wildlife. Why would any judge in the land consider any request that kept you from a high-walled cell with a plug in the middle to catch your bodily fluids when you finally stop contorting in pain? Your legal team have nothing. *You* have nothing. No wonder your team lodged an insanity plea — this request does nothing but add to that claim.'

Henry took his time to reply. 'I got to learn a little about the police, about your rank structures. Being an inspector must be a thankless and cheerless existence. You're not high enough to be shielded from the flak from the troops at the bottom, you're just right to take the flak from the more senior officers and you have no *real* influence at all. You're here as a pair of ears *Inspector* George Elms, nothing more. You *aspire* to be my Malakh. Your opinion is nothing to me. *You* are nothing to me. My proposal is already with your force, addressed to those who actually matter. You are required simply to add my desire to reveal the location of the missing remains. Now it would seem that *you* are wasting *my* time.' Roberts lurched to his feet and loomed over George. The prison guards both took a step closer, one at each shoulder. One of them looked a little panicked.

George did his best to appear indifferent. 'The problem with knowing nothing but a life with money is that you get very used to getting your own way. You're in prison, you're a murdering piece of scum and you will be tossed in whatever dark corner the judge has ordered. You will be forgotten about and then you will die. In pain and alone. Me, on the other hand . . . I'm now going to return to my life and my sea view and I won't be giving you another thought. Run along now, I'd like to get back in time to see the sun setting on the sea. It's quite spectacular this time of year.'

Henry lunged, his giant hands still trussed together. He stopped inches short of George's face. George stared him down. He didn't flinch. Henry's faced twisted into a smile.

'Shame,' George said, 'I was nearly able to add another charge to your rap sheet there.' He turned to address the prison guard who had hurriedly spoken into his radio and now had a hand on Henry's shoulder. 'Can you chuck this one back into his hole? We're done.' A third guard appeared. He had a boyish face that flushed red. He looked out of breath.

'See you soon, *Inspector*.' Henry stood back up straight and suppressed a cough. He allowed himself to be led away.

George was still furious when he made it back out. He had gone through the numerous security protocols in silence, desperate to go through the final door that led out into the sunshine. His car was parked a few hundred metres from the entrance. He sat in the driver's seat and rested his hand on the keys. Sweat still ran down his forehead. He snatched his hand away, scooped up the mobile phone that he had left in the compartment under the armrest and got out again. There was a row of shops nearby with a café among them. He walked in and ordered a mug of tea. The café was almost empty. It was nearly 11 a.m. He turned on his phone and it pinged with a message from 'MAJOR' — George's nickname for his boss, Chief Inspector John Whittaker, who had reached that rank in the army and seen action in Kuwait and Afghanistan. He was just a few years off retirement from the force now and he gave George the impression that he had half an eye on his plans to move to the sun in Cyprus when the time came. No doubt that was why George had been sent a hundred miles from their shared office space in Langthorne House Police Station to talk to some crackpot who fancied himself as God's right-hand man. George reckoned today was what was known in policing as a 'tick-box exercise.' Where the police have to complete certain tasks purely so they can say they have. The Major's message said simply, *Call me*.

George made it to a table where he began squashing his tea bag in its mug. His phone rang and the Major's name flashed up.

'Jesus, man. Give me a chance!' George grumbled before answering the phone. 'Major.'

'George, old boy! How the devil are you?'

'Funny you should mention the devil. I think I just met him.'

'More like God, I thought? I read a summary. That's right, isn't it? The man thinks he's God?'

'I think he sees himself as seated at his table at least. Thanks for this job. I assume I have just wasted a day so you didn't have to?'

'Well, what is the point of rank if you cannot abuse it, I always say?'

'I'll have to remember that one. What do you need from me? I assume some sort of report summarising the ramblings of our friend and then we can all get on with our lives?'

Whittaker hesitated before replying. 'Can you speak freely, George?'

George looked around the café. He was sat as far from anyone as was possible. He was pretty certain no one could hear him but it was a public place. He never trusted places he didn't know.

'Not really, Major. I stopped off for a cup of tea. The prison service were as accommodating as ever.'

'Good. I hoped as much. In that case you can just listen. There was a meeting this morning. It seems I wasn't in possession of quite the whole picture. Roberts's legal team have made a further approach. You know they have requested a move, somewhere that he can see out his final days?'

'Yeah, he said as much. Obviously I laughed in his face, Major. I assume your meeting was filled with much laughter too?' George was suddenly uncertain.

'Not so much. I mean my initial reaction was the same, but there are elements of this proposal that might have legs. It's with the Home Office, George. This runs high — as high as it gets.'

'Why would they even entertain it? We all know what the man is.'

'We do. But now the Home Office know what he can offer.'

'Money?'

'How did you guess?'

'But the message we would be sending . . .'

'It would appear there is a way of diluting that message, George. It's early days — nothing has been agreed. Look, what was discussed should not leave that meeting, but I see it as need to know. His proposal is that he funds his own end of life care. The secure unit that will house him is being built to a specification approved by the government. He pays the costs of that build, the wages of the staff and every other operating cost. And when he departs this world there is a state of the art, secure medical facility that the government can claim as a big win from Roberts.'

'A big win? What about how it looks when the world realises that a serial killer is getting special treatment?'

'That's one spin. There are plenty others. You know as well as I do that prisoners getting palliative care can be taken to hospital-'

'And most don't. Most never leave the hospital wing. They've got all the facilities they should need, why are we considering this at all?'

'I think you have to understand the pressures here. Roberts's legal team are breathing down everyone's necks. They're complaining daily about his medical care and they've been petitioning for hospital treatment since he was first diagnosed. They've already made it clear they will be launching legal proceedings if he dies in prison.'

'On what grounds?'

'Human Rights. And look, there won't be a breach to his rights, the prison services aren't doing anything wrong, but they could do without it. I think that's the point here – we all could. Everyone just wants this problem gone. This move might just suit us all.'

'Including Henry Roberts.'

'Yes, including him. Imagine if we do move him to a mainstream hospital. That'll be a huge operation. A man chained to a bed, five prison guards on overtime covering him twenty-four hours a day and the ward of a hospital largely cleared. It's a huge pain in everyone's arse, George and he's offering quite an alternative.'

'I still can't see it happening. It's not going to sit right with anyone, surely?'

'Well, it's not just the government who could be on board. There are a number of snouts in the trough, including our own police force. They have got wind that they can claim any costs that come from policing this venue directly back from Roberts's estate. Without any scrutiny on what those costs actually are.'

'A blank cheque?'

'Pretty much.'

'What costs? If this were to ever happen, the prison service would run the place, nursing staff would do what they do. What police costs?'

'Well, there's the part that could cause us all the grief. The part where we would need to be up to speed on the investigation that put Roberts in prison in the first place. We would need a good knowledge of the victims, who they were and more importantly who their families are. If they got wind of his movement, if anyone did, we could have a real situation on our hands.'

'You're talking like this could actually happen, Major? His message to me was about telling us where he buried the two missing bodies. He thinks he can use that as a bit more leverage.'

'Shit! Well, that is something. I know that was asked for as part of the negotiations. He obviously sees that as the final piece. Did he actually say *buried*?'

George peered around the café again and then lowered his voice further. 'Well, no. He didn't actually use the word *buried*. That's some assumption on my part.'

'Politics though, George . . . think about it. That would be quite a result. He's also laid out in his legal proposal that he will be refusing any further treatment that may prolong his life. So we need to consider that he is proposing to foot his own medical and security bill, sign over his estate to medical facilities across two counties, top up the coffers of a police force facing more and more cuts and give up the location of two victims, bringing closure to a case that still captures the media's imagination. There was a lot of pressure around this case. The victims were pretty, white, working-class young women. The public really cared.'

'Now you're talking like you think this will happen!'

'I'm talking like I don't want to be caught out if it does. We need to understand the risk from the victims' families. There's a lot of work to be done. I want to meet with the team up in Herefordshire who led the investigation sooner rather than later. That team may not know this is on the table. I don't think it will go down well.'

'Jesus! I imagine it won't. You said *need to know*. Why do I need to know any of this?'

'You're a detective, George and a bloody good one. What do you think?'

'And I was naïve enough to think I was just a pair of ears. Passing on what he told me. What more do you need?'

'We need to go to Wales. I've managed to find us some accommodation up there, a place called Symonds Yat. It suits our needs. It's the village where Roberts lived.'

'When?'

'Well, George, since I figured you're kinda half way there . . .'

'Now?'

'Ha! Don't be ridiculous! Not right now, George! Finish your tea first.'

Chapter 2

Symonds Yat, despite sounding like the most Welsh place George had ever heard of, turned out to be very much an English village. Bordering Wales, it lay among steep, dramatic hills with the River Wye slithering through its middle. The details of his rushed accommodation had come through via email. Symonds Yat was a small village; it had a campsite, a couple of pubs and a few businesses offering adventure on the River Wye or in the Forest of Dean, which finished where the village started. George passed plenty of B&Bs, but his accommodation was a house — a holiday let. Rather ominously, it could only be let for a week at a time. George considered that was the reason it was booked in the first place.

He parked on a raised gravel bank under signs that read *Wye View Villa*. He stepped out of his car into a pleasant evening. He was high up on one side of the valley and the sun was dipping low behind him, slashing the forest opposite in half. The bottom half was the dulled grey of the river and the brown of the muddy banks and tiled homes; the top half was a vivid green where the sun was still strong across the canopy of trees. It was breathtaking. George walked up a steep path and pushed at a low gate. The springs creaked and the gate crashed back against a rubber bung. He could hear a dog barking, small and yappy. It was getting closer. Suddenly it burst into sight — a Jack Russell. It stopped short and, barking incessantly, bared its teeth.

'Sharkey! SHARKEY! Sorry about him!' A woman's shrieking voice. She appeared from George's right in a faux leopard skin top over leggings. Her hair was dyed brown but showing its natural grey at the roots. She had a cigarette on the go and oversized sunglasses that covered most of her face. The dog ignored her completely. She nudged it with her foot. Its bark changed to a growl and its teeth stayed on display.

'Hopefully his bark is worse than his bite?' George said.

'He doesn't bite so much anymore.'

'Oh. Not so much, well that is a relief. Has he eaten tonight? He looks hungry is all.'

The woman laughed. 'Oh yeah, he's eaten all right. He won't leave me alone of an evening until he does. Hang on.' She bent down and picked him up. She tucked him under her arm. His growl seemed to worsen.

'You're renting Wye View, I assume?' She gestured at the house beyond George. He took the opportunity to look at it closely for the first time. It was a whitewashed semi-detached house split over three floors. The middle floor had a good-sized balcony. There was a wooden bench out front on a patch of gravel. It looked like the perfect place to sit and take in those incredible views.

'Yeah. I guess I am.'

'You sound surprised about it! You here on your own?'

'No. I have a . . . friend joining me later. I was thinking they might be here by now.' George wondered what she might think when a man who was as near as dammit sixty and still held himself like a sergeant major came marching to the door in his day suit. He thought fast. 'We like our hiking. Something we've always done, you know? It gets us away from the wives. I hear its good round here.'

'Ah, yes. We get a lot of hikers. Mountain bikers, too . . . climbers . . . kayakers. This was voted in the top ten places to visit for the outdoorsy-type in Britain.'

'Sounds ideal. So which one are you?'

'Me?'

'Yeah. Are you the hiker, the biker or the boat thing?'

'I'm the retiree. I sit and watch from up here. That's about as active as I get!'

'Sounds very sensible.'

'Well, nice to meet you er . . .'

'George.'

'George. I'm Valerie. I live here with Clive — he's my partner. Well, my latest one at least!' She chuckled, George joined in. 'This entrance bit here is communal. I try and keep hold of Sharkey best I can but he does like to come and see who's coming in. It's good for me, for security, like. But just shoo him away.'

Sharkey was still showing his teeth. George didn't fancy pushing his leg out towards them. 'I'll bear that in mind.'

'I assume you're here for the week then? Did you get the instructions when you booked? He leaves the key in the porch there. You should be able to just walk in. We're a very trusting bunch round here. We don't get any trouble, see. Just as well, the police are pretty useless!' She chuckled again. So did George. He walked to the house, leaving the woman remonstrating with Sharkey over where he had chosen to urinate.

The key was actually hanging in the door. George moved through it and into the big kitchen that was straight in front. There was a handwritten note welcoming him and offering a pint of milk in the fridge. There were also some neatly arranged leaflets for things to do in the area. George flicked through them: a beauty spot, a tin mine tour, guided forest walks, a steam railway and afternoon tea.

'Sounds like a cracking idea to me,' George said and he clicked the kettle on.

George walked his drink out to the front bench to make the most of the view. The swathe of light was now almost to the top of the treeline. Soon it would be dark. The email had said that they had meetings planned for the next morning. Whittaker had signed off by saying, *you might beat me by some distance as I have some loose ends to tie up before the trip*. George already knew his chief inspector well enough to interpret that statement. He reckoned he could expect him the next day — and he would most likely be late for any meeting. George finished his tea and freshened up. He found a local pub right on the banks of the river. He was back after a couple of pints and sure enough, the Major still hadn't materialised. At 11 p.m. he put the key in a pair of wellington boots in the porch and sent a message with its location before going to bed. He smiled to himself. The amount of times he had given security advice, telling people not to put a key under their mat or anywhere so damned obvious. Symonds Yat seemed like such a quiet, safe place, just as the neighbour had said. He hoped that was the case, it sounded like the local police weren't up to much.

Chapter 3

There! He'd caught a glimpse of her. He always got a flutter in his stomach when he found her. The station was busy — rush hour. The 07:20 to Ludlow was already idling on the platform with a low buzz, its doors hanging open. Men and women with their suits, briefcases and shined shoes stepped aboard, the girl among them. She was two carriages up from where he stood on the platform. But today he was going to get closer. Maybe even close enough to hear her voice. He imagined how she might sound: well-spoken, cheery. He imagined how she might smile when she saw him, how she might play with her hair, cross her legs towards him like he had read in the books. He licked his lips and boarded the train.

People were shuffling along, trying to find seats alone. Most of those already seated had headphones in or were already bent into newspapers or novels. As he moved through them they took no notice; they had no idea of who he was or why he was there. He pushed through the first set of doors which clattered shut behind him. It was a beautiful train: solid, made of real materials like wood and metal — part of the old stock. They would be replacing it soon. He had seen the new trains: all pointed noses, plastic, wipe-clean surfaces and automatic doors. Soulless. He was half way through the next carriage.

He could see her!

She was sitting down, facing his approach, and reading something on her phone. He walked into her carriage. There were a few vacant seats — one directly opposite her! He couldn't sit there, not yet. He would build up to that. She was on the left side, he moved to the right. He could still face her. He wasn't directly opposite but it was a good view. Perfect.

The train jerked as a gear was engaged. He heard a sharp whistle from outside. It prompted hurried movement on the platform through the window. A flustered-looking woman threw herself through the door. She was fat and her face was blotched red with exertion. He did nothing to hide his disgust, his lips turned up in a sneer. Her eyes met his and then snatched away immediately. She moved to a seat that faced away from him.

He turned back to the seated blonde. She always looked elegant, but today even more so. He ran his eyes over her. He started at the brilliant red heels, then took in her long legs. They were crossed, left over right, and gripped in black tights. She had on a smart black dress that was pulled tight across her thigh. The top of the dress cut in round the neck. She had a white blouse beneath with three buttons undone and a wide, red belt round her middle. Her hair was down today and tousled. Sometimes she wore it back in a single ponytail. Sometimes she straightened it. Tousled was his favourite. It showed off her hair the best. It was blonde, but had light and dark tones that mingled together. Her hair shuffled against her dress and cascaded over her breasts when she flicked the fringe out of her face. She smiled. Those beautiful blue eyes lit with humour behind black-rimmed glasses. Something on her phone was holding her attention, making her laugh. He felt a pang of jealousy — more than a pang, it was hard to control. He wanted to go over there and snatch the phone off her, then sit right opposite her and become the thing she was focused on, the thing she was smiling at.

Patience.

The train moved off. She peered out of the window momentarily and then her eyes dropped back to her phone screen. She had a bag between her ankles. She reached down and pulled out a white cable with headphones attached. She didn't normally listen to music. She huffed, suddenly annoyed. Her attention back to her phone. She lifted it to her ear.

'Hey, you okay?' she said.

The voice . . . there it was! Beautiful. Just as he had imagined. She giggled a little and her annoyance fell away immediately. She moved to tuck a long strand of blonde behind her ear. Maybe she was talking to a boy? A boy*friend* maybe. The pang was back, but it was stronger this time. It was more like a fury. It swept through him and he had to plant his feet on the ground so he wouldn't step over to her. He wanted to demand to know who it was and why she was talking into her phone rather than talking to him. She didn't even know he fucking *existed!* She would. Soon enough.

He closed his eyes. He thought that if he didn't watch those perfect lips smiling into the phone, forming words and giggling, a beautiful song sung to another; if he didn't see it, he could pretend that she was just talking out loud. Maybe she was! Maybe it was her way of giving him a message — if she was shy, perhaps? He listened closely.

'No, I can't tonight. I'm staying late at work for a social. Amy's been trying to organise one for ages and people keep letting her down. I said I would go tonight, even if no one else did . . . No, it won't be a late one, I'm back at work tomorrow morning, just a few drinks . . . It won't be anything like that! That was just the once. I'm just sorry you had to be there to see it . . . No, I won't! I'll be on the last train home. That's the problem with living out in the sticks see, you can't get back into *historic Ross-on-Wye* after 10 p.m.! They shut the gates . . . Yes, that's right. Okay then, I'll speak to you later. Sorry!'

The call ended. He still didn't open his eyes. His breathing had quickened, he was panicking under the surface. She was getting a later train. Tonight! This was his opportunity. The train would be quiet, dead quiet. She would be all his. If he *wanted* her! His mum always said to him *you can get anything you want. You just have to want it enough.* He wanted her enough but he wasn't ready. His mum was expecting him back and she couldn't look after herself. He'd made no arrangements to be home late. She knew he was out riding the trains today; he did it every day. But he was always back by six. Back in time for tea. Back on the busy commuter train. With her.

His routine was set in stone. Monday to Friday on the trains, out with her and home with her. Then cursing the weekends, wishing them away. There was that one fortnight where she hadn't been on the train. He'd got so worked up that the conductor had called him an ambulance for the next stop. They had given him oxygen, told him he was having a panic attack. He wasn't panicking — it wasn't that. It was his heart; it was bursting — he had needed to see her again! She did come back — three days later in a shorter skirt than normal and no tights. Her top half was a crisp, white blouse and tanned skin. Her hair was lighter and she had a new wristband. It had beads on a black strap. It looked handmade. He struggled to get it out of his mind that someone had made it for her, a holiday romance perhaps?

Finally, he opened his eyes. Her headphones were in. She was sat back in the seat, her eyes upwards, her head rocking with the gentle movement of the train. He looked at her exposed neck. It looked so soft, so smooth. He wanted it. He wanted his hand round it. He wanted to control her, to peer deep into those eyes, for her to do everything he told her to. And she would. He had known his day was coming for a long time. Maybe he *was* ready. He had been patient, waiting for the right time — and this was it, surely? She had been giving him all the signs. It was time.

Chapter 4

Dennis Coleman immediately looked hostile. He had opened his door just a crack, enough for George to make out one eye, a chubby cheek flushed red and a balding head with a swathe of brown hair.

'Dennis Coleman? I'm Detective Inspector George Elms.' He lifted his badge to eye height. It was the same width as the crack in the door. Dennis pulled the door open a little more. George could see he was in cargo shorts and a jumper that was tight over a protruding gut.

'Where's the badge from? Certainly isn't local. What is this?'

'You're right. Lennockshire.'

'Lennockshire?'

'The south coast. You can't miss it. If you end up in the sea you've gone too far.' George tried a smile. He did his best to look reassuring. 'If I was a betting man I would say that you were not expecting me.' There was no way he could have been; George had made a last-minute diversion. He took his badge away. Dennis looked him up and down for the third time.

'What do you want?'

'Just to talk to you. Nothing to worry about. The way I understand it one of your old problems has become my latest one.'

'What problem?'

'Henry Roberts.'

Dennis's reaction was instant. His eyes flared wide, and he inhaled sharply. 'He's in prison.'

'He is.'

'For the rest of his life.'

'He is.'

'So what's the problem?'

George made a show of looking around. Dennis Coleman lived in a tidy-looking bungalow dug into the hills of Ross-on-Wye. Every dwelling George had seen in this part of the world looked like it had started as a wrestle against nature. Everything was dug out. In Dennis's case he had noticed a sheer face of rock in the back garden that was easily visible from the road. It was like a permanent reminder from Mother Nature that he was living there with her permission. This particular excavation had five similar looking houses in a neat row.

'Do you mind if we maybe do this inside? I don't know your neighbours. Specifically I don't know how good their hearing is.'

Dennis still hesitated. He did one last scan of George and then stepped back.

'I still don't understand what you could need to talk to me about.'

'Thank you.' George stepped into the hallway. Dennis didn't move any further. There was no move through to the kitchen, no cheery offer to put the kettle on and definitely no move to the lounge for a soft seat. Dennis stood still in the middle of his hallway. The daylight was restricted where curtains were drawn in other parts of the house.

'I was hoping you might be able to tell me about him. I understand you were the detective sergeant at the time. You're listed as one of the main players actually—'

'In Roberts's case?'

'Yeah. I met him yesterday. We had a very brief chat. But I like to know a bit about people, you know? Knowledge is power an' all that.'

'Why are you even talking to him? He's in the prison system. We did our bit.'

George was thinking fast. He hadn't expected to be met with such suspicion so soon. Dealings with police officers were usually simple. Coppers liked to help coppers and they rarely needed preliminaries. George still hadn't caught up with John Whittaker. He had no idea how much he should be revealing. 'He's in a high-security lockup down in my patch. I think you put him there, so I'm sure you were aware of that already. I work with the prisons quite closely and we're running a pilot down south along with Probation. We found that we were getting criminals who were being released having been influenced or inspired by other prisoners when they were inside. I think some of these lifers have got nothing better to do than to play mind games with other people in there.'

'Roberts is talking with other prisoners? He should be in solitary surely? Or at least limited to other cons with the same sentence.'

'I agree.'

'So why isn't that happening?'

'I think his contact is limited. The pilot was more set up for terrorist offenders. There was concern that some cons were being radicalised in prison. We had a couple convert to Islam and then get involved in plotting terror attacks when they got out. Some white supremacists too — with the same end game. But Henry Roberts is such a high-profile prisoner that he has a bit of a following. I think some of the younger lags may even admire him.'

'Jesus. It's a sick world. But the easiest way is just to stick him in a cell and close the hatch. I heard they were talking about appealing again, to get him moved to a secure hospital. From what I know about them places, he'd be worse off at a luxury hotel. He needs to stay where he is. Or in some stinking hole somewhere.'

'Again, I agree entirely. But if they don't do that I need to know a bit of what you know. I want to limit his influence as best I can. I think you can help.'

'I thought I knew evil, boss . . .' Dennis flailed.

'*George*. Just George is fine.'

'George. I thought I knew evil. You know, when you start this job you very quickly have to confront things. People stabbing people, raping people — murdering people. I've seen all that. It never really bothered me. I mean, you have the shock value the first time over, right? We all get that. But I got numb to it.'

'We have to.'

'I wasn't numb to Henry Roberts. That man, he got underneath my skin, George. He gets inside your soul. I thought I had seen evil — I hadn't. You deal with these murders — victims shot, stabbed, beaten to death. Run down with a car, I once had. But there was always a reason. A jilted husband, a running feud, a pub fight. Roberts doesn't need a reason. He just wants to hurt people.'

'I like him more already.'

'You know what he did, right? To that girl?'

'No, actually. I mean, beyond the fact that he killed her. I read something about burns being found on the body, but the actual cause of death wasn't in the briefing I got.'

'She had burns, yeah. The one we did find.'

'And that was the cause of death?'

'You should know. If you're part of this, if you're dealing with this then how come you don't know?' Dennis's voice carried anger again.

George shrugged, 'I can't tell you much more I'm afraid, Dennis. I got sent down here to find out what I could. I get the impression there is a lot about this fella that's need-to-know.'

'We all signed something. Something that said we wouldn't talk about it.'

'For this case specifically? We all sign the Official Secrets Act, Dennis. You mean when you walked away?'

'No. When he was charged we all signed it. We agreed not to talk about this case. About the deaths. About what we knew. If you're here just to find out about that then you're wasting your time. You're not press, are you? You know impersonating the police is a criminal offence, right?'

'Blimey, Dennis! Of course I do. I'm not here to lie to you, mate. Let me tell you what's happened here — the way I see it at least. I got a call yesterday from my chief inspector. I was at home. He tells me that he needs me to do a prison visit to get a feel for a prisoner as part of working out the influence he might have on other prisoners. I come out from the prison and give him a call, and he suggests I come up here to learn a bit more about him. I get no guidance on how that's supposed to happen, who I should talk to — nothing. I get a list of a few names of people that were involved. You're one of them. I can go if you want, Dennis. I'm not here to piss you off and I'm definitely not here to impersonate anyone else! I don't need any information on what happened to those girls, I've got other people on my list. I can't help but feel like I've been stitched-up a bit here! I'm unprepared and a little out of my depth and I just want to find out what I can. That's it really. If you can help, great, if you can't I'll go back with whatever I have.'

Dennis was studying him closely. He stayed silent so long it was almost uncomfortable. 'She was nineteen years old. The girl we found. She was burnt, yeah, that was part of what happened to that girl. But not all of it. I can't talk about what happened. All I can say is, it's some ancient thing I'd never heard of, cracking open heads to let demons out type stuff. Henry Roberts was playing God with their lives. And I'm certain he enjoyed every second of it.'

'Sounds horrific.'

'When they sat us down and made us sign to say we would never talk about it, I was relieved. I never want to talk about it. I've never said it out loud. I went through a real dip after it all. I didn't handle it very well. You're not dealing with a normal man. He is outside of humanity. Don't ever lose sight of that. I spent a lot of time in the same room as him. I know you've met him. He might not have talked to me but he didn't need to. Those black eyes . . . there's nothing there but hate.'

'We didn't get on. I'll tell you that much.'

'I don't know what's going on down there but you can't have him out in the general prison population. Not even for a second. He's a big man. He has charisma. He could have an influence. I don't know how much and I'm not saying he has the will or the ability to create another like him, but even if someone had a tenth of his evil rub off on them . . . I mean, you'd have a real problem there.'

'Sounds like it. Sounds like you did a great job getting him off the street, too, Dennis.'

'It was my last job.'

'You're retired?'

'I wasn't due to. I had eight years left when I started on that case and just five to do when I finished it. After the court case, I walked. I did try to go back to work. I lasted another few days but . . . I just lost it, you know? It was a tough time. The force did their best to get me back on the level but I couldn't get past it. What that man did. That there is that much evil in the world, George . . . I had my eyes opened. Suddenly I felt like there was nothing I could do to combat evil like that. For a police officer that's not something you can work through. I was scared of my own shadow for a while. I'm still trying to get past it. Once you get to that point, there's no way back. I just want to stay here and pretend it doesn't exist. It cost me forty grand of my pension and a wife.'

'It does, though — exist, I mean. And it needs people like you and me to cage it. Imagine if there was no you, Dennis. If you hadn't done what you did. If Roberts was still out there now.'

'We wouldn't have stood a chance. We got lucky as it was. Somehow his last victim got away. She was some athlete, a pro-biker. He got confident picking on her and it was a mistake.'

'And what about him? Before all this I mean. I understand he is a man of means?'

'Of means? Money? More than a hundred million, I heard, but no one's really sure. The Roberts family are part of the history of this area. They've always had land, some had titles in the past. I think Henry might have had a title passed down. If so, he doesn't use it.'

'And he's the only heir?'

'He has a brother for sure, and I'd guess a fairly wide extended family who might have benefitted when his parents passed. They say a lot of the money was all offshore and buried in barely functioning companies and trusts. But Henry manipulated his dad and then worked on his mum. He made sure all other potential beneficiaries were written out. That was what I heard at least. Just him left at the end. Maybe it's another example of his hunger for power. He wanted control of the fortune, for his relatives to have to knock on his door and ask if they wanted money. Money is power. People bow down to it. Perhaps Henry saw that as a way of feeling more like a god.'

'Absolute power corrupts absolutely,' George mused.

'I prefer *evil bastard*. Some people are just born that way. You couldn't man-make a Henry Roberts. He was forged in hell itself.'

'Now who sounds like the religious zealot?'

'You need to spend a little more time with him. You'll see, George. He's not to be messed with and he's not to be underestimated. If you came all the way up here for my advice be sure to take it back with you. This man has to stay locked up. Preferably in a windowless room. Evil like that . . . it can spread like wildfire. You can't let that happen.'

'Thanks. For your time, I mean. I'm sorry to drop in like this and to bring this all back to the fore. I didn't realise it had left such a lasting impact.'

'I loved my job. I always wanted to do it too. Good versus evil, right? Twenty-five years in, that man made me realise that good can never win. It can only hope to control. It sounds like you're a part of that now, George. Now we've got him locked up, you throw away that damned key.'

George stepped back out into the sunshine. The door clicked shut behind him with no further word and before George had had time to say his goodbyes. He walked back to his car. His phone had an email from Whittaker. He wasn't going to make it that day either. George was starting to accept that he wasn't going to make it at all.

'Another stitch-up!' George muttered. He took in another elevated view of the river. This one was from the other side of the valley, back to Symonds Yat and was every bit as breathtaking. He turned towards the bungalow he had just left. The curtains were all tightly pulled shut. It had to take some sort of evil to convince a man to shut himself away from such beauty.

Chapter 5

Mary Pope sat still and straight in her daughter's bedroom. She could hear the clock ticking in the hall downstairs, steady, unrelenting. Every tick had a slightly different tone. The sort of thing you wouldn't notice unless you sat and really listened. She knew that she sat in here too much, that it wasn't healthy. At first the counsellor had encouraged her to do so. He'd told her that it might help, that she should focus on the good times, the joy that Chloe had experienced in that room. She looked around it now. It was just as it had been left a little over three years before. The bed was as it had been made by Chloe, who had pulled the sheets roughly back and plumped the pillow so her mother wouldn't moan. Some dirty clothes were kicked under the bed, out of sight. No doubt she intended on dealing with them later, but Mary knew that she would have ended up finding them, tutting at her daughter's laziness and moving them to the wash bin that was no more than ten paces away.

Chloe Pope was just nineteen years old when she didn't come home. Close to finishing a gap year before going off to read medicine at Cardiff University. She was very bright, the cleverest the Popes had ever produced. She would have made a great doctor too. She was smart, dedicated and had real attention to detail but, above all else, she cared — too much. Mary lifted heavy eyes to the posters still clinging to the wall: Greenpeace, anti-fracking, the animal rights protest marches she had attended in London. Mary had always said to her that if she picked up too many of the world's problems they would start weighing her down. *You have to look after yourself before you can go and start sorting out everyone else's problems.* Chloe would just smile. Her dad said she had a big heart. He also told her that she needed to be careful. 'Such a big heart and caring for everyone,' he would say. 'Someday that heart might burst.'

Mary missed Chloe so much that *her* heart felt like bursting. Chloe had had a wonderful life ahead of her. Now it was gone. It had taken Mary a couple of years to accept that. She wouldn't listen to anyone who said that Chloe wasn't coming home. She held out hope that maybe she was off somewhere trying to make a difference in the world. Perhaps she'd slipped under the radar in case her parents wouldn't approve. Then she would walk back through the door and announce that she was on the run for criminal damage to a Japanese whaling vessel or something. Mary knew that the people around her believed for a long time that she was still waiting. They were worried about her, worried that she would never be able to let go. But in truth she knew from day dot that Chloe was gone, that her giant heart had been snuffed out. She and Chloe had had that precious mother-daughter bond, and she had felt it break.

Colin had seemed to take it better. Her husband was pragmatic. He talked about turning her bedroom into an office from which to run part of his business. He said that he might as well use the space to create something good. To Mary it sounded callous, like he wanted to paper over her memory. She could appreciate now that it was all part of his coping, part of his moving on, and that it needed to happen. The counselling had helped them both with that. It helped her understand that everyone was different and that Colin was hurting just as much as she was. Though she felt less alone, counselling could only get them so far, only stop the pain so much, only dress open wounds. What they really needed was for their daughter to be found. They needed someone to bury. *Closure.* She couldn't say how many times she had heard that word, how many people had told her how much better everything would be once she had it. Maybe they were right. Anything was better than how she felt now: lost and in limbo, her life frozen in time, like her daughter's belongings, while she stared out of the window at the distant trees, wondering if one of them marked Chloe's final resting place.

She could see the Forest of Dean from their window. In the early days, she had spent hours in that forest every day. She had been part of the search while she still clung to the hope that they still might find her daughter alive. Now, she couldn't set foot in there. She was still convinced that her daughter was in there somewhere but, over time, she became unable to cope with being surrounded by the trees. Now when she saw the shuffling branches or heard the chorus of raindrops tapping against the leaves she imagined what her daughter might have experienced — the last things. That other girl, the police said, had been killed where they found her. They were pretty sure of that. So Chloe was likely to have been killed in the woods too.

The knock on the door nearly sprung her off the bed. Her body was so tense. She didn't seem to be able to relax anymore. She was sitting at the bottom of Chloe's bed and could see through the open door into the landing. She wasn't expecting anyone. She couldn't remember her last visitor. When Chloe had first gone missing there were people here all the time. The police, well-wishers, neighbours, friends — her sister. They stopped coming a long time ago. Mary knew why, she knew she was difficult to be around. She had forgotten how to relax, how to smile, too.

The door thumped again. This time it was firmer.

Mary stood up and walked through to the bedroom at the front of the house. She could see a figure. He had stepped back from the front door and was looking right up at the window. She ducked quickly to one side.

'Mrs Pope?' The smaller window was open. The blinds shuffled in the same breeze that had carried his voice. She was rooted to the spot and her breath quickened. She hunted around the room for her phone. She would call Colin, tell him to come back. She wasn't very good on her own. He was out doing the shopping. He would only be ten minutes away.

'Mrs Pope . . . I'm Inspector George Elms. I'm a police officer. I'm sorry to bother you. I was hoping for just a few minutes of your time. You can stay up there if you like? Just shout down. Or you could throw something if you would rather? You'd have an easy shot from there. No eggs, though. I have an allergy.'

She froze. There were a few second of silence, then the voice started up again.

'. . . or cats! That's another allergy. They make my neck itch. Please don't throw your cat . . . or anyone else's cat.'

Mary moved back to the window. She looked down through the blinds. The man was still standing a few paces back from the house, looking up at the window. 'What do you want?' she managed. She was aware that her voice was weak. The man lifted his hand to his ear, she took it that he couldn't hear. 'What do you want?' she called out, louder this time.

'I bought some biscuits. There's a shop just down the way — you probably know that already. I've got nothing to drink them with, see? I wondered if you might be able to help?'

'What? What are you on about? Biscuits?' What was this man talking about?

'They're Jammie Dodgers. Or a version of, I think. They were cheap. There, I said it! They're not for you, anyway, Mrs Pope, if I'm honest. I was hoping you would give me five minutes of your time. Maybe a cup of tea. And I could eat the biscuits.' She could see a wallet with a glinting metal badge in its middle.

Mary walked down her stairs. The man was an outline through her front door. He was still standing away from the house. He had a packet of biscuits held up in one hand when she opened the door. His police badge was in the other. She didn't open it wide, she was ready to push it shut immediately. He kept his distance. Mary appreciated that. He was in a shirt and tie, formal trousers and a jacket. The tie hung low, his top button was undone. He had a warm smile.

'Have we met?'

'Well we have now.'

'Before though? I met a lot of police—'

'No. No we haven't met, Mrs Pope. I am DI George Elms. I'm from another force, down on the south coast. We're a bit late to the party but we now have some involvement with Henry Roberts and—'

'You don't speak his name! You don't speak his NAME!' Mary slammed the door. The glass rattled in the frame. Her legs nearly buckled under her and she struggled to breathe. She could feel the panic rising up; it threatened to consume her. She remembered what she had been told. She slammed her eyes shut and concentrated on her breathing. She got it back under control. It took her a little while, it always did. Maybe ten minutes. There hadn't been another sound from the other side of the door. The police inspector must have left. Tentatively she pulled the door back open. He was still there. He was sat on a wide tree stump, left over from when Colin had cut down a tree in their front garden. The policeman didn't say anything. He gave her time to speak.

'Sorry. I'm sorry,' she said.

'You don't need to be sorry, Mrs Pope. I do, however. I'm pretty sure no one has called ahead like I asked them to. I'm pretty sure you weren't expecting me and I'm pretty sure that Jammie Dodgers might have been the wrong choice.'

Mary burst into tears. She was so unpredictable these days, even she didn't see it coming. Relief maybe. The tension finding the quickest route out of her body. Her body shook suddenly, it was laughter now! She couldn't stop it. It took her over. She laughed hard, she couldn't suppress it. Mary gathered herself together. 'You must think I'm crazy,' she said eventually.

'Not at all.'

'I'm sorry.'

'Stop saying that. *I'm* sorry. Now, that's the last time either of us have to say it. Agreed?'

'Okay then.' She pushed the door open wider. The inspector stood up. Mary stepped away and into the kitchen. She was aware of him following her into the house. She heard him pull the door shut. 'You'll be needing a tea, then. To go with those Jammie Dodgers.'

'Oh. Well, if you're offering!'

'You're a cheeky one, I'll give you that.'

'I get called a lot of things in my own force, Mrs Pope. Cheeky is not the most common.'

'Mary — please, it's Mary.' She clicked the kettle on. Then she turned to face the inspector and leant back against the kitchen bench. She made sure her feet were firm on the ground, that she had a good base. 'Is this it then? Did you find her? Is that why you're here? Did you find Chloe?' Mary covered her mouth with her hand. She bit hard on her bottom lip.

'Oh no! I'm so sorry, Mary, that's not why I'm here.'

She took a moment to compose herself. She turned away and pulled two cups out. 'It's okay. It's just the first thing I think of. You know, every time I see a police officer. Every time the phone rings, or the door knocks. One day it will happen.'

'I think you're right,' he said.

'I know what you want to speak about. You said that your force has some involvement with that animal. He's rotting in a prison cell, I was assured of that, Inspector . . .'

'George.'

'George, sorry. I was assured of that. I was told he was living out his days in solitary. What involvement could you have?'

'Firstly, I should say you're right, Mary. He's locked up, he's in a cell and I would guess that most of that is in complete isolation. That's the way that animals like him are treated. It is not a nice environment from what I've seen. I haven't had much to do with him at any point, but my bosses have asked me to assist the prison service. It seems we have a mutual problem. There are concerns that he can still have limited access to other prisoners at certain times and through correspondence. We want to make sure that he can't have any influence on them.'

'Influence?'

'Yes. Animals like our subject, they get off on power. It is a big part of why they offend. It might be the main reason. When they are locked up, they still crave that power over others. One way they can still scratch that particular itch is to manipulate and influence people around them. I have been sent up here to get a good understanding of him. That way we are better prepared to stamp out any influence he might have. I was given a list of people to speak to up here — police officers mainly. I do have to be honest, Mary, you were not on the list. But how can you get an understanding of someone, of the impact they had, without speaking to the people affected the most?'

'I suppose you have a point. But I don't know what I can say about how you deal with him in prison. I mean, it's obvious to me, lock him up and throw away the key. Why should he ever have human contact again? I can never have contact with my Chloe. He did that.'

'I know that. And I agree, that's the easiest way, but there are human rights issues—'

'Oh to fuck with all that!' Mary's hand jerked to cover her mouth. 'Sorry, I'm so sorry . . .'

The inspector smiled broadly and he waved his hand. 'Don't even think about it. I was going to say I don't care about human rights — at least not in this instance. My opinion of someone like this is that they should lose all human rights the second they begin acting like an animal. But I am very conscious of his solicitors. They use that legislation on a daily basis to launch appeals and to generally try and make their clients' lives more comfortable. I don't want him to have a single comfort he isn't entitled to. Not a thing. To be sure of that I have to play my part.'

'Okay. I think I see. I don't think I could do your job.'

'You have to be able to see the bigger picture sometimes is all.'

'And not have a potty mouth. I never normally swear.' She still felt genuinely rattled by her own profanity.

'And I swear all the time. Far too much. Just because I see the bigger picture doesn't mean I have to fucking like it!'

Mary chuckled and pushed a cup of tea towards the inspector. She brought her own to her lips. She looked at George Elms over the top. He had day-old stubble and his shirt was a little wrinkled. He was handsome, though, and had a warm face and a calming manner. Mary felt like she could talk to him, like she could trust him. She knew she could be too quick to do that.

'What do you need to know, then?' She said.

'I don't know really. I didn't really come here with an agenda. I wanted to talk to you about how this has affected you, if you knew anything about the man who did it. Before, I mean. And if he was known in the village. Anything that might help me understand him better.'

'Well, I knew of his family. I think everyone did. Generally they've always kept themselves to themselves but they couldn't *not* be known. They lived in a big estate. You're always going to be interested in the gentry living in your village. My ex, he used to go to the shoot up there occasionally and I think Malcolm Roberts was often there too.'

'Malcolm?'

'He was the father. He was quite well liked. I mean, no one really knew him but a couple of times he helped out with a few community bits and pieces. He stepped in to finance a swimming bath that was facing closure. There were a few other things — he used to let the locals run a village fete and some fayres on his land. That sort of thing.'

'And the son. Did he carry on those traditions?'

'I don't believe so. Malcolm died a few years ago and the arrangements that were in place for the fete kept going. I don't know who sorted that, if they had to get permission or if it just carried on because it always had. Then, when the girls started going missing we asked for permission to search their land, you know. We were told it was no problem, the guy who managed the estate even joined the search party. I mean, we had no idea . . .'

'Why would you? He's an intelligent man. He didn't want to arouse any suspicion.'

'He was different, though. I knew that much.'

'Different how?'

'Different. They were a very traditional family. All privately educated, all went on to get good degrees at good universities. But the youngest son, he dropped out of school early, I think. He had a reputation for being rebellious. He spent a lot of time away from the village — in London, I heard. I hadn't seen him for a long time then, when I did see him again, he had tattoos and a shaved head. He looked anything other than gentry.'

'Do you know why there was such a change in him?'

'I don't know if there was. I think that he just got to the point where he couldn't live their way anymore. He obviously had something in him that was being suppressed up there. I saw him for the first time in a while around the same time as Chloe . . . well, around when she went missing. Of course no one made that link at the time. It wasn't until that brave girl fought him off and got away . . .' Mary inhaled a breath. She was holding up well, she couldn't talk like this normally. Certainly she couldn't talk about Chloe like this.

'She described his tattoos, right?'

'She did. She's some pro-biker, mountain bikes I think. She wasn't from around here but she managed to get a good look at a tattoo on the top of his head. Angel's wings. Of all the things . . . It went from there.'

'Did you get any reaction from the family? Have you ever had any correspondence with them?'

'Not really. It was dead quiet after the arrest. I was on to the police every day. I know they were doing their job and they couldn't make him talk about my Chloe . . . I know they wanted to. I got on well with Sergeant Coleman, but even he had to tell me to stop the calls at one point. I think I upset him. I know he was trying his best. He was just as frustrated as I was.'

'I've met DS Coleman . . . Dennis. Only briefly, mind. This case has really affected him, Mary. I think he would have done everything he could.'

'You spoke with him? I got told he had left the police. He used to live in the village. I know he moved away when all of this was going on. I heard his wife left him. I used to see her at church sometimes but she stopped going. I guess he was under a lot of pressure. They both were.'

41

'He told me he wasn't working for the police anymore.'

'He's okay though?'

'He seemed okay, sure.'

Mary took another swig of her tea. He was certainly easy to talk to but she was still considering how much she should share with him. 'I did go up there. To the manor house. After he was arrested, I went up there and knocked on their door.'

'At the family home?' He asked.

'Yes. I haven't told anyone. Not the police anyway. I can't get into trouble, can I?'

'Not for knocking on someone's door you can't.'

'She wouldn't come and see me. His mother. I thought I could get to talk to her. I thought I might be able to appeal to her to speak to him. To ask him to tell her where . . . where I need to look.'

'What happened?'

'She wouldn't even come to the door. She wouldn't speak to me. I think maybe she thought I was angry at her. I wasn't. I mean, I know I can't blame her for what happened. One of her staff told me to leave. They said they would call the police.'

'Did you try again?'

'No. She died a couple of weeks later. I felt terrible when I heard. I thought maybe it was all the stress. I guess I added to that.'

'You did what anyone would have done — her included, no doubt.'

'Thank you.'

The inspector suddenly seemed restless. 'I've taken up enough of your time, Mary,' he said. 'Thank you for talking to me. I will leave a phone number in case you have any questions. I'm not involved in the investigation up here so I can't help you with the search for Chloe. But I know what can happen . . . you get a visit out of the blue from a police officer asking questions and suddenly, a bit later on, you have more questions about why. Don't hesitate if you need to ask.'

'Thank you. My husband's due home a bit later. He may call. He's not always had a good relationship with the police. He's very angry, Inspector, and he doesn't handle it very well.'

'I can understand. There's nowhere for him to direct it. We don't mind bearing the brunt of that to an extent. It will get easier with time.'

'I've been told that enough times.'

'I can imagine you have. It sounds like people trying to appease you, I know. But there's truth in there. I'll leave the Jammie Dodgers, so you can tell your husband that we're not all bad!'

'I will do.'

The inspector walked across the hall and towards the door. She skipped ahead to get the door. She could see he was lingering on a cross she had on the wall.

'Do you still go to church? I know you said you saw the sergeant's wife there.' He asked.

'I lean on the church more so now than ever. I don't get there as much, for one reason or another. But it's become even more important in my life.'

'Did Chloe go too?'

'She did. From a very young age. They've always been very welcoming when it comes to children. It can be like a crèche at the back on a Sunday!' Mary chuckled. Memories suddenly flashed through her mind of Chloe as a toddler, crashing around at the back, making the congregation smile quietly to themselves and to one another. The vicar would raise his voice to deliver his sermon, thanking Chloe for her part. They would all laugh. No one ever minded. Even then Chloe seemed to have the knack for making a whole room smile.

'That's good. It must be a comfort to you. Knowing that Chloe had her faith.'

'She did. But I think it was being tested, Inspector. It's one of the things that bothered me straight after . . . well, when she went missing. She had stopped going to church. She wouldn't talk about why, either. She just got upset, like *angry* upset. I'd never really known her like that about anything before. Colin said it was just a teenage girl acting out about being forced to do something. I mean, we never actually *forced* her. I wanted us all to keep going — as a family. But I respected that she didn't want to go anymore. I only hope she found her faith again . . . at the end. I just hope . . .' Mary had held herself together well. She was losing it now. The tears fell thick and fast. They forced her to shut her eyes. She felt the inspector touch her on the shoulder. She opened up to him. He embraced her fully, she felt him wrap her up in his strong arms. She pushed her face into his chest. He smelt like fabric softener. His voice was gentle in her ear.

'It's okay, Mary. In those circumstances, under those stresses, we'd all find our faith. Even if we didn't have any at all before. He would have been with her and she would have known it.'

She backed away a little and sniffed. 'Thanks, Inspector. I'm so sorry.'

His warm smile was back. 'What did we say about that word?'

* * *

George made it back to his car. He was still shaking his head. He hated being so in the dark, so unprepared. He tried Whittaker's number again. Finally he picked up.

'George!'

'Where are you, Major?' George was aware that he sounded gruff. It was intentional.

'You know me and honesty, George — hand in glove. So, here goes. I'm in my office in Langthorne House. I had every intention of following you up, old boy, but things are moving down here. I've been in one meeting and out of the next. Now I need to go to London. You've caught me packing a change of pants as a matter of fact.'

'An overnighter?'

'God, I hope not!'

'So why the change of clothes?'

'Meeting the Home Secretary. We all know just how much she likes the police force, George. I can imagine it will be a very short, sharp meeting. And then the change of underpants will be required.'

'About Roberts? You still think they are considering his move?'

'Considering it? I think we have moved past that, George. Like I said, it's all moving rather quickly. I need you to pick up what you can about the victims and their families. We need to establish what threat there is that they might turn up on a Langthorne cliff top with lit torches and pitch forks. If this does go pear-shaped I will need more than a change of underpants.'

'How would it be your fault? Just tell them it's a bad idea. That this piece of shit deserves to rot in a hole and we can't police the threat. Job done.'

'Except he's offering them money and power. We both know that's all these people care about.'

'Then you need to be insistent.'

'It's like I said, George, his legal team are going to get him moved to a hospital, and soon. If he moves to this other place instead it saves the taxpayer coughing up for his medical care. Now he says he will divulge the location of the two missing women. That's a big political score. Add to that the government getting a cutting-edge secure medical facility that will be left when he goes *and* he's refusing all treatment — so he's basically agreeing to die. They're winning all round. They will be criticised, no doubt about that, but it's not a difficult one to turn back round. They would be criticised for treating him on tax payers' money as well and even more so if they had to pay an expensive legal battle after Roberts has gone.'

'You sound like you're starting to agree with it.'

'I sound just like you should: accepting. We need to look at the positives, George. When the senior team and the Home Office make a decision we don't get consulted, we just get told to make it happen. And trusted to make sure it doesn't get leaked.'

'You know that's exactly the reason I never wanted to get promoted. Ignorance is bliss, Major.'

'Very true, old boy. Can't say I'm disappointed that my retirement is creeping closer. Soon I get to pretend that none of this happens, that the people in charge only care about the people they were put there by.'

'I'll get the files on the victims and I'll head back. I'm only a few minutes from the police station. Your schedule has me in a meeting with Emma Rowe — she was the SIO for the job. I can't say I'm looking forward to it, Major. Not if she's anything like the other people I have spoken to up here.'

'I spoke to her on the phone. She seems very nice, actually. Have they given you the cold shoulder up there, old boy? You really did need me — someone with a bit of charm!'

'It's not that so much. You should see it up here. It's a little village with a little community and it has been all but destroyed. It's like they're locked in the grip of a shared nightmare. I just met some poor woman who is still waiting for her daughter to come home three years on. It's been hard, Major, especially as I've been lying to them all about why I'm here.'

'Finding those missing girls will go a long way to getting that village over this. We need to grit our teeth a little, George, take from this what we can. You can be involved in speaking to the families when it's done if you want to.'

'No, that's okay. I think the team that ran the investigation should give them the news. Assuming there is any. I'm not convinced he'll stick to his side of the bargain.'

'I think the terms are the point of this meeting. It will be airtight.'

'Sounds like it's all in hand. I'll go back to pretending it isn't going on. I'll be back later today.'

'Yeah, George, about that . . . I figured you could have another night up there. Have a night out on the company, you know? There's no need to rush back today. I won't be here anyway.'

'Out with it, Major.'

'Say again?'

'You need something else.'

'You made an impression, George. On a serial killer. I'm not sure how you should take that. Anyway, he's never spoken to us before. To the police, I mean. He spoke to you. You have the relationship, and he'll need to be told that we have an agreement.'

'I'm not doing it.'

'You might have to.'

'There are any number of people who could make themselves available to sit in a room with that piece of shit. Or just tell his solicitors.'

'He asked for you. In three years he has only ever said a few words and that was immediately after his arrest. He won't speak to anyone else. We just need to get this over the line. A warranted officer needs to witness him sign his name. That's it.'

'What do you mean, he won't speak to anyone else? I was sent because you couldn't make it. He was going to speak to whoever turned up yesterday. It just happened to be me!'

'And it still does.'

'Jesus, Major! He's asked for me because he wants to gloat. Because I pissed him off. He wants to see my face when I tell him.'

'You might be right, George, whatever. This isn't about pride — not for you — this is about doing your job. Get it done. You have an appointment tomorrow. I figured you could do it on your way back.'

'Because I'm half way there, right?'

'Exactly.'

George rubbed his face. He had been absorbed in his call but he looked left, towards the house he had just left. There was movement at the same top window. It would be Mary. Still stuck in limbo. Something needed to change for her.

'Fine. I'll tell him and then I'm out.'

'Thank you, George. I do appreciate it. While I have you, would you like me to pass anything on to the Home Secretary?'

'If she fired me, would I still have to sit in a room with that man tomorrow and watch him gloat?'

'Yes, George.'

'I see. Well, no then.'

Chapter 6

The 21:10 from Ludlow squealed as it came to a stop. The last train back to Hereford.

There was no sign of her!

He was panicking. He could feel it rising up in him again, just like before when it had gotten so bad he couldn't move. It was a more modern train than this morning. The doors all opened in unison. It was shorter than the commuter train. He could see all four of its carriages. There was some movement on the platform: an older woman who was already sat down reading a book when he got here and a middle-aged man with a backpack and hiking books, clutching a flask. They moved to board the train. He looked up at the clock. Every second clacked by loudly. Time moved on. Less than forty seconds and it was scheduled to leave.

Where was she?

Suddenly he heard the clicking and scraping of someone running in heels. *It was her!* She appeared to his right. She ran right past him and slowed to a walk as she approached the train. She stopped at the door. She looked a little unsteady as she reached out for a yellow pole. She pulled herself on. He followed her into the carriage. He flushed with a sense of relief and of excitement at the same time. He had to suppress a grin.

The two people he had seen on the platform were already on and settled. He stood in the doorway, waiting for her to choose a seat. She turned so she was facing in his direction. She lifted her right foot and tugged her shoe off. She threw it onto a seat with a table in front while she reached down for the left. She sighed loudly as she moved into the seat. She pushed her head back against the headrest. She had a layer of moisture on her forehead that was just visible in the light. Her fringe was sticking to it. She smiled to herself; it looked like relief.

He took his seat. His position was similar to the one he'd adopted that morning. He was at an angle to her, across the other side of the walkway. He could see her well. There were some other passengers who must have been on the train already, but not many. Maybe five in total in his carriage and they were dotted as far apart as they could get. He looked at them all in turn. They were all listening to music, reading books or magazines, or staring idly out of the window. No one was taking any notice of him.

The door fell shut. The train moved off. She had her eyes closed now. She might even be asleep. It was a forty-minute journey; there was plenty of time to get some rest. He couldn't rest, though. He couldn't even relax. He could feel the excitement building in him. He wanted to clap his hands and tell everyone that his day had finally come, that he was *so* ready. But he needed to be quiet. He needed to be invisible.

The forty minutes seemed to take an age. She woke up for the last fifteen minutes. She looked at her phone. She tutted as she jabbed at it impatiently and then threw it onto the table. The screen was dark. It had to be out of battery. She stretched as the train pulled up. He could see the place sign on the platform beyond her: LUDLOW was underlined in orange.

She picked up her shoes and walked onto the platform barefoot. He waited a few more seconds before he moved off the train. She was slower than the rest of the passengers, she pulled her suit jacket tighter, did up one of the buttons and folded her arms over her front. A bag hung off her forearm. She still looked a little unsteady. The train station was quiet and the lighting was poor. The other passengers dissipated into the surroundings. She walked out of the entrance and towards a car that was ticking over, its lights dipped. They lit up fully as she walked towards it.

A taxi! He hadn't considered that. She always walked to her car. She parked it in the streets nearby, wherever she could get a spot. She seemed to prefer Holgate Road, maybe because it was one of the few streets that were lit. She had parked there this morning. He'd never considered that she might not be driving home tonight. Of course she'd been out for drinks — *how could he be so stupid!*

He needed to think fast. She was at the car. He was close enough to hear voices, a rushed conversation through the passenger window. She moved to the back and tugged the door open. He reacted by jogging over himself. The driver looked at him. The window was still down. He hadn't considered what to say.

'Cooney?' He said, hurriedly, then cursed inwardly for giving his real name.

'No, mate. Sorry, I got my fare. Do you want me to see if someone's on the way?'

'Er, yeah, please. I called ahead.' He could see the sign on the roof carried the number and *Wye Taxis*. 'Wye Taxis, right?' he said.

'That's us. You say your name's Cooney? Where are you going?'

'Symonds Yat,' he said, hurriedly.

The man pulled his phone from where it was suckered to the front window. A woman's voice called out from the back.

'You're going to Symonds Yat?'

He leaned forward a little more. *She was looking right at him!* He couldn't speak. She was smiling at him, it was so beautiful. Perfection! All of those months watching her, seeing her talk to other people, smile at other people, and now she was smiling at him. She was looking right at him. She had spoken to *him*!

'Symonds Yat?' she said again. Her smile dropped away, she looked unsure.

'Yes, that's right. I get your train, you might have seen me about?'

She pursed her lips. 'No, I don't think so. But you don't see people on them things, do you? Do you want to share?'

He looked at the driver who had his phone in his hand. He shrugged. 'I'm dropping at Symonds Yat, mate, it don't matter to me how many.'

He straightened up. He stood still for a few seconds. He needed to. He was trying to calm his beating heart and his shallow, quick breaths. He felt like he might explode. He pulled the back door open. She was scooting over. Her dress rucked up a little on those long legs. She was smiling again. He tried to return it. He tried to look comfortable — normal even. He knew he wasn't good at that.

The car moved off. The interior was drenched in her scent: day-old perfume with a tinge of wine. He just wanted to breathe it in.

'How long have you lived in Symonds Yat?' she said.

He had to break out of his daydream. 'All my life,' he said. It sounded hurried; he took a breath.

'Really? I've only been there a couple of years. We moved there when I was sixteen. I remember being absolutely horrified. I mean, there's nothing there for a sixteen-year-old girl, right?'

'Oh, I don't know, really.'

'I suppose you don't! I mean, you've probably never been a sixteen-year-old girl!'

'No.'

She laughed. He couldn't. It was awkward. She moved to talk to the driver. He knew his opportunity for conversation was gone. It didn't matter. Soon he would have her full attention.

Chapter 7

Hereford Police Station was immediately familiar to George, despite him never having been there before. Police stations, it seemed, were built to a set template. It was a solid-looking, brick-built square with blue touches around the long, equidistant windows. It was elevated, built in the middle of an expanse of grass that dipped steeply down to the pavement. A man on a ride-on mower looked to be dicing with his own safety, clinging onto the steering wheel as the mower lurched sideways down the bank while he stuck to his lines. His expression was calm at least and it did nothing to unsettle the cigarette between his lips. George pulled into a visitor bay in a small car park at the front. He could see the main parking area for police vehicles behind a solid metal gate with security sensors for access.

The front counter staff gave knowing nods when he gave his name. They checked his ID and sat him down. In less than a minute a man walked up to the front counter and extended his hand. He had a tiny frame. His shirt was tucked into trousers that were sucked in, like he had no waist at all. His hair was receding around the edges. He looked cheery enough.

'You must be Inspector Elms? I'm DC South. I've been asked to come and collect you.'

'That's right. Hopefully you are expecting me.'

'Emma Rowe asked me to come down. She's the DI here for Major Crime. She seemed to know all about you.'

'Well, let's hope that isn't true.'

George was led to the stairs. It was two floors up.

'I don't like lifts.' DC South grinned over his shoulder as George tried to keep up with him. In contrast, George was a fan of anything that made life easier. He was still lagging behind when the detective pushed through into a meeting room where a number of faces turned to him instantly as he entered.

'You must be Inspector Elms?'

The voice had come from a sharp-looking woman in a black trouser suit. Much of her brown hair was swept up into a tight bun, leaving just enough to form a fringe. She stood at the front of the room, leaning on the back of a chair. She carried herself with authority. Her expression was stern.

'I am.'

'I'm Emma Rowe. Sit yourself down somewhere, George, and I'll be with you shortly. I know why you're here. The people in this room are generally those who were involved in the case. We can give you what you need. We're just running through what we have on today. Help yourself to the tea and biscuits.'

'Great, thanks.'

Emma looked back to where DC South sat with an open book filled with handwritten notes. He pushed his glasses onto his nose.

'Andy, where were we?'

George had clearly interrupted them. It was hardly his fault. He reached out for one of the tall thermos flasks in the middle of the table and pressed the pump. It squeaked and hissed as the hot water came out, and George felt very aware of himself. Someone pushed a plate of biscuits towards him. He decided he liked this police force.

'The stabbing incident at The Fox pub . . .' DI Rowe was back to business. 'Did we cover that?'

'Almost. So, a couple of lads who we know from the Hells Angels are in there. One of them gets into a bit of verbal with a random bloke, who leaves shortly after. The biker is then stabbed on his way out around an hour later. We have people there now trying to sort out the CCTV. Early indications are that there's nothing from inside.'

'Okay. So uniform are doing their bit with that. I see the CID DS has already set out the forensic strategy and it seems sound. I don't see us picking up that job unless he takes a turn for the worse. The last I heard it was a punctured lung, right?'

'Yes. Initially they thought it was life threatening but they've stabilised him now. He's not expected to die.'

'Fine. Is that about it?'

'That's about it.'

'So we have the rape job to close off today. I want that case file ready for court by the end of this week. I know it's only on the reserve list from Monday but we could still get caught out if we suddenly get a courtroom. We all know that the key to getting a rape case home is in the confidence of the prosecution. I want us ready. Over-prepared.'

'Yes, ma'am,' came a chorus of voices.

George swigged at his tea. He was positioned at the back, directly opposite Emma Rowe. There were five detectives at the table: three on his right, two on his left. They were all smartly dressed and they were all scribbling down notes. Most of them hadn't touched the biscuits. George was impressed. He reckoned Emma ran a tight ship.

'So, I mentioned it briefly, team . . . George Elms at the back there is from Lennockshire Police, all the way down on the south coast. George, did you want to tell the troops here what brings you all the way up here?'

Hell, no. That was the last thing he wanted to do. George leant back and did his best not to look like a rabbit caught in headlights.

'Yeah, sure. If I'm honest I'm not entirely sure what my home force would like me to achieve from this visit but we're running a bit of a pilot on our high-risk prisoners. One of them is Henry Roberts. He's in Belmarsh — put there by you good people, of course.' George took a second to survey the officers. They were all looking at him intently. Some shuffled in their seats. A solidly built man sat opposite him bit down on his cheek. George continued. 'We're concerned that he might have an influence on other prisoners — or just anyone he could communicate with, in fact. We want to make sure we have a good understanding of him and of what he did, so we can do our best to limit that influence.'

'And they sent you up here?' The solidly built man opposite fired the question. 'Could they not have just asked for the file?' This was the last thing George wanted: having to lie to a room full of detectives under questioning. These people were lied to for a living.

'They sent me up here to ask for the file. I think in the future we will just send an email request or pick up the phone, but this is brand new. I'm leading the pilot and Roberts is our prime subject of concern — our prime subject after those locked up for terrorist offences, at least. We've been running something similar around terrorists for a while. You'll appreciate that a terrorist who has a strong ideology will often seek to groom and radicalise from within his prison cell so that we have prisoners being released that are a far bigger danger to the community than when they first went in. Roberts is our first prisoner outside of terrorism who could be classed as somewhat similar. From what little I know, he was driven by a desire outside of normal criminal motivations. He didn't kill for money or any other obvious gain. His victims were random and murdered to appease his need to feel powerful. We must assume he still has that need and we're concerned that he might seek to create disciples to get his power fix.'

'Is he not in solitary then?' The question came from somewhere on George's right. He wasn't sure who.

'Yes — I mean, for most of the time. But he does get out into the general population. There are a number of reasons for that, I understand. Medical facilities are communal, some of the meals are communal — although mostly he eats alone in his cell. He is allowed to use the chapel as well — he still has rights around practicing his religion. I'm sure you have the same opinions as I do about his rights, but unfortunately the prison service has to do what the law dictates.'

Emma finally jumped in to save him. 'I have someone going over the material. I'm sure you can appreciate there is a lot of it, George. This was a very involved case. I have some stuff that you can take now, but the rest won't be ready for a few more days. I'm sure you understand that we are very busy. As I'm sure you are too.' George got the message loud and clear. This was a pain in their arse and they didn't want to be doing it in the first place.

'I can indeed. That's fine. Whatever you can do for me.'

'Right then, team, I think that's it. I'll be speaking with you all in the next day or two. You all have your jobs around this rape case, I just want to be sure we are on track. Any issues, you can come to me. Jane, you need to be running this as the disclosure officer, okay? I want to know if you're not getting what you need.'

The officers filed out. George stayed seated. Emma moved closer. She sat down and looked at him intently.

'Thanks again,' he said. 'I know what it's like when you're running a busy department and you get asked to look back over something you thought you had put to bed ages ago.'

Emma stared at him and bit down on her bottom lip. 'You're a good liar, George. I can see why they sent you up here.'

He couldn't help his surprised reaction. 'Say again?'

'What's going on with Roberts? *Really?* Because I don't buy the bumph you just gave to my team. Now . . . I understand need-to-know, I understand why *they* might not need to know the real reason for you driving two hundred miles to pick up a file, but *I* want to know. I *deserve* to know. I led that team through this. It was the worst episode of my career — all our careers, I would imagine. I lost two officers. Both quit on the day it was finished. Pretty much collapsed under the weight of it all. Is there an independent investigation? Is that why you're here? The first thing they do when they have a problem with an investigation is to get another force to review it, right? I mean, normally they go public too, they say that's what they're doing. But they don't always. Are we being investigated?'

'Jesus, no!'

'You're not lying to me now, George?'

'That was no lie. There's no investigation that I'm aware of.'

'So you were lying earlier.'

'You didn't give me much of a choice.'

Emma smiled. She stood up. The coffee flask was down the other end. She filled a cup and gestured at George.

'Sure, I'll have a refill.'

'I didn't give you much choice, you're right. Good leaders are transparent, George. I didn't want you coming up here, snooping through the files and leaving without so much as a word of explanation. I've seen that happen before. It sparks speculation. Speculation is always bad.'

'I'm not sure I've put a stop to the speculation, Emma. I don't think they believed me completely.'

'I'm sure you're right. But they will if I back you up. They will believe me. And they'll help in any way I ask, so that you get what you need.'

'So you want me to explain the real reason I'm here in exchange for the information I need?'

'The information is yours. I want you to tell me the real reason you are here out of respect. I want you to consider that you are back in Lennockshire and in your office. Consider that I walk in and ask you for the casefile on your career case. The one that damned near destroyed you, your team and your community. You'd want me to tell you why, right?'

'I would. I'd insist on it, in fact.'

'I'll top up these drinks. You can start whenever you like.'

George took a second. She was as sharp as her suit. George liked her. 'You should know right from the off that I'm being kept in the dark too. I certainly don't know everything. I got approached a couple of days back by my boss — who's a man I know and trust. He tells me to go to the prison to meet with an inmate. There's no real brief, just that the prisoner has asked to speak to the police. I was also asked to get a feel for him — whatever the hell that meant.'

'Sounds like a stitch-up already.'

'Exactly what I thought. The prisoner is Henry Roberts. A real nice fella is Henry. We didn't get on too well—'

'He did speak to you then?'

'He did. It seems there's something he wants. So now he'll speak to us. I understand he didn't speak to your lot at all?'

'*I don't murder people, I set them free*. Eight words I can never forget. It was his immediate reply when he was arrested. The only words he ever uttered. His defence team gave us a few statements that were definitely written by Roberts. It was all religious mumbo jumbo. Some crap about being God's disciple. They're all in the file.'

'He does seem to see himself as very special. But the crux of it is that he is not a well man — physically. He has stage-four cancer somewhere unpleasant. I don't know the details, but he's looking at a few weeks, maybe less, before he takes his rightful place in hell. He wants to die somewhere other than a Category A prison. Now, at this point you need to promise that you will stay calm. I'm just the messenger.'

Emma slopped the cups down on the table. She turned away from George to the window and pushed her fists tightly into the small of her back. 'Go on.'

'He wants a sea view.' George felt ridiculous just saying it out loud. He waited for a response.

Emma didn't give him one. Her attention seemed to be out of the window.

'I thought it was some sort of joke at first. But it now appears he has a strong chance of getting his move. I'm told he's a wealthy man. He's built a place in our patch. I live in a town called Langthorne and he's acquired land on the clifftop there. He's built a state-of-the-art medical facility to Home Office specification where he has asked to be allowed to go to die.'

Emma spun on her heels, strode over to George and loomed over him. 'Utterly ridiculous! The man's a killer and in prison!'

'He is. I know. I did what I was told and I reported back. I thought it was a tick-box exercise, some human rights crap. But there's more to it. He will sign the medical facility over to the government. It will be fully functioning for whatever use they can get out of it when he's gone. I know this stinks, Emma, but there are some positives.'

'Some positives? Positives are going to be a hard sell up here, George, I can assure you of that. The way you're talking, this is happening, isn't it?'

George shrugged. 'The Home Office are making that call ultimately. That's how high this goes. I've made the same assumption you have, though. I've spoken to the boss a couple of times and he's talking like it's a done deal.'

'Ridiculous! British justice! The press will tear us apart over this. *That* makes me angry too. Who do you think they'll call for comment when they hear about this development? It won't be the damned Home Office, I can tell you that! It'll be *me*. And no one's told me a damned thing about it.'

'I agree, Emma. What can I say? I totally agree. Personally, I think you should be part of the conversation around this. But my opinion doesn't matter to anyone.'

Emma shook her head. 'What positives? You said there were positives. Because right now I'm really struggling to think of anything that even comes close.'

'Roberts wants this badly. Part of his deal is that he tells us where the bodies of those two other girls are. I know that's going to be big up here. For you and for the families you worked with.'

Emma looked back to George for a second and then shook her head again. 'It won't soften the blow. Not if we have to tell those same families that he's been moved to his own luxury facility with a sea *fucking* view! What is this world we live in, George? Tell me that.'

'I really don't know sometimes, Emma. I really don't know. It's not about justice, that's for sure. I think this could be a big political score for the government. There's been a lot of pressure all round to find those bodies. I also know that my home force have a blank cheque to claim expenses for policing his transport and his time there. Your force might benefit too. And, the icing on the cake for the decision makers is that he is refusing any treatment beyond pain relief. He is basically agreeing to die.'

'Win-win then, right? Except this monster still gets to exert his power. That's what this is all about, right? For him at least. You said it yourself a few minutes ago . . . this man feeds off power. This is perfect for him. The only thing he has left to do is die and now he's managing to dictate how and where that happens.'

'I agree. I hate it.'

'Do we get to have any kind of opinion on this?'

'An opinion we get. An influence is far less likely. There's a meeting today. At the Home Office. I think a decision will be made today.'

'This is going to happen, isn't it? You don't meet there to talk about whether something happens, you meet to talk about how it happens. He's winning. Christ, George! He's getting his own way again!'

'I'm sorry. I'm in the middle of all this. It's not even been made clear to me how much of all this I should know, how much I can share, or what the hell I should be doing. The main concern from my bosses are the victims' families getting wind of the move and turning up in Langthorne with an axe to grind — or more likely to stick in Roberts's skull.'

'What about the media? Are they going to be told officially?'

'I don't know. I get the impression they'll be kept in the dark for now. I reckon there'll be more than a few people praying that this man dies pretty damned quick. Then the government will release it as a good news story. "The man's dead, he told us where the bodies of his victims were buried before he died and we got him to fund a brand-new medical facility that benefits us all." You can see how that could be very easily spun into a good news story.'

'I can. Bastard politicians! Someone should leak it.'

'As long as that someone isn't the person who has just been in a meeting with me and someone I wasn't supposed to tell in the first place.'

'I wonder if Herefordshire Police are even being represented at this meeting. We're a small force. We get walked on all over again. I saw it when the investigation was going on. They wanted to send officers from other counties down. We had to fight them off. I should have let them come. They could be having this shit now. They could be left feeling like this.'

'Look, Emma, I'm really sorry. You hit the nail on the head. This is a stitch-up for me. I had no real idea what I was getting involved in. I just need the case notes. Maybe a summary of the murders and then I can get out of your way. In fact, don't worry about the summary, I can piece it together from the file.'

'Oh, you can have your summary, George. Chloe Pope was the first girl to go missing. It was a standard missing person search at first — if you can call anything we do standard. We were told it was out of character, but girls at that age . . . well, you know. But then we found Josh Haines's body and his girlfriend, Ellie Smith, was missing. Ellie went missing on her twenty-third birthday. She went out for a meal with Josh at the Ferrie Inn in Symonds Yat. Josh was found in the driver's seat of his car early the next morning. He had been stabbed more than thirty times and his heart had been cut from his chest. The hearts of Ellie and her boyfriend were never found. We found an engagement ring box in his pocket. We didn't find a ring. Forensics would later put Roberts inside that car.

'The investigation moved on when we found the remains of a third girl, Lucy Moon. We know Henry Roberts murdered her. We also know that he made sure it was indescribably slow and painful. What was left of Lucy was buried at a beauty spot overlooking the River Wye. He marked the shallow grave with a large, wooden cross. Her remains were found by a hiker — or at least a portion of them was. It seems that some of the wildlife picked up on the smell and dragged her right thigh a couple of hundred metres away from the burial site. Henry was linked to that by DNA. She wasn't clothed when she was found, but her clothing was found nearby along with his . . . tools. The clothing was attributed to the body and had on it the DNA we needed from him. CSI reckon she might have put up a good fight at some point. Certainly she was very close to him for a period of time. He was either fighting her or raping her.

'With regard to how he selected his victims, the rail connections are a definite link. They were all local to Symonds Yat or the surrounding area. Lucy Moon was on her way home from work when she went missing. She used the train to commute back to Hereford. She disappeared between the train and her car. We have CCTV footage that shows Roberts as being on the same train. He was in the same carriage. He got off at the same time. He was a few metres behind her when the camera lost them.'

'So Chloe and Ellie are the two girls that are still missing?'

'Yes. And Josh Haines's heart. Lest we forget.'

'Jesus . . . it's strong evidence.'

'Strong enough to charge. Strong enough to convict. After a hell of a bun fight, mind. Roberts let it all play out. A team of very well-paid solicitors pulling every single minute detail apart, their client never uttering a word. There were other links though — more generic stuff. Some of it was circumstantial, but together it was enough to satisfy the jury. The team did some great work. We could link the murder tools to Roberts. The murdered girls were all from Symonds Yat and they all had daily routines that we believe he was able to take advantage of. We also did a lot of work on profiling the victims. We showed they were all around the same sort of age and they were all of the same type.'

'Type?'

'Young, slim and pretty. Attractive overall. And blonde hair. That seemed to be his thing. His last victim, the one who got away, was a pro-biker. Lucy Mackenzie — another Lucy, but she got far luckier than her namesake. She fought him off. She gave a good description of his vehicle and of him — specifically a distinctive tattoo. She also managed to scrape some of his DNA from his face. It matched and we had our man.'

Emma suddenly stiffened.

'So he wasn't known to the police before this? He just suddenly pops up and murders four people?'

Emma wasn't listening. She moved quickly to the door and pulled it open.

'Emma?'

'ANDY!' Emma called out across the floor. Andy South, the detective with no waist, appeared at the door. She ushered him in. The door closed behind him.

'You okay, ma'am?'

'Our missing person. From last night. Go again with the description.'

Andy was holding his day book. He flicked it open. 'This was from uniform patrol . . . *Annie Cox. Female, white British, twenty years old, slim, 5ft 8in, blue eyes, blonde hair.* Parents think she was wearing a grey suit jacket and a black dress. But they couldn't be sure.'

'Is she pretty?'

'The missing girl? We have her social media page out there if you want—'

'Is she pretty, Andy?'

Andy pursed his lips. 'She looks like a bit of a stunner to me, ma'am. Just don't tell my wife.'

'And she commutes, right?'

'She does. She was catching a later train. Uniform are doing some enquiries around her workmates. It looks like she had a drink and someone walked her to her train. She should have made it on but CCTV will confirm that.'

'Have we taken that on?'

'The missing person? Well, no. Do we suspect foul play?'

'Maybe assume we do — just until we make some headway.' Emma moved back to the door. She held it open. A clear sign the conversation was over.

'Am I missing something, ma'am? I know you want us all focused on prepping for the rape trial, is all.'

'I know. I just want to be sure that everything's being done. We don't need to take it on completely. Just stay in touch.'

'Understood.'

The door pushed shut and Emma looked back over at George.

'It's the same description as Roberts's victims,' George said.

'Exactly the same.'

'He's very much locked up. I saw him in prison. Yesterday.'

'You did. What was that you were saying about him influencing people?'

George wasn't sure. 'You're thinking copycat?'

'I don't know what I'm thinking. I know he's locked up. All this time and I still can't shake what he did from my mind. Maybe the two detectives who walked had the right   idea.'

Chapter 8

Liam Cooney sat on a wooden chair. It was rickety and smooth from when he had rubbed it down and painted it white. His mum had complained ever since that she would fall off it one day. It was the chair she used when she got out of bed. It took all of her effort to sit up, to put her legs out and to stand. She would use the chair for support. Sometimes she would have to sit in it for a few minutes while she got her breath back.

He stared at her now, lying in her bed. She was so still, so silent. He had sat there most of the night. Watching her. Her colour had changed. Quickly at first, but even now her pallor was getting greyer, as if the colour were still draining away. He kept going back over the events of the previous night in his mind. When he came in late she had complained immediately, saying that she couldn't move without him and that she was running low on oxygen. She was on a bottle downstairs in the lounge so she could watch *Midsomer Murders*. She liked that. Her machine was upstairs, it fed her through tubes tied off round the back of her head. Two prongs ran up into her nostrils, constantly feeding her oxygen, keeping her levels sufficient to stay alive. Without the machine, she couldn't last long. She had suffered with a chronic pulmonary disease almost all his life: emphysema or something similar. For as long as he could remember there had been people coming in to look after her — until, that was, he had turned eighteen. Then it was all down to him. He needed to be there a lot of the time and it got worse, to the point where she could hardly move around the house without him. She couldn't wash or use the toilet on her own. It wasn't right. No mother should live a life like that. No son should see his mother the way he did.

Last night he had been merciful. He had told her that. He closed his eyes. He could still picture her face when he said he was going to show her the mercy she deserved. He got her into bed. She waited for her oxygen, for him to move the tubes into position. He didn't. He told her that it was her time. He showed her the pillow he had bought specially. It was big and soft, white with pink flowers. She always liked pink flowers. She begged him not to. She didn't seem to understand. She told him she didn't want to die. She was so stressed. Her arms and legs thrashed a bit at first, but she was so weak. He held the pillow for longer than necessary. He had felt her life go. And then she wasn't stressed anymore.

Her face! He smiled now at the memory. When he lifted the pillow off, it was beautiful. She was so peaceful. She was free.

He couldn't wait to write. He sat down and typed out the words; he was descriptive — it felt good to remember the details. His typing was so clumsy; his hands were still shaking from the excitement. It felt so . . . *good*!

He remembered what he had learned, what he needed to do when it was done. He plugged the oxygen in and waited all night. The text took him hours to get right. He was careful. He knew it was early, he was supposed to wait until everything was ready. But he couldn't wait. The woman on the train . . . God put her next to him in that cab. It was time — he just *knew* it.

The police were prompt. He called 999 just after eight a.m. He checked his watch when they knocked; it was barely ten past. He answered the front door.

'You called an ambulance, son? They are on their way.' There were two police officers. The one who spoke had a sergeant's chevron on the front of his uniform. His name tag read *PS Alan KEMP* in big white letters.

'Come in! Can you help me?' He ran ahead. He bounded up the stairs, his heart still full of joy. He pushed the door open and stepped back. He wanted to see their faces when they saw what he had done. They moved in quickly and he moved in behind them. His mother was facing up. Her skin was still the same grey tone. Her lips purple in contrast. They caught your eye. One of the police officers put two fingers together, he pushed them into her neck. He stood over the other side of the bed. The officer looked up. His eyes ran over the oxygen machine — it was the size of a bedside cabinet but on wheels. Wires from it ran across the floor and chased up the bed. Then the officer looked at him sadly.

'I'm sorry, son. I don't think there's going to be much anyone can do.'

He threw his hands over his face. Both of them. He sobbed behind them. He felt a light touch on his shoulder. It was Sergeant Kemp. There was a shout from downstairs; the ambulance crew had arrived. They were shown in. He was led out. Someone made him a cup of tea. It was almost an hour before more people turned up. They wore black suits and they carried a stretcher up the stairs. Sergeant Kemp came down to see him. He spoke in a low, sad voice. He told him he was sorry. He said they were going to have to take her away now. He said he had taken her wedding ring off. He handed it over. It was a dull gold. He ran it over in his hands a few times. He didn't know what to do with it. He stuffed it into the front pocket of his hooded top.

He was still in the living room when the men in black suits walked back past. The stretcher was heavier now. It carried a long, black form on it. His mother. Finally she was at peace. She was *free*. His heart fluttered with excitement again, his hand fell to his back pocket, feeling for his phone. He would finish up and then send another update as soon as he could — for, truly, he was merciful!

Sergeant Kemp and all of the police officers left shortly after. The sergeant had asked a few questions while the other officer bagged up a lot of his mother's medication. They both said again how sorry they were. They shuffled uncomfortably from one foot to the other. He was given phone numbers to call if he needed to. Then they left. The silence was glorious. The machine that had hummed, gurgled and hissed as it constantly fed his mum with oxygen was silenced along with her constant dry cough and the rasping voice that he had come to so despise. There was nothing here now but the silence.

He made himself a hot drink and a sandwich, making sure he made an extra one and wrapping it in a sheet of greaseproof paper. He took a small bottle of water out of the fridge. He tidied up his cup and his plate. His mother had always hated it when he had left anything out. He slipped on his hiking boots and pulled open the back door. The sun felt warm. Spring was starting to assert itself. The garden was long and thin. There was a row of conifers halfway down; his dad had cut an arch in them before he died. His dad had liked the garden. It was a little overgrown now. His dad's shed was at the very bottom, past the old coal shed. On the other side of the lawn was a rough area of scorched earth where he liked to set fires. He unclipped a heavy padlock from the shed door and pulled it open. It wasn't large, but there had been enough room for his dad to use it a workshop. He had liked to work with wood and was a cabinet maker by trade. His lathe was silent and dusty now — just a home for spiders that scuttled from the sudden flood of light. He stepped in. To his right was the workbench, adapted from an old war-time Morrison shelter, it had a solid metal top and sturdy legs. It hadn't taken much to turn it into the perfect place to store a body. The work surface was hinged to act as a flip-open lid and this was secured with a padlock. He'd also found a solid, Victorian clothes iron in the shed and lifted this on top as extra weight. He closed the shed door and shut out the sun before switching on the light. He unclipped the padlock and heaved the iron from the bench lid. It flipped up.

'It's okay! They're gone!' he said. 'And they've taken her with them!'

The energy-saving bulb took a while to warm up to its full power and didn't quite reach into the depths of the box. His eyes were still adjusting. He heard a scuffling sound, then a murmur. Though he'd given her quite a dose she was now coming round. There was more light now and he could see her. She was lying on her side, her head turned towards the noise. She blinked at the light. Her beautiful blonde hair fell over her face. She smacked her lips and made a moaning sound. He reached in his pocket for the extra sandwich.

'Here. I brought you something to eat. And some water. You must be thirsty?'

She still couldn't form words; she sounded a little more distressed.

'It's okay. You can take it. I brought it just for you. And don't worry, no one will be coming back now. It's just you and me!'

She managed to half sit. Her body was still twisted towards him. He reached out to push the hair out of her eyes. She jerked violently at his touch. He could see her eyes now, the pupils were large black discs. That would be the sedative. He hadn't wanted to give her that. It seemed so cruel and demeaning to someone so perfect, to take away their consciousness in such a manner. But he needed control and he hadn't wanted to hurt her. He couldn't have explained that. She would never have listened. So he did what he had to do. Now he could take his time. He could make her see. She could understand better who he was and what he was doing. How he could set her free.

For now he unscrewed the water bottle and pushed it into her soft lips. 'Drink. It's just water.'

She reached for it. Those perfect lips pursed and hunted for the fluid. A little spilt down her chin and he wiped it gently away. Her skin was so soft. He would always be gentle with her. When the time came, he was going to take his time. He was going to be sure she was ready and that she knew what was coming so that she could savour it. She took hold of the bottle herself. She tipped it back and glugged at it until it was empty. She breathed out in a sigh. He held out the sandwich.

'Cheese and pickle,' he said. She reached out for this, too. Her eyes seemed a little more controlled; she seemed to focus on the food. She took a bite and he watched her intently: those lips; those eyes; the way her cheek dimpled slightly with every chew. She clearly was God's finest creation. Another few bites and the sandwich was devoured.

'I'll be back,' he said. 'Soon.' She was still sat up. He pushed the lid so it fell gently onto her arm. She made another noise as if she was unhappy. She was starting to become more lucid. Soon she would be able to talk. 'Move your arm,' he said. 'Move your arm out of the way. It's not time yet.' He leant on it. It didn't budge. Suddenly she made a louder noise, like a scream but it was guttural — as if she had no control. All her grace and beauty fell away. She sounded just like his mother.

'Move your arm!' he said. He pushed down on the lid. There was still resistance. The lid pushed up towards him. She was trying to get up, to get out! He lifted the lid. His right arm thrashed forward and his fist connected firmly with something solid. He glimpsed her hair whipping from her face as her head was thrown backwards. The lid fell shut.

He was breathing heavily as he sat on top of the lid, running his fingers over the solid metal. 'I don't want to hurt you. But you need to do as I say. Okay? OKAY?' He heard nothing. He pushed the bar back in and locked the padlock. This time he didn't notice how pleasant the sun was as he marched back up the garden and into the house.

Chapter 9

George had found St Dubricius's Parish church right on the banks of the Wye. The grassy churchyard was so close to the river that some of its randomly scattered tombstones almost threatened to topple into the water. He walked to the edge. The water was clear and it ran quickly, the current stretching out the reeds that clung fast to the floor. It was perhaps forty metres wide at this point. To his left the water lapped against a muddy flat; its levels were low. He turned back to the church.

He hadn't noticed any clear signs of life. There was one other car, a small Ford hatchback, but he had passed it a bit further up the road. His was the only one in the small, gravel car park.

George was surprised when the heavy wooden door pushed open. Where he was from, churches were locked more than they were open. The building opened up in front of him, as beautiful within as it was from outside. He pushed the door back shut.

'You can leave that open if you want!' a voice called out from the direction of the altar. George couldn't see the source at first, then a man came into view, about as casually dressed as a vicar ever got: corduroy trousers, a shirt with dog collar and a thin jumper. 'We should let in some of this lovely spring weather after the winter we've just had.'

George moved back to the door to pull it back open a little.

'I can imagine the winters are harsh around here.'

'That they are.' The vicar walked the length of the church and stopped a few metres short of him. He looked George up and down.

'I'm George Elms. I'm a police officer. There's nothing to worry about. I just wanted a quick chat if possible?'

'I know who you are. This is a very small village, Inspector. Talk to one, talk to all. I got told that on my first day here, twenty years ago. I've never forgotten it.'

'You're not from the village then?'

'Originally? No. A city boy. It's taken most of those twenty years to find my place here. People don't trust outsiders easily!'

'I'll bear that in mind.'

'And so I've heard a lot about you.'

'So you've heard I'm not to be trusted?'

'I've heard that no one really knows why you're here. Which means that whatever story you're selling isn't ringing true.'

'I see. Well, even I draw the line at lying to a man of the cloth.'

'I'm sure you do, Inspector.'

'Please, call me George.'

'Then I'm John. John Lawrence if you need to write anything down. But just John is fine. I've spoken to the police a few times over the years.'

'Mary Pope. She's the one who squealed me up, right?' George smiled mischievously.

'Mary is one of mine. She's a regular. Always has been. A little more so, though, since young Chloe didn't come home.'

'I'm sure the Church have been a great comfort.'

'I think so. Only so much we can do, though. But it wasn't Mary. It was her husband, actually. A little upset, I think. Now, won't you come in?' John turned away and George followed him down the aisle towards an impressive stained-glass window that dominated the chancel. The wooden pews to either side of them were in stark contrast: most looked dishevelled, the paint flaking; there were gaps where some were missing. He must have seen George looking over at an upturned pew that rested on top of another.

'They're both going away today. Restoration. The river . . . she is both our best friend and our worst enemy.'

'The river did this?'

'She does it fairly regular now. Through the summer we are the number one choice for weddings and christenings. That river is the backdrop for a thousand smiling newlyweds. But the winter shows her bitchy side. We've been flooded quite badly in two out of the last eight years. Seems like we're just recovering from one when the next tide comes in.'

'Global warming?' George offered.

John shrugged as he led George through a vestry door. 'You read the history books on this place and it's always been a feature. No telling if it's worse or better. The collection plate you walked past, it's for flood defences. Feel free to offer some assistance. Tea?' The vestry had a desk, lots of leather-bound books and a changing area. It also had two monitors showing what looked like a live picture of the outside of the church. The main entrance was shown in grainy detail, as was the car park where George's car sat.

'No, thank you. This doesn't strike me as the sort of area where the church might need CCTV.' George gestured at the screen.

'It never used to be. We got a little bit of trouble down here after someone in the press wrote a story linking the church to what happened to those women. A few cars were stoned in the car park. There was banging on the church doors when we were holding services. Nothing to worry about. I'm convinced it was just local kids who saw it as an excuse.'

'Enough to get the CCTV system though.'

'It wasn't enough for me. The women who run some clubs from here put out an appeal. They raised the money and the system was fitted. I never saw the need. I don't think we need anyone looking over the church. Not anyone earthly anyway. But it made the people here feel a bit safer. I don't even know how to work the thing.'

'That's okay. I'm not here to ask you to review your CCTV.'

'No. As I understand. You're trying to get to grips with our most infamous resident. Am I right?'

'That's it.'

'I won't bother asking why. I'll save you the dilemma of lying to a man of the cloth, as you put it.'

'I'd appreciate that.'

'I'm afraid I can't help much, really. Just like I told your colleagues, I knew him. He came here a number of times. But right from the start I could see that he was on the wrong path. He wouldn't be told. He wanted to learn but he didn't want to be taught. You know what I mean?'

'I'm not sure I do.'

'Well, he came here with what seemed like a lot of love in his heart for God. Which is good, of course. But it was *only* for God. He spoke ill of his family, of the community, of everyone really. I tried to teach him that God is about understanding. He's about loving people at least as much as He is about being worshipped. But he wasn't interested in that. He had studied his bible but had interpreted it the way he wanted to and there was nothing I could do to persuade him of any other way.'

'So, a devout Christian but a little misguided?'

'I wouldn't even say Christian. He was closer to the Old Testament faith in some of his interpretations, but he was all over the place, really. The differences can be subtle but very important. Generally I don't mind that. As long as you have love in your heart for God you are on the right lines. But we didn't always see eye to eye. I thought he came to me to ask for my guidance but he wouldn't listen. He just wanted me to reinforce his interpretation. I couldn't do that. He wouldn't hear that he might be misinterpreting or misunderstanding. I could show the path, but only he could choose to take it.'

'And he didn't.'

'He stopped coming after a few months. I'd been used to him coming every day. Then he just stopped. There was no falling out, no point when I realised that he might not be coming back. He just didn't. I don't know what changed. I thought perhaps he had moved away.'

'What was he like? As a person, I mean?'

'You mean, did I think he might be a serial killer of young women?' John's tone carried a warning.

'This isn't your fault, John — what happened. Serial killers don't walk around with it stamped on their heads. Henry Roberts is an intelligent and cunning man.'

John's body language changed again, like he was standing down from his offensive. 'I know that. We all know that when the devil appears he doesn't always have a tail and horns.'

'He might have an angel tattoo and a passion for God, though.'

'He might.'

'I think some people are just born that way. They have that in them, the ability to do unspeakable things,' George said.

'*Born that way* goes a little against what I stand for, Inspector. But I appreciate the sentiment.'

'No offence. The things I've seen . . . it makes it difficult for me to think that a God would make a conscious decision to create someone like that. I think I take comfort from thinking that sometimes nature just gets things wrong.'

'Whatever gives you comfort. The Lord is mysterious, he can send things to test your faith, your resolve. I thought maybe Henry was my test at first. I mean, here was a man who loved God every bit as much as I do, but he was lost, desperately looking for a way to serve Him best. He was very intense. That's the best way I can think of to describe him. I remember trying to be careful when I spoke to him. Everything was literal. He could get fixated too, and he wouldn't accept the lack of a clear answer.'

'And religion isn't like that?'

'It isn't. It's a lot of interpretation. Of reading and listening to other people. Henry certainly didn't want to do that.'

'Did he have any friends?'

'Friends? What, at the church? No, he isolated himself very quickly. The congregation here — before Henry, at least — they were, typically, of the older generation. People that might be coming towards the end of their own lives. They find comfort in the Church, in understanding the afterlife. That doesn't make them zealots or even very knowledgeable about their faith — it's more about the coffee mornings, bridge clubs, a bit of company and maybe repenting their sins before it's too late. Henry was frustrated by anyone who didn't adore God in the way that he did.'

'So people stayed away from him? Did they fear him?'

'I think maybe they did. Looking back, certainly. You get a lot of little old ladies popping in for their Sunday sermon. Henry was an imposing man. A big build, a full beard and those dark eyes. Some of the regulars actively avoided him. This was long before anything happened.'

'But his appearance was what scared people — not his demeanour?'

'A little bit of both. It was that intensity again. There was no such thing as a casual conversation with Henry.'

'And what about you? Did he scare you?'

John took a moment. 'Intimidated. He intimidated me. Sometimes, when I disagreed with him — if I told him his interpretation was wrong — he would make me feel uncomfortable. Scared? Maybe.'

'Did you ever see him with anyone? Outside of the church?'

'I didn't ever see him outside of this setting. I'm a regular in the pub, at the local store and around the village. I never saw him anywhere but here.'

'Since he left town, have you kept the same clientele as before? The "little old ladies," as you called them?'

'Pretty much, yes. A few more have sought guidance after what Henry did, when it was revealed what he had done under our noses. And, of course, those poor girls . . . their families and friends have become a part of our community — the church community, I mean.'

'Are you aware of anyone who presents in a similar way to Henry? Anyone with that passion or with a bit of a skewed interpretation?'

'Where are you going with that question, Inspector? We are not a breeding ground for serial killers up here. This is a small, beautiful village with a small, beautiful community of people living in it — good people. We are trying to get back on our feet.'

'You're right. I'm sorry, that was worded badly. Henry Roberts strikes me as an influential sort of person. Do you think he had anyone's ear? Someone he might have influenced?'

'Is there something we should know, Inspector? This village has suffered a cancer marring its beautiful landscape. That cancer was found, it was cut out and removed. I can't even imagine what the reaction might be if there was some suggestion that it hadn't been removed completely. You need to be very careful in what you are saying.'

'You're right. And, John, there's nothing to it. Just me being overcautious. I'm sure you can understand. I popped in here on my way home anyway. I promise, I shan't be causing any more trouble!'

'I appreciate that. Safe trip.' John stood up. He moved through the church towards the main door.

'This isn't the first time you've been asked these sorts of questions, is it?' George mused. The two men stepped out into the warm sunshine.

'It is not. The police made the religious link early on, long before they knew about Henry. I don't know how. Maybe they found something at those crime scenes. I took question after question. I opened up my attendance books. I even found myself looking at my congregation differently. It was not a good time for me. My role in this world is not to suspect and certainly not to judge, Inspector. That is for a far higher authority. I'm here to guide and to teach.'

'And did you get questions about Henry having friends?'

'I had a lot of questions, Inspector. Think of a question and you can be sure I was asked it.'

'I'm sure. Well, I'm sorry to have taken up your time. And for dredging up memories of what was clearly an unsettling time. Please, forgive my intrusion.'

'You're in luck, Inspector. I am all about forgiveness.'

George was fiddling with his wallet. He held out a ten-pound note. 'For your collection.'

John held out his hands. 'There's no need. I feel like I put you on the spot a little. I can't expect a man just passing through to have concerns for our little village.'

'Please, take it. You need all the help you can get if you are trying to hold back the forces of nature.'

John relented. He took the note. 'I suppose I asked for that!'

Chapter 10

George threw his jacket onto the back seat of the car. His phone was tucked away in the arm rest, his wallet pushed into the glove box. The prison staff would just take it all off him anyway. All that was left on him was his police badge with his driving licence pushed into the back — two forms of ID. George was again parked in the street close to Belmarsh Prison. This time, however, he was against the old, stone walls that made up the perimeter of the huge site.

The traffic was busy. Normal people going about their normal lives in the warm sunshine of early spring. Some would be at work, some on their day off perhaps — all of them would be building towards their future. Planning their summer holiday or their next birthday, maybe booking time off for Christmas or even a career change. Step the other side of the four-foot wide, stone walls, push into the deepest confines of that solid building and you had men who could contemplate nothing more than the walls themselves and the rotation of the evening menu.

George knew a little bit about life inside. He had spent some time as an inmate at a remand prison, and not too far from where he was standing now. He knew what it was like to be frozen still, while everyone else got on with their lives around you. You couldn't see it — or not much of it through the tiny, square windows distorted by wire — but you could *feel* it. George had been in that position but with the hope that one day he would walk free. He couldn't begin to imagine what it was like for the men who had nothing. No hope of freedom. No chance. And yet he wished more than anything that he could walk into the confines of that prison and condemn Henry Roberts to stay there for the rest of his life. No chance. No hope.

But his message today was different. The Major wasn't long off the phone and the decision he'd reported came as no surprise to George, though it hadn't stopped him beating his steering wheel in frustration as he queued to come off the M25 to head towards central London. He'd calmed down enough to agree to meet with Henry Roberts. There was some paperwork for him and his solicitor to sign that needed witnessing by a representative from the Home Office. George Elms would be acting as that representative.

The twelfth security door seemed somehow heavier than before as he was led along the same corridor. It was the same atmosphere: dust and heat charged with frustration. He made it to the same room with the same magazine. Only this time he had some company.

The solicitor stood up as George entered. He wore black trousers pulled too high by braces so that the hems were a good inch from the top of his heavily polished shoes. He was a tall man; lean, with glasses and thinning hair that had been swept over to cover a bald spot. His white shirt was spotted with sweat. He had dark features. His sleeves were rolled up. The dark hair on his arms was slick against his skin. He offered his hand. George took it up; the man's grip was limp and his palm sodden.

'I say, I reckon they should turn the heating up in this place!' He snorted laughter. He rubbed his hand against his trousers and sat back down. 'You must be Inspector Elms?' The man looked down to read the name off some paperwork that was laid out on the table.

'That's right.'

'Excellent. I'm Alan Smythe, of Smythe, Smythe and Alexander, solicitors of law. From just up the road there.'

'You got the short straw then?'

'The short straw?'

'Smythe and Alexander had better excuses, did they?'

'Oh! Oh, I see. Yes, indeed they did. My father started the business — he's long dead now, of course, and Alexander was his partner. Alzheimer's for him, I'm afraid, so very much the silent partner. I guess it is just me left from the title.'

'I'm sorry. I didn't mean to be flippant.'

Alan waved him away. 'Don't mention it. He gave me a good start in this world but we were never close. Now, the matter in hand here today should be a very simple one. It would seem that we have presented a case that has been accepted unequivocally. The details are all in this document, do you need time to read through it or . . .?' Smythe was sweating profusely: it ran down his forehead, was smeared on his glasses and his shirt was sticking to him. George wasn't comfortable either.

'I don't think so. What do you need from me?'

'Well, nothing, actually. You simply need to be present when Mr Roberts signs the document. You're not here to agree or otherwise with its content, just verify that you were here. A bit of a waste of your time, really.'

'You're the first person to show any concern about that.'

'I'm sure. Right then . . .' Smythe moved away. George watched him. He spoke to the guard. He was careful to put his back to George, his voice lowered, his arms by his side so he gave nothing away in his body language. Solicitors were all the same. Whether they meant to or not, they always played matters close to their chest. He sat back down. 'He should be just a moment.'

George took a seat too. He couldn't help but notice that the solicitor was sipping from a cup of tea. There was no time to make a point. Roberts stooped through the door, then stopped still.

'Inspector! I told you I would see you soon, right?'

'You said just that Henry.' George bit down. He just needed to watch him sign. Then he was out.

'You can't fight the will of God.' The intensity in Roberts's eyes remained. He stared down at George. He was sweatier still. He still wore a prison-issue tracksuit — top and bottom. The backs of his hands were shiny under the lights. He was pale and clammy. He sat down in front of George.

'Not long now, Henry. Let's hope you make it all the way down there. You're not looking so well.'

Henry coughed. It cut through his smile. The room waited for him to recover. 'Don't you worry about me. The Lord has a plan for me and it isn't dying here. I will make it, and then when the time is right I'll take up my place by His side.'

'How are they treating you, Mr Roberts?' Smythe cut in. He took a seat next to his client. George couldn't imagine how much he was being paid to represent this man. George couldn't conceive of any amount that would be enough for him.

'They've been just fine. But this place, it's not for me. When are we moving? Will it happen straight away?'

'Not straight away, Mr Roberts. There are some logistics to be worked out. We need to be sure it all goes smoothly. Just a few days.'

'Ah, yeah.' George saw an opportunity he couldn't resist. 'The logistics. See they've put me in charge of the move. So there are a few things I need to get done before I can move you. But rest assured, I mean, I will be working day and night to get it done. Well not night. Not tonight at least. I've got a thing, see. And I'm on a rest-day tomorrow. Then Thursday I'm in meetings. But, I will be straight on it. When I can.'

Roberts's stance was the same as the first time they had met. Sat at the table, his back straight, his hands out in front of him. They were held together by the solid steel of the handcuffs. He leant forward. His hands pushed forward as did the man himself, screwing up the paper document. Smythe tried to reach in, to pull the paper out of the way. Roberts locked eyes with George. Neither man would break contact.

'This decision has been made far above you, *Inspector*, and you will be expected to deliver what they agreed immediately. This is the Lord's will and you, like them, are powerless to stop it. Now . . . make sure you are watching closely.'

He backed away a little and smoothed down the paper. He picked up the pen that Smythe was holding out. He needed to put both hands down on the paper to write. His signature was huge, the letters finishing with a flourish. He underlined it firmly and stood back up almost immediately.

'Now this is your moment. God is forgiving. Surrender to his will.' He turned and stooped to walk back out of the door.

'Will do, Henry!' George called after him. 'I'll be back in touch real soon. Don't you die in the meantime, okay?'

* * *

George turned the radio station off the second he got back into the car. He drove hard and fast and in dead silence. His phone ringing dragged him out of a sort of trance. He moved to answer it and he realised that he was covered in sweat. His heater was still showing as 'on.' He flicked it to 'cold' and pressed the screen.

'George Elms.'

'George . . . Emma Rowe.' Her voice was loud through the speakers. He turned her down a little. She sounded stressed.

'Emma, are you okay?'

'Did you speak to the vicar?'

'The vicar?' George's mind was still back in the high-security wing.

'The vicar. Symonds Yat. Our vicar down at St—'

'Oh, yes. Beautiful place. I dropped in.'

'You dropped in because it was beautiful, did you?'

George felt himself squirm. 'Well, no, actually. I mean, obviously you know I was up there to get a good picture. I thought that the church was a good place to finish.'

'What did you tell him?'

'Tell him?'

'John Lawrence. We talked a lot during the original investigation, and not always in a good way. He wasn't happy with the police involvement at his church.'

'Okay.'

'So, what did you tell him?'

'I didn't really tell him anything. I was there to ask him questions.'

'Did you ask him if we had any more? If there were any more serial killers attending his church?'

'Don't be ridic—'

'Because that's the impression you left him with. I'm not sure what Langthorne is like as a place, George, but this is a very small community. Everyone here knows everyone else. You cannot go round shooting your mouth off. Did you mention that there might be a copycat? About the girl that has gone missing?'

'No! Of course not! I just asked him if Henry had any friends. It was a generic question.'

'Well, he saw right through it. We have to keep a lid on this. We cannot have any suggestion that there may be more problems in our area. Do you understand?'

'Look, I understand. And anyway I am out. I am very nearly home. I just thought I would pop in and ask the question. I saw the look in your eye when that Andy South fella went over your missing person. It was a relevant line of enquiry. I'm still a detective, so I asked it. I also asked the prison to provide me with any letters that might have been sent to Roberts and any visitors that have been there. Unfortunately Roberts's legal team have been all over them so they couldn't give it to me there and then. They need the right form apparently. I will be scanning that up later today and I should have it by return. Do you want me to forward anything on to you or not? Seeing as how we are *both* detectives.'

The line was quiet. George suspected Emma was taking her time to think, to compose her answer. He hoped she wasn't letting her anger build. She came back calmer and quieter.

'The mountain biker. In her first account, before we interviewed her on tape . . . she mentioned someone else.'

'Someone else?'

'When she was attacked. She was dragged a fair way towards a van. She can't be sure, but she thought the van backed up a tiny bit when they got close. She thinks she might have seen movement at the driver's side. We pushed her on this and she was never sure.'

'So Roberts might have been working with a getaway driver?'

'It's possible.'

'And you think he might have given himself a promotion in Roberts's absence?'

'I daren't even consider it right now, George. But we cannot rule it out. When you get those letters and the names of who's been visiting him, I do want to know. As a matter of urgency.'

'That's fine. I'll call you straight away.'

'Fine. And you don't breathe a word, okay? Lord knows why I'm telling you this.'

'Not a word. And the Lord moves in mysterious ways, Emma. Your vicar told me that.'

'Sounds like a cop-out to me.'

'To me, too. And I'll stay the hell out of your village, okay? I don't want to be upsetting people.'

'If they get wind of more women disappearing, George, there won't be anyone left to upset.'

Chapter 11

George pulled into the area of hard-standing at the rear of a large, white building. It looked freshly painted. He could see Whittaker hurriedly ending a call on his phone. George was surprised by the building. The façade was older than he had expected — of a 1950s vintage, perhaps — and its look overall was that of numerous care homes in the area. For some reason, George had conjured the image of a new build. He was way off the mark. The drive led up the side of the house. George could see large windows to the side and the rear. He guessed they would be just as big at the front where they would look out to sea. They weren't actually in Langthorne anymore. The town was some way below them. This was the village of Capel-le-Ferne, whose chalky, raking coastline formed part of the celebrated white cliffs of Dover. Capel was also home to a Battle of Britain memorial; with such a commanding view of the Channel and the French coast it would have seen some spectacular action during the Second World War. George knew the area well. All the houses that tentatively looked over the cliff edge were large and detached. Most of the occupants were retired and affluent. The house he had parked outside was the first in the row and on the Langthorne side of the village. Here, he was over a hundred metres above the sea and the views were uninterrupted. The gardens finished with a low fence and a sharp drop. Access from the road to the row of houses was gated off — private to the occupants.

'Very nice,' George said. Whittaker assumed his usual stance: hands behind his straightened back, his chest out. A sea breeze toyed with his tie.

'I know. It's bloody shit all this, George. Absolutely bloody shit.'

'It is at that, Major.'

'So, I figured it made sense that we have a chat here. This is Roberts's property — at least, it is for the next few weeks. Or shorter with any luck. I wanted to show you around before he takes up residency. I will warn you, though . . . we have colleagues here from the prison service. They are ultimately responsible for everything that occurs once you walk through that front door. I am aware of that fact because they've made a point of telling me three of four times already.'

'Are they not being accommodating?'

'Accommodating, yes. Will they appreciate any advice or feedback regarding security or layout? I can say definitely not.'

'I see.'

'They are the experts, apparently.'

'I'm quite happy for them to play expert. I told you, Major, I don't want anything to do with this. When it all goes wrong, when the media and the families find out, I want to be able to back away with a finger pointed at other people.'

'I'd like to do the same, George. My concern is that there will be more fingers pointed *towards* me than away.'

They walked to the large front door. 'But you oppose this, too. I assume you made it clear in your meeting?'

'I said nothing. Never got a chance.' Whittaker stopped. 'I had a good look around that table yesterday, George. I had a bit of a moment. They were all talking, accepting the risks, talking about outweighing cons with pros — the usual stuff — and do you know what I realised?'

'Go on.'

'No one even knew who I was. And no one cared. And I was the only police officer in that room.'

'Sounds dangerous.'

'Sounds ominous. Standard rule of politics, George. They need to be sure they have a scapegoat in place — just in case. They might as well have asked me to come wearing a bell with bags tied across my back.'

Whittaker pushed open the front door to be met by a stern-looking man in a suit. He looked beyond Whittaker and stared at George. 'Can I help you?'

'This is Inspector George Elms. He should be on the approved list,' Whittaker said.

The man flicked open a folder. 'Do you have ID?' he demanded. He was small and weaselly-looking. His suit was slightly too large, as if he had borrowed it from his dad for the day.

George smiled. 'Yes.' He made no more movements.

'May I see it?'

'You first.'

'Sorry?' The man looked flustered.

'That's okay. Take your time.'

'Why do you need to see my ID?'

'I know, right?' George chuckled. 'A little explanation goes a long way, doesn't it?'

'George, G4S have been tasked with the security. The door locks are all on a computer system. They're not working yet. Until then our friend Simon here is doing the job.'

George showed his ID. Simon wrote something down. He fiddled with something then produced a white sticker with a barcode on it and the word *Visitor*.

'You need to put this somewhere visible,' Simon said.

'State of the art,' George grinned.

The main door led through to an entrance hall that was more like an enclosed square box. There were numerous black panels, retina scanners and cameras that would allow security personnel to verify who was entering. George could see that the security measures to enter the building were going to be thorough, but right now, nothing was working. All the panels were dark. The only sign of any power was a small red dot on the door in front. Whittaker ran a card over it. It turned green and he pushed it open. He held the door for George.

'This is an airlock corridor. Part of the inner security apparently. The solar panels you might have seen on the roof? They run the core power. They can't be switched off.'

'Can't say I did. Does that mean that he will be able to just walk out when the sun goes down?'

'Funnily enough, I asked the same thing! Apparently he would be able to, yes, but it would need to be down for more than a month. I guess if it's pitch black for a month something terrible has already gone wrong.' Whittaker moved to the door further down the corridor. He turned back to George. 'You have to shut that one for this one to open. Your standard airlock I'm afraid, George.'

George moved forward. He heard the door click shut. He had come across airlock corridors in the more secure areas of police stations. They were designed so they couldn't be rushed. A simple design, but effective. Whittaker opened the next door so George could move into the main part of the building. It was nothing like what George had been expecting. Where the exterior had been familiar, the interior was anything but; any original features inside were all but missing, stripped away and replaced with modern metal and white finishes. It was clinical and modern — it made George think of a high-end dentist's.

'I'll show you the cell to start with.' George followed Whittaker through to what would have been the main lounge. Straight away there was an obvious structural change. The ceiling was missing. As were any supporting walls. The room now opened up over two floors with just a few supporting pillars dotted through the centre. The far wall was pretty much all window. Looking through it, the garden was an area of flattened grass with sharp borders. The turf was fresh. George could see the joins where it had been recently rolled and pressed down. It sloped gently down to a fence made of such a thin mesh that it looked more like a shadow. The sea dominated the view beyond this. It shuffled and moved and was divvied up by three rough lines of differing shades of blue. There was something about watching a big body of water that George had always found to be calming.

'What people would do for this view?' George said.

'Kill for it, I suppose,' Whittaker snorted.

'This is all wrong, Major. I know I've said it. I don't know what I was expecting but my last hope was that all of this would be something akin to what he deserves . . . not like this.'

'I know.'

'Is that why you brought me up here? To show me his luxury accommodation, to make sure that I'm properly pissed off?'

'Of course not. Although I would understand why you might think that after the last couple of days. There are some people I would like you to meet and they happen to be here today. I figured it made sense. Let me finish the tour and we'll do some introductions. You might actually find some modifications that you do like.'

George noticed a steel structure that was closed in on three sides and pushed against the window. Whittaker turned to George for a reaction. 'The cell,' he said.

'The cell?' George was puzzled. There was a door on the side he could see. It was very similar to the cell doors he had seen in prison. The locking mechanism was the same. So were the flaps for communication and observation. It was locked open. He pulled it open further. It felt like it had the same weight too. Inside, the position of the bed was different: it was central and it was raised. It had metal padded tubes either side of it that were locked shut. There were holes drilled along its length. They looked to George like they were designed to secure the occupant's arms. There were wires trailing through the solid-looking ceiling that gathered on the bare bed. Whittaker rattled one of the tubes.

'Apparently this is the first bed in the UK that is signed off as being able to give the prisoner medication without his consent. Previously there was no way of doing it.'

'We don't want to be giving him any medication, though? I thought that was part of the agreement?'

'Oh, it is. But they used Roberts's money to develop it, so I guess they thought it was right to put it in here. The prisoners on hunger strikes, or refusing anti-psychotic medication . . . now we can give them their shot without the human rights people claiming it as a form of torture. It's something about the way the arms are secured in here. It uses pressure points so the arms can't be moved. Or something like that.'

'Am I supposed to be impressed?' George wasn't even looking. He had walked beyond the bed, to the end of the cell. To that window. It dominated the far end; it was the whole wall. The bed was split, the end furthest from the window was raised so it would propel the occupant towards that view.

'I guess not.' Whittaker moved to stand next to George. 'Have you ever seen anything like it?' Whittaker said.

'No. Nor would I ever dream anything like it. I don't understand it. Why would they build a cell in here? Surely the whole place is the cell. There aren't going to be other prisoners in here, right?'

'Not with Roberts. It was part of the agreement. The plan is to divvy it up for a lot more occupants when Roberts is out of the way. I think the Home Office were trying to atone by building this one. They can insist he is still in a cell with identical dimensions. This is the result.'

'And the hanging wires, the hospital-style bed and the view? Does that help them atone too?'

'I listened to the arguments in the meeting, George. The point that they kept coming back to is that he would soon be moved to a hospital anyway. That's a massive security operation, a massive headache and a massive expense. The prison system simply can't cope with giving that sort of care. This avoids all that. He would have been transferred to a hospital, he would be in a bed just like this one and the wires . . . those are for the medicines and fluids.'

'I thought he was refusing any treatment when he gets here?'

'He is. He's waived his right to chemo or surgery, or anything that might make any sort of difference. This is just set up for oxygen and pain relief. He's insisted he doesn't need that either, but we all know you can say one thing about pain and then another thing when it comes to it. Human rights again, George. We have to have something to help ease the pain.'

'Let's just hope it isn't long before he's permanently numb.'

'We had the latest medical report in the meeting yesterday. I don't think you have long to wait to get your wish.'

'And this was agreed yesterday, was it?' George stepped back out of the cell. He could only imagine the considerable structural work that had taken place to be remove the guts of the house without it folding in on itself. The top floor was now a mezzanine. He could see a bit of it, enough to see a bank of monitors, a desk and some seating. Back on the ground floor there looked to be a sort of holding cell too. Its door was directly opposite Henry's cell but this just had a long bench along one of its walls. There was a ground-floor extension, too, that George had noticed on the way in. The entrance to that was now barred by another heavy-looking security door. It had a black box on the wall next to it with a flat panel that again looked like fingerprint access.

'Gentlemen!' George turned towards the voice: a young man, his cheeks flushed red. He was dressed in a suit, but looking a little more comfortable in it than the security guard. His hair was messy with gel and pushed over to one side. It looked like he had gone to considerable effort to appear that he had gone to none at all.

'Ah, George, this is Daniel Callaghan. He's director of operations at G4S. This is his baby, really.'

'More like a problem child, I would say! Please, call me Dan. Impressive, though, isn't it?'

'I'm not impressed if that counts?' George said. It did nothing to stop the man's beaming smile.

'Well, lucky for you, you won't have to live here.'

'I'd love to live here, Dan. But I couldn't afford it. Clearly I don't deserve it.'

The smile dropped away. 'You'd swap would you? Your life for his? Your situation for his?'

'No. And I'll tell you something else I wouldn't swap, I wouldn't swap his cell for this one. You know what that man did, right? Only everyone seems to be smoothing over that.'

'I'm sure we've all had that internal dialogue. We all know who he is. My job was to make this place happen. Other people have the job of deciding who gets to stay in here.'

'And you started yesterday, did you?'

'Yesterday?'

'The decision was made yesterday, right? That's what we're being told. How long has it taken to get to this point? I mean the structural work, the security bits — not to mention the purchase in the first place.'

'Eighteen months. I can only tell you when I was commissioned to deliver this. When decisions are made, whether they are made, or what those decisions are, that's not my remit.'

'It's convenient, isn't it? How the decisions that make the difference are always someone else's.'

'It is for me. Now, if you'll excuse me, gentlemen, I need to get back to it.'

George didn't watch him leave.

'I know you're upset, George, but we need to be playing this clever. This is happening. We have to accept that and then we need to be sure that it happens smoothly. There can't be any problems.'

'Why do we? They're asking for problems. This is happening — I get that. But it has been happening for a long time. We're only involved now because we have to be. Because they need us to do the dirty work. Sitting outside this place at all hours, while he gets to sit up and look at his view.'

'I agree. It's not ideal, George. It's not even acceptable. Not when you consider the risk they want us to manage. But the meeting was clear, the prison service is taking care of his transfer and his security when he gets here. They're bringing his medical team down from the prison and they will be staffing the inside of this building. All of the people working here are the same that have been working with him at Belmarsh so they can keep the circle of knowledge small. They've all been sworn to secrecy. We're just the people on the outside keeping the peace. The *what ifs* are ours. Nothing more. Our problems start if this gets into the public domain.'

'It will.'

'I know that. Everyone knows that. But if it happens when he is here already or, better still, when he is dead, then it can be managed. We can't have a circus around his transfer. That doesn't play out well.'

'I'm sure it doesn't. Well, I was hoping to get back to some police work. Any objection if I go and pick up with my team and my caseload? Like you said, this is someone else's problem — for now at least.'

'It is. No objections from me. There is another fella I wanted you to meet. He might cheer you up a little bit.'

'How so?'

'He's the man who will be making sure Roberts dies.'

* * *

Doctor Assan was leaning over a stainless steel desk in one of the upstairs rooms. He had his back to George and Whittaker when they entered.

'Doctor Assan,' Whittaker said. The man snatched around, as if the sound of his own name had wrenched him out of a trance. He held a startled grimace, his body was stiff and his nostrils flared. He looked to George like a man under stress.

'Chief Inspector . . .'

'John.' Whittaker jumped in to help him. 'And this is Inspector George Elms. He met with our patient a couple of times. I think he was hoping you could give him some good news.'

'Good news? I'm afraid there is little to be positive about. He is gravely ill, Inspector.'

'That's what I meant by good news.'

The doctor's grimace dropped away enough for a weak smile. 'Ah, yes. This is a most unusual case. The first I've had perhaps, where everyone is happy for the patient to die.'

'What's the prognosis? Don't spare me the gory details,' George said.

'Henry Roberts has stage-four cancer. His primary was in his bowel but we were able to operate on this and remove his tumour. He then had a six-month course of chemotherapy so we could be sure we had killed off all of the cancer cells. It looked positive — for Mr Roberts, at least. But then the cancer came back. This time in the lymph nodes of his lower back. This is serious, but things can be done. We were making preparations when we discovered a shadow on his lung. The cancer had spread. The cancer that will kill him is the one on his lung. His breathing capacity is being reduced — daily. He is weak, Inspector. I looked around at this place, at the security. This is not necessary. This man should be on a ward, in a bed. He will need some severe pain medication. This cannot be managed well here.'

'I agree with you. Except for the bit about the pain relief.'

'I will do my best.'

'What's a normal day for you, doc?' George said.

'Not this. This is not normal.' The doctor gestured out towards the house. It buzzed with people. George could count at least three tradesmen all going about their business in the building. The whole place had the feel of being in a rush to get finished. 'I work in private hospitals. Mostly in London. I specialise in cancer. End of life treatment, really. The prison work was just something I took on to expand my CV. I thought it might open some doors.'

'So, you're not the man I should ever hope to see walking into my room to give me some news?'

'I suppose not, Inspector.'

'How long do you think he'll last?'

The doctor shook his head. 'We cannot do anything to stop the spread across his lungs. His end will come when they start taking on fluid, when they cannot provide the oxygen necessary to keep him alive. This may not be a good death.'

George grinned. 'There, see! You can give good news.'

There was a shrill tone and Doctor Assan grabbed his mobile phone. What he saw on the screen seemed to make him even more tense. He excused himself and Whittaker led George back downstairs. He walked past the cell, through the door with the fingerprint scanner and into the ground-floor extension. He didn't scan his prints. The door was limp in its metal surround. The extension looked to be a communal area. It was made up of soft furnishings, a kitchen and an expensive-looking coffee machine with a plastic funnel on top that housed whole coffee beans. Whittaker made for it.

'Not quite the facilities you would normally expect in a prison.' George huffed.

'This is for the staff. That's the impression I get, at least. I think the prison service was given the opportunity to kit this place out on someone else's budget and they've made the most of it. You can't blame them for that. We'd have done the same.'

'So the prison service will keep hold of this place after Roberts. Is that the plan?'

'That was the discussion in the meeting. They will build more cells. It will become a place where prisoners with medical issues can be effectively managed. It will take away the need to take them to the general hospitals. I think the prison service have been crying out for something like this for a very long time.'

'He's playing on that desperation. Roberts, I mean. This is a man who knows how to get what he wants.'

The coffee didn't take long. Whittaker put it down on the table in front of where George was still standing. Whittaker sat down. George eyed him suspiciously. He flicked from the chief inspector to the steaming mug.

'What?' Whittaker leant back in his chair.

'I told you I was leaving. You ask me to meet Doctor Death. Then you make me a coffee. This all feels like it's building to more bad news.'

Whittaker grinned. 'No such thing as bad news in this job, George. It's all an adventure, right?'

'And my adventure isn't over quite yet?'

'Not even close.'

George pulled out the chair and slumped into it. 'What more do you need from me?'

'Henry Roberts. He's given up the site for one of the missing girls. For Ellie Smith.'

'*One* of them?'

'Yes. One of them.'

'I thought it was both? I thought that was all part of the deal?'

'It is, you're right. He's giving us Ellie Smith and then Chloe Pope after.'

'I thought he was in a hurry to move? And what is he saying? That we either do what he says or the deal's off and he doesn't move? We'll go with that one then! Fuck him, he can stay and rot where he is.'

'You know how important those sites are. For the political aspect of this, I mean. I think Roberts knows that too.'

'And for the families. I don't care about the politics. That doesn't matter to me a jot. I'm taking small comfort in the fact that the families get something out of this. That's all.'

'The families then. It's massively important for them. We're going to retrieve Ellie tomorrow. Early. It's really important—'

'We? You mean "we" as in the *royal* we, right? Like the police?'

'Me and you, George.'

'Why the hell do I have to go?'

'I was just going to tell you. It's really important that you at least go to the site. It's part of his conditions. He's—'

'His conditions? Roberts? Why am I suddenly part of this? I just met the guy! There's a whole other police force that put him there. I'm just the twat who turned up to listen to his rantings.'

'I know what you are, George. But, for the first time, the police have a contact that Henry Roberts is talking to. We can't lose that, George. He's insisted that you go to the site. Then he'll tell you where the second one is. But only you.'

'Fucking hell, Major!' George pushed off the table. He walked quickly to the window and fixed on a small boat that bobbed against the waves. From this distance he could just see a flash of the white surf.

'You need to get your head around it, George. I know it doesn't sit comfortably with you. It doesn't with me either. We do what we're told for a couple of days. We play this man's game, do what the politicians need and then we're done. He can have his view and he can have his death. And one should follow the other pretty damned quickly.'

'I just don't . . . it's control again! He craves it, we know that much, and we're just handing it over to him. He's thoroughly enjoying himself, Major, and I'm at the centre of that. That's what I can't get out of my head. Why can't we just tell him that I'm going? He wouldn't know any better.'

'I don't want anything going wrong. I don't want him striking up a conversation with you about the colour of the scenery up there or the rare plants that are growing over it or some other crap and working out that you didn't go. I don't want anything to threaten this. It makes no difference anyway. We go up tomorrow. It's a day out in the woods. We're meeting the locals who will take us to the site. As soon as that's done, we can come away. CSI and the search teams will do their bit and then we can go back and meet Roberts for the last time. We'll listen to his bullshit for just a few minutes, just long enough for us to get the other site out of him and then we're done. I'll pass the details up the line and another family gets their daughter back. You will have made that difference, George. You said you saw one of the mothers, you said she was waiting for her daughter to come home. You can make that happen.'

'I don't see this being the end of it. Every time I do my bit you're asking me to do something more. You know I don't mind normally. I'll do whatever you ask, whatever is needed of me. But I catch bad people. That's what we're all here to do. I don't move them somewhere nice when they've already been caught. I don't get used as part of their games.'

'That's what I like about you, old boy. You're here for the right reasons. But we have to play this game, this time. Give me one more day, George.'

George sighed. 'Look, I appreciate that you're asking at all. I know you can just order me up there. If it was anyone else I would dig my heels in, Major. Let's just get this done. It needs to be an early start though. I'm taking my daughter to the cinema tomorrow evening.'

'Excellent. I'm glad you've come round. I was giving it one more go and then I was going to order you up there. Now, pick up your bottom lip and let's get the hell out of here, shall we? You've got a caseload on back at the office.'

George chuckled. As they walked back through the house he took one last, lingering look out through the huge glass window. He tried to focus his mind on Mary Pope. On repairing some of the devastation at least. That was his job now.

Chapter 12

Whittaker wrenched open the car door. 'What sort of time of day is this, eh, George?'

'Five a.m., Major. I thought you army boys were used to the crack of dawn?'

'I retired, George, remember? I figured the police would be a bit like getting a little Saturday job to tide me over.'

'Of course you did. May I suggest an early stop for a cup of coffee, then?' George pulled out of a marked bay at the front of Langthorne Police Station. 'I assume I'm heading back to the same village? That area at least. The Forest of Dean?'

'No actually. We're going a little further afield.'

'Further?'

'Yeah, not much. We're going over the border into Wales.'

'So not the Forest of Dean?'

'No. Still a forest, I think. Afan Forest.'

'Afan Forest? Do you know where that is?'

'I have the postcode for where we are meeting the people that do. Don't you worry, we'll get there.'

'Might have to skip the coffee then, Major. I need to be back down here at a reasonable time today.'

'I know. You're taking Charley out to the cinema. Is she choosing?'

'She has already. I think the film is described as a *High School dance epic*.'

'I see. Are you sure she's choosing?' George joined in with Whittaker's chuckle.

'I'm sure. And even if I enjoy it, I won't admit it.'

'Well, don't worry. I've made arrangements. We should be in, find what we need to find and then out.'

* * *

George found the car park four hours later. The entrance was via a sudden break in thick woodland. He had to slow as he pulled onto the grey shingle and exposed rock that made up the surface. The scenery really opened up and he could see they were at the base of a steep tree-lined bowl. The parking bays were defined by long, filed-down tree trunks that were fixed roughly together with exposed joints. There were a few parked cars scattered around. Most had some sort of bike rack. He saw two mountain bikers head off as he approached. He pulled in next to two identical-looking trucks. They looked brand-new, their bodies lifted high over thick, knobbly tyres. Both had *Warrior* emblazoned on their respective rumps. A cheery-looking woman in waterproof trousers and a fleece walked over with her hand held out.

'George Elms?'

'That's right.'

'Nice to meet you, sir. I'm Becca Moors. I'm on the tactical support team by day, but I do a bit of search and rescue in my spare time. Round here mainly. We're all volunteers but no one knows the woods like we do.'

'Sounds like we're going to need you.'

'I think you're right. I've had sight of the map you people want us to follow. It's barely a sketch.

'Oh, really? I've not seen it myself. Is it going to be a problem?'

'Only if it's not where we think it is. There are some landmarks that we're pretty sure we know between us. I'm confident we can get you there.'

'Well, we are in your hands. We struggled just to find the car park!' George turned to the sound of another engine. A Ford rolled up next to them. Emma Rowe stepped out. She looked more casual. It didn't suit her so well. She was in dark jeans, a fleece top and hiking boots. George smiled at her as she walked over. She smiled back but it looked fraught; it barely reached her lips and it fell away quickly.

'Hey, Becca,' she said. 'George.'

'Morning, Emma. Apologies. I wasn't expecting you or I might have brought the biscuits this time. This is John Whittaker. The chief inspector I told you about who had me stitched up from the start.'

'Ah, yes. We've spoken on the phone. Nice to finally meet you, sir.' Emma's smile now looked a little more genuine. She shook Whittaker's hand. 'He did say that too, sir.'

'I bet he did. The problem I have is that I can't really deny it. This was a bit of a stitch-up to be honest. In my defence, I didn't realise quite how *much* of a stitch-up. Not that it would have changed a thing, of course.'

'It might have made you quicker to send me if anything,' George said.

'You might be right. Still, it didn't quite work. I still ended up here.' Whittaker suddenly sounded awkward and hurried. 'Not that this is a bad part of the world, Emma. It's lovely here. You know what I mean?'

'I do. Don't worry, sir. For the record, I would rather be anywhere than here today.'

George's gaze lingered on her. She carried herself with authority and grace, but she didn't hide stress well. George believed her. She really would rather be anywhere else.

A rugged-looking man came out of the second truck and stood next to Becca. He was just as cheery and was also in waterproof trousers and hiking boots. George was in his standard formal trousers with tired leather shoes, a cheap shirt and an even cheaper tie. He had a long jacket that hung open. He suddenly felt unprepared. The man smoothed out a large map on the bonnet of one of the trucks, then introduced himself as Dan. He moved a finger to a central point on the map.

'This is the car park, where we are. Afan is like a bowl, as you can see. The sides are covered in trees and trails. That's why the bikers love it here. Our site is up one of the sides, much higher. Up here.' His finger moved to the top left of the map. Any paths or roads seemed a long way off, even with George's basic understanding of maps. 'We can drive some of the way. The rest is a hike. I don't think it's too far off the track, but I'm not going to say that in case you all end up getting very upset with me.'

'Okay. Are we going to follow you up?' George looked back over to the family hatchback that he had managed to rent for the day. Becca must have seen him because she started chuckling.

'Not in that! We'll take the trucks up. Dan is going to take the lead. He's our EGT camera man. Emma needs it filmed. Where did you want me to start from, Emma?'

Emma's own gaze had been lifted to the hills. 'Sorry, Becca?'

'The recording. You said you wanted it filmed? Dan here will be in the front truck with his camera. Where did you want him to start from?'

'Are we leaving now?'

'We can. We're ready.'

'Then he can start now.'

'From here?' Becca looked a little taken aback.

'Yes, I would rather he got too much than too little.'

George sat in the front of the second truck. Becca took the driver's seat. Whittaker and Emma were in the back seats. Dan was being driven in the lead truck. George looked out. He could see numerous trails leading away from the car park. All of them were uphill. They moved back out onto the road at first. The climb was gentle. Nothing his hatchback couldn't have handled. It was a few miles before they turned onto what was more like a forest path. The Warrior bumped and dipped over the rutted trail, but it was easy enough. George took in the scenery through the window. The further they moved into the Afan Forest, the more dramatic their surroundings became. George had been in woods before, forests even, in England. But they were nothing like this. This was otherworldly stuff. It was stunningly beautiful and changing all the time. They moved past trees on the outskirts with trunks that were gnarled and matted. They looked like they had been standing as guardians on the outside for centuries. Further in, the trees got taller and thinner but much closer together. Some were wrapped together, their slender trunks tightly intertwined, jostling to reach for the sunlight. It was so dense that the light dipped to twilight levels. George was trying to follow their progress on the map. He quickly gave up. Luckily for him, the lead Warrior ploughed on as if the driver was confident of where he was going. George moved back to staring out of the window. Nature continued with its show. The dense greens and browns gave way to reveal a sudden cliff of solid rock with water slithering down its front. It was twenty metres tall and appeared from nowhere. And they were still climbing.

The going became harder: the track less of a track at all; the rocks more pronounced and obtrusive. He could see brake lights ahead. They stayed on; the lead truck had stopped. The passenger door pushed open and Dan stepped out, his camera levelled. It was pointed forward and he walked straight ahead.

'This is it, then,' Becca said. She pulled on the handbrake and killed the engine. George stepped out. He immediately regretted his choice of clothing again. The floor was coated in long grass and mulch. It was damp. He followed the group. His trousers soaked through almost instantly. They had stopped on a gradient, the trucks pointing up. He walked past them. The tree canopy was a little thinner at this height and he could even see the sky. They found a path of sorts. Comprising compressed mud, pine needles and sharp rock, it was barely wide enough to walk on — probably a wild animal run. It pushed back into an area of dense trees. Dan was still leading, capturing every step on camera. George could hear him giving the occasional line of commentary. The terrain changed again. The track ran out and underfoot was now a vivid green moss. It was springy to the step and, when George moved off it, it recovered immediately as if he had never been there. The moss got thicker, its colour even brighter and coating everything. The tree trunks and branches, the flat rocks, every inch of ground was lurid green. It was as strange as it was beautiful, like photoshopped reality. George was a few steps behind the two guides and Dan with his camera.

'I'm too old for this, George,' Whittaker said.

'I was thinking the same, Major.'

'Don't be ridiculous, man! You're not even forty yet!'

'I meant about you!' Both men chuckled. George turned to find Emma. She was a few more steps behind. He didn't think she had any desire to catch up with them. He was just about to call out and check that she was okay when he heard a shout.

'This is it!' He looked up. Dan held his camera steady. Becca had given the shout. George walked up to her. Beyond where she stood he could see a circular clearing where the ground levelled out. They were at the top of the incline. George could see the trees sloping away now, back towards where they had started. It was even clear enough for him to see the trees on the other side of the bowl. Just about every inch of the clearing was coated in the same moss he had just walked on. The exception was a small, round tree stump right in the centre.

'This is it? Any idea where we need to look?' George scanned the area then called back to Emma. 'There was a big cross the last time, right? Marking the grave?'

'The grave, yes.' Emma moved forward a few paces. When she stopped she was still a few feet short of George. Her eyes flicked around the clearing. They rested back on George. 'This isn't where he buried her,' she said.

Becca rustled the map. 'It's the place on the map—'

'This is where he killed her,' Emma said.

George turned to see her step back. 'How could you know that? It's a load of moss and a tree stump in the middle of nowhere. What do you know that we don't?'

'That's not a tree stump.'

The stump was maybe ten metres away and George moved towards it. He nodded at Dan who turned his camera back on. Dan said the time out loud and stepped beside him. It took just a few paces for George to see that Emma was right. It wasn't a tree stump, it wasn't even wood. It looked like it was made out of a rusty metal — copper, maybe, or brass. It was on four stumpy legs and the moss had made a start on curling around the bottom of each. As George got closer he thought it looked like a water tank, or maybe even two grafted together somehow. It had a distorted shape, a wide, rounded bottom that pinched up to a slim neck that was off-centre. The moss underneath it was thinner than everywhere else and a slightly different shade of green. He was close enough to see a line in the metal surface. It ran all the way around the side like the whole structure might come apart. George held back so Dan could move around it with the camera. He paused the footage and lowered it.

'Any idea what you're filming here?' George said.

'Not a clue. I was hoping you might.'

'No. But I know someone who does. Don't touch it for a minute.'

Emma had moved quite a distance back through the trees. She was facing away. She looked like she was taking in the view of the forest on the other side through a break in the trees. George's approach was loud with the cracking and snapping of twigs and branches underfoot but Emma did not turn around.

'Emma, any chance you could help me out with what I'm doing up here?' George said.

Emma's shoulders shook. Her head dipped forward, she sniffed loudly.

'Are you . . . okay?'

'Sorry, George. I didn't want to come up here today. But I didn't want to ask anyone else. It wouldn't be fair.'

'What's going on, Emma? Are you speaking in riddles on purpose? What's the matter?'

She turned at last, her face flushed, her eyes filled with tears. 'What did you see?' she sniffed.

'What?'

'Up there. What did you see?'

'What did I see? Something that looks like a water tank. The sort we've all had in our lofts at some point. But it's odd. It looks like it's been beaten out of shape. I thought I was coming up here to find the shallow grave of a murder victim. What's going on?'

'Have you ever heard of a Brazen Bull?' Emma's voice was so low George had to lean in to hear her words. She shivered.

'What? A brazen what? What's this about, Emma?'

'Don't worry, I hadn't heard of it either. I mean, why would you? But I know all about it now. I know all about it because of Henry Roberts.'

'So, tell me about it. I assume I need to know.'

'Oh, you do, George! Ancient Greece. They had a problem with petty crime. It was everywhere. The ruler at the time wanted a new method of punishing and executing criminals. He wanted to make them suffer in the worst way possible before they died, so that he could send a message.

He wanted a device so terrible that no one would ever commit a crime again. Out of pure fear. The Brazen Bull was it. The inventor showed it to the ruler, explained how it worked, what it did. Legend has it that he was so appalled by what he saw that he ordered the inventor to be the first victim.'

'That's what that is up there? A Brazen Bull?'

'Of a sort, yes.' Emma walked back past George, back towards the clearing. The group had stayed on the outside. George walked behind Emma. He could hear the group chatting as they approached. They laughed in unison. The laughter dropped away immediately as Emma walked through them. They must have seen her expression. They all had questioning eyes for George. He ignored them. He continued after Emma. She stopped a metre short of the device.

'The Brazen Bull was traditionally made entirely out of bronze. For lightness this one will be like the others. Made of copper. It has a thick skin but it's hollow. It would have been shaped like a bull in Ancient Greece. I guess Roberts didn't have the time or the skill to emulate that.'

George turned to the group. They were all looking beyond him. Emma had their full attention.

'The victim was stripped naked and forced inside the bull. It is just about big enough to take a nineteen-year-old, naked female. It would have been locked shut. She would have been in the pitch black. Roberts then built a stack of wood under the bull. We don't know at what point he would have done that, but for the maximum effect it was suggested that he did it once he had his victim trapped inside. When he had enough wood he would have set it on fire. Roberts would have controlled how big the fire was. The metal, of course, would heat up. Copper is an excellent conductor of heat. The bottom would become hot to touch at first, but the whole thing would heat up. And it would get hotter all the time.' Emma paused for a moment. She lifted her head to where the sun drifted through the canopy. 'Can you imagine the panic, George? Can you imagine what that must be like?'

'Jesus . . .' George said.

'The metal would keep getting hotter. He could have doused the flames to prolong it, or fanned them to speed it up. But, at some point, it would have started to scald. Those young women, George . . .' She paused. She fought off breaking down. 'They would be sweating heavily. They would be soaked. Their own sweat would heat up too until it boiled on their skin. The nerves on their hands and feet would be burnt away first — it's not a quick process. It would have been almost a relief when it finally happened. But you can't keep all your weight on your hands and feet forever. At some point you're going to collapse. In the dark. In more pain than you can imagine.' Emma turned back to the group. She fixed on George. 'He cooked them alive, George. In the pitch black. Alone and terrified. As slowly as he could manage. That's what you're dealing with. That's what devastated my team and that's the man that we locked in a stinking cell. You need to understand who he is. Everyone does.'

George was reeling. His mind trying to form the right response. 'The press . . . the media . . . they just said they were burned. It read like it was after — like he was trying to get rid of the evidence. Then he buried what was left of them.'

'The media didn't get all the information.'

'What did they get?' George was still flailing, trying to make sense of what he thought he knew.

'What they needed. Nothing more.'

'Why?'

'Because we didn't have the bodies. Because Roberts didn't confess. The judge, the CPS, the police . . . we all agreed to keep the details secret until we had closure. Technically the investigation is still open and Roberts's defence team are still making noises about an appeal.

We're still looking for those missing girls. And if anyone showed knowledge of what happened here, or Roberts did at any point, it would show that they were involved for definite.'

'By anyone, you mean an accomplice?'

Emma sighed. 'We never got a word of explanation, no admission of guilt, nothing. We can't say what happened here for sure. I expect the full details might be released when Henry dies, especially now we have the missing girls. But his death might mean that we never actually know what happened.'

'So was anything actually buried? At the other site?'

'Yes, what was left of Lucy Moon when he had finished.'

'What was that?'

'Imagine, George, imagine roasting a pork joint. For hours — days even. The flesh falls right off the bone . . .'

'Jesus . . .' George managed again.

'Seems he wasn't there to help.'

'So, you just found her buried bones?'

'Most of them.'

'Most of them?'

'So the bit about the animals carrying some of it off, that bit was true?'

'No. We got them all, just not at the same time.'

'Not at the same time?'

'No. What was missing, we found when we arrested Roberts.'

'He kept some?'

'He was wearing them.' Emma walked back towards George. She didn't slow down. He stepped aside, his mouth flapping open and shut. He was trying to speak. He wanted to say something, he just didn't know what. She kept walking. George watched her until she was out of sight among the trees.

Whittaker was looking right at him. He was shaking his head. 'What the hell do you make of this then, old boy?' he managed. 'What are you thinking?'

George turned back to the solid-looking metal 'bull.' The belly dipped low, the spindly legs holding it a few feet off the ground. Plenty of room for a good fire underneath. The moss was a different colour where it hadn't quite had the chance to re-establish itself through the earth that would have been scorched underneath.

George felt suddenly very cold. 'Well, he didn't do this on his own.'

Chapter 13

George pushed through the interior of Belmarsh Prison, his teeth gritted, his eyes to the floor. It was a struggle for him to be here. He was having to make a real effort to keep his composure. He didn't know if he could sit opposite that animal. Not now. The descent down the Welsh hillside and the drive to Belmarsh had given him ample time to dwell on what he had seen in that beauty spot. The journey had largely been awkward small-talk. They had tried to talk about it, but neither he nor his boss could find the right words. For George at least, the only emotion left in him was anger. Whittaker lagged a few paces behind as they made their sombre walk through the oppressive corridors. Normally they would have been side-by-side, exchanging banter. Whittaker, with his grim sense of humour and enjoyment of a wind-up, typically thrived on a prison visit — to a place where their efforts could be seen to score the occasional victory. Not today, though. Both men proceeded through the twelfth door, their heads still bent, their voices silent. The two prison guards showed them into the same side room. George recognised the same solicitor, Alan Smythe, sole survivor of Smythe,

Smythe and Alexander. This time there was a recording device on the table.

'We'll go and get him for you,' one of the guards said.

'Can we have a minute or two first?' Whittaker said. Both guards nodded. Smythe also took the hint and excused himself.

'You want a tea?' A guard stuck his head back in to ask the question.

George looked up. Today's two guards were fresh faces and they seemed to constitute an upgrade from his previous experience.

'Yes, please. That would be lovely,' Whittaker said.

George looked up at the door as it clicked shut when Smythe, a blur through the toughened glass, pushed his back to it. George noticed the heat for the first time since arriving. The room was as unbearable as ever but that door closing suddenly made it feel even more uncomfortable. It seemed smaller today, tighter. His stomach was turning over, the rage turning to disgust. He felt he might vomit and his back ran with sweat. It turned his thoughts to what Emma had said. *Those girls would be sweating heavily. They would be soaked. Their own sweat would start to heat up, too, until it boiled on their skin.*

'We need to talk, George, before he comes in here. I can't have you leaping over a table or doing something equally stupid. We're here to do a job.'

'I want to. I really want to. I can't get it out of my head . . . what he did . . . I've never seen anything like that.' George flopped into a chair and dropped his eyes to the floor. He heard the chair opposite scrape.

'Horrible business, George. Are you okay?'

'Not really, Major. Sometimes the world just makes me sick and weary.'

'I know what you mean, old boy, really I do.'

'I should have known there was something more to all this. When I saw the state of that DS. I could tell he had taken it hard, Emma and her team, too. I thought it was a bit of a small-town mentality, you know? Like, maybe you don't get much violence up there and they don't see too many dead girls. I was wrong about them.'

'It's okay to be wrong sometimes, George. Even you.'

'You sound just like Emily Ryker.'

'You mean I sound like somebody else who knows you well?'

George lifted his head. 'I'm okay, Major. I'm not looking forward to sitting opposite this piece of shit. But we're in and out, right? He just needs to tell us that what was left in that . . . thing . . . was all that remained of that poor girl. Then he gives us the other site. Then you can task someone else with going to find it and we can go and get on with our lives.'

'That's it. You're going to be okay to do that?'

'You mean without using my bare hands to speed up his prognosis? I make no promises.' George could tell Whittaker was lingering on him. 'Look, don't worry. I know how to get a job done.'

'Back in the army days we had a job to do. I can't tell you where in the world this was, George, but let's just say it was another world altogether. We were sent to sweep a village school. A gang of rebels had taken it. Hell of a firefight. They left pretty damned quick. We had to sweep the building to be sure they were gone. They had gone, but the school had been in use when they went in. By the time they left, no one was alive.'

'Jesus, Major, I can't imagine.'

'Well, I don't have to, George, unfortunately. I can conjure up the images from that place any time I want to. And, of course, any time when I really *don't* want to. We walked through that place and it was like hell itself. They were grouped together in the classrooms, all at the back, by the windows. You could see where they had been trying to get out. They never stood a chance. It was a primary school, George. I didn't lose anyone getting inside that building, but by the time we stepped out the other side I had lost all twelve. Physically they were fine, but their heads were gone. Not straight away. We did our job, but those men were never the same. They were big blokes, George — brave and strong. Like bloody tigers. Too big, maybe. Too strong. They didn't talk to one another. They didn't talk to me. They didn't talk to anyone. Sometimes we all need a bit of help to work out the world. It's a shithole, George. There are people in it that are from a place we can never understand. I'm not one of those who say you have to learn to accept it. Luckily for us we don't have to, because we're police officers. We get to make a difference. We hunted down those men that were in that school and we rid the world of every last one of them. And because of that, I can live with it. I can live with what I saw because I can tell myself that I cured the world of that little part of it. Today . . . what we saw . . . we can play our part in caging it. We can make sure it never gets an opportunity to hurt anyone again. We just sit in front of him for a few minutes. We listen to his shit and we're out. Don't let it eat away at you. You're part of the cure, George. Take heart from that.'

'I always have, Major. It wasn't so much what I saw today, it was what we didn't see . . . what those girls would have gone through. And then he just leaves her in there so a few years later all we get are some stinking remains, a few bits of bone. Forensics are going to have to scrape out what's left. How can anyone think so little of another human being? It was so beautiful up there. I've always loved the woods. Things like that can taint somewhere forever.'

'They can. I won't even bother saying that you should try not to let it. From now on, when we walk through a forest we're going to think about those girls. There's no point pretending we won't. That's okay. Just don't let it be the only thing you think about. Make sure you think about what you did to stop that, about how you're the reason it won't happen again.'

The knock at the door made George jump. A guard bustled in and put two teas down. He dropped them hurriedly on the table — the cups were too hot in his grip. He wore a pained expression and rubbed his fingers. George's mind flashed to a female resting her hands and knees on searing metal, in the pitch black with nowhere to go. He shivered.

'Are you ready for him now?' The guard said.

'Yes. Thank you,' Whittaker replied.

Roberts was led through thirty seconds later. Two guards flanked him with an arm each. It looked like they might be holding him up rather than controlling a threat. George certainly didn't feel threatened. He wanted Roberts to be bigger, to be more of the man he was when he was first imprisoned — so he could be angry, so they could go toe-to-toe, so it would be more evenly matched. Instead, Roberts looked pathetic. He slunk into his seat directly opposite George. His eyes were down, his face twisted into a grimace, as though the act of sitting down was causing him pain. Smythe was back in the room too. He slunk into the corner. George stayed seated. Whittaker stood over his shoulder. He reached down to press the record button on the device on the table. It beeped confirmation.

'I am Chief Inspector John Whittaker. I am here with Inspector George Elms and this is a recorded conversation with convicted prisoner Henry Roberts. This is being recorded for evidential purposes, which means you do not have to say anything today, Henry, and you need to be aware that anything you do say may be used in evidence. You are tried and convicted in relation to this matter so this recording only becomes significant with any future appeals or challenges to your sentence. This meeting and its recording is as per an agreement with your legal team. Do you still consent to this meeting being audio recorded?'

'Yes, of course!' Roberts grinned widely.

'You have agreed to reveal the location of your victim. We are not here to discuss any other matters and we will not do so. We will not ask you any questions outside of that. We will write a short summary of what you have told us, which you will be given the opportunity to sign as correct. Your solicitor is here to oversee, but also in case you have any questions. Should you wish to speak to your solicitor we will leave the room and the recording will be stopped. Do you understand?'

George kept his eyes down while Whittaker covered the formal points. He was concentrating on his breathing. He used the liquid in his tea as something to focus on. It fidgeted against the sides, picking up every movement from the room. Roberts didn't reply, and George sensed Whittaker shuffling beside him. The silence continued. George felt compelled to look up. Henry Roberts was staring right at him. He was close. He was leaning forward on his scrawny neck. His cheeks were more sunken than even a few days before. He smiled as George made eye contact, those black eyes tore right into him. He was studying him intently, his head rocked to one side, his lips curled into a sneer.

'You went there, didn't you?' Henry said.

George sniffed. He straightened his back. He shuffled a little further away. 'I don't think you listened to a word that was just said did you, Henry? There's an agreement. Do your bit and we'll go and do ours.'

'I didn't think you would! I thought you would come in here and pretend to have been. I would have known though, George. What did you think?'

George turned his attention back to his tea and took a swig.

'Are you wasting our time here, Henry?' Whittaker said. 'You need to start talking about why we're here or we'll be leaving. I think your solicitor can tell you what that means for your deal.'

'Mr Roberts, can I urge you to discuss the matter in hand only, please? They police are only concerned with the final location. Once this meeting is complete, I can immediately push for the next phase. To get you moved.'

'It's a beautiful spot up there beyond the woods. Don't you think, George? I spent a long time up there.'

'Was she in there? Was that all that was left? And the other girl, where is she?' George growled. He had to bite down hard to stop any more words coming out.

'Tell me what you saw, Inspector. Describe it for me.'

'This is not my time to speak, Henry.' George swallowed hard. He knew Henry wanted him to lose his control. He focused on the recorder in the middle of the table. He kept reminding himself that it was all evidence, that Roberts was putting himself at the scene, something he had never done before. It probably wouldn't make any difference, but it gave him some satisfaction at least.

'Did you see the mouth? At one end of the bull. I twisted the metal to make a mouthpiece. It's shaped like an instrument. It *is* an instrument! Oh, Inspector, you should see it in action! You should *hear* it! The voices inside, the bellows, the cries for help and then the cries of discomfort. They drift out as the softest sound, like a beautiful chorus sung just for you. It mingles with the birds, with the shuffling of the trees. Nothing artificial about that sound. It's wild and pure. It's the soul, Inspector. It's beautiful when it goes.'

'You've had your fun, Henry. You've got your captive audience. Now . . . where is she?'

'Who?' Roberts was beaming, his face showed pure delight.

'Chloe Pope. The girl you tortured and murdered. You can sit there with a big grin on your face all you like, Henry. I don't really give a damn. Where is she?'

Roberts sat back. 'Ah, the police! Black and white.'

'Last chance, Henry. Remember, your deal walks out with me. And your deal was both of the girls.'

'But you found her already! Miss Pope was there too, Inspector.'

'What are you talking about?'

'The remains. You found the remains lying deep in the belly, didn't you?' Roberts leant forward. He was so close, George could smell his odour. The guards stepped in close behind him. 'I didn't have the time to wait for her to cool that time. Test what you have and you'll see. They were both in there. Not at the same time, Inspector. Not to start with. One watched. Pick which one you think. That was something, Inspector! Oh the fear! It was accidental. Necessity. But having two! It was so . . . beautiful!'

George felt a hand on his shoulder. It had a grip. Tight enough to have some control. He was now aware that he had risen up a little, his thighs locked in a squat. The hand pushed him back down into the seat.

'We're done then.' Whittaker's voice drifted over George's head. He wasn't focused on anything. He was aware of more speech in a deep baritone. He sensed Roberts was talking to him but he wasn't listening to the words. Then Roberts stood up in front of him. He was just a wide blur. He was led out of the room. George was vaguely aware of other movement.

'George? It's done.'

George shook his head free. It was Whittaker. Everyone else was gone.

'Let's get out of here shall we, old boy?'

Chapter 14

George walked hurriedly to the door. He always got a nervous, excited feeling when he was picking up his daughter. Tonight, though, it felt a little muted. He almost wished he wasn't seeing her. Not because he didn't want to — he yearned to spend every available hour with her. He just felt like the day had sucked the joy right out from him. He was still rattled. He just hoped he could move on and forget what the world was capable of for the few hours he was in the company of his daughter.

'Daddddddddddeeeeeeeeeeey!' Charley yanked the door wide open before he had a chance to knock. She barrelled into him. She wanted to hug and bounce at the same time. George swept her up. All his anxiety, all the horrors of the day, every piece of that sealed metal tomb — it was all gone. He held Charley in a tight squeeze and lifted her off her feet.

'How you doing, chicken?'

'Good. You're late!'

George checked his watch. 'Three minutes, Charley! I mean, that's not bad.'

'Mummy said you would be late.'

'I'm sure she did. And I'm very sorry, Charley. I promise it won't happen again. Is your mother here?' George looked into Sarah's family home. Sarah and Charley were back living in it for a short time, at least until Sarah and her new fella, Ronnie, managed to find a place. George tried not to think about that too much. It was a big former farmhouse in a rural setting on the outskirts of Canterbury.

'She got me ready. She said she couldn't come and see you. I've got everything I need.' Charley held up a small bag that was hanging across her shoulder. She was wearing a fleece top and had a jacket draped over her arm. Sarah always came to the door for a quick chat — just pleasantries. Sometimes it was awkward, but they were getting on a little better. At least George had thought so.

'She say why?'

'No, Daddy. Can we go? What time does the film start?'

'Yes, honey, don't worry, we've got plenty of time.' George called into the house: 'Sarah? SARAH! You in there? Is there any sort of handover with this package?' George tried to sound jovial. He looked back at his daughter. 'What about your nanny? Is she here?'

'No. She's out. Shopping, I think.'

'SARAH?'

'Okay, George! Okay, hang on!' The stairs were right in front of the door and Sarah's voice came from the top of them.

'You okay?' George persisted.

'Yes, of course.' Sarah didn't seem to be coming any closer.

George stepped in. He could see Sarah's legs. They were trailing down the stairs. She was sitting on the top step. 'I thought you would come and say hello is all.'

'I don't have to, do I? She's nine now, George. I don't think she likes her mother hanging on her back the whole time.'

'I'm sure she doesn't. What's the matter?'

'Nothing, George. I just said that.' She seemed agitated, and George knew when he was being told half-truths. He certainly knew his wife. He stepped in a little further and pressed the switch in the hall that lit the stairs. Sarah tried turning away. It was too late.

'Where's the bruise from?'

'Why are you giving me the third degree, George? I'm not one of your criminals. I don't need to answer your questions.'

'Who did that to you?' He moved further in. Sarah turned back to face him. Her right eye had a black tinge with a brown smudge lower on her cheek — a black eye, maybe a day or two old, and her nose was red and swollen

'It wasn't a *who*, it was a *what*. I bumped it getting into the car.'

'You did that getting into a car?' She was lying. Everything about her screamed it: no eye contact; her body turned away from him; she was rubbing at her neck; her head even shook a little as she spoke — a subconscious tick. It was all too common: a mouth saying something that the body contradicted completely.

'Did Ronnie do this to you?'

'Don't be ridiculous, George.'

'Did Ronnie do this to Mummy, Charley?'

'George!' Sarah ran down the steps and put her arms around their daughter's shoulders. 'Don't say things like that in front of Charley, please!'

'No. Mummy said she bumped her eye when she was getting in the car.'

'Like I said. It was a freak accident is all,' Sarah said

'But he does shout a lot.'

'Charley!' Sarah scolded. 'That isn't true. Everyone argues from time to time. But this was nothing to do with him.'

'At you?' George said. His question was directed to Charley.

'He shouts at everyone!' Charley said.

'Is he here?' George said. He was trying to stay calm. He knew he wasn't managing it very well. He could feel the heat in his cheeks and was aware that his breathing had quickened. He had bunched his fists.

'No, he isn't here. He's working late. They've got a big project on the go. He'll be back a bit later. This is nothing to do with him, George. Don't you go making anything of it. I was in a rush. I caught my face on the car door. I feel like an idiot, okay? I'm very embarrassed — and I had a hunch you might misinterpret things — so I didn't come down to see you. Now you need to get out to see your film.'

George didn't talk anymore to Sarah. He couldn't. He put Charley in the car and they drove off. Charley was excited. She chatted non-stop. It had only been a few days since he had seen her last but she was full of stories about school, boys and her dancing lessons. These were usually the best times. He would always make sure the first hour or so was time that they could just spend talking together. Today he had planned for them to have a meal first and then a film at the cinema. He should be chatting with her. He should be just as excited. But now his mind was back at the farmhouse. Filled with that bruise and thoughts of another man shouting at his daughter. They made it to the restaurant: TGI Fridays. It was Charley's favourite and she bounded through the door. They were shown to a table. George got his daughter settled. He left her blowing bubbles in her coke and took a few steps away with his phone in his hand.

'George? I thought you were out with your daughter tonight?' Emily Ryker picked up on the first ring. She was George's intelligence officer, or at least she was assigned to his Major Crime Department. They were very close. Too close at one point before George and Sarah met. That was very much ancient history but George still respected Emily as the finest intelligence officer he knew. If ever he needed answers, she was the woman who could provide them.

'I am,' George whispered.

'Okaaaay . . .?'

'I know this is a bit out of the blue, and we've had a similar conversation already . . .'

'But?'

'But did you ever find out anything about Ronnie Giles?'

'Ronnie Giles. The architect. Your ex-wife's new partner?'

'She's not my ex-wife, Ryker.'

'Okay, fine. So your wife's new partner?'

'Yes.'

'We did have this conversation. You might remember it? It was the one where I told you that I can only use police systems for *crime* enquiries. I probably also mentioned that those systems are tracked, so they know what I'm looking at and when. The only thing they don't know — but they will ask me to explain — is why.'

'I remember that. I get that about police systems. But you're the best I know at open source research. Facebook, Companies House — all that stuff.'

'What do you need to know, George?'

'I just need to know where he works. That's all. Nothing incriminating, nothing about his criminal history or past domestic incid—'

'Assuming he has any.'

'Assuming he has any. Can you do that?'

Emily sighed. 'When for George?'

'How long is *High School Musical 3*? I really have no idea!'

'Are you kidding me?'

'I know you're at home. I know you're off duty. I'd really appreciate it.'

'Should I dare ask why?'

George considered this for a second. 'No. Probably not. I just need to know if I'm right or not.'

'You're always right, George. Even when you're not. It's your worst trait.'

'Thanks for pointing it out.'

George's mood improved a little during the meal. Charley's enthusiasm for life, her innocence and her cheeriness, it captured his heart as usual. He found himself wishing, not for the first time, that Charley would never have to grow up. The film was entirely as expected. An American high school dance troupe winning a competition against all odds with a lot of singing and dancing was never going to be something George could be enthusiastic about, but Charley enjoyed herself and nothing was more important.

When he dropped Charley back, her nan answered the door.

'Hey, Joan.'

'George. Did she have a good time?'

'I think she did, yeah.'

'She told me you were letting her choose the film. How did that go?'

'As expected.' They shared a chuckle. Joan was a good woman. They had always gotten on well, even though she'd found herself in the middle of her daughter's marital issues.

'How's Sarah?' George tried to sound casual. Joan's expression was immediately serious.

'She said that you saw her bruised eye. She said you got upset about it.'

'Of course I did.'

'She banged it on a car door, George. These things happen.'

George lingered on Joan. She didn't give a reaction, but she wouldn't meet his eye. 'They do, Joan. Do you think that's what happened?'

'That's what she told me.'

'That doesn't answer my question.'

'Well, it should do, George. She told me what happened. She doesn't lie to me.'

'And Ronnie, did he tell you the same?'

'He wasn't there when we talked about it. Recently, he's been working a lot more to be honest. I wonder if he's been staying there rather than coming back here. I don't think he's unhappy, I just think they need their own space.'

'I'm sure they do.'

'Look, George, she's an adult. She's always been able to take care of herself and she's never stood for anyone's crap. If she wasn't being treated right she would deal with it. Don't you think?'

'I suppose, Joan. She dealt with me alright.'

Joan chuckled again. 'Well, there you are. It's nice to see you again, George. We'll get this little madam to bed for now. See you soon?'

'You will. I'm picking her up again on Saturday. Is Sarah not home? Are they out?' George gestured past where she stood at the open door.

'She's in. In the bath, I think. Ronnie's working late again. They've got a big contract on the go at the moment. They've all been working late into the night.'

George walked towards his car. He heard the door pushed shut behind him. He was back on his phone. He dialled the number for Emily Ryker.

'You sure you want this?' Emily asked, skipping all pleasantries.

'Of course.'

'It wasn't difficult to find. He's working for an architects in Canterbury. They're quite open on their website about who they employ. He's one of their faces.'

'I'm sure he is.'

'They're at the University Campus in Canterbury. The Innovation Centre there.'

'I know it.'

'I thought you might. One of the units. I don't know which one specifically. There's an accountants, some sort of consultancy and a few other desk-based start-ups. It'll be busy during the day. The sort of place where you could easily make a scene.'

'Make a scene! What do you think I intend on doing, Ryker?'

'Like I said, I don't want to know. And you didn't get any information from me.'

'Understood. And don't worry, I won't be going there during the day.'

The call ended as George got back to his car. The university campus was just a few miles away on the other side of the city. He started the car and made for it.

The campus was large. The entrance was off a steep hill. There were neat lawns on either side of the road that meandered through the grounds. The pavements on either side were lamp-lit but the grounds beyond were in darkness. The Innovation Centre was separate from the main university buildings. It had its own car park to the back. The main reception looked to be shut up for the night and only one of the units showed any lights. George couldn't see anyone moving inside as he swept past. He parked close to it. He could see four other cars, well spread out. Each had a layer of moisture on their windscreens as if they had been there a while. There was movement now, from inside the lit unit. A man stood leaning over a desk. George watched as he straightened up, removed his glasses and rubbed his hands through his hair. He looked tired. His collar hung open. George had met the man briefly and only once, but it was definitely Ronnie. He couldn't see anyone else in there. He had to be working late on his own. Each unit had its own rear door access that led straight out into the car park. He could see it was hanging open slightly. It was a warm evening for the time of year.

As George moved to the door, Ronnie's attention had remained downwards, but then he moved suddenly away from his desk and towards the back of the office. George could see a number of desks. They were all higher than in a standard office and with stools in front of them rather than office chairs. The computers were more like large-screen televisions that were at different angles on stands jutting out of the desks. Ronnie had been bent over one. Now he was pouring out a drink from a coffee pot. George hadn't really thought about what he would say. He'd intended on thinking it through first but he was here now and this was his chance. He stepped quietly inside.

The room was lit harshly by strip lighting. Ronnie still had his back to George who watched him put a mug of coffee on the desk. His sigh turned into a deep yawn as he opened the drawer and pulled out a sachet of sugar. When he leant back on the desk, George's eye was drawn to the knuckles on his right hand. They looked red; the middle one seemed a little misshapen, even swollen. He then swung around quickly. 'What the—'

George reacted instinctively. He caught Ronnie half turn. He took hold of his right shoulder and pushed him back so he was facing the coffee machine. He grabbed his right hand and forced it downwards. George's knee was the same height as the drawer. He shoved it as hard as he could. The drawer slammed shut on Ronnie's hand and he screamed out in pain. The drawer bounced back out and George lifted his foot this time. He kicked it back shut as hard as he could. Ronnie dropped to his knees and screamed again. George took hold of the drawer. He slammed it again into his hand. Ronnie tried to snatch it out. George caught him by the wrist. He pushed it back and held it. He slammed the drawer again with his knee. And again. George finally let go. Ronnie fell to the ground, took up a foetal position and brought his right hand up to his face. His fingers were at different angles, his knuckles flushed white. He screamed again.

George grabbed him by the hair. 'Shut the fuck up!' He wrenched Ronnie's head backwards so that he could look into his eyes. Ronnie was sweating, his face wore a shocked expression. 'George? What the hell are you doing?' His face was red, his eyes watery.

'The next time you lay a hand on my wife or child, I won't stop until I break something you can't fix. Do I make myself clear?' George hissed through gritted teeth. He still had hold of Ronnie's hair. He felt him nod. George's jaw was locked so tight he could hardly speak. 'Now put your hand back in the drawer.' The drawer had bounced back open. It was just above Ronnie's head. He looked up at it.

'Please! Please, George! No more!'

'Put your hand back in the *fucking* drawer, Ronnie.'

'I'm sorry, okay. I'm sorry. It escalated! It won't happen again. I get the message, yeah?'

'PUT. . . YOUR . . . HAND. . .' George spoke slowly. He steadied himself. He knew he was losing control. He took a moment. 'Put your hand back in the drawer.' His voice came back quieter but with no less menace.

'What the hell, George? You're a police officer! You can't be doing this!'

'That just means I know how to dispose of a body, Ronnie.' George let go of the grip he had on Ronnie's hair. Ronnie got to his knees. He was still facing away. He bent his head so his forehead touched the wooden surface of the units. His right hand reached out. He rested it on the lip of the drawer. He held it there.

But George was already walking away. As he reached the door, he glanced back to see Ronnie still on his knees, his shoulders shaking as he sobbed. George turned away and made for his car.

He fell into the driver's seat, his heart racing still; his breathing was shallow, his palms clammy on the steering wheel. He drove fast out of the car park. The tyres screeched. He made it out of the campus and turned hard left to roll down the hill back towards the city centre. He was trying to breathe, trying to get himself under control. Trying not to turn the car round and go back there to finish the job. He shouldn't be driving, he wasn't concentrating. He turned off the main road and pulled up. He turned the engine off and angled the mirror in the sudden silence. When he peered into it he saw that his eyes were wide, his lips pulled back over his teeth in a sort of snarl. Driving away from the campus, he'd thought he was furious. But the man looking back at him now was something very different. He was terrified. His heart still beat hard and fast, his hands were trembling as they moved to his phone. He scrolled shakily through his favourites. Emily Ryker picked up on the first call.

'You do know I'm off duty, right?' She sounded angry.

'Ryker . . .' It was all he could manage, his voice was breaking as he said it.

'George? George, are you okay?'

'I'm just as bad. I'm just like him.'

'What's the matter? What happened?'

'Shit day, Ryker,' he said. He lifted his hand to rub at his face. It fell over his mouth. The whole day and every emotion of it rushed back at once and overcame him.

'What do you need?'

'Can I come round? Can I come to you?'

She hesitated, but just for a second or two. 'Of course. I'll make sure the kettle's on.'

Chapter 15

Liam Cooney had waited long enough for the darkness to come. Though it was twilight, the lights down to the garden had clicked on and that was good enough for him. He moved quietly but still peered over to his neighbours' gardens. The fences on either side were tall but they dropped with the gradient. The grass was too long; his feet swished through it. His mum always liked it when it was freshly mowed. He should have cut it a few days earlier. He didn't like to leave it. It would be so long by the time he made it back.

He pulled open the shed door. The lawnmower was in the corner and he briefly considered firing it up. He shook his head. That would be silly. It would look out of place at this time of night. He turned in the doorway and peered back out at his neighbours' houses one last time. Some had lights on; most already had curtains drawn. They were all settling in for the night. No one cared about him. They never had before.

He pulled the shed door shut, swung the catch across, clipped a thick padlock through it and pocketed the key. Satisfied, he turned on the light and looked over at the bench. The stout Victorian iron he had left resting on top had moved slightly, leaving fresh scrape marks. She must have given it a real shove. He was impressed; she shouldn't have been able to move it at all. She had spirit. She was a fighter. He pulled the rope from his pocket and tested its strength. It was thick, coarse and worn. But it was strong. No way anyone was getting out of that when he knotted it up tight.

He hauled the iron off the top and heard a scuffling noise. She was awake in there and she was moving. He checked the windows. They were all covered over. He undid the padlock that kept the box lid down. The catch had enough give for the lid to lift just an inch. Liam considered that it might have even given her hope. But she was never getting out. The lid yawned open. The bottom of the box was hidden by shadow but he could just make out her limbs. And her upturned face against her blonde hair.

'Are you okay?'

He heard a whimper. She moved. Slowly. The box wasn't big enough for her to move a lot. He had read up on it: when you suppress people's movement, their limbs can't move properly — they stiffen up. It takes fifteen minutes or more for the blood flow to fill the muscles again. She wouldn't be able to move well to start with. Perfect.

'Please . . .' she said. That voice again. Soft, gentle, beautiful. He liked it when she pleaded with him. He wanted to get closer. He yearned for her to whisper it right in his ear. He squatted over her.

'What did you say?'

He turned his face. Her lips were a few inches from his ear.

'Please. Please let me go.' He could feel her breath against his cheek. He closed his eyes to the pleasure. He stood back up. His face was a wide grin.

'Your freedom is coming. I'm going to make sure of it! I was up in the house and I suddenly thought — I don't even know your name! What is your name?'

'Please!' The voice was a little stronger.

'Your *name*? What should I call you?'

'Please, just let me go.'

'Your NAME!' His anger flared. It bent him double, his face close to hers again, his eyes forced wide. He could feel his heartbeat in his temple. He swallowed. Straightened back up and took a breath. He still couldn't control it. Even now.

'Annie. It's Annie. Please, don't hurt me.'

'Annie!' He said. He stepped away and closed his eyes. 'Annie,' he said. He inhaled deeply. Perfect. It was all perfect. 'You need to come with me, Annie. You understand, right?'

'Are you going to hurt me?' Annie had managed to rise to a sit. She was rubbing her legs, probably trying to get some feeling back into them. The blood would be rushing to her legs, causing them to tingle and itch.

'You need to do what I say, Annie. I think we can get on. I think we can be good for each other, but you have to do what I say. Do you think you can do that? If you're good to me, Annie, I will be *so* good to you. I will be so good!' He stopped talking. He felt himself welling up. The emotion had crept up on him. It took him a little by surprise. He took a breath and pushed it back down. He focused back on Annie. She was sitting up with the light on her face. Her hair fell over it a little but she lifted her hand to push it back behind her ear, the way he had seen her do it a thousand times before: on the train, when she got into her car, when she walked with her head bent and her headphones in. She was doing it for him now. All for him. When she moved her hair he could see her face. Her cheek around her eye was swollen, it was an angry red and her eyelid looked like it was a little more closed than the other.

'What happened to your eye? To your face?' He could feel the anger building in him again.

'You know what happened. What do you mean?'

'What happened? Tell me what happened.'

'You hit me. Are you taking the mick?'

He shook his head. He couldn't remember! He couldn't remember hitting her. She was lying! That must be it. He wouldn't have hurt her. She was perfect.

'Who hit you?'

'*You* hit me. Why are you talking like that?' Her voice was stronger. She sounded like she was getting upset. Her tone was harsher. He didn't like it. He liked it when she was soft. He shook his head. Sometimes he could get angry. He could black out, his mum used to tell him — she would have bruises too. He would get so angry, begging her to tell him who had done it, who had hurt her. She finally told him. She said it was him. She said he got so angry she didn't recognise him. She said his eyes went all funny. Just like a bathroom window, she said. He was so sorry. He said so all the time. His mum . . . she said it didn't matter, that she knew it wasn't his fault. She said he could hurt anyone when he was like that.

'Where are we going? I just want to go home.'

'You can't go home. Not yet. We're going for a ride. You need to come with me.'

'A ride? I don't want to go for a ride! I just want to go home! Please! Just let me go home.'

'No!' he snapped. He knew he had. He didn't want to get angry. Not at her. He didn't want to leave any more bruises on her. They needed to get going. 'Hold your hands out. Put them together and hold them out.'

'No. Please, please just let me go.'

'Hold your *fucking* hands out!' He was angry again but this time he sucked in air straight after. Like he was taking back the words. His mum hated it when he cursed. She wouldn't listen to it. She would tell him; she would say that you shouldn't talk like that, that you shouldn't use *them*

141

words. Sometimes he would get angrier, they would argue, he would come back in the room and his mum . . . she would have new bruises.

Annie stood up. She looked shaky on her legs. 'I'm going home. You can't keep me here.' She moved forward. She lifted her leg to get out. She wasn't listening to him. She wasn't doing what she was told.

His hand plunged for his waistband. He'd brought a knife, the biggest he could find. It was a zombie knife, one of his own. He had got it from the internet. It was a sharpened, steel arc that could gut her in an instant if he wanted it to. He moved closer to her. He was on her quickly, his left hand grabbed a fistful of hair. He pulled back hard and her face lifted to the light. He pulled the knife round so it flashed in front of her eyes and settled on her throat.

'You're coming with me. You're going to do what I say. Do you understand?' Her puffy eyes were wide and didn't blink. They flicked to meet with his. She jerked her head. He pushed it away. He felt disgust. He rubbed his hand down his jeans. It was damp with her sweat.

'We need to get going. The next time you say *no* to me I *will* slit your throat. Are you coming with me now?' He picked up the rope and ran it through his hands, licking his lips.

'Yes,' she said.

Chapter 16

George woke up fully dressed in a bed he didn't recognise. His head was muzzy, tinnitus fizzing loudly in his ears, and he was aware of a bright block of sunlight across which a shadow moved.

'Alright?' It was Emily Ryker's voice. George squinted. Her form was still backlit by the sun.

'Nope.'

'That'll be the hangover. I'll make some breakfast. It'll be downstairs.'

The shadow departed. He still needed to squint when he sat up. The curtains looked like they had been pulled roughly open. He was in a double bed — Ryker's, he guessed. The other side was flat and made; he must have slept alone. He swung out his legs and paced to the window. Ryker lived right on the coast. Her move to the south of the county was only supposed to have been temporary — one week, a couple of weeks, a month tops. That was three years ago. Officially, hers was still a temporary attachment, and her job role had never been sorted, so she still rented places. George thought he knew her well enough to suggest that she was always going to be scared of laying down roots. He reckoned that was why she never pushed to have her contract resolved. It remained the perfect excuse *not* to settle. He stretched at the window and concluded that she should stay, even if it was just for that view. The English Channel practically lapped at her door. Her backyard ended with a low wall where the promenade started, and on the other side of that were the pebbles. He turned away. Sea views had become something of a sore point. He walked down the stairs and into the kitchen.

'Coffee. Strong.' Ryker slapped a mug down in front of him. It read KEEP CALM AND FOLLOW SPURS. Tottenham was Ryker's football team.

'How come I get the Spurs cup?'

'What would you prefer? There are some little floral china numbers in the back of the cupboard left by the little old dear who was here before me.'

'I like a china cup, actually.'

'I bet you do. It wouldn't feel right though. They're not meant for people like you: wearing yesterday's suit, swigging black tea to cure your hangover.'

'I suppose I can't argue with that.'

'Scrambled eggs okay?'

'You know I recently told someone I had an egg allergy so she wouldn't throw them at me. One of the stranger fibs I've told. She . . . you know what, it doesn't matter. Eggs? Yes, please, Ryker.'

Emily rolled her eyes, 'I swear you're getting stranger. I'm sure I don't need to know your morning-after stories either. Just call a taxi and leave like everyone else!' Emily laughed. It seemed forced.

'It wasn't a morning after. We'd just met actually. Not even . . . honestly, forget it! And thanks.'

'Don't thank me. Two minutes in the microwave, George. You won't get no Jamie Oliver shit round here.'

'I don't mean for the eggs! I kinda chewed your ear last night. Turned up out of nowhere.'

'Drank all my whisky.'

'Drank all of your whisky . . . Ah, that explains it.' He reached for his head.

'Don't worry about it. You need to talk out shit like that. Whittaker was right, you know. It can fester.'

'That might explain the smell.' George sniffed his shirt in disapproval.

'You can have a shower if you want but you'd have to get back into those clothes. If you really want a change I've got a size-ten off-the-shoulder number that might go with your shoes.'

George snorted into his mug. 'Nah, I figure I'll get back home to my own clothes. I'm a size twelve, see.'

'So what are you going to do now?'

'Now?'

'Yeah, about this Roberts piece of work. You flip-flapped all over the place last night. One minute you were moving on, forgetting about the whole thing, the next you were turning up at the court of appeal yourself. Where are you now?'

'Ah. Sorry about the flip-flapping. It always happens when I'm on the whisky. I'm going up there.'

'Up there? Up where?'

'Back to Symonds Yat. I want to talk to the SIO again. I just want to bottom out this missing person.'

'The SIO? This Emma you were talking about, right? The inspector?'

'Yeah.'

'What for?'

'I don't know really. Closure probably — for me, I mean. I might be able to help.'

'So might the other hundreds of officers who are actually warranted to work in her police force, George. We're a long way from that particular coal face. Think how we would react if we got officers from other forces turning up and demanding to help. They would all get a pill. Police forces don't mix well.'

'I know that, Ryker. But this is different. I could feel her desperation. We've all been there. When we need something to happen but we're too scared or too proud to ask for help. I think she wants help.'

'From you?' Emily chuckled.

'Well, she doesn't know me, does she?'

'She can't do. Are you sure it was help she was after?'

'In all honesty, I've got no idea. I figured I could go and see her. I need to speak to her anyway. I need to keep her up to date on what happened with Roberts — what he said. They won't know yet. Whittaker said he would leave it to me to tell her. It wouldn't feel right doing it on the phone.'

'No, well, you can't poke your nose in so easy over the phone!'

'It's not about poking my nose in, Ryker. I told you, I saw that site yesterday. There's no way one man does all that alone. Drags that . . . that thing through those trails. Then gets two young women there too. It doesn't work.'

'And then you've got another girl missing in the same circumstances . . .'

'Exactly.'

'Time for Super George to swoop in and save the day.' George flashed angry. He bit hard so he didn't react but he stared Emily down. She raised her palms in surrender. 'I'm just saying. You need to be aware that it's going to look like that. Sometimes you police with your big size tens, George. You know that as well as I do. We put up with it down here because we have to.'

George felt his anger drop away just as quickly as it came on. She had a point. 'You're right. She needs updating. That's my reason for being there. I'll see how she is, see how they're getting on. I can offer my help at least.'

'And if they turn you down?'

'The size tens, Ryker.'

Chapter 17

George felt a little better for the freshen-up and change of clothes at his flat. When he got back to his car, he checked his phone. He had missed a call from Whittaker and made a mental note to call him back at some point. He didn't want to do it yet. He wanted to be far enough away from Langthorne that it would be difficult for Whittaker to call him back. Not that he thought he would. It was a reasonable move to go up and talk to the Senior Investigating Officer for a job like this in person. The update was not one he was looking forward to giving. He also had an email from an HMP address — Her Majesty's Prison. He scanned the content hurriedly. The body of the email acknowledged his request for copies of all correspondence to prisoner Henry Roberts. It said that he hadn't received or sent any letters, but they attached all the prisoner's logs. That was something more than he'd asked for — unusual for HMP. Maybe they'd felt like they had to send something? High-risk prisoners like Roberts had a constant log running. It would mostly be handwritten and was a running record of his day that was filled out by whichever staff members were on duty. It would include things such as his meals, any medication and his general routine. It would also include anything of note. It probably wouldn't help, but George thought it might break his journey up by finding a coffee stop an hour up the motorway and giving it a read.

He also wanted to send a text message to Ryker. He looked at a blinking cursor for a good minute or more. He didn't know what to say. He settled on: *Thanks for hearing me out last night. I guess I needed a rant. Sorry to intrude. And about your whisky.* He sent it before he could think any longer about the content.

An hour and a half later he was in the queue for an overpriced services coffee and Ryker still hadn't replied. He considered sending another but changed his mind quickly. He was pretty certain he hadn't done anything to upset her. She was probably just busy.

He walked his coffee over to a table against a window and opened the email from HMP again, this time pressing on the attachment. It took a while for his phone to work. He took the opportunity to look around, checking there was no one close. Most people appeared to be passing through and the few sitting anywhere near him were taking no notice. The attachment finally downloaded and he opened up the prisoner log. It was small on his phone, so he zoomed in as best he could. It was a scanned handwritten document: the dates and times were down the left-hand column; the wider column captured Roberts's movements. Every aspect of his life was recorded. It made for pretty bland reading. Henry Roberts was given three meals a day. Mostly he had these in his cell and, from the small cross-section George scrolled through, it seemed they often came back untouched. He didn't interact with staff at all. His demeanour was recorded as *withdrawn* or *sullen*, but *no concern* was written after each entry. He continued scrolling through the same daily routine: breakfast at 07:30 hours, nurse visits at 08:30, 12:00, 16:00 hours, and a supervised visit to the prison chapel at 18:00

hours that usually lasted around an hour. Some nights were punctuated with a medical visit, too. He noted from the signatures that there were just two different nurses. The names were largely illegible but he could make out a few *CB*s. It looked like Roberts was reading a lot of books, but he did very little else. He closed the file; there was nothing of any interest to him there. He checked his watch. It was nearly 10 a.m. He needed to get back on the road.

Emma Rowe met George personally this time. He was back at the front counter of Hereford Police Station. She looked a little more relaxed than the last time he had seen her. She was back in a smart trouser suit. It seemed to suit her better than the jeans and hiking boots.

'How are you, George?'

'Long time no see!' he quipped.

'I know. Lucky you. You get the joys of Hereford twice in a week. You could have just picked up the phone, though, George. I'll be honest, I was expecting just a call.'

'I know. I've never been a big fan of the phone. Not when something's important.'

'Sounds ominous. I know what you mean, though. We'd better get a coffee on the way then.'

George took a tea. There were more biscuits too, a good selection. He declined. Anyone who knew him would have seen that as a sure sign of bad news. Emma didn't know him well but she was still watching him expectantly. Like she knew he wouldn't drive two hundred miles just because he didn't like phones.

'We met with Roberts. Straight after our last visit here. I'll be honest, it probably wasn't the best time. It was hard.'

'I can imagine. Don't beat yourself up about that, I wouldn't have been able to do it, I know that much.'

'Someone had to. The Major came with me.'

'The Major?'

'Sorry, Whittaker — the chief inspector.'

'Ah. That would make sense. I assume he's army. If ever a man carried himself like a major . . .'

'Exactly so. It's like there's a steel rod from his heels up to the back of his head.'

'They all have the same.'

George was stalling. Emma wore an expression he recalled seeing on his mum's face whenever he was building up to telling her he'd misbehaved. It somehow said that it was okay to tell her, to get it off his chest. 'Henry Roberts didn't give up another site.'

Her expression changed instantly. From benign interest to anger. 'That was the agreement though, right?' She was clearly battling to stay calm.

'The agreement was that he gave us the location of the two missing girls. He's done that Emma. They were both there.'

'Both there? At that site? Did we miss something? The forensic team are still there, do I need to—'

'We didn't miss anything, Emma. He left both the girls together. They are still in that contraption.'

'The Brazen Bull.'

'Yes. They're in there together.'

'At the same time? Is that even possible? I'm not even sure they could fit.'

George shrugged. 'He didn't give too many details. I'm not sure how they ended up like that but he said we will find remains in there and they will be a combination of our two missing girls. It doesn't change anything for the forensics team, does it? They will recover everything as they see it. It'll all be bagged and tagged and then identified back at the lab.'

'No. It doesn't change anything from a forensic point of view. They'll need to know, obviously. But, for me standing in front of those families, for me telling them what happened to their little girls, it changes everything. He didn't put them in there together, George, did he? He couldn't have.'

'No,' George conceded.

'So, one of them was second.'

George hung his head. He had made a conscious decision not to tell her about Roberts's comment. The thought of one of the girls waiting for her turn turned his stomach over. He didn't feel the need to inflict that on Emma. But she was too sharp for her own good.

'I guess so.'

'He made one of them watch, didn't he, George?'

'He . . .' George floundered.

'He told you that, didn't he? And he enjoyed telling you. That was why he insisted on speaking to you. You know that, right?'

'Yeah, I know that. I don't know why he's got such a hard-on for me but, yeah, he wanted me to hear his news personally.'

'That's who he is, George. He took great delight in watching my team fall apart around him. The more we found out about him, the more we struggled to stay together and the more he fed off that. You know what you are to him, George? You're an opportunity. An opportunity to watch someone brand-new break in front of him all over again. Because of what he did. It's all about his power over his environment, over the people around him — over the people who try to control him.'

George sighed. He took a few seconds, it was unusual for him not to have a reply ready on his lips. 'I take it you read psychology?'

'I did, as a matter of fact. A long time ago, though. And we were never warned about people like Henry Roberts. I'd never have believed that people like him could ever exist.'

'I know what you mean. He's a new one on me too. I thought I had pretty much seen it all.'

'And for his crimes? We gave him his sea view.' Emma stood up from the table. She paced to the window where he'd seen her a couple of days before. George reckoned that was her thinking spot.

'I'm not sure I know what justice looks like for someone like Roberts.'

'The fires of hell, George. That's all there is.'

'Let's hope it won't be long until he gets there.'

'Indeed.'

'What happened with your missing person case, Emma? Has she turned up yet?'

Emma suddenly stiffened. 'No, not yet, George.'

'You're worried about her.'

'Missing people are always an element of concern, right?'

'Most of them don't worry me in the slightest, Emma. But when you get someone missing and you know in your gut that it isn't right, that they aren't a teenager sneaking out to see a boyfriend or a kid in foster care trekking back to their natural parents. Then you get worried.'

'Well, she is neither of those things, it's true.'

'Where are you with it?'

'There's a whole team working on it,' she was quick to reply.

George held his hands up. 'I don't doubt it. And very capable they all are too, I'm sure.'

'I'm sorry. I didn't mean to snap. I need to protect my team. It's a strange atmosphere, that's all. There are different pressures to normal circumstances. Nothing about this has been *normal*. There's a huge elephant in the room whenever we get together. The last time we investigated missing women like Annie Lowe they were in the clutches of Henry Roberts.'

'But this time she can't be.'

'No, she can't be.'

'But his accomplice? That's a possibility?'

Emma walked over to the opposite window, where blinds fell from the ceiling down to the floor. She turned them in. 'There has never been a shred of physical evidence of an accomplice, George. It was a throwaway comment from a witness who was terrified and confused.'

'That scene yesterday, Emma. It wasn't created by one man. No way. You must have thought that too?'

'I don't know, George. I don't know what to think. You didn't see Henry Roberts before the illness got hold of him. His reputation as "The Bull" was quite apt. He was a man-mountain. Strong as . . . well, as a bull.'

'But that isn't why you named him that, is it? And I assume it was you? Did someone slip up and it got out to the media? That was a nice save, saying it was due to his size.'

'What does a nickname matter? The point stands — he's as strong as a bull.'

'Strong enough to carry an industrial-sized copper water tank the distance we walked? And then two struggling women?'

'It's doable, right? If he made three trips. It would be doable.'

'It's unlikely.'

'We can't deal with unlikely, George!' Emma snapped again. She moved back to her thinking place.

'Of course you can't. You have to deal with the facts you have, especially when you're under the sort of pressure you must have been under. I've been there. The press, the management — they just want a result. And when they get it they don't want to hear that it might not be a complete result. After all the effort it took to get Roberts through that custody door, the last thing you needed was the thought that there might be someone else involved too.'

Emma sighed. 'I shouldn't have mentioned it, George. I haven't mentioned it to anyone else. I would appreciate it if you did the same. This girl will turn up, I'm sure. We're just hypersensitive up here.'

'And if she doesn't?'

'Then it's still none of your concern.' Emma's tone had an edge again. This time there was no apology. George had outstayed his welcome.

'Well, I should leave you to your investigation. I got news back from the prison. He didn't write or receive any letters and no one visited him. He's been living a pretty miserable and solitary life. Nothing more than he deserves, of course.'

'I don't think we can talk about what he deserves really, George, do you? He's too wealthy to get what he deserves.'

'You're right. I'll stay in touch. Let me know if you need any help.'

'I will.'

Her office door closing behind him the second he stepped out told him that he probably wouldn't be the first person she called if she needed a chat.

He walked back out into the fresh air and leant on his car. He didn't feel right driving back to Langthorne, when there was a live investigation going on. But it wasn't his investigation and the SIO had just made it very clear that he wasn't required.

He suddenly realised how hungry he was. He would need to eat before he headed back. He remembered passing a pub that looked like it did a good lunch. It was nearby, in a small village called Symonds Yat, near some grand estate. He started the car and headed towards it.

Chapter 18

The Roberts estate was not difficult to find, despite the only visible part being a big, farm-style gate. It was pulled shut and closer inspection showed it to be padlocked, too. The gate itself was the giveaway — or rather it was the six-foot long, white sheet draped over it with the word *SCUM* written in blood red. George could just about fit his car off the road to park in front of it. He could see the new-looking CCTV camera bolted to the side of a stout tree. The branches around it had been cleared so it would have a direct view of the gate. He wondered who was left to monitor it.

He would get his answer just a minute or so later. He vaulted the gate, leaving the car nudged up against it and walked up the drive. The view opened up as he rounded the corner. The leafy trees gave way to flat lawns and a row of what looked like shop fronts in a converted stable block on the left side. From this distance they all looked shut up. One of them was boarded up, giving locals yet another canvas on which to spray their profanities. He heard a car engine behind him and turned towards it. A small, white van pulled up close to him. George had to step back to read the name and tag line: *ABLE SECURITY: Able to keep your property secure.*

'Hello, can I help you maybe?' The driver's window was lowered to reveal an overweight man bunched up in the cabin. His face was red and clammy, and he looked harassed in general.

George reached for his warrant card. 'I'm a police officer. I'm based out in Hereford. We're running an investigation into some tagging.'

The man's piggy eyes flicked from the warrant card back to George. 'Tagging?'

'Yeah. Graffiti, you know? The kids, they all have their own tags. Up in the city there's hundreds of thousands of pounds of damage from one offender in particular. He uses a specific tag. We've got some intelligence that he might be from this area.'

'They send CID in suits out for tagging these days, then?'

George shrugged. 'Budget cuts. And we're talking high value.'

'Well, there ain't no one living here now.'

'I know that. I know whose place this is. You can't work at Hereford and not know, right? I saw the graffiti on the gate, there's some more over there. I spoke to a couple of local officers and they reckon there might be some more up at the main house. If I can find the same tag out here, that just firms up my intel is all.'

The man licked his lips. He looked out over the steering wheel. 'There is more, yeah. You want me to take you up there?'

'That would be great. Thanks.' George walked to the passenger side. When he opened the door the male was leaning over to push a dozen sweet wrappers, an energy drink and an empty tube of Pringles from the seat. They all fell into the foot well. George thanked him again and sat down, being careful where he put his feet.

'Graffiti, eh?' the man said.

George made a listening grunt.

'I nearly joined your lot, you know.'

'Oh right.'

'Yeah. I got through all the tests an' that. But I got a high blood pressure score. They wouldn't let me in for that. They said it wouldn't be good for me.'

'Yeah, they can be strict like that.'

'I don't get it, but it didn't matter. I got this job pretty much the next day. It's practically the same thing, right?'

George couldn't be bothered to disagree. 'I suppose it's similar, yeah. Do you get much trouble on the estate?'

'Nah. At the start like, when he was first put away, it was quite busy. I was up here most of the time. It made the old lady feel better to have me up here, I think. You know, for protection.'

'The old lady?' George played dumb.

'Yeah, the Roberts lady. His mum. Of the one what done the murders.'

'Ah, I see. Was it just her up here?'

'Yeah. She used to moan about it. She said it used to be a busy place 'cause they had all the shops up and running. There was a team of people just doing the grounds and I think some staff in the house. In the end she had a cleaner and one gardener. Some old fella. She died out of the blue, really. I seen her a couple of days before. She looked fine to me.'

The house approached. The drive twisted and trailed around but the scenery suddenly changed. Neat hedges and formal gardens gave way to a solid, redbrick building. George was taken with just how big it was. He hadn't known what to expect, but this was larger — far larger.

'Blimey! These people knew how to live, right?' George cooed.

'Yeah. Who knows what you would use all those bedrooms for?'

The van pulled right up by the front entrance. This was a significant structure in its own right. It jutted out of the front. It was square and solid with a huge redwood door with a central brass knob and pillars either side. A huge white lintel had something engraved on it: *A.D. 1707*. The house was over four storeys. The first three had rows of perfectly identical square windows, the fourth layer was in the slant of the roof and its windows had pointed tops to complement the sloping roof behind. He walked back far enough to see six chimney stacks. The west side of the building looked like it had been extended. It was another solid-looking square with larger windows and newer, redder bricks.

'Luckily they've extended over there. Otherwise they would have been falling over one another,' George quipped. He was talking out loud to himself but the security guard was closer than he realised.

'Yeah. That's just storage now. The old man used it as a workshop type place at one point. He was into his metalwork according to his missus. Some of it is still in there. Sculptures an' that. I never really got art.'

'Metalwork?'

'Yeah. Odd stuff it is. Weird. You can see it through the windows.'

'Have you got a key?'

'I do, yeah. Only for that bit though. I think they've forgotten. The lady, like, just before she died, she put me a kettle and a fridge out there for when I was here a lot. I still use it as a tea stop, but I'm not out here much. Lucky for you I was here today!'

'Lucky for me.' George smiled.

'But I thought you was here for the graffiti? I can show you that. There's some on the other side.'

'That would be great. But I'm fascinated. You wouldn't mind showing me around a bit, right? I mean, the bits you can see? I've never been anywhere near a place like this and on *our* wages we probably never will again!'

'Sure!' The man smiled broadly. He seemed delighted with the comparison. They walked to the west wing. It was well established, probably a hundred years old or more, but next to the rest of the house it still looked a little out of place, as if it felt awkward posing next to its older sibling. It had its own entrance around the side. The guard led the away. His body language suddenly changed.

'Well, this ain't right.'

George caught up with him. He had moved through a large door — similar in style to the front door. Only this one was hanging open. Part of the door had broken away and there were clear tool marks where the lock was. Someone had broken in. The guard clumsily pushed through it.

'They can't get at much in here. I'm just worried about damage or squatters. You get a hell of a time getting squatters out, you know.'

George stopped to survey the place while the guard moved some distance in until George couldn't see him. The room was completely open plan. With all the windows, George had been expecting a number of segregated rooms. The ceiling was high, the floor a dusty concrete. It was dimly lit. The windows all had solid shutters with steel winding mechanisms to open them. George moved to the one closest. The mechanism whirred and squeaked and the sudden light lit up the Able Security guard, who looked out of breath.

'I've done a quick look round. I can't see any damage or anything. There's nothing to nick, really. They ain't even touched my milk!'

George walked out into the huge space and his movement kicked up the dust. Thick and acrid, it got to the back of his throat and he coughed. On the far side he could see silhouettes of dark objects that looked like they were laid out next to one another. He moved towards them. The light from the open shutters near the door didn't reach this far so he opened another. The mechanism was harder on this one and he grunted with the exertion. The sunlight fell upon a row of sombre-looking copper tanks. Each was distorted in some way, with one end pulled up into a slim funnel. Some were conjoined together and the body of one was pulled out so that it looked like it had a couple of misshapen legs. George sucked in a lot more dust all at once and coughed hard. By the time he had recovered the guard was back with him.

'I told you. Weird, ain't they? I never get art.'

'I need to make a call.' George moved back across the room. He bundled through the splintered door, which hung limp as he moved back out onto the gravel. He filled his lungs with the spring air as he tried to work his phone. Emma picked up on the second ring.

'George.'

'When you searched his house, did you film it? You would have done EGT, right?' he spluttered. He took another breath. He needed to be calmer. He was certain that something as important as this would have had an Evidence Gathering Team sent in to film the location before anything was searched or moved. But he needed to be sure.

'What?'

'The Roberts house. Where you searched, did you film it? An evidential film?'

'Jesus, George, I know what EGT is! Why the hell would you ask me that?'

'Please, Emma, just answer me.'

'I thought you were heading back. Where are you right now?'

'Emma — this is really important. Please, humour me for just a second. I will explain.'

'Yes, George, of course we did. I never watched it myself. It wasn't used in court. We used some stills.'

'The stills. Were they of more Brazen Bulls?'

Emma took her time. Her voice came back quieter. And angrier. 'We used a lot of evidence for this case, George. I'm sure you can imagine. But, yes, we found a number of similar contraptions.'

'He practiced, didn't he? At the house. Until he got it right.'

'Where are you, George?'

'I'm right, aren't I? Why weren't they seized? As part of the investigation. They're evidence, right?'

'They are, yes. It was a decision at a higher level than me. Some were seized, George. We still have six of the damned things in storage. No one knows what to do with them now. They were all very similar to the ones we found out in the woods. A decision was made that we just needed to take photos of the others. We took DNA from them to cross the Ts. The defence never argued that he made metal . . . well, whatever you might call them. They confirmed he had a fascination with metalwork.'

'How many were there?'

'What?'

'Left. How many did you leave?'

'For Christ sake, George! I don't know.'

'Do you still have the EGT tape? To hand?'

'It's in storage, the actual tape. We had a digital copy on a shared file. It will be in the network. I could probably—'

'Watch it, Emma. Can you do it now?' George could feel his stomach turning. He moved over to a row of bushes in case he had to vomit. His breathing was quick and shallow. He was feeling a little light-headed.

'It's not that easy. Hang on . . .' George reached out for the bush. He let the branches run through his fingers. Beyond it a blossom tree was shedding a rich pink bloom like gentle snow as the breeze blew. Nature's beauty. It was in such contrast. He strained to hear a muffled conversation down the phone where Emma was talking to someone else. She came back after a couple of minutes.

'We've got it on the shared file. Its forty minutes long, George. What do you want from me?'

'Can you get to the bit where they film the workshop? Where the copper tanks were?'

'I don't know. Hang on.' He heard her bark instructions at someone. She came back to him. 'Yeah. We're just walking into the extended bit. It's pretty much empty.'

'Do they film the copper tanks individually? I need you to tell me how many there are, Emma.'

Emma huffed, making her frustration clear. 'Right. Here we are. We're getting a detailed viewing of each one, George. Stand by.'

George took his last breath of the fresh air. He moved back through the door to the workshop, back into the open room. Immediately he could feel the thick dust moving to the back of his throat again. The guard was to his right. A kettle hissed. He called out something. George ignored him and moved back to where the copper tanks lay. He squatted down at the end of the row.

Emma was back. 'Seven, George. Looks to me like there are seven all in. Yep. Confirmed. Now, what's this all about?'

George pushed his fingers into the fresh, rutted tracks that ran through the concrete floor all the way to the door he had just entered. They were unmistakable as drag marks. He slunk to a sitting position.

'Someone's been to his house, Emma. There's one missing.'

Chapter 19

There it was again. A solid thump from the back. She shouldn't be able to do that. She shouldn't be able to do anything. He had tied her up good and she was secured to a down-pillar that was bolted to the chassis of the van itself. It happened again. He swore loudly. Signposts on the left side counted him down from three hundred yards to the next exit off the motorway. He took it. He came to a roundabout, turned left and the next thump was the loudest yet. By the time he pulled the van over hurriedly on a muddy bank next to a sturdy-looking metal gate, he was furious. He slammed the driver's door and stomped to the rear doors. He pulled one open so hard it rocked on its hinges. The road was busy; cars were passing both ways. He had angled the rear so it was facing into the field. One last check. He was sure no one could see in. The interior light came on with the opening of the door. She was still there, where he had left her, her hands so tight around the post they showed white. Her eyes were wide open, washed out and red, and they met his own. Movement caught his eye as the tank rolled lazily into the middle of the van.

'Ah!' All his anger immediately drifted away. 'I thought it was you! I thought you were banging my van!'

He hadn't tied it right. He could see the rope at the top, where it had been secured to the opposite side of the van to the girl. It had come loose and it had just enough leeway to roll out and then thump back against the side of the van.

He climbed into the back. It took just a few seconds to loop the rope back over it and tie it off firmly against the side — tighter this time, and he knotted it twice to be sure. He turned to the girl. She was still looking at him. He had her full attention now, just like he'd known he would. He smiled broadly. Even with blotchy eyes, her hair messed up and a gag pulling at her cheeks and making her mouth hang open she was still beautiful. He reached down and rested his palm on her soft, white skin. She felt wonderful too. Soft, gentle and warm. Perfect. She closed her eyes to his touch. Savouring it maybe? He moved his lips closer to her ear.

'Don't worry. Soon you will be free. I'll show you freedom like you never dreamed possible!'

He stepped out of the van and slammed the door shut behind him. He checked his watch. He needed to get back on the road.

Chapter 20

'George! How goes it up there?' Whittaker sounded cheery on the other end of the phone. George was anything but.

'I'll explain all later, Major. We have a bit of an issue up here. I need to talk to Roberts. I know you have contacts at the prison. Can you make it happen?'

'Roberts? Henry Roberts? I can try and sort that out for you, George. I am a little surprised though, friend? The last time we spoke it seemed to me like the last thing you might want to do.'

'I still don't want to. I can assure you of that. But I'm going to need to.'

'I'll make some arrangements. When did you want to sit down with him?'

'Today.'

George heard the Major suck in a lungful of air. 'Today! Well now, that does give me a bit of a problem. Today is moving day, George. It's quite an operation, as you can imagine. You're lucky I kept you out of it. We have all sorts of top brass down here flapping about, making farting noises. It's not pleasant. I have to say, old boy, getting you in front of our subject will not be easy. I would go as far as to say not possible. Tomorrow some of the heat might be off us long enough to sort something. It can't be that urgent, surely?'

George rubbed at his face. It *was* that urgent. Maybe leaving it a day would be a good thing. Something that he could use to his advantage. George reckoned Roberts knew who had their missing female. He just *had* to. He also knew that Roberts would be delighted to be asked about it, to have the power to decide whether he told them or not. He was equally certain that Roberts would never tell them; why would he? Not without something to offer in trade. It was too late to put a stop to his move. George couldn't prove that he knew anything anyway. His legal team would never let the move be delayed while George couldn't actually prove any links. But he *knew*.

'Okay, Major. Can you get me that sit-down for as soon as possible? I really want to speak to him. Until then I'll stay up here and see what can be done before that conversation.'

'What's going on, George?'

'The short version? We have a missing person. A female. She fits the profile of the Roberts's previous victims perfectly. It's massively out of character and everyone's very worried.'

'Okay . . . I'm missing something here, George. Henry Roberts definitely didn't abduct a girl in the last few days. He has an airtight alibi.'

'Sorry, yeah. I know he didn't. Roberts's last victim, the biker who got away . . . when she was giving her evidence she couldn't be sure that the van wasn't being driven by someone else. A second offender.'

'A second . . . shit, George! And you're inclined to agree it would seem?'

'No one was sure. But there is other evidence around this girl's disappearance. Circumstantial stuff, for sure, but enough for us to take it seriously.'

'And you think that talking to Roberts might help? He would love that — you know that, right?'

'I do. I can't say I relish the thought of talking to him about it but we are going to have to at some point. You never know with him. I might be able to play on his thirst for power. I don't expect him to help, but I'm certain he knows where this female is.'

'I assume you are staying up there to help with the search?'

'I am. I'm on my way to the missing girl's house. We're going to revisit the parents.'

'We?'

'Yeah, Emma Rowe is meeting me there.'

'Ah, so she's letting you help, then? You must be getting better with the old charm offensive.'

'Well, no actually. I didn't give her a choice, Major! I think deep down she's actually a little relieved I'm here. I can tell that by the way she told me to fuck off!'

Whittaker laughed heartily. It was catching. George felt some of his nervous tension ebb away.

'Only George Elms can find an invite in a *fuck off*! Yup. Go easy with her, George. She seems like a good egg to me.'

'Oh, she is. I get the impression she doesn't want to involve her team in all of this just yet. I don't think she wants to have the conversation where she suggests that they have another Henry Roberts on their patch.'

'Another Henry Roberts. It's been a few years though, George. If that were the case, where has he been all of this time?'

'I agree, and I don't know. Strange coincidence that this girl goes missing just as he gets his move.'

'And we both agree that detectives aren't keen on coincidences, right?'

'Right.'

George ended the call. He was sitting a few hundred yards from the address where he had told Emma Rowe he was going. He hadn't waited for her answer but he knew she would show. This was a sensitive address where he could do a lot of damage. He saw a car pull onto the drive. He guessed it might be hers. He edged forward and walked up towards the house. Someone was looking out. He was committed now.

The house looked around thirty years old. It was detached with brown uPVC windows and guttering. It had tiles that came half way down the front in a fancy pattern. A handsome place. The door was answered before George could knock by a blonde woman with a slight build. She had her head bent and wore an oversized jumper, the sleeves covering her hands, just the fingers poking out. He guessed she was around fifty, maybe a little younger. She looked meek, vulnerable almost.

'You must be Inspector Elms,' she said. Her voice suited her demeanour. George strained to hear it.

'I am. I assume my colleague is here already?'

'Yes. I'm Annie's mother. You can go through. Don't worry about your shoes.'

George moved into the lounge as directed. An angry-looking man turned to him immediately. George guessed he was the dad. He was much taller than his wife. His chest was puffed up and his arms were by his sides but they were stiff and held away from his body, as if he were ready for a fight. His hands were fists. He stared George up and down.

'Maybe you can tell me exactly what you're doing to find my daughter?' he spat.

George offered his hand. 'Inspector George Elms,' he said. The man ignored him. He turned to where Emma was stood near to the front window.

'Is no one going to answer me?'

'I've told you already, sir. I have a team of officers working on finding your daughter. We are doing all we can.'

'So why are you here? And two of you? That's two more that could be out looking for my daughter, am I right? We've had police here pretty much non-stop since she didn't come home. I'm fed up with it. When you came out the first time it made a lot of sense to me. The officer — what was her name? Whatever. She told me why. She told me that you search the house, Annie's bedroom — that you look for any reason why she might have gone missing. That all made sense. But you didn't find any. That should have started the alarm bells, right? She's never done this before. She's in trouble. I can feel it. She's out there somewhere, in trouble, and you people keep coming round here telling me how much you're doing—'

'My colleague has told you that we are doing all we can.' George cut in, his voice a little louder and more forceful. Emma was staring at him, as if making it clear that George needed to answer the man.

'Talk is cheap. Do you have any idea how this feels? To be sat here waiting? I went out earlier, with other people from the area. We were looking for my daughter in the woods, in the rivers, in sheds and outhouses. We were looking everywhere. Have you any idea what it's like to be out there, terrified that you might find your daughter . . . I can't even say it.' He slumped to a sit on the sofa. George gave him a second to compose himself. His body language changed. He finally relaxed a little. George sat next to him.

'My daughter was missing. She's a lot younger than Annie. She was six at the time. The difference was, I knew she had been taken. And I knew that I might not get her back. I can't explain the feeling. It's like a constant pressure, but from the inside, pushing out. I've never felt anything like it before or since. I'm not saying that is what has happened to Annie, but from experience, I know exactly how you are feeling. You are the most important people to us now. You are some of the last people to see her. And you know her best. *If* she has been taken by someone, the statistics tell us that it'll likely be someone

169

who is known to her. The people that can best tell us about the people she knows are you and your wife. So I make no apologies for coming back here again and again, and I will keep coming back until we have exhausted every last avenue. Every last enquiry. Is that okay?'

The man huffed. His stance softened though. 'You know what it's like then. Did you get her back? Your daughter?'

'I did. It was the worst time of my life. But I kept myself as calm as I could manage and I did everything I was told by people who knew what they were doing, who were emotionally separate from the investigation. You can't make the right choices on something like this when you're so wrapped up in it. You won't be thinking rationally. You can't possibly.'

'When I get hold of whoever has taken my baby girl, I tell you, I won't be thinking rationally then.'

'I wouldn't expect you to. She works in the city. She commutes there every day. That's right, isn't it?' George wanted to move him on.

The man nodded. 'Yeah. That day she was getting a later train. She had a few drinks after work. She wasn't keen on going. She said that to me. She was sat right where I am now. She said she wasn't really bothered but she felt like she always said no. So she went.'

'And did you speak to her during the night? On the phone, by text or any other way?'

'No. I mean, I'm her dad, aren't I? No twenty-year-old girl talks to her dad when she's on a night out.'

'They don't, you're right,' George said. 'Tell us about her friends. Does she have friends in the area that you know of?'

'Yeah, she's a popular kid, you know. Especially with the lads. It's a bit of a running joke. I keep saying I need to get myself a shotgun. I was a twenty-year-old bloke once. I know why she's popular.'

'Was she out with her friends on the night she didn't come home?'

'Workmates. I don't know them so well. She talks about them a bit, but first name stuff. There's an Adam, a Matt, two Mels. That's about right, isn't it?' He looked over at his wife.

'Adam. He's her boyfriend. Well, I think they're seeing each other. I did tell one of the officers. I don't know where he lives.'

'She has a boyfriend?' The man shook his head. 'I guess good old dad will always be the last to know.'

Emma rounded on Mrs Cox. 'What do you know about the boyfriend?'

'Adam. That's about it. I get the impression they work together. I don't know if they're at the same place. She works in insurance. She never seems to be at the same place. She mixes with other companies a lot, I think. Her desk is in Ludlow.'

'Do you know his surname? Or any nickname, or pet name? Anything that might help us work out who he is?' George said.

'You think this Adam could be involved?' The dad spoke. He was back to raging up. His chest and arms tensed.

'We need to speak to him. We don't know anything, but we should assume he was out with her last night. Or at the very least in contact with her.'

'I'll find him for you. He might not be any good to you by the time I've finished with him!'

'That isn't very helpful at all. And so far you *have* helped. Let us do our job. It is far more likely that this lad can tell us something that leads to us finding your daughter than him being involved in his disappearance.'

'Christ, Ken! Let them do their job. We don't know what's going on, do we?'

'No! No we don't and neither do these clowns!' He threw his hands in the general direction of George and

Emma, and stormed out of the room. George heard some banging noises in the kitchen then the sound of a back door slamming shut. George assumed that he had left the house. It was for the best.

'He'll be fine when he calms down,' his wife said.

'He's angry. I would be too. Trust me, we have no issue with him acting out at all. He needs to vent that somewhere. I'm quite happy for it to be at me. I'm sorry, I didn't get your name?'

'Joanna. Joanna Cox. Ken is Annie's dad.'

'Okay thanks, Joanna. I'm sure we have contact details for you already, but do you mind if I take your number? Just in case I think of something that might help.'

'Eh, no. Of course not.'

'Here.' George passed her his card and a pen. 'Just scribble it on the back. Do you know if your daughter was on any social media at all?'

'I think so, yeah. They are all on it, aren't they? Kids these days?'

'They do seem to be, yeah. Are you on any social media?'

'No. I don't know what I'm doing with it. I tried Facebook once but I couldn't make head nor tail.'

'Does she have a computer here or a tablet or anything?'

'She has a laptop-tablet thing. It's, like, an all-in-one. But she uses it for work. She has it with her. At least, she did have . . .' Joanna was starting to break. She had done well so far. Better than George had expected. She was stronger than she presented.

'Okay, no problem. We need to leave you alone, Mrs Cox. I know this is hard for you. One last thing . . . Did your daughter have any nicknames, any pet names that her mates would use? Or maybe even that you used?'

'She . . . at school she was Annie, spelt *A—N—I*. It stood for something, I think. They were just girls being silly, you know. They were in a band, her and her mates. I gave all the details of her close friends to the other police officers. They're a bit of a distance from here. We moved when she finished school. For Ken's work.'

'Understood. Thank you. That's been very helpful.'

George waited for the front door to shut and to be far enough away from the house before he spoke.

'We need to find that boyfriend. I have an intel officer who is a bit of a bloodhound to say the least. I can give her a call?'

'A bloodhound she might be, but she's a two-hour car journey away, George.'

'For the online stuff. Social media. It's how you find kids these days, right? Or at least find out about their lives.'

Emma shrugged. George was relieved she wasn't putting up walls to him trying to help anymore. 'Sure, it can't hurt.'

He was already dialling when he got to the end of the drive.

'George. Let me guess? You need something.' Emily Ryker sounded slightly amused.

'It doesn't count as help if it's your job, Ryker.'

'Oh! I'll remember that next time you call off-duty!'

'I literally cannot remember the last time I did that!'

'You have a short memory, George. Short enough to forget last night, and the night before that. And the night before—'

'Fine. You got me.'

'How are you today anyway? You doing okay?' Ryker loaded up the sarcasm. He ignored it.

'Yeah. I'm getting stuck into finding this girl. You know how I like something to focus on. I need your help, though.'

'Of course you do. I have a pen and paper. What do you need?'

'Our missing girl — we've just found out she had a boyfriend. Her name is Annie Cox, she might use A.N.I.' — he spelled the initials — 'on her social media. His name is Adam something. I need his details. I don't care how you get them.'

'Okay. Where does she live, where did she go to school, where does she work and how old is she?'

'Shit, Ryker. She's twenty. We're in Symonds Yat, near Wales. Does that help?'

'Not a whole lot. Do they work together?'

'They might.'

'Well, thanks for the help!'

'If it was easy, Ryker, I would have called up some Welsh biff to do the checks, wouldn't I? Now come on, show us what you've got. I'll send you the running log, you'll get all of her address details, date of birth and anything else they've put on there. You've found people with less to go on.'

'True. I'll get straight on it.'

'I knew you would.' George ended the call. He was aware of Emma on his right shoulder.

'Welsh biffs?'

He could feel himself blushing. 'I had to make her feel wanted.'

George was relieved when Emma smiled. 'You really like to push your luck, George, don't you?'

'You have to do what you can with luck. Lord knows we need it.'

'What are your plans now?'

George sighed. 'I don't know. I'm not a fan of waiting around but there's not much more we can do. I spoke to John Whittaker a little while ago. If anyone knows who has this girl it's Roberts, right?'

'He's a line of enquiry,' Emma conceded.

'Then we need to talk to him.'

'If we did, you know he won't tell us anything, right?'

'I don't *know*. I mean, yes, that was my first thought. We're probably wasting our time. But we have to do it. We have to ask him the question. Like you said, it's a relevant line of enquiry.'

'Okay. And I assume that falls to you, seeing as you're still the only police officer he's actually spoken to.'

George sighed. 'It does.'

'He's going to enjoy that too. You turning up with your cap in hand, begging for information on a missing girl. That will be a huge thrill.'

'The power thing? I know. I'm not sure how I'm going to play it yet. One thing I do know is that I can't turn up with my cap in hand. Asking him to help is a waste of time. We can't offer him a deal, he's already got what he wants — he moves today. I'm going to need something else. Something that he can't refuse.'

'Any ideas?'

'Not yet. Luckily it's a long drive down there.'

'Are you going now?'

'No. I would but, like I say, he moves today. When I spoke to Whittaker earlier it didn't look like it was going to be possible to get in front of him. I'll stay up here tonight. Let's see if we get anywhere with the boyfriend and then we'll go from there. What else do we have going on? I assume CCTV reviews from the trains, etc.?'

'That's all in hand. Let's get back to the nick. We can talk to the team doing the work and find out where we are.'

'Sounds like a place to start.'

'But, George, for now at least, let's keep any Henry Roberts link to ourselves.'

George watched Emma until she got into her own car. He pulled his phone back out of his pocket.

'What now, George!' This time Ryker didn't sound so jovial.

'Sorry, I couldn't really speak earlier. I need to give you some car details too. A part reg. Can you do what you do with it?'

'Part reg. You never come to me with a complete picture, do you? Everything's always cracked, broken or incomplete with you.'

'You're the fixer, Ryker. Like I said, anyone can run a full registration number. It takes Emily Ryker to piece together part of one!'

'What have you got?'

'A white van. I can't tell you much more than that as regards the description. It looked like it was transit sized, but I could only see a small section of the back. Just enough to see the last three letters — *POJ*. What are the chances?'

'Chances of what? Getting you the vehicle? Depends on a lot of things going right, George. Where did you see it?'

'On a CCTV camera in Symonds Yat. It was at the estate that belongs to Henry Roberts. It might just be our man.'

'I'll do what I can. Why couldn't you speak earlier?'

'Eh? Oh, Emma was right next to me.'

'Emma Rowe, the SIO up there? You couldn't speak in front of her? Surely she needs to know if you have a suspect vehicle?'

'I don't have a suspect vehicle. I have three letters and a visible white panel that is probably part of a van. I need you to get me more.'

'Why are you holding back on them, George?'

He took a second. He wasn't sure, really. This was her investigation and she seemed very switched on. 'I just want to be sure I have the whole registration. I want to know it's a van for sure. I don't want coppers out there in marked cars stopping all white vans, or media appeals around those three letters. Anything that could scare our man and make him change his vehicle or push him underground. Or, worse, force his hand. I have to believe that this girl is still alive, Ryker. From what I've seen she won't be harmed until the environment is just so.'

'And you don't trust them to do that? You're not the only one with a brain, you know. I know you think you are sometimes—'

'They're terrified, Ryker. I know what you're thinking! I know in the past I've kept information out of a lack of trust. That isn't it. This whole force, this whole community . . . they're absolutely terrified. Fear makes people do strange things.'

'Leave it with me. I'll do what I can as quickly as I can. Sounds like they're right to be scared up there, George.'

'Oh they are, Ryker. They definitely are.'

Chapter 21

Once they got back to Hereford Police Station, George made for the uniform sergeant who was leading the missing person investigation. He was a cheery-looking man, both his beard and glasses were neat and thick.

'We're doing all we can to find her. Usually you get a lass of this age and they turn up looking a bit sheepish, you know. They stayed out one night too many with their boyfriend or girlfriends. I suppose you get to a point where it's gone too far, where you don't want to just pick up the phone and call your parents 'cause you know you'll be in trouble!'

George nodded, despite disagreeing with just about every word. 'And have you got the CCTV from the train yet?'

'Yes. The transport police are pretty good round here. We get a bit of bother on the trains. They're pretty slick at getting the stuff downloaded. We normally deal with it, see. The other forces they make them deal with it but we're so far out we tend to take it on. They really appreciate that.'

'Has it been viewed?'

'It has. We found our girl. The train CCTV is very good. We know that she got on. She nearly didn't, mind! Nearly missed it. She got on the train and then she got off at her normal stop. She was alone the whole time. The footage is clear but she's not directly in front of a camera unfortunately. She looks like she plays with her phone then falls asleep. There's really nothing to report.'

'She was on her own?'

'Yeah, the whole time.'

'Was there anyone near her?'

'There were other people on the train. But they were spread out, as you would expect. She didn't talk to anyone and no one talked to her. We've taken a few stills from it so you can see what she was wearing. We've got some of the other passengers too, but they're not great. We spoke to her workmates and she was wearing the same thing when she left them.'

'So she disappeared between getting off the train and getting home?'

'She must have.'

'That's not a girl who's stayed over at her boyfriend's or her girlfriend's for an extra night then, is it? That's a girl who was on her way home.'

The sergeant's smile fell away a bit. 'I never thought of it like that. I guess that's why you're the detective, right?'

'Did you find the boyfriend yet? This Adam fella?'

'Adam?' The sergeant looked confused.

'Yes. We spoke to the mother earlier tonight. She said she had told some other coppers about Adam. Annie is seeing someone called Adam apparently. No one seems to know a surname or any other details. Did anyone at work know anything about him?'

'Oh. Well, no one's told me about a boyfriend. There are a lot of officers involved, see. We've got all the waifs, strays and sick-notes out doing what they can. You know what it's like! We've got no resources so we just put out

179

who we can. It is all being collated. I'll get it together and have a good look through, see what we've got.'

'That sounds like a good idea. I'll leave you to it.'

'Cheerio!'

George closed the door behind him and exhaled. He walked back to where Emma was in her office. She was hunched over her computer.

'Your team should be leading this, Emma.'

'What? Leading what?'

'The missing person. I just spoke to the uniform skipper who's currently running it. He seems like a lovely fella but he's not the man to find her. Is he?'

'Well I have a couple of DCs overseeing, George. To be honest we shouldn't really have that much.'

'What do you mean, you shouldn't have that? This is a possible abduction, right? Down where I come from Major Crime would be—'

'Then go back! Go back to where you came from, George. You're only here on my goodwill! Because I could do with some help, but if you want to start dictating how this force should work like the one you've come from then your help isn't needed any more.'

'Okay, okay. I'm sorry, you're right. I'm sticking my nose in. Just explain to me why Major Crime are not leading with this so I can get back in my box.'

'Because, George, no one is saying this is an abduction. On the surface this is just a girl, barely out of her teens, who has not made it home from a night out. We get them reported every day. I've got four other missing persons reports, two from foster care, one who didn't make it back from a party and one who's suspected of heading to London to meet an older boy. All of them are at risk. All of them need finding and you could say that they are all possible abductions. My team can't lead the search for everyone. That is why it is a uniform function until we get some sort of confirmation of foul play.'

'This is different, though. Surely you see that? Annie Cox isn't missing from foster care. She isn't sneaking off to see her boyfriend or to go to a party. She's a young professional who we know was on a train on her own and who went missing somewhere between stepping onto that platform and her home address. She's never been missing before and she is an exact match in description and MO to three other girls who were murd—'

'Enough!' Emma's voice was almost a shriek. He himself had been getting louder. He came back a lot softer.

'And a Brazen Bull is missing.'

Emma stood up. She walked back to her thinking place. She didn't face outside the window. She turned and stared at George. 'That house has been targeted for damage and break-ins more times than I can remember. We've stopped responding to the calls there. The security guard has become a pain in the arse, calling us up every five minutes just because he doesn't want to squeeze his fat arse out of that van of his. We both know how much a copper is worth, George. You've got some chancer who's gone in there and taken one of the copper tanks. I reckon they'll be back for the others too, now they know they're in there. There isn't a man, woman or child within twenty square miles or more, who doesn't know that place is sitting empty. We're putting two and two together without a shred of anything to prove it. I've entertained your abduction theory and I've even fuelled it a little — I should have kept the details to myself. But this is nothing more than a missing person investigation until someone can tell me different.'

'We have to consider it though, right? Forgetting the copper tank. We have to consider that Annie Cox never made it home from the train station having been seen to be travelling alone. How do you explain that?'

'I can't. Not right now. Isn't that just the way all missing persons start out? And the vast majority end up being nothing more than an innocent misunderstanding or someone who maybe doesn't want to be found for a day or two — for whatever reason. Then they turn up. No harm done.'

'No harm done!' George could feel his temperature rising. He wanted to grab the woman and shake her. He wanted to make her see. He took a few moments. Emma turned away from him so she was facing out of the window.

'I know you don't want this to be true, Emma. I know you, your community, your team out there, your whole police force, you don't want to be considering that you didn't get it all when you got Henry Roberts. Your vicar talked about cutting a cancer out. Maybe something was left. Someone. And that someone is out there now, with a twenty-year-old girl hostage and a stack of logs under that missing tank. In fact, forget the tank. I accept that the missing tank could be a chancer thief nicking copper — who only took one. But Annie Cox is not some silly little girl staying out at her boyfriend's.'

'We're running this missing person investigation the same way we run them all. There's no reason to run it any different. I owe it to those four other missing people, to my team, to my police force as you so eloquently put it. I owe it to them to be consistent and not to be ruled by *your* gut feeling.'

'Tell me you don't have it too? You can't tell me it's just me! I've seen you work, Emma, you're as sharp as they come. Does this feel right to you? Any of it?'

'This conversation is irrelevant and it's over, George. It's been a long day. Maybe we should start fresh tomorrow. My uniform colleagues will be working through the night. They are aware that Annie is their priority. Maybe they will make some headway.'

'Tomorrow? Tomorrow I will be going to see Henry Roberts and I will be asking him who has Annie Cox. And I will be doing that with nothing to offer him. All I will achieve tomorrow is delighting Henry Roberts. If you could only put your team of detectives on this, they could get us a lead, something that I can at least pretend that we—'

'GEORGE!' Emma suddenly exploded. She had been facing away and it caught George out completely. She was red faced. Her eyes bulged. Her chest rose and fell. He had gone too far.

'Fine. Okay, I'm sorry. I'm not here to make your life more difficult. I should know my place.'

Emma's head fell forward in a sigh. 'We'll start again. Tomorrow.'

George agreed and left quickly. He waited until he was out of the building before he let rip with a series of profanities into the swiftly darkening sky. His phone buzzed as he got back to his car. Emily had found Annie Cox's Facebook and Instagram pages. They featured the same male a number of times. He had a surname — Faith. Adam Faith. George couldn't help but curl his lip. It was very apt. Adam Faith's Facebook page also listed his occupation as a PE teacher at a secondary school in Monmouth. He would be simple to find. He forwarded the message on to Emma. She could send whoever she wanted out to follow that line of enquiry. George knew it wouldn't matter anyway. Adam Faith hadn't abducted Annie Cox. Adam Faith wasn't going to kill her if they couldn't find her in time. But someone else had that intention.

Chapter 22

She could only jerk her head. Her hands were still trussed up tight against the side of the van. Her mouth was taped up too. She breathed heavily through her nose in her panic. It suited his needs; the deeper she breathed, the quicker and deeper she took down the substance. He felt her slump unconscious. It wasn't a big shot but he still took the rag away instantly. He just needed enough time to fuel up the van.

The van was parked down a quiet country road he had picked out when he saw the sign for the dead end. It was better than he'd imagined. Down the end of the lane was just a turning circle surrounded by trees and woodland, the houses having run out fifty yards back. Complete privacy. He pulled back up to the main road and turned left. In less than a minute he passed a service entrance to the Eurotunnel site on his nearside. He went straight over the next roundabout and the petrol station was on his left. The traffic passing through was steady but there were plenty of pumps. He pulled up to the one at the far end. He could see movement at the window: a young girl serving someone. He fixed on her as the diesel pumped. Even from this distance he could see she was attractive. She was slim, not very tall but perfectly formed. Her blonde hair was tied off and ran behind her back. The pump shuddered and cut out. His tank was full.

It was busy in the shop. There was a queue for the four tills. The blonde girl was at the first one. Someone shuffled forward to her and she smiled warmly. He took a few steps. He wanted to be closer. He heard someone huff in his ear. He'd stepped right in front of them as he'd bustled in. He'd not even noticed. He didn't care. He gazed back at the girl and she looked up suddenly, as if she could sense him staring. Maybe she wanted him to. Whatever, he ducked into an aisle and bit down onto his knuckles. He ostensibly browsed the ready-meals and sandwiches. He'd just come in to pay for the diesel. *But she had seen him!*

He moved to the back of the shop. He needed to find something to buy, an excuse for ducking down the aisle rather than going straight to the tills. A door opened that he hadn't noticed nestled in a row of fridges. A man in the filling station's uniform stepped through and nodded a greeting. He ignored him. The man walked away briskly like he had somewhere to be. The door, in contrast, was swinging shut slowly. His eyes were drawn to a white piece of paper fixed to the middle of the door. It had strips of highlighted pen through it. He moved closer. It was the staff rota: a table of names and dates with shift start and finish times. The top two names were the only females: Sadie and Gill. He only had a couple of seconds before the door clicked shut. He took in what he could.

He picked up a packet of crisps. Something he could take to the tills. The queue was shorter by now, just one person in front of him. There were three tills in operation. The blonde was directly in front of him but he couldn't get a clear view. The man in front was short but wide. He was dressed head to toe in high-visibility orange. He wore safety boots and had *HIGHWAYS* emblazoned across his back. He stepped forward towards the blonde. Her till was free.

"Ello darlin'!' He was brash; he talked like he didn't care who was listening. His stride was a wide swagger. The girl smiled, but it was a nervous smile and she flushed red. The colour seemed to rise up from her chest and neck. She said something back but her voice was too low to travel.

'Yeah, number four! An' a lucky dip. Seein' you in 'ere I suddenly got the feelin' this might be my lucky day!'

He was starting to panic now. At the third till someone was still pouring items onto the counter, but at the next till along, the woman there was nearly done. They were making small talk before she left. The Highways man was done too. But he was still talking. He held a drink and some crisps in his hands. He had stuffed the lottery ticket in his pocket. He was promising to take her somewhere special whether he won or not. He laughed out loud with it.

The tension was so bad that his stomach twisted and his breath was shallow. This was just how his panic attacks would start. He wanted to shout out. He wanted to *lash out* and with something sharp. He wanted to run it through this wide fluorescent orange back. He would silence the mouth at the other side of it forever.

'Can I help you?' His violent reverie was interrupted by an urgent voice and he felt a tap on his shoulder — someone making him aware from behind. The woman at till number three was leaning forward looking expectant. He cursed under his breath and stepped towards her reluctantly, his head down. Suddenly his periphery filled with a thick shape — a blur of orange. He stopped still.

'Sorry, bruv!' The Highways man stepped across him. He kept his eyes down until he passed. He lifted them to meet with the lady behind till number three.

'Bit full of himself that one!' She turned to her right to address the girl at the first till, 'Sadie! I think he liked you!'

He chanced a look over. She was still smiling nervously but the red tinge to her skin was deeper, more pronounced, like she burned with embarrassment that the Highways piece of shit had even spoken to her. He could understand it. But she shouldn't be embarrassed. It wasn't her fault. He lingered on her. He was closer now. Close enough to see that she had subtle colour to her lips and he could see the detail in her hair. It fell down her back in an elaborate French plait. She wore a white shirt that fitted snugly over her breasts and tucked into a black skirt around a slim waist. She had a brightness about her. A purity. 'Sadie . . .' he murmured.

'You okay, love?'

He snapped back to the older woman in front of him. He mumbled his apology, put the crisps on the counter and gave his pump number. He paid in silence and walked as quickly as he could back out to his van. He pulled the door shut. His hands shook as he rested them on the steering wheel. He watched the Highways marked van pull off the forecourt in front of him. The man with the swagger went with it. But he would be back. He had seen a load of their vehicles just up the road where a section of the motorway was dug up. This was the closest garage.

He moved his van a short distance to the area marked *staff parking*. It was round the side of the building. There were two doors, solid-looking and firmly shut. These would be the staff doors, he reckoned. He just needed to confirm. He'd waited only ten minutes when the furthest door swung outwards. It had a push bar on the inside, the sort that would lock shut if you pushed it closed. An overweight man in a shop-issue white shirt and black trousers stepped out. He lit a cigarette, took a long drag and lifted his head to blow the smoke back out. It whirled and raced around his head before dissipating into the late afternoon. The man didn't seem to take any notice of the van in the staff parking area.

He still waited for the man to finish his cigarette and go back in. He didn't want to draw attention to himself. He didn't want anyone to be able to say that they had seen a van hanging around by the door if questions were asked.

When the door finally slammed shut, he pulled away and left the petrol station.

Chapter 23

George actually slept soundly, something he rarely did at the best of times. Somehow he had managed to purge all the worries, the frustration and the horrific images — either that or it was just a reflection of how tired he was. He had slept with the balcony door open and he was still close enough to hear the gentle shushing and gurgling of the River Wye. Perhaps this was the sound that had lulled him to sleep. He stepped back out on the balcony just after 5 a.m. He nearly didn't set the alarm. He couldn't remember the last time he had needed one. Today he was glad he did. The view was even more beautiful at that time in the morning. The sun was still hidden behind the valley so the whole image was presented with a grey, misty hue. The river still made its noises at the base of the hills and the trees swayed in a gentle wind. The whole scene was shuffling along in perfect time and it was all natural — not a soul in sight.

In fact George didn't notice other traffic until he was well on the way to Gloucester. The sun was still low enough for him to pull the visor down and he was surprised to hear his phone ringing through the car speakers.

'Major! What the hell are you doing up at this time of the morning?'

'Well, what would you know? I got woken up by a bloody text message, didn't I? Lord knows who would send one of those at five bloody thirty in the morning.'

'Oh! Sorry about that. I assumed it would quietly sit on your phone until you sat up with your morning tea.' George had considered waiting before sending his message, but he was a man who liked to do things while he was thinking about them. It was just a few lines to tell Whittaker that he was heading back, that he still wanted to speak to Roberts but he was going to make a diversion. George guessed that it was the diversion reference that had prompted Whittaker's call. His chief inspector knew George's reputation better than anyone and, in the past, diversions often meant trouble.

'No. It had the effect of forcing me to make the damned morning tea in an effort to appease *the enemy*. My wife is not a woman who enjoys a text message tone as an alarm call, George.'

'Well, that I can understand. Please, pass on my apologies!'

'I will do no such thing. I fear that would serve to just prod the beast. Which, I might add, is something that now appears to be even further away following your antics.'

'I see. Well, thank you for making me aware.'

'Too much information, George? You can't complain now. You wake her, you upset her. You have to accept the gory details of a nonexistent love life.'

'Is that why you called, Major? To talk about your enforced celibacy?'

'Well, no actually. But it feels bloody good to get it off my chest, old boy!' Whittaker laughed. He had a powerful guffaw when he really laughed. George couldn't help but smile himself. He was still thundering down the motorway.

'So, how can I help?'

'Your message. You're heading back. You mention a diversion — anything I need to know about?'

'Not really, Major. I had a bit of a run-in with Emma up here last night. They're still treating their missing girl as a standard misper. I think I understand why, but they really shouldn't be. Emma knows it too. She has a good nose, I can tell. She must have the same gut feeling as me — all the signs are there.'

'A run-in? Did you leave on good terms? We're still going to need a working relationship with them, George.'

'Yeah, of course. We didn't fall out. I backed off. I could tell I needed to. I just need her to see. But she's so stubborn, Major . . .'

'I can't imagine what you mean, George, never having had to manage anyone like that before.'

'Point taken. I'm only stubborn when I'm right, though, Major. That's when I dig my heels in. I think she's digging her heels in because she doesn't *want* to be right. She's burying her head. The whole force is. No one wants to be the one who admits that they've got another abduction. Another girl in real danger on their ground.'

'And now you've got to go and talk to Roberts with nothing more than a prayer. I know you said you wanted to avoid that.'

'I did. That's what the diversion is about.'

'Go on?'

'I was reading back through everything that we have. I looked at his custody notes. He's had consistent medical staff the whole time. While he was at HMP there were two nurses and the doctor we met down at the secure unit in Langthorne. The same personnel are going to be continuing with his care. I figure that the nurses probably know him as well as anyone. Certainly they would know what he wants or needs. He might even have dropped his guard around them enough for them to give me something I can use. Anything!'

'I can hear the desperation from here, George. You're not talking about withdrawing or withholding treatment, are you? Or to use its proper name — torture?'

'Now there's a thought! But no. Unfortunately I wouldn't get that past my line manager. But Roberts has needs. Everyone does. I know he got his move, his view and his place to die, but there might be something else. It's a long shot, Major, but I am all out of ideas.'

'Okay. So how does that look? You drop round for a cup of tea with the nurse and ask her what you can use in exchange for him telling you who he was working with and who might now have abducted another young girl?'

'Well, when you put it like that . . . I don't know, Major, if I'm honest. I'm not sure what it looks like. I just need to get in front of her. We can have a chat and go from there.'

'It can't do any harm.'

'I need your help, though. From the operation order covering his transfer it looks like the nurses are working opposite shifts and the doc is kinda fitting in as and when. Two females, I forget their names. I want to speak to one of the nurses away from that place. They might be more relaxed talking to me in their own homes.'

'Where there's no CCTV? No record of the conversation even?'

George smiled at his screen. 'Am I really so transparent, Major?'

'Like a cell window I saw recently.'

'Well, fine! Can you confirm whoever isn't working today and where they live? I think they're both in the south London area. I'm aiming on getting there for when one of them gets in from her night shift.'

'You didn't get any information from me, George.'

'Of course.'

'I have boxes of files around this fella. I know the working patterns and staff details are in there somewhere. I will hook them out and send them through to you.'

'Ideal. How was moving day? And leave out the bit where that animal first walks into his cell-with-a-view.'

'Fine, actually. We never got anywhere near him to be honest, George. The prison service did all the transport and the hands-on stuff. The place was finished with about twenty minutes to spare, I think. Some of the security bits are still out of sync, but no one's too concerned. Even from a distance, George, he's not a well man.'

'What is the latest?'

'He's deteriorating. The doc reported that they drained some fluid from his lung so he was strong enough to move. Without treatment, it's going to fill back up and stop him breathing. He's too weak to be treated anyway. It might be days now.'

'So we're running out of time here, Major. Can he still speak?'

'To you? I bet he'd love to.'

'I bet he would. I need to see him today.'

'Let me know when you're done with your nurse friend. I'll try and make it happen this afternoon. I did some groundwork yesterday. There was some resistance to it, though. Everyone's shit scared of his solicitors. Would it be a formal chat? Something under caution?'

'I'd rather it wasn't. I don't really want to be reminding him of his rights.'

'I thought you would say that.'

'Thanks, Major. Send those details through. I'll stay in touch.'

* * *

George was on the outskirts of south London by the time the Major sent address details for the nurse due home from her night shift with Roberts. He diverted immediately. It was a nice street: tight housing but tree-lined and with bay window features and patterned fronts. The nurse's name was included: Camille Bisset. *CB*, he mused. She was a French national, apparently, but a long-time UK resident. Her house was in the very middle of the row. Though her neighbour's property was pristine: hanging baskets bursting with colour, neat slatted blinds and a spotless front door, Nurse Bisset's frontage was not quite so appealing. The curtains were drawn tightly and there were no obvious signs of life. George knocked firmly. He left it a minute until he knocked again. He stepped back and looked around. The traffic going past was steady and there were a couple of people out on foot. No one was taking any notice of him. He checked his watch: 8:30 a.m. Plenty of time for her to have finished her shift at 7 a.m. and to be back by now. He didn't think it was enough time to be home and asleep. He knocked again. He followed it up by squatting and peering through the letterbox. He could see through to a kitchen at the back, some stairs off to the left and some mail on the floor. No real belongings. It didn't have the feel of a house in use. He stepped back again. Further this time so he could see the first floor. More drawn curtains. The windows were all sealed shut. He turned to the sound of a door closing behind him. Someone stepped away from the house opposite.

'Excuse me!' He called out. A young woman stopped in the midst of a long stride. She seemed to be in a rush.

'Can I help?'

'Do you know the young lady who lives here at all?'

'And who are you?' She was clearly annoyed.

'Sorry.' George hurriedly crossed the street. He pulled his warrant card from his pocket and held it out. 'I'm a police officer. She's not in any trouble at all. I had an appointment to see her this morning. She's helping us out with some enquiries is all. Have you seen her today?'

The woman shrugged. 'No, not for a while. I know Dee next to her — the house with all the flowers. They seem quite close. I've seen them talking often anyway. I haven't seen her for a few weeks if I'm honest. I still see

Dee. Actually, I think your appointment might have moved out.'

'Dee, you say?'

'Deanna, yeah. Directly next door.'

'Thanks for your help.' He moved back across the road.

Dee wasn't answering either. The expensive-looking blinds were angled so he couldn't quite see in. The sort of deliberate angle if you were heading out for the morning. George wasn't getting anywhere here. He wasn't hopeful that his nurse was here anyway. He wrote a note on his own business card asking for a call back. He dropped it through Deanna's door. He hoped she would see the police reference and be spooked enough to call him straight away.

George gave the address one last look and walked back to his car. His attention moved to his phone.

'George. How did it go?' Whittaker picked up fast.

'It didn't. She's not in,' George replied.

'Ah. She can't have gone straight home. Are you going to wait around?'

'No. I don't think it's a current address.'

'I see. That's the address I have. It's the only address I have. Do you want me to put a call into the prison and see if their HR team have any update?'

'No, don't worry. They'll just ask why. I'd rather the prison were out of the loop when it comes to me pumping their staff members for information that is verging on a breach of medical standards. What about the doctor? Did you have an address for him?'

'I do remember seeing one. But he was with Roberts all day yesterday. He'll probably be back there today. There's a fair bit for him to do.'

'So I might be able to speak to him later when I see Roberts? If he's there, I mean. Doctors are more used to being tight-lipped, I probably won't get too much out of him anyway.'

'You might be right. Let me follow up on yesterday, George, and make sure I can even get you in there first. That's proving to be more of a challenge than I expected.'

'Understood. Work that charm you keep telling me about.'

George's next call was to Emily Ryker.

'Patience is not really your thing, is it, George? I was going to ring you when I was finished.'

'Now you don't have to.'

'Who says I'm finished?'

'What have you got so far? I'm parked up and trying to work out where I should be going next, Ryker. I wondered if you had anything that might help.'

'I might have. I'm still trying to flesh it out down here, so don't go off half-cocked. If you'd waited until I'd finished I could have given you definites.'

'What have you got?'

'The part reg. I ran it through the national ANPR system. I got a lot of hits. I narrowed it down a bit — to your neck of the woods, wherever the hell that is. I got very little. There aren't many fixed ANPR points on the road network up there. The Severn Bridge is about it really.'

'Very little is *something*, right?'

'Very little is nothing, actually. The part reg hits I did get weren't white panel vans. They were any number of other things. That was the best I could do out of hours last night. This morning I was able to talk to someone who has access to a much juicier database.'

'Only an intel officer could ever refer to a database as *juicy*.'

'Oh trust me, George, this is some juicy shit. This is the one that shows ANPR hits for the private companies. A lot of car parks now for theatres, airports, venues, councils — you name it, they all monitor their car parks by ANPR. It's linked to your parking ticket. Not to mention petrol station forecourts and so on, and so on.'

'And?' George sat up a little straighter, he could sense the excitement in Ryker's voice.

'And they log the details. I got a hit on a van. At a supermarket two days ago. A white, Renault panel van — MC17 POJ. It's on the outskirts of a place called Ross-on-Wye. That's right in among it, right?'

'It is, yeah.'

'I made a call to the supermarket this morning. I had a little bit of to and fro — I had to give them the old, *do you know who I am*. Anyway, they've burned the CCTV. It should be ready for you to collect by now. I got them to view it quick, too. They would only watch a few seconds. It's the camera that covers the car park. It shows the van pull in, it shows a white male get out and enter the store. They assured me they'll get a still of his face — the cameras are good in there apparently and they could see that he went in. They were going to go and check the other cameras and come back to me but seeing as you jumped the gun you can take that up with them.'

'That's brilliant, Ryker! Outstanding. I guess I shouldn't expect any less from you, should I? Can you send me the store details? I'll call the SIO and get that picked up.'

'No problemo. It gets better, too. And when I say *it* gets better, I mean *I* get better. I ran the van on PNC. It's registered to a hire car company in Ross-on-Wye.'

'So we can get details on who has it?'

'We can. I'm on it. But they might not do that over the phone. That'll probably need one of us stood there in uniform. Hire car companies are generally very wary about giving out details over the phone.'

'I knew you were the right person to call, Ryker. You're gonna find this girl on your own and from two hundred miles away!'

'Funny you should mention the distance. With the full registration I was then able to run it on the nationwide ANPR system again. This is where your problem comes.'

'Problem?'

'Yeah. Your plates are gonna be a clone, George. An identical-looking van also pops up at a petrol station and then again at the Dartford River Crossing. Suddenly that's a long way from where you are.'

'The DRC? Do we know which direction?'

'Southbound.'

'Southbound DRC. When? Are the times right?'

'Well, yes and no. I mean, it's the next day so it's possible. But why would the van leave Ross-on-whatever and then effectively head south — right towards us here?'

'On the same day that our man is moved in the same direction. Coincidence?'

'Ah, shit. Is this the bit where you tell me what you detectives think about coincidences? Spare me, George, I've heard it all before. No one knows that he was even being moved — that's what you told me — let alone the day it was happening.'

'Unless someone did.'

'How? No one in Herefordshire even knew until a couple of days ago.'

'Roberts knew.'

'Roberts? He did. But no visitors, no letters in or out, no contact with the outside world and no one who cares enough anyway. How could he get word out?'

'I don't know, Ryker. I really don't know. Good work on the van. Any more hits?'

'Not as of a few minutes ago. I have an alert in place.'

'Excellent. Look, send those details through. I'll give Emma a call and get someone out to the hire car company and the supermarket. That's good work, Ryker.'

'I know.'

'Of course you do.'

He checked his watch as his phone fell silent. It was still early, but not too early to start making calls. He hesitated about calling Emma. He didn't want to get into a conversation with her about how he had got hold of the information. He just needed her to get someone out on enquiries — without delay. His phone beeped with a message from Ryker. It had details of the hire car company and the supermarket. He pressed to forward it on. He selected Emma's name and sent it. He followed it up with a message he hoped would be simple enough.

'URGENT — Emma — this is the van that may contain your missing person. Can you get someone to go see the hire car company for a name? The supermarket have CCTV that will contain an image of him too. I'll explain shortly!'

He pressed to send. The phone made a noise confirming it had gone. Immediately the message showed two ticks next to it. Emma had received the message. The phone announced that she was typing. His phone vibrated.

'Okay.'

That would have to do. She was obviously still upset with him, but none of that mattered for now. As long as she got that enquiry started. He considered calling her, just to smooth it over and to make sure she was on board. He made a decision and moved his hand to the car key. If that van was heading south he should be doing the same.

It was another forty minutes of motorway and silence before his phone rang again.

'Hello?'

'Is that George Elms?'

'Yes.'

'Oh. Hi, this is Deanna Dean. I think you put a note through my door?'

'Ah, yes I did. Thanks so much for calling me back.' George was feeling tired all of a sudden. He shook his head. The sign for the Maidstone services flashed past. He would let her tell him that she didn't have a forwarding address for his nurse and then he'd stop off for a coffee and freshen up.

'That's okay.' She sounded unsure, a little fragile almost. Like she was waiting for him to announce terrible news.

'Look, Dee, it's nothing to worry about, okay? It's actually nothing to do with you. I was after your neighbour. We had an appointment this morning for a chat. She's helping me out with our enquiries. You have a nurse next to you, right?'

'Cam?'

'Camille Bisset, yes.'

'Yes, that's right. And she made an appointment to see you there?' Deanna suddenly sounded very unsure.

'Well, yes and no. We made an appointment but I didn't check the address because I'm horribly incompetent at times. We have that place on our system. It never crossed my mind that she might not be there.'

'Ah, I see. That makes sense. She moved out about four weeks ago or something, I think.'

'Are you still in touch with her?'

'No, I'm afraid not. What makes you think we were in touch at all? She just used to live next door.'

'Okay, no problem. I spoke to another neighbour. Someone over the road. She said that you guys might have been friends is all.'

'Oh, I mean, we weren't really friends. She was nice, but when we spoke it was just to say hello over the wall. And she helped Tommy with his costume. She's very talented, see. A little too talented actually.'

He started to slow for the slip-off to a rest and a coffee. 'Costume? She's a nurse, though, right?'

'I think so, yeah. But she said she used to work for a studio. One in London. She obviously loved it. I just don't think it was regular enough or something.'

'A studio?'

'Yeah. She said she did makeup there. A proper makeup artist. It came up when we were talking about trick-or-treating. At Halloween. Tommy was going out. He's my ten-year-old boy. She said she would do his makeup. I'll be honest, I didn't like it. Like I said, she was *too* good. It was supposed to be a bit of a laugh, a bit of fake blood round the lips and silly string. She took it real serious. He looked like the walking dead by the end of it! I didn't like it at all, seeing my son like that. He looked ill!'

'Ill?' George sat bolt upright. He felt his stomach turn over. His voice rasped from a throat that was suddenly closing up.

'Yeah, very ill. Pale face, black lips, black round his eyes. It was awful! She meant well, though, so I didn't say anything.'

George cleared his throat the best he could. 'I'm sure she did. Did she say where she was going? When she moved?'

'She didn't, no. I don't have any forwarding details I'm afraid. We were just neighbours.'

'Of course. Thanks for your help.'

'No problem. I don't think I've helped at all, have I?' She chuckled down the phone.

'Well, it's not the answer I was hoping for, but you've been great.' George pushed the accelerator and moved back out into the outside lane. The services flashed past in a blur of colour. He didn't feel sleepy anymore.

Chapter 24

George could see Whittaker at the rendezvous point agreed over the phone: the pub car park of The Valiant Sailor in Capel-le-Ferne, less than a minute from the secure unit housing Roberts. Whittaker stepped out of the back of a police van as George pulled up.

'What is this all about, George?' Whittaker stiffened his back. He looked agitated. 'Do you have any idea of the politics involved in a stunt like this?' He *was* agitated.

'I do. This isn't a stunt, Major. Did you make contact with anyone in there yet?'

'No. I used the dedicated line — no answer.'

'No answer?'

'Well, no, but that's assuming it's actually ringing in there. They were still putting bits together when I left. I told you, I could have just knocked on the door and avoided all this. I'm not overly concerned.'

'I am, Major. We shouldn't have put him in there until it was ready.'

'Come on, George. The man's come here to die. He's as weak as a kitten. They had to stabilise him to transport him down here.'

'I get that. Did you bring a team?'

'I got what I could. I had a tactical team that were relatively close by. They were in the middle of dismantling a cannabis cultivation. They're a bit pissed off. I couldn't really tell them why they're here.'

'Are they ready to go?'

'Yes. But what do you want them to do?'

'Just like you said. We go up to the door and knock.'

George got back into his car. The Major walked to the van. George could see the officer in the driver's seat. He shook his head, then he turned and looked at George. He looked confused. He quickly turned away again. The Major stepped back out. He walked to George's car and sat in the passenger seat.

'We'll follow them down. They'll do the knocking.' Whittaker got in the car.

'Understood.'

The house came quickly into view. The perimeter fence was new. It was lower than George would have expected on a secure unit, but he knew they were trying to stay under the radar for now. No one wanted to advertise that the new occupant was a Category A prisoner at this stage; eight-foot razor wire might well have done that. The vehicle gate was sturdy however. The van stopped at it. George could see cameras hanging down to driver height. An arm came out of the van and pushed something on a silver panel. George waited. It was maybe thirty seconds until the same arm came out again. Another thirty seconds passed. Then it was a minute. The van shook. The side door popped. Boots hit the floor as the team stepped out. The woman wearing sergeant's stripes walked to Whittaker's window.

'We're not getting any answer, sir. On the intercom, I mean. It just rings. Did you want to try the phone number you have again?'

Whittaker turned to George. His anger seemed to have given way to concern. 'This is what you were expecting, wasn't it?'

'We just need to get in there, Major.'

The tactical team vaulted the gate in turn. A couple of them took long, clear-plastic shields. They jogged towards the building. The lead man carried a heavy enforcer and a wrecking bar. George followed them over. Whittaker was a little slower. The team stopped at the main entrance. George looked at the enforcer. It was used for smashing through wooden and UPVC front doors. He didn't quite know how they might gain entry into a secure unit if no one was letting them in.

He needn't have worried. The lead officer pulled at the door. It swung outwards immediately. It was supposed to be locked tight. It caught them all out, they were too close and they had to shuffle backwards. They stepped in.

'What the hell?' Whittaker exclaimed. George ignored him. He moved into the lobby with the tactical team. The first thing he noticed was the darkness, then the silence. It hadn't exactly been operational the last time he had been here but the silence was more prevalent. The panels and cameras for scanning prints and retinas were still dark, but it was quieter. He got the feeling that it wasn't just the security that wasn't working. He looked at the door to the airlock corridor and remembered that it was powered differently and, sure enough, there was a small red light. He looked through to the airlock and briefly considered that they wouldn't all fit, that they might have to go through in two groups. A gloved hand pushed at the first door, for entering the corridor. It didn't budge. George looked into the gloom. He could just make out the other end of the corridor and a slit of light where the door was propped open. He squinted. There was something jammed in the bottom of the door. He couldn't make out what it was.

'You can't open this door. The far one is open,' he said. The window in the door was small. The tactical team bumped into one another and craned their necks to see through. The sergeant stepped back. She ran her hands down the steel sill of the door. It was flush to the steel rim. 'There's no way we're getting a rabbit in there. I assume the glass is reinforced? That's assuming anyone could fit.'

The rabbit. A hydraulic arm with a claw at the end that could be pushed into a gap in a door and then pumped to split the two apart. It was an effective opener in the right circumstances. These were not the right circumstances.

'We need another way in,' George said.

The team turned towards the front door. George stayed in the lobby. He pressed himself back up against the window. Whittaker stood next to him.

'Do you have a torch I could borrow?' George said. The nearest officer nodded and pulled a torch from a pouch on his belt. He handed it over. George pushed it up against the window.

'What's going on, George?' Whittaker was craning to see in himself. The torch lit up the scene a little better at the far end of the corridor. 'Where the hell are the security guards?'

'I can't see much of the inside, Major. I might be able to vouch for one of the guards though.'

'You can see one? What the hell is he doing?'

'At a guess, he's propping the door open, Major. With his head.'

George and Whittaker moved back outside. One of the team had returned for bolt-croppers and they were making a start on a side gate on the west side of the building. The fence was a little higher here, some barbed wire along the top. It was subtle, but this close George could see the lethal little barbs. The team quickly gave up on the gate and moved on to the fence. It was a thin mesh of steel. They would need to cut a gap. It was slow going.

The team's movements were noticeably more urgent. Whittaker was shuffling from foot to foot next to him. George felt calmer. He already knew there was nothing inside to rush for. They were too late.

It took nearly ten minutes for enough of the fence to be cut. The team pushed through the last bit and jogged to the other side. George stooped through the gap. The Major was already ahead of him. He watched the team move round the building. The new turf was soft underfoot. That big window at the rear loomed above them. George pushed himself against it as the team moved to the double doors that were off to the side. The doors were caged in by the same steel mesh used in the fencing. They made a start. George turned his attention to the glass window. From this side, it was heavily smoked, but he could just about make out the interior. He moved to the far left, to look into the cell. It was empty. The bed had ruffled sheets and an upturned beaker with water pooling beneath it. Signs of a disturbance maybe? The restraints were undone but they looked out of use rather than cut or forced. He moved across the window so he could take in the open-plan lower level. Nothing much was out of place here, no further signs of disturbance. He could see a couple of pizza boxes stacked on a table top, a jug of water and more beakers. Everything else looked like it was where it should be. He couldn't see much of the upstairs, the mezzanine level. He took a few steps back to take in the whole of the back. The tactical team were still cutting through the mesh to get to the only door that was visible at the rear of the building. George could tell they were struggling. Whittaker was standing over with them. George turned out to sea, his vision lifted beyond the thin, mesh fence.

'George!' Whittaker's voice. He sounded excited. George turned to him. The team were pushing through the fence. He jogged towards them. The back doors hung open. They were in.

Despite that huge window, the house was dim. The alcove and offices tucked off the main, open-plan room were silent and dark. One of the officers flicked a light switch — nothing happened. The sergeant barked at George and Whittaker to stay outside. The tactical team started in formation, moving through the house, room by room, void by void, searching for anyone or anything. George and Whittaker both ignored the instruction. They moved into the ground floor. George was close to the cell door. It hung open. He moved to the pizza boxes. A local supplier. There were just crumbs left.

'Contact!' A shout from the tactical team. George and Whittaker exchanged a quick glance then moved towards the voice. They were in a small area that led through to the first of the airlock doors, the door that George had seen from the other side. Two of the team were kneeling down. Others were turning away. The sergeant turned right back towards them.

'Oh God!' She gagged a little. George kept moving. He got closer. A young girl in nurse's uniform. Navy blue scrubs, the soles of her flat shoes were lying towards him. The blood was thick on the floor. The blood pool was a little disturbed where she had been dragged a few feet to act as a door wedge. There were no other signs of disturbance, no obvious defensive wounds. George had seen scenes like it before. This wasn't a fight. This was a woman who never even had the chance to fight. The blood was localised as if it had flowed smoothly out rather than there being any splatter. She might not have even seen it coming. And she was definitely dead. George could see the eyes now. They were looking down her body, towards where George was stood at her feet. The angle of the head was unnatural. He could see the slit across her neck. It was jagged, untidy and deep. So deep that George reckoned that was why she was at an angle. He'd damn near cut her head right off. The other members of the team were turning away one by one. Their half-hearted attempts to find a pulse, to consider CPR, had all come to an end. There was nothing anyone could do. George couldn't turn away. He was transfixed by those sorry eyes. She looked young to him, no older than thirty. Such a waste of a life.

'What a mess we have up here, George!' Whittaker was on his shoulder.

'It's gonna take some clearing up, sir.' Suddenly his attention jerked to a loud banging noise off to their left. The tactical officers were milling about, but they all snapped to it too. Then there was a voice — a cry for help. It was coming from the holding area George had seen on his tour. The door to it was shut this time however. One of the team wrenched it open. Immediately people poured out with excited wails and cries as they saw the police uniforms.

'Oh thank God! Thank God!' A well-built prison guard was first out. He stumbled and the tactical team held him up. George stepped up to him.

'What the hell happened?'

The man shook his head, like he was shaking it free. 'He was so weak . . . one minute he was so weak, we were waiting for him to die — then he just raised up like he was possessed! I've never seen anything like it. There was someone else here too. It was just a pizza delivery — I didn't think nothing of it. I thought someone had got one in! We never stood a chance. He was going to kill us all!'

'Who?'

'The guy with the pizza. He had a gun, for fuck's sake! He never said nothing, just waved it around. But Roberts . . . he got a knife, a huge fucking blade. I got no idea where it came from! It was a big, curved thing. Like a sword almost. He said no one had to get hurt. He said we just needed to get into the holding cell. That was it. We did what we were told. We all got families to get back to, you know?'

'What about her?' George gestured at the body surrounded by blood.

'I dunno, man! It was like she wasn't listening, like she wasn't hearing what he was saying. She went a bit crazy. She started shouting at him. She said he wasn't going nowhere. She tried to use a phone. She's foreign. I couldn't understand some of what she was saying. I tried to calm her down, but she weren't having none of it!' He looked down at her, at the scene in general. 'Oh God! Look at that shit!'

'Did Roberts do that?' George said.

'He must have. We were all forced into the holding cell. She was fighting with the door, she wouldn't let them close it. I tried to calm her down and pull her in but she wouldn't listen. Suddenly she was just dragged out. The door was slammed shut. I didn't even hear anything. He must have just cut her straight away. Oh God!' The man broke. His eyes began leaking tears, he put his hand over his mouth and he moved forward. George stepped aside and he stumbled through the back door that still swung open.

'We need to keep some control of him, George!' Whittaker said.

'We do, but I think he needs some air.'

George turned away from the mess on the floor. He stepped away from the sobbing group and the tactical team who were calling with urgent tones on their radio. He stared into Henry Roberts's empty cell. He was aware of Whittaker standing at his shoulder.

'Jesus, George, what have we done?'

Chapter 25

George was glad when Whittaker shut the door to his office. He wanted it shut, shut to the buzz of the Major Crime floor, to the ringing phones, to the questioning looks from the quickly gathered team of detectives. Whittaker's phone rang too. The sudden, shrill tone cut through George and made him jump. Whittaker turned it down. He didn't pick it up. George was relieved. He needed a few minutes to gather his thoughts.

Neither man spoke. Whittaker fussed and fidgeted over making some hot drinks. When he'd finished and put a mug down in front of George it seemed to be the cue for him to say something. 'The first thing we need to do is bring everyone up to speed.'

'Have senior management said the same? They're going to want some control over who knows what and when,' George said.

'We've lost control, George. We've lost Roberts. The second that man stepped out into the sunshine we lost the luxury of a circle of knowledge. It doesn't matter who gets hold of this now. The beat coppers, the media — the more the merrier. The more eyes we have out looking for this man the sooner we might be able to get him back.'

'He knows that.'

'I'm sure he does. We can assume he has a plan.'

'He does. You don't orchestrate something like that without considering what happens next. Are we to assume his plan means moving back out of our county?'

'Quite possibly. But this is our mess, George, we need to be cleaning it up.'

'I'm not quite sure this is our mess, sir. Right from the start—'

'Yes, George, I know. Spare me. That will all come out in the wash and when it does it will still be my head — or at least my force in the spotlight. That's for later. Right now we need to find this guy.'

There was a soft tap on the outside of the door. George snapped towards it as if stung. Emily Ryker pushed it open and waited. Whittaker gestured her in. George had called her on the way back. He hadn't told her much, just that they needed her to meet them in Whittaker's office. And to cancel any plans for the next few days. From the grave look on her face, he could assume she was up to speed.

'Emily, thanks for coming down.'

'Of course. You all okay?'

'Not really, Ryker.' George said. 'We've got a bit of a problem on our hands.'

'What happened?'

'We don't know just yet. We were starting to piece a few bits together. We knew Roberts was getting help. I got a sniff that he might not be quite as ill as we hoped. I was starting to put it together. I was too late.'

'If we suspect inside help, I'll get an intel cell going for all the staff.'

'We have a team of detectives talking to the group from the house now. But I'm not sure they're going to be able to tell us too much. I'm still convinced it's the staff who *weren't* there — that's the place to start.'

'Then you might be pleased to hear that I think I found your nurse.'

George's back stiffened. 'Where?'

'Not so far from where she used to live. I have a contact at the Department for Work and Pensions. They couldn't find her — she's not claiming benefits. But her boyfriend is.'

'Boyfriend?'

'Yeah. I found her social media and that linked to a man who appears to be her boyfriend. We were able to do a search in the Dartford area and find him. He registered for his benefits at a new place recently — a flat. It's a lot smaller than Camille's previous house, but from the land registry people it looks like she's buying this one rather than renting.'

'Like she might have had a cash injection recently.'

'Exactly like that. There's a little more to it, too.'

'More?'

'I searched Companies House. Camille Bisset registered a business three weeks ago. She's the only listed director. The Beano Café. It's part of the same building.'

'As the flat?'

'Yes. They live above it. I found the filing for the accounts. It's profitable. But just okay, nothing amazing.'

'So what, she's a qualified nurse who now fancies making bacon butties for tradesmen and for a smaller salary? That's not right, is it? I need to go and speak to her.'

'Now?' Whittaker exclaimed. 'I can only imagine the amount of work that has come out of today. We're going to need a full debrief, George. I would rather you weren't at the other end of the county when we're trying to work out a strategic plan.'

'I know that. That's why I need to go now. If I stay here I'm going to be in the queue to get swabbed, to get my clothes seized, to have a full body-map and an interview. We don't have time, Major. With respect, that house gives us more questions than answers. All the answers are out there. This missing nurse, she's trained to make people look ill with makeup — movie standard. She's had a decent cash injection too. She has answers. More than fibres that might be stuck to my trousers. We know who murdered that nurse. We need to know where he is now.'

'Fine, George. But I need some sort of result. And quick.'

'I'll speak to her and then I'll head back in so we can get our heads together. Who knows, it might be clearer by then.'

'And what about Emma Rowe? She's got an active investigation up there that links in. She won't even know yet,' Whittaker said.

'No. I need to speak to her. I've tried calling but she hasn't picked up yet. I'd rather not do it over the phone anyway but she's not even giving me the chance to do that.'

'I'll try. There's a strategy meeting today in London — this afternoon. I'm supposed to be attending and she pushed to be put on the list. I don't know if she was added but if she was she may be in London already.'

George scooped his car keys off the table. 'Major, if you do get hold of her, consider asking her to meet me. I would still rather tell her to her face.'

'Meet you where?'

'The Beano Café. Ryker here can give you the address. Just hold off on telling her too much.'

'You want me to call her and tell her to forget about her strategy meeting with the Home Office and head down the road to meet you at some greasy café? And without telling her why?'

'Yes. I think we can assume your meeting is off anyway. Just tell her it's really important and it really needs to be done face-to-face.'

'You know I'm the senior officer, George, right?' Whittaker's tone carried a warning. George knew he could get above his station, and he'd been pushing Whittaker today. He knew that too.

'Of course, sir. And if you tell me to do something else I will do it immediately. I'm merely suggesting the best course of action.'

'I'll speak to her, George. I'll see how it goes.'

'Thank you, sir. I appreciate it.'

'You've suitably atoned, George. So now you can stop calling me, sir!'

Chapter 26

'What the hell is this, George?' Emma Rowe looked furious. He could understand her reaction. Her mood was only going to get blacker too, he was sure of that. He knew that Whittaker had got hold of her by phone, he was aware that she had been told that the meeting was cancelled and was also assured that she didn't know why. Whittaker had told her to meet with George for some answers. He had warned him that Emma was beyond furious, as she didn't appreciate being treated like someone on the periphery. George had received his update straight after Whittaker's call with Emma. It was twenty minutes more before Emma called him. She'd surely been ringing around, trying to find out what she could from other sources. He would have done exactly the same in her position. When she did finally call it was obvious that she was still in the dark. That was probably the only reason she'd agreed to do anything he asked at all. He didn't even try to appease her, he didn't answer any questions. He just guided her into a tight, residential street in Croydon, South London. When she arrived he was leaning casually on his car with his arms folded. He was directly outside a dingy-looking café. He wasn't trying to be aloof; he genuinely didn't know how to tell her. When she stepped out of her car he spoke quickly, before she had the chance to tear his head off.

'I'm sorry, you should know that from the off. This is not about keeping you out of the loop, this is about making sure you are aware of everything.'

'What the hell are you talking about? What is all this about? Do you have our girl or not?'

'I'm closer. I'll explain everything.'

'This is bullshit, George. I could be half way back by now. You know I can't afford to be taking a day out from what I've got going on.'

'Just let me buy you a coffee.'

'What? Here?' Emma still looked furious. She took a step back to take in the frontage of the café. It was tired and dirty. George knew she was on the edge. He stepped inside, not entirely convinced that she would follow him. He watched her through the glass door. She muttered something then slipped her phone out of her pocket and checked it. She shook her head. But eventually she did step in.

'You have five minutes and then I'm back on the road.'

'Sounds fair.' George walked to the counter, where a man greeted him. He ordered two coffees.

'I bring it over!' The man was so cheerful he almost sang. George turned round. The café was cluttered with tables but only two were occupied: one against the window by an elderly-looking man with a leg stretched out across the aisle that looked like it was giving him some pain; the other against the far wall by a young woman with her back to George. He moved in her general direction. Emma followed but she stopped when George fell into the seat directly opposite the woman. She looked up in surprise, first at George, then at Emma standing to the side of him. George waited for her attention to move back to him.

'Can I help you?' The French accent was immediately noticeable.

'Did you never wonder what he did, Camille?' George replied.

'Who are you?' The woman's back visibly stiffened. Her eyes flicked between George and Emma.

'Henry Roberts. Did you ever wonder what he actually did? You must have wondered? The details of it, I mean.'

'I . . . I do not know what you are talking about.' She stood up, her chair scraped on the floor. George held out his warrant card. He stayed seated and looked up at her. She fixed on the card. She didn't sit down. She didn't walk away either.

'We've ordered more drinks,' George said.

'Am I under arrest?'

'Not if you sit back down.'

She dropped slowly back into the seat. George leant in. 'He killed three women. Young women. Teenagers. That bit you definitely do know, right?'

The woman's eyes dropped to the table. She shrugged. 'We all have our jobs. I am a nurse at a prison. I do not ask the patients if they are good people, I know the answer already. If I am not under arrest I can leave then, yes?' She stood back up.

'Have you ever heard of a Brazen Bull?'

'George!' Emma growled. The woman looked at her.

George continued. 'It's an ancient torture method. It's one of the most painful ways to die, by design.'

'Are you with this man? What is this about?' The woman spoke directly to Emma. George persisted.

'It's a bull. Or at least it is bull-shaped. It's made out of metal — copper in this case. It's hollow, and its belly hangs low to the ground. Imagine for me, Camille, that you are forced into the belly of a copper bull. You can't get out, no matter how much you struggle.'

'George! Is this really necessary?' Emma snapped. George just needed her to give him another minute. He continued.

'You're naked, Camille. Lying in the bottom of this metal bull. You don't know what's going on, it's pitch black. Then, someone lights a fire underneath it. Copper is a good conductor of heat. The metal starts to get warm. Maybe you don't know why, but you can probably hear the crackle and the hiss of the burning logs. You're panicking, Camille, can you imagine how much you would be panicking? You lift yourself off the bottom, away from the heat, you try to hold yourself up. Maybe you could jam a foot higher up. But the metal's getting hotter and the heat is spreading. As it gets hotter you start to sweat. Soon you're drenched in it. But it's getting hotter and hotter. Soon the sweat boils on your back, Camille, the air is so hot it scalds your throat. You're being fried and boiled alive at the very same time.'

Camille flopped back in her chair. Her head dropped forward. Her mouth hung open, her eyes puffed red and filled with moisture then a thick tear rolled down her cheek. She lifted her hands to wipe it away. She kept her face covered. *'Quelle horreur!'*

'You didn't know, Camille. No one did.'

'I *can* imagine!' she moved her hands away. Both eyes were leaking tears now.

'What did he offer you?'

'What?'

'Henry Roberts. Think about it, Camille, about why I am here, about what I might already know. This is your chance to talk to me off the record before we have to make any of this formal. What did he offer you?'

'I do not know what you mean.'

'I know about your past, about your ability to make people look unwell, close to death even. It was your job once. I know what you were doing for him, Camille. Now you need to tell me why.'

Her gaze flicked again from George to Emma. George had sensed that Emma was standing straighter beside him. He didn't look directly at her but he was relieved she was still there at least. Camille's body language changed: she seemed to wilt in front of him; her back curved forwards; she needed to put her arms on the table to support her weight.

'Oh God! They know where I live! And they know where my sister lives!'

'Who does? Who knows where you live? Henry Roberts? If he's hatched some plan you just need to help us out, Camille, and we'll make sure he goes back to rot in his—'

'It is not HIM!' she shrieked. It made George jump. 'It is not him. I do not know who, I do not know, okay? I was never told and I never asked. I know about the bull thing. They did not call it what you called it, but they told me about it. When they said it, it was worse. I still have the nightmares. These people . . . they told me I would get the same. A man talked to me, he told me that I needed to do what I was told. They gave me money, yes, but this is not why I do this.'

'What man?'

'I do not know.'

'Where did he talk to you? What does he look like? Tell us what you know, Camille, and we can help you out.'

'He . . . I did not see him. He wore a mask at first and made me turn around. I thought he was there to hurt me, to rape me maybe. He told me that I would not be hurt if I just listened to him. He said that he had money, it was good money, but if the plan failed I would lose a lot more than just the money. I did what I was told.'

'And what was that?'

'Some makeup, yes, but some drugs too. Makeup can only do so much. It was very important that he looked very ill. The drugs, the makeup and he was eating almost nothing every day. He is still weak.'

'So the cancer thing, it's all fake?'

'Not all, no. He has cancer. Very treatable, I think. But the doctor does the tests. I think it is. Otherwise why give the drugs to keep him weak?'

'So what's the story with the doctor?'

'The same story as me, maybe? The same people threatening the same things? We never actually talked about it. I only knew what I had to do. Sometimes I saw the doctor had a phone — a mobile phone. This is not allowed. This was for Henry, I think. Maybe even he was behind it all? Everyone maybe. The people building the house, too . . . some of them . . . all of them . . . I do not know. The locks, the alarms and the CCTV is all signed off as good. But I heard them talking. It does not work. The house is not finished. It is not ready.'

'So, Henry Roberts walks out? That was the plan?'

'I do not know. I was told to make him ill enough to get the move and to keep him weak while he was there. I do not know any more.'

'When?'

'I don't know.'

'Camille. If you know anything more . . .'

'I swear, I do not.'

'When do you work next?'

'Tonight! I am working every day now until he . . . Until the end.'

'What end?'

'I do not know. My employer says until he dies, but I know he might not. I just wait for my instructions.'

'But you're not sleeping? Today, before your shift?'

'Not yet. I may sleep for a few hours later but I get to sleep some hours at night — when he sleeps. Last night I had five hours sleeping maybe.'

'Who is working the day shift?' George was suddenly on the back foot a little. He had a scenario in his mind that he had convinced himself of. That this woman knew what was going on, or part of it at least. That she was going to

220

stay away from that house today, because she knew today was *the* day. But now George wasn't so certain that she knew much at all.

'The day shift? My sister. I told you, they know about her too. They know where she lives. They say to me, that they would hurt her. She knows nothing. She is there now. Do you need to talk to her too? There are no mobile phones but there is a number for the house. I can—'

'Your sister?' George was suddenly reeling from flashbacks of those dead, sorrowful eyes. 'So she's in on this too?'

'No! Like I say, she knows nothing. We work together but she does not do medicine. She always works with the doctor. And these people, they know what she is to me but they promised they would leave her out of all of this. I begged them to. But they said she was in danger too if I did not do what they asked. She does not even know the danger there. I tried to get her to leave, to take another job, but she would not. She asked me why one time. We argued a little. She said I did not like working with her. I could not tell her the truth. I can tell her when this is all over. If I just do what they say I can keep her safe. You will help, please? You will help keep her safe?'

George sat back. He was thinking fast. He knew she needed to know. But if he told her now she would fall apart and she would be no use at all.

'I think she is okay there,' Camille said. 'It is the people outside — they frighten me. When we are inside we are okay. Henry . . . he can be sweet. I know he is big. He is scary to see. But when you get to know him he can be . . . nice.'

'He isn't nice, Camille, you have to trust me on that.'

'I know who he is. I know what he is and what he has done. But he is okay with us. He is very nice to my sister.'

George shifted tack. 'Tell me about this café.'

'This café?'

'Yes. How is it yours?'

221

She shrugged. 'I do not understand. They said it was the best way to do it.'

'To do what?'

'This is how they get me the money. I did not want the money but they said it would be . . . compensation. They gave me some money to buy this place — the flat and the café. When it was done they said they would come back and buy it back from me. They would pay £20,000 more.'

George sat back. He'd heard the story before. It was a common method for criminals to hide payments for 'favours' or to launder money. You lend someone the money to buy a business. They register as the owner and then in a few months the criminal comes back and buys it for more than was lent, often more than it is worth. On the surface it looked like an entirely legitimate and small-time buyout. No one would blink. The money to make the purchase might also be layered in offshore accounts or an investment business with a structure so confusing you would struggle to see where it came from in the first place. It might not though. Maybe they hadn't been so careful.

'How? How did they give you the money to buy it in the first place?'

'They set me up a business account. They put money in it so I could buy it and a little more. I did not have to do anything. I just signed some papers.'

'Do you have any account details?'

'I have a card. The money is mine. They said that. They said they will just put more money into it when I have done what they ask and I move out. You have to know, I do not want the money.' She suddenly went quiet and dipped her head forward. Her hands reached under the table. George's instincts took him to his feet. He tensed up. Her hands moved back above the table. She dropped a purse and a black object onto it. It was a simple-looking mobile phone. She scrabbled in the purse. She slid out a card and threw that down.

'This is the card. And this is the phone. They gave it to me. It is how they talk to me. You can have it. There is nothing on it, no numbers, they do not text. I cannot call them. It is no use.'

George relaxed. He turned the card over so the account details were facing up. He pulled out his own phone and took a picture of the front.

'I will just be a few moments.' He snatched Camille's phone and put it in his pocket. He made eye contact briefly with Emma. He walked across the café to the door and stepped out. He let out a huge breath. Immediately he was back fiddling with his phone. Emma followed him out. She took her own deep breath. He looked at her. She was fixed on him.

'You okay?'

'Not really, George. We need to talk.'

'Yes we do. I need to make a call and then I'm with you.'

He held the phone to his ear. Emma looked like she was having an internal battle to stay calm. Her face twitched like she might explode at him. She seemed to change her mind and she turned away. Her hand came out to steady herself on the wall.

'George.'

'Hey, Ryker!' George kept his eye on Emma as he spoke. 'I've sent you a picture of a bank card. It's a business account. Right now it's our only lead. Divert what you need to divert, whoever you need to look at this. Find out what you can.'

'Understood. I'll get on it. Are you okay up there?'

'We're doing what we can.' George turned away. He lowered his voice a little. 'What's the latest from the house?'

'Jesus, George, what can I say? I was just in with Whittaker. He's getting it from all angles. They're taking statements, forensics, you name it. The first accounts all tell the same story though and it matches with the one you told me. Someone turned up to help your mate Roberts and between them they get control of the place. They tell anyone there to get into a lockable room. The girl stands up to them and she gets her head all but cut off.'

'Any CCTV from anywhere?'

'Not from the secure unit. Nothing inside or outside was working. We have found the gun that was mentioned, though. It was left out the front, stuffed in a hedge. It's a dud. A reasonably accurate copy. Accurate enough that you wouldn't argue with someone holding it. I guess Roberts doesn't have any use for real guns.'

'No, he does seem to have got his strength back.'

'And then some.'

'What about the doctor?'

'He was there. He's been arrested. Which is right but it may cause us some problems.' George knew what she meant. He was key. They could only assume that his medical records had been faked for a prolonged period of time. It seemed like he had been providing the link to the outside help too via a mobile phone. They needed what he knew. Now he was under arrest they would have to wait for formal interviews where he would be given the choice not to answer any questions at all. The system was certainly not designed for urgent situations like this.

'And what about his family?'

'Protective custody. To be fair to Whittaker, it was his first thought.'

'Okay, good. The nurse, the victim there. They're sisters.'

'Who? What do you mean?'

'Day nurse and night nurse. One got the other the job. It's early doors but the nurse up here knows a bit. If she is to be believed then she was threatened and paid. It wasn't just her life that they threatened her with either. It was her sister's too.'

'So, she knew it was going off today? And what, she left her sister in harm's way?'

'I don't think she did. She knew something was going on, but they told her as little as they could.'

'Does she know? About her sister, I mean?'

'Know what?'

'That she's dead? That Henry Roberts used her head as a draught excluder.'

'Jesus, Ryker!'

'Poor taste? Really? Coming from you, George Elms?'

'You're not the one up here trying to think of a way to break the news. No, she doesn't know.' George turned to check that Emma was still out of earshot. 'And that's before I tell Emma Rowe that we lost Roberts.'

'She still doesn't know?'

'No, she doesn't.'

'Another shit day, George.'

'Ain't it just?' George pressed to end the call. He wasn't listening anymore. It was like it had suddenly hit him all at once, the adrenaline, the emotion, the reaction to a murder scene. His mind had clicked into detective mode and only now was he stopping to consider the enormity of it all. Roberts was free and someone's baby sister was dead.

'You gonna talk to me now, George?' Emma said.

He blinked hard and struggled to begin. It felt like his throat was closing up. He stooped forward, his hand moved to his abdomen, it churned and ached. 'Yeah,' he managed. 'Henry Roberts . . .'

'What the hell is going on?' Emma was angry but it was tinged with concern. George was almost bent double. He used the wall to straighten back up.

'He's killed again, Emma.'

'What are you talking about?'

'Roberts.'

Her eyes flickered as they stared into his. She was looking for the lie. She didn't find it. She covered her mouth with her hand. 'When?'

'Today. And he'll kill again, Emma. I know he will.'

She turned ashen, the colour emptying from her face. Her eyes lost their focus and her head shook slowly. 'He's out, isn't he?'

'They both are.'

Chapter 27

Whittaker's office was not the sanctuary it had been earlier that day. The noise and confusion they had managed to shut out before was now very much in the room. George thought it might even be inside his head: his ears were roaring; his tinnitus was always worse when he was stressed.

He had driven as quickly as he could to get back there, with Emma sitting silent in the passenger seat. They left Camille at the café, just as soon as George was able to organise a uniform patrol to get there. She would be taken to the nearest station where she would be safe and where she could give her full statement. Technically, she was still under suspicion of being part of this whole thing but George had been looking into her eyes when she spoke to him. He had seen her reactions. Some things you couldn't fake; she had been telling the truth. He had repaid the favour and told her his truth. She wilted to nothing in front of him. Crying for her sister on the floor of her new café. George had sucked it all up: the misery, the loss, the desperation, just like he always did. Then he walked away.

George, Emma and Whittaker stood around the chief inspector's desk. No one spoke. There was a brief rap at the door and Emily Ryker bustled in without waiting.

George thought Ryker looked just as shocked as everyone else. He looked from person to person. This was a room full of people not easily rattled under normal circumstances, but this had caught them all on the back foot.

'Hey. The boss said you wanted me here,' Ryker said quietly to Whittaker.

'We need everyone we can get with a sane and rational mind right now,' he said.

There was a shrill tone, and Ryker snatched her phone up to her ear.

George looked through the partition window, across the Major Crime floor. It was starting to fill up. Any detective doing anything other than this job had been called back in. They would be asking for help from other counties, too — anyone able-bodied with a warrant card if George had his way. It didn't matter how Roberts had escaped, not right now, just that he had. George didn't dare think what his next move would be.

Ryker finished her phone conversation quickly. She was flustered.

'Everything okay, Ryker?' George said.

She ignored him and spoke to Whittaker directly. 'Sir, do you have a radio?'

'Yes, of course.' Whittaker gestured at the handset in a charging cradle on his desk. Emily snatched it up.

'Traffic are behind a van. They got an ANPR hit from their onboard camera. White van, same reg. It deviated when they got behind it.'

'Where?' George said.

'M20 — London bound. It's pulled off the motorway. They haven't made any attempts to stop it yet. It's Maidstone rural.' Emily fidgeted with the radio. It suddenly erupted with excited voices. They announced that that they were going to attempt to stop it. George guessed that traffic had followed it until the armed backup could arrive. Everyone in Whittaker's office was utterly silent as they exchanged looks. The radio hissed back into life. '*Vehicle is stop, stop!*' Sirens were clear in the background. The radio fell silent again.

Chapter 28

The two armed officers approached the van from the rear, their side-arms clutched firmly in both hands, lowered but ready. The two unarmed traffic officers tucked in tightly behind them. The armed officers split. One made for the driver's door, the second strode beyond to get a view through the windscreen where he saw the driver. He gestured at him to show his hands. Both officers had a view of him but from different angles. The driver didn't respond immediately and they both bawled at him to comply. The engine was still ticking over. The officer closest to the driver's door wrenched it open. He barked at the seated man not to move then reached in and grabbed the keys. The man was bundled out of the van and put face down. His hands were cuffed behind his back.

Attention turned to the rear of the van. An officer reached out for the handle to the rear door. He rested a hand on it. He waited for a jerked nod from his colleague who was a step further back.

His gun was levelled. The door swung open.

* * *

Annie squinted and blinked in the sudden flood of light. She tried to lift her head, but her neck was stiff and shot with pain. Her wrists were sore. They were bound tight with coarse rope that further hindered her movements. She turned her head away from the light and saw the girl lying next to her. She had been making noises in the darkness, in reaction to the thuds and movements of the van. Just moans, nothing discernible. Annie had given up trying to talk to her.

She tried to look back up at the doors. The whole of the back of the van was a fiery white. The sun was at the perfect angle to beat down into her eyes. A figure stepped across, casting enough shadow for her to make out some detail. It was someone new. She didn't recognise him. He was taller than her captor. Taller and broader. A full beard dominated his face. His hair was long too. It fell round piercing, dark eyes that stared straight at her. The younger man appeared next to him. This one she did recognise. He was beaming, delighted.

'What do you think?' he said.

'Perfection.' The man's beard shook as he spoke. His voice was deep, almost a growl. His eyes were still fixed on her and he licked his lips.

'I told you, Henry, didn't I? I said she would be perfect!'

'You did.'

Suddenly the daylight was gone. The slamming of the door made her jump. The female lying next to her moaned. She almost formed words this time, then sighed heavily. Annie heard two more thuds. The engine started back up and the van started moving again.

* * *

Ryker was listening intently to her phone. The radio had been silent too long and Whittaker had instructed her to call for an update. After a few seconds she shook her head, her eyes dropped to the floor and she exhaled loudly.

George turned away. He walked a few paces to a shelving unit and brought his fist down hard. Something bounced off, he heard it hit the floor but didn't see it. His eyes were tightly shut.

'Okay. Thanks for letting me know.' Ryker ended her call.

George suddenly felt unsteady. He pulled a chair towards him and slumped into it.

'It's not our van,' Ryker said. 'Nothing in the back. The driver checks out. It's a Highways van and he's a Highways worker. It's likely they've had contact with it, though — the suspect plates have been stuck over the existing ones. Not very well either by all accounts. The driver just didn't notice.'

'Do we know where he's been, where's he stopped? Anything?' Whittaker sounded desperate. George felt it too.

'He's being spoken to now by the officers. He's not long dropped off a couple of other lads but I've got no more than that. It'll all be covered.'

'They'll have been careful,' George said, miserably.

'Yes, George! It's a long shot, but we have to give it a go!' Emma interjected. 'We have to hope that they made a mistake somewhere. Stop being so fucking negative!' She leant on the wall, her hand to her nose as if she was fighting back tears. 'I'm sorry, George, okay? I didn't mean to have a go.'

'Don't be,' George said. 'We need a next move ourselves, here. We never really expected to get this bloke with a traffic stop, did we? We need to dust ourselves off. Ryker, where are we with the financial checks?'

Ryker still looked deflated. 'I er . . . I spoke to my contact over the phone. Right from the start she wanted a signed superintendent's authority to be snooping around in someone's accounts. It's highly regulated. I convinced her to at least make a start. I told her I'd be able to get the authority. Without it she can't give me anything we can use evidentially. She found some activity that she could only tell me about off the record.'

'Activity?'

'Yeah. Large amounts of money going in and out of that business account. Amounts that wouldn't make sense for a café. What stood out were four transactions in four days, all were for fifty thousand pounds each. They were all moving from that account to the same place.'

'To where?'

'It looks like a trust of some sort. A charity, she thought.'

George scowled. It wasn't uncommon for criminals to use trusts to wash their money.

'What trust?'

'I don't know the exact details. It was a Christian fund. The address was a church back up in Emma's area. It was a funny word, I wrote it down somewhere, it'll be back at my desk.'

'St Dubricius's?' George said.

'That's it!' Emily said.

'That's Roberts's church,' Emma said.

'It is. Where I upset your vicar, remember?'

'You did. So what's the link there? I guess it might make sense for him to give his money away to the church. It's all he cared about.'

'It would if he was staying in prison. But he always intended on coming out. And why now? Ryker, when were the transactions?'

'She went back twenty-eight days. She needs to go further really, considering he's been in prison for a couple of years. But without those authorities we're getting nothing more. Those transactions were a couple of weeks old.'

'I was there just a couple of days ago. We need to go and see him, Emma. That's good work, Ryker. Was there anything more?'

'Not without the right authority. I spoke to the boss, here. We're being warned off doing much round this — am I right, sir?'

'Absolutely,' Whittaker said. 'There's a big hoo-ha, as you can imagine. They don't want us anywhere near it right now. The brass from headquarters have set up their own resources to run an investigation into how Roberts was able to walk away from a secure unit in the first place. I would rather they didn't know that we were looking at finances. Everything we do needs to be under the radar, please.'

'Don't worry, Major,' George said. 'You know me and the radar. I'm barely a blip. Emma, I think we need to go and see your vicar friend.'

Emma looked pensive. 'He doesn't like me, George. He told me he doesn't like you either. What if he complains? He did before. That's hardly staying off the radar, is it?'

'It's fine. We'll be a couple of hundred miles away from here so nobody else will have got to him yet. We need to be swift, though. And we need to make sure we get everything first time. Do you have his home address?'

'There'll be one on file. He gave statements.'

George turned to Whittaker. 'Major, we need to get back up the line. I can't do much here at the moment. If we're about to come under a lot of scrutiny, that can only hinder us.'

'Well, you are far more likely to be left alone in Symonds Yat. I'll do my best to attract the heat for the time being. I don't think it will be long though before people realise that you were the main police contact with Roberts.'

'Thanks for reminding me.'

'Well, whatever. If you're not here, you can't be asked about it. Go and take the holiday you had booked. There's no reason not to.'

'Holiday, Major?'

'The cottage up in Symonds Yat. It's still booked out for another couple of days. I suggest you use it.'

George couldn't help but grin. 'I'd forgotten all about that place.' He checked his watch then looked at Emma. 'If we leave now we might be able to get to catch our vicar today.'

'We might.' Emma looked unsure. 'I don't see him giving us any information, George. We shouldn't put all our hopes on that conversation. Roberts was a devoted parishioner. On the surface, him doing what he could to make a donation could be plausible.'

'I agree, *on the surface*. But John Lawrence made a mistake. He gave me a little glimpse under the surface.'

'How so?'

'He asked me for money.'

Chapter 29

The monotone roar of rubber on tarmac was the only sound accompanying their journey up the M4. George was in a hurry. Emma looked through reports and logs for the first forty minutes of the journey and said nothing. George had expected questions, criticisms maybe, frustrations definitely. He got silence. When she put her paperwork back in the bag tucked between her feet, she turned towards the window and that was where her attention stayed. The silence was becoming awkward. He was hunting for something to say — the right thing to say. It was Emma who spoke first.

'Do you think she's dead already?' She was still facing the window and her voice was low.

'No, I don't think she is.'

'He likes to savour it, doesn't he? The whole thing. From start to finish. He probably enjoys this bit as much as the act. The build-up, I mean. He definitely enjoys the fear. And she will be scared, George. Can you imagine how terrified she must be right now? Assuming she's still alive.'

'No. I can't, to be honest. And we shouldn't be trying to either. We need to focus. Roberts is still weak. He has to be. I know we've been deceived about his condition but he's still barely eaten in months. He'll take a while to recover. And I think he'll want to be stronger before he does anything. Like you said, he'll want to savour it and . . .' Emma had turned to look at him. 'And what, George?'

'I was just going to say . . . it takes strength to do what he does. I've thought about it — far too much to be honest. I'm pretty sure I couldn't do it. Dragging that bull, and a girl fighting for her life.'

'It's possible though. With two of you. Once you find a remote enough spot you can take your time. Rest up,' Emma said.

'Plenty of remoteness around Symonds Yat. Do you think he'll head back there?'

'I do. It might make sense to go elsewhere if he's considering the odds of getting caught, but I don't think he is. He knows the area around there. That remote spot he's looking for? There are hundreds of them, and I bet he knows just about every one. I don't think getting caught has crossed his mind. Yes he's been clever around the van but I think it's just to get him back to where he wants to be.'

'So he should be easy to find?'

'I didn't say that. We just need to be sure . . .' This time Emma ran out of steam. George didn't push her. He reckoned he knew what she was going to say.

She sucked in a deep breath and seemed angrier. 'We can't let it happen, George. Not again. The first time around we were chasing shadows, we had no clues at all. Then we got a break and we had him in a cell. He was chained to a fucking bed. Tried and convicted, but for those girls who were already gone . . . we can't let it happen again. We had him!'

'I know that, Emma, I know. There's another reason I don't think he's hurt her yet.'

'What other reason?'

'Something he said to me when I visited him in prison, after we found both those girls and he told me how they had died together. I wasn't going to talk to you about it but you guessed anyway. He did make one of those girls watch. And he loved every minute of it. It *is* about fear with him. Fear, control and power. He feeds off it. And I think he found his sweet spot when he had those two girls together. When he spoke to me, when I looked into his eyes, I knew that if he ever got the chance again he would be sure to have two.'

Both of them fell silent again. Neither needed to speak. They knew what it all amounted to: they were running out of time. And Roberts needed another girl.

They stopped for coffee. George didn't need the drink as much as a break from the silent car — something else to do or say unconnected with this whole mess, even if it was just ordering a black coffee to go. He sensed Emma's relief when he suggested it too. She didn't stay with him in the services. She got a bottled water from a different outlet. George wondered if she used the water as an excuse to go somewhere else, to be apart for a little while. Forty minutes later, she still hadn't opened the bottle and he knew he was right.

Emma's office was still and stuffy when they finally got there. She pushed the windows open and woke her computer. There was a stack of box files on a table that was separate from her desk with a couple of seats around it. They all had 'Op Example' written on their spines.

'Op Example?' George said.

Emma stopped what she was doing. She rested her eyes on the boxes and sighed. 'The Roberts murders. That's what the name generator brought up. They'll be a new Op now, of course, down in Langthorne.'

'Yep. The force just love giving things titles. Op *Bad* Example I would suggest.'

Emma managed a smile. Nothing more. She looked tired suddenly. George was feeling it too. She looked beyond him through the partition window to the banks of desks where her detectives sat. George had only seen a couple on his way in. The early shift carried the bulk of the numbers. It was well into the late shift now where it was resourced just for cover from Major Crime.

'Are you worried about how you're going to tell them?' George said.

'Terrified. Of course I am.'

'Did you want me to do it? I mean, it's nothing to do with you, what happened. That way it keeps some separation from you.'

She shook her head. 'I appreciate the offer, George, but I'm going to have to manage the fallout from all this. It should be me from start to finish.'

'Just like it was last time?'

'Yeah, except it isn't finished, is it?'

'We will finish this though. Between us all. When are you going to tell them?'

'Tomorrow. There's a morning meeting every day. It's the only time I can guarantee getting everyone together.'

'What if this gets out before then?' George said.

'I thought about that. I spoke to John Whittaker earlier. I called him from the services about that very issue. Your lot are keeping a lid on it for now. It's been made very clear to him. Apparently they're concerned they might force Roberts into doing something if they release the information to the press.'

'That's ridiculous. Roberts has his own schedule. We won't prompt him to do anything earlier, we can only hope to delay him.'

'I agree. I said the same. I also told Whittaker your theory about how he needs some time to recover. He didn't disagree but, reading between the lines, I think there's hope that this can be nipped in the bud before anyone has to have a press conference at all.'

'The one where they admit to letting a Category A serial killer walk away from prison.'

'It doesn't seem possible, does it?'

'It doesn't. Just a couple of days ago I went to see him at Belmarsh. That place is a fortress. He barely stood a chance of seeing a blue sky again, let alone walking to his freedom. I said from the start that it was where he belonged. When we let him have a little control over his environment he was always going to take more. He played us all. And very well.'

'He did that. With help. I don't know what scares me more . . . Roberts, the devil we know or . . .'

'Or the one we don't,' George said. 'I think he was planning his escape from prison before he even got sent there.'

'You might be right. That's not going to soften the blow tomorrow, is it? When I stand in front of my team and tell them he's outwitted us all.'

'Not you, though. Not them. The only people he *didn't* outwit were your investigation team. You need to lead on that.'

Emma sighed, longer and harder than George had heard before. 'Maybe you're right. I'll give it a go.'

'I'll be there. With you, I mean. I'm happy to step in and take the flack as the bumbling, foreign force who messed up their job.'

She chuckled a little, 'I think you'll play that role well.'

'I've made a career out of it!'

The laughter increased. The silence that followed felt somehow less awkward. Both seemed content to be lost in their thoughts.

Emma spoke first. 'What else is there, George? What more can we do?'

He pulled out the note book in which he had listed outstanding actions as he saw them. 'The van that was hired. We were doing some CCTV bits around that?'

'Oh! Did I not update you? I had a missed call then an email. I didn't call them back. The CCTV was reviewed. It's not very clear. I asked for some stills to be taken off it and put out on all the briefings. We haven't gone public with it yet. Hang on . . .' Emma played with her computer. It took a few seconds to activate. 'Here.' George walked round to get a better view of her screen. The camera looked like it was fixed high up, behind a counter. It pointed down at a steep angle. It captured a white male with a slim build. He didn't look that old, maybe early twenties, but George was guessing at that from an overall impression. He wore a light hooded top. The hood was up. It had a blurred motif on the front. Something on the left breast. The image was poor quality overall. Certainly he couldn't make out any facial features. It looked like he was in black tracksuit bottoms and white trainers.

'Is there a video clip?' Experience told him that stills were not the way to *see* someone. You need them to be moving. The way they move, the way they hold themselves, that's what can be recognised.

'I did ask for that. This should be it.' Emma scrolled through her emails. She clicked on another attachment. The screen went black for a second then the video started. Their man hovered by the door. To George he looked like he was building himself up to something. A few people moved in before him. Finally he stepped in. He kept his head bent and he didn't look up at any point. George was in no doubt that he knew where the camera was. His walk, the stiffness to his movements, telltale signs of someone who was tense, rigid almost.

'It's no clearer,' Emma said.

'It isn't. But from that I would say that he has been there before to recce the place. There will be a clearer image of him. From earlier but who knows when.'

'I'll get someone back down there from my team to go through it.'

George started pacing. 'I wouldn't bother. It's not going to be enough to ID him unless he's already well known to us. And the time it would take to go back through every minute of CCTV they have stored . . .

That's assuming he has been there in the period still stored on their system. I think we'll have better uses for your team, Emma.'

'Okay. Tomorrow morning, when I tell them what is going on, we will get one of two reactions. They will either collapse in front of me or they will all instantly want to know what they can do. I think I know my team. I think they're all going to want to be out doing something to get us closer to getting this animal back behind bars.'

'I'm sure you're right.'

'We are going to need to give them something to do though, George. That will be key to this. If they're sitting round thinking about it too much we will have problems.'

'Understood.' George was back to flicking through his book.

'The doctor. His interview is key. I've asked Whittaker to update me when it's done. There might be some leads we can follow up on. Maybe more financial stuff, too — they'll look at his accounts for sure? We still don't know enough around those. You and I will speak to the vicar about the same thing. I've had success in the past with following money. I'm sure you've had the same.'

'I've hit a fair few brick walls, too. Roberts is used to having money — probably used to hiding it too. Those sorts of people usually are.'

'I'm sure you're right, but we have to try. Is there a family accountant? Anyone they used? Might be a good place to start.'

'I don't know. I'm not sure if that was picked up as part of the initial investigation either. It was never about money.'

'I think it is now. It took a lot of money to get him out of that prison. Maybe some of your team could have a look at that. They might be able to get a superintendent up here to authorise more intrusive checks. Someone who isn't quite concerned about an IPCC enquiry.'

'That makes sense.' Emma was shaking her head, however.

'Do you not agree?'

'No, I do. It's not that. I've gotten used to criminals doing all sorts of terrible things for their own financial gain. I can understand that. Crime for money makes sense to me. I think that's one of the reasons why this hit us so hard — this was about Roberts enjoying killing young women. And in the most hideous way he could imagine. We have to stop him, George.'

'I know. We will. We just need some luck. Fortune favours the good. That's a thing, right?'

'It's brave. Fortune favours the brave.'

'That can't be true. Tomorrow morning you'll be addressing a room full of incredibly brave people. People that stood up to the Bull. And yet we certainly haven't had any luck.' George felt his phone vibrate in his pocket. The screen read *Ryker*. 'Maybe this is our fortune right now — hey, Ryker!'

'George, can you speak?' She sounded urgent.

'Of course. Wassup?'

'I've been monitoring inbound emergency calls. I had a word with the FCR. I asked that they let me know of anything even remotely related to vans or girls. I've been getting tagged in everything from vans parked over drives to girls seen throwing stones at a supermarket in—'

'Ryker!'

'Sorry. I'm babbling. There's a call log. Here in Langthorne. It might be nothing. I've sent it to your email.'

'It won't be nothing. It's obviously got you interested. Can you forward it on to Emma? We can look at it on her screen.'

'Yeah, doing it now.'

'What's the summary?'

'A young girl working at a petrol station down here in Langthorne. She finished her shift at around 20:00 hours last night. Her car was parked ten metres from the exit door. She said goodbye to a male colleague and left to go home. She has since been reported missing. Her car is still on the forecourt.'

'Young girl?' He made eyes at Emma. He could see she had opened up the log on her screen. She scrolled through it.

'Yeah. Seventeen. Not long passed her test. It was her first time driving to work, George. We've been given a picture from the parents. I've scanned one. It should be with you.'

'Last night? Before Roberts got out?'

'Yes. While he was still tucked up in bed. But we know his mate was in the area.'

The picture opened up on Emma's screen. A young girl's image appeared, she wore a beaming smile. Her long blonde hair fell either side of her pretty face. She had high cheekbones and piercing blue eyes that were filled with joy as she held up a brown and white puppy dog. She looked so carefree and happy. So innocent. George knew she was perfect. He struggled to speak.

'Thanks, Ryker. We'll have a look through the log and we'll come back to you.'

'Okay. We've got CCTV enquiries going. The staff car park isn't covered, we know that much already. But any vehicle going in or out will have been captured. They have ANPR. I'm doing what I can around that. It's out of office hours now though, so it might take a little longer.'

'Understood.' George could feel his energy draining away. There were a thousand things that needed doing. He knew that, but he had just driven two hundred miles away from that garage. This enquiry had just gotten a whole lot bigger. 'Who's at the scene?'

'I've spoken to Whittaker. I've told him that I think it could be linked. There wasn't much going on there until then. Now we have everyone there.'

'Okay, good work. We will need everyone who works there tied down. There needs to be some proper questioning going on. They will have seen our man. He will have been in there.'

'Leave it with me, George. I know what needs to be done.'

He finished the call and his tired eyes met with Emma's. 'We have no idea where he's gone. We have no idea who he's with. We don't know the van anymore.' George was mumbling, thinking out loud.

'A couple of things I do know.' Emma still had the image of seventeen-year-old Sadie Edwards on the screen. Her name was written in bold under the picture.

'What's that?'

'We need some rest, George.'

'Rest! How can we rest?'

'We need rest, George. We're no good to anyone exhausted. We need to think again when we're fresh. Let's start again tomorrow. Early.'

George couldn't disagree. He wanted to speak to the vicar. He wanted to go through his accounts, to question him on every detail. But he would need to be sharp to do that. 'You said a couple of things.'

Emma sighed. 'I did. The other thing I know is that Roberts now has his second girl.'

Chapter 30

George's legs burnt with fatigue as he climbed the steps up to the holiday cottage. As he paused for breath at the door, he heard the patter of clawed feet, followed quickly by yapping and then a growl. Sharkey had arrived baring his teeth.

'You came back then?' The Essex twang was recognisable straight off, as were the leopard skin leggings. 'Thought you'd had enough, seeing as how I didn't see you again.'

George summoned up a tired smile in greeting. 'Hey! Nice to see you again. I think Sharkey would rather I never came back.'

'You can ignore him. I told you that last time. He's all show.'

'And teeth.' George gestured at where Sharkey was still showing a full set.

'That's all he is. A set of teeth. How did the hiking go?'

George was aware that she was looking him up and down. He stood in a shirt and trousers, a tie hanging limp a few inches short of where his top button was undone, and formal black shoes. He didn't look much like a hiker.

'Good. There are some incredible trails around here.'

'There are. Is that where you've been today?'

'No, I got called into work today. It can happen. I was hoping to come up here for a complete break. Things never quite work out how you want them to, you know what I mean?'

'I do. What is it that you do for work?'

'I'm in insurance. An actuary. I set the pricing for your policies. That doesn't mean you can hate me for it though. I set the base price. I have nothing to do with the profit they lump on top!' George's standard answer complete with snorted chuckle was delivered seamlessly. He had lost count of the amount of times he had given that line at social functions, to boyhood mates or just whenever he didn't want a conversation about being a police officer. It was about perfect: just interesting enough to be a real job, but boring enough for no follow-up questions.

'Ah, I see. That's important enough for them to call you up on your holidays is it?' She chuckled, seemingly satisfied.

'Not to me it isn't. Well, I've got an early start in the morning. Who knows, I might actually be able to get a hike in!'

'Good luck with that. I hear it's going to be another warm one tomorrow. We don't get too many of them round here — you make the most of it.'

'I'll try.' George was already walking towards the house. He heard the woman encourage the dog not to attack him. He was grateful for that.

The key was where he'd left it. The milk was still there, too. In fact, nothing had moved. Why should it have done? It was still his to use for another couple of days. He made a cup of tea, cursing that he hadn't stopped off for something a little stronger. He considered the pub. It was only a short walk but he dismissed the idea. He wanted an early night.

He had brought some reading material home; specifically, Dennis Coleman's daybook. All the formal statements and supporting material was there, everything that was submitted to the Crown Prosecution Services summarising all the evidence. George didn't want the polished summary in the format required for court. He wanted the doodlings and thoughts of a good detective. George had a theory about that. DS Coleman was a mess. He had fallen apart. To George, that smacked of a *good* detective, the sort who couldn't accept that he hadn't been able to help those girls. For so much to have been taken out of him he must have obsessed over this case. Bad detectives don't obsess, they just accept their failings and move on. George understood what it meant to obsess. He also knew that the thoughts and feelings of an obsessed detective were worth far more than a polished CPS case summary. The book was A4 sized. And two thirds full. The writing was scratchy. *Op Example* was written on the front and took up all of the cover. The first few pages were written out in the VOWS format: every part of what Dennis knew at that point categorised as either *Victim, Offenders, Witnesses* or *Scenes*, a classic discipline. George skipped past this section. He wanted the material from later on: when Dennis felt he was chasing his arse; when he was out of plausible ideas; when only the theories were left.

While he leaned on the kitchen bench with the notebook, George became gradually aware that the old house had a chilly edge — like houses often did when they'd been sitting empty. He considered the log fire and the sofa but changed his mind. A hot shower and his bed seemed like a better idea. He would take his reading material with him. Hopefully a combination of reading and the sounds of the river would lead to another good night's sleep. If he was to make any headway, there was another long day to awaken to.

Chapter 31

George pulled into a visitor's spot at the front of Hereford Police Station just before 7 a.m. Once again Symonds Yat had come through as the perfect place for a good sleep. He did indeed feel refreshed. Sleep had come despite him spending his last waking moments with the notes of a sergeant desperately chasing a serial killer. He was flicking through them again now but was no longer taking it in. He was killing time; without Emma, he couldn't even get into the building.

A car pulled in and he thought he had spotted her. Sure enough, she appeared on foot less than a minute later.

'Morning, Emma.'

'Morning. Did you sleep well?'

'I did, actually. I seem to sleep a lot better up here than I do at home.'

'A reason to stay?'

'Who knows?'

Emma walked quickly past George, away from the entrance they had used previously. 'Did you see someone on the steps?' she called out.

'Someone where?' George hadn't seen anyone around at all. He wasn't even sure which steps she meant. She walked around a wall and turned back on herself. George followed. When he rounded the wall he could see some stone steps in front. They led up to the doors to the front counter, which was closed this early in the day. A man in a black woollen hat and gloves sat on them. It wasn't a cold morning, but it had been a chilly night. George reckoned he had been there a while. The figure stood up as they approached. George jogged to catch up with Emma.

'That's odd? Don't you guys have a bat phone?' George referred to a facility at most police stations. A phone positioned at the front for people that turn up to make a report out of hours.

'We do. It's on the wall. I think I know who it is.'

'Anyone you need to worry about?'

'It's Chloe Pope's dad. He used to be here a lot. In the early days. I haven't seen him for a while. He can be a little ... spikey. You just have to go easy on him, okay?'

'I've no intention of being hard on a grieving father,' George said.

'Mr Pope!' Emma called out.

The man rubbed his hands together and dug his chin into the front of his jacket as if he was cold and he wanted them to know it. 'Colin. I thought we agreed on that,' he said.

'We did, you're right. It's been a little while, Colin. How are you doing?'

'Is this George Elms, by any chance?'

'I am indeed.' George held his hand out to shake. Colin eyed it for a second. Eventually he took up the offer.

'You don't understand the problems you caused when you came up like that.' He stared at George. His jaw rippled a little. He looked agitated.

'Problems? If I caused any problems I'm really sorry. I didn't come up to see you to cause any problems—'

'What did you come up for then?'

251

'George here is—'

'Is it true?' Pope was getting more and more wound up.

'Is what true, Colin?' Emma asked softly.

'You're moving him? To somewhere cushy? So he can be more comfortable? Is that fucking true?'

'Now, Colin—'

'Yes or no?'

'There's a little more to it than that—'

'Yes, then! How could you do that? That piece of shit should be in a fiery pit. Not—'

'Who told you that?' George took his turn to cut in. He felt himself starting to flare up too.

'What the hell does it matter?'

'Did you just find out?'

'You people aren't listening to me! You've never listened to me. If you had listened to me at the start, when I first said that Chloe was missing, when I first called it in, maybe—'

'Answer the question, Mr Pope!' George snapped. 'There's a far bigger investigation right now and we don't have time to be fucking about. Unless you feel you need to be under arrest to answer any of my questions? That can be arranged.'

'Under . . . why are you having a go at—' His demeanour changed. He was suddenly on the back foot.

George pressed him. 'Who told you and when?'

'My wife, she used to go to the church. She heard it there.'

'Used to? That makes no sense. You mean someone from the church came to your house and told her?'

'The church came to her, yeah. The main man. He came up and talked to her. He comes up a lot. So she can still do her bit now that we can't get her there.'

'Can't get her there?'

Colin Pope had now completely backed down. He sighed, shook his head and came back quieter.

'Agoraphobia. A fear of being out of that place. Ever since . . . well, ever since. She was part of the search. We both were. But it messed her up. It started with a fear of the woods. Then the trees in the garden. A little bit of wind . . . the moving branches — she would just freak out. I had to cut them all down.' His eyes had lost focus, his head had slumped and his voice was brittle with desperation. 'You can imagine how someone with a fear of trees might struggle around here. This place is made of trees.'

George remembered sitting on the tree stump in the Popes' front garden. 'So she doesn't go out at all?' George's tone was softer too.

'No. I tried to move her to the city. I thought it might help. She said she wouldn't go. She said "what happens if our Chloe comes home? If we're not there, she might run off again." I know it's silly. She knows it too. But how could I argue with that? I did used to. I used to tell her what I thought she needed to know. I used to tell her that Chloe was dead, that she was never coming back. But every time I said it out loud it broke her heart. It feels like I've loved that woman my whole life. I didn't want to be breaking her heart no more. So I stopped. She's not coped. Not at all. And now we hear that you're moving that . . . that thing. So he's more comfortable?'

'And John Lawrence told you that?'

'He did. And good for him, or—'

'He's dying, Colin,' Emma said.

Colin Pope stared at Emma intently. 'Dying? Who?'

'Roberts?'

'Dying how?'

'Cancer, I think. I've not really been too well informed about the whole thing. The prison service is dealing with it all. He's being moved to palliative care. They struck a deal with him. He gets to die in a place that isn't a prison cell, and in exchange — he tells us where Chloe is.'

Colin stood up, perhaps too fast. He looked unsteady. George stepped towards him. Colin held out his hand out to stop him.

'And did he? Did he tell you?'

'He did,' Emma said.

'When?'

'A few days ago.'

Colin's tears were sudden, like they had been just behind the surface the whole time. 'You didn't tell us?'

'We don't know what we found yet, Colin. But we did find something. No, we didn't tell you. That was my decision. I think it was the right one. There are tests we need to do to be sure. You and your wife have been through enough. It would have been another couple of days or so, and then I was going to come up and talk to you both. The last thing I wanted to do was turn up with hope. Just hope. I think you've had enough of that. I wanted something definite. I wouldn't have put it past that piece of shit for this to be another one of his games.'

Colin's head was shaking slowly from side to side. The information was sinking in. 'There wasn't much then? Left, I mean?'

Emma took her time. 'A lot of time has passed, Colin.'

'So there won't be anything to *see*? Nothing to see for ourselves? I think Mary . . . I think she's going to need that.'

'DNA testing will be one hundred percent, Colin. There'll be no doubt. The circumstances too . . . how we found Chloe, where we found her. There'll be no doubt at all.'

'Can you tell me? Can you tell me how you found her? Can you tell me how . . . how he . . .'

'We'll sit down, Colin. With your wife. When I have all the facts. We'll take as long as you like. I'll answer every question you can think of. But I think we need to do that when I have all the answers.'

'She died alone and terrified. That's all I keep thinking about. Is that right? Can you tell me that at least? Was she alone? Somewhere remote like that other girl?'

Emma did now look over at George. He returned her stare. He kept quiet.

'She wasn't alone, Colin. That much we know for sure.'

'She wasn't?' He bit down on his bottom lip.

'No. The two girls . . . we think we found them together.'

Colin sucked in air. His head lifted to the sky. 'That makes me feel better . . . that actually makes me feel a little bit better. She wasn't on her own! She had someone else there. Someone that wasn't him . . . someone *human*.'

'Colin, we need to get back to work. We have a lot to do but I promise you I will come and see you both the second I have something definite — in a day or two.' Emma started walking purposely towards the station entrance.

Colin turned to George. He offered his hand. This time the handshake was returned with a lot more vigour. 'Thank you! Thank you so much for finding her!'

'I'll take your thanks for the team up here, Colin. I'm just an imposter — but I know they'll appreciate it.'

George caught up with Emma where she was waiting for him behind the wall. She was fidgeting and looked angry. 'I thought I said we should go easy on him?'

'I don't like letting people walk over me.'

'He's a victim. We can't forget that. His life will never be the same again. Him and his wife, they've been a pain in the arse to us at times, but they're victims. They are what we are here for. To protect them.'

'I totally agree. But they don't get to walk over us, there's no point in spending our energy placating people who can't be placated. They want their daughter found and they want the man that did it in chains. We're not getting any closer to that while we're taking questions we can't

255

answer on the steps. I feel for the man. But we don't appease him answering his questions, we appease him by getting results.'

Emma lifted a hand to her brow as if she was nursing a headache. 'This is such a mess, George. I didn't know what to say. I didn't consider that he wanted to talk to me about Roberts. I thought it was more questions about Chloe. I thought I might be able to give him some positive information for once and that would be that. He caught me out. I couldn't tell him the whole truth.'

'You're right, you couldn't.'

'How did he know about the move? How could he know that?'

'I don't know. I'll put a call into Whittaker and see what they're telling people down there now. That information shouldn't be out, but this was always going to be difficult to keep a lid on.'

'I'll be the one who has to manage it up here though, George.'

'I know that. We've got your team meeting this morning. How much do you want to tell them?'

'Everything. I don't want to hide anything anymore. I've kept this from them for long enough.'

'They'll need to keep it to themselves. For now at least.'

'I'll tell them that. I trust them. They'll just want to do what they can. We've got a busy day. We'll get this meeting done first. We can get some of the work delegated out.' Emma started walking towards the door that would take them in. George lingered behind. She stopped at the door. 'Are you not coming?'

'I want to go and see DS Coleman first. Then we need to go and speak to the vicar. In that order. Can we consider putting your team meeting back? I know it's important but I think this could be too.'

Emma scowled. 'Dennis? You want to go and see Dennis? I appreciate that he should be spoken to, I was intending on doing it, but not before I've spoken to my team'

'I think he can help us, Emma.'

Emma shook her head vigorously. 'He was a good man. But he can't help us anymore. He took it hard. This investigation finished him off, George. Trust me, I tried to help him.'

'No one knows more about Roberts than Dennis. I looked at his notes. They tell the tale of a man obsessed.'

'It all but destroyed him. We turn up at his house now and tell him Roberts is on the loose and we will finish the job.'

'I don't think so, Emma. I have some questions that only he can answer. I think he was close to really understanding Roberts. We need that.'

'I thought John Lawrence was your key man? That's who you came all the way up here to see.'

'He is. But there's no point in speaking to him if I haven't spoken to DS Coleman first. I only realised that last night.'

Emma sighed. 'I don't like it. You need to handle him sensitively, George. Can you even do that?'

'I don't know any other way!' George chuckled.

'I think I just saw that, George. I really don't know why I was worried.'

* * *

The road to Dennis Coleman's house was well worn and, like everything else, it was cut out of a steep hill. The left bank dropped away at an alarming angle and George could almost touch the bank on the right. The car pitched and bounced as the wheels found places where the tarmac was subsiding. He swore as a high-sided box van appeared at the other end. It looked like a delivery van from a local supermarket. George needed to back up. He couldn't expect the van to do so. He reversed almost all the way back to the adjoining road before there was space enough for the van to ease past. George wound down his window and the van driver did likewise.

'Did you just deliver to number four, mate?' George asked. 'He's my brother, see. I've been trying to call him but he never answers. I was just starting to get worried!'

'Number four, yeah.' The van driver was cheery. 'He's up there alright.'

'Ah! Great! I hope you dropped some teabags. The last time I was up here he didn't even offer!'

The delivery driver leant out further and lowered his voice. 'I dunno about tea, mate, but you'll be alright for something a bit stronger!'

'Oh right. Well, at least I know why he wasn't answering his phone then!'

The driver waved cheerily as he continued past.

George looked over at Emma. 'At least we know he's in.'

'I could have told you he would be in. Him being in isn't the problem. Him answering the door is the problem, George, and I can promise you he won't.'

George edged back up the hill. 'He'll talk to me. He did last time.'

Dennis's bungalow was just as George remembered it. No car on the drive, no signs of life at all from the outside. Every window covered with closed curtains or blinds. He knocked the door first. Emma stayed back leaning on the car's open passenger door. George knocked hard and long, and then stepped back. Nothing moved. To one side was a gate in a six-foot tall slatted wood fence. He gave it a rattle but it was locked.

'Dennis!' George shouted. 'Dennis! It's George Elms. We spoke a few days ago. I need your help, Dennis!' George pushed himself up against the gate. There were gaps in the wood. He could just see through. A small window on the side of the house was open slightly. He lifted his foot and was able to get his toe in enough to get some grip. He pushed up and grabbed hold of the top of the gate with both hands.

'What are you doing, George?' Emma was walking over to him.

'We need to speak to him. I don't think we're knocking on the right door.' He lifted his other foot higher still. George scaled the gate and dropped down the other side. It was bolted on the inside. He slid back the bolt and the gate swung open.

Emma stood in the gateway with her arms folded. 'Maybe he just doesn't want to talk to us, George.'

'Then he needs to tell me. I'm no mind reader, Emma.'

George walked along the side. The small window was frosted and an extractor fan turned slowly beside it. He guessed it was a downstairs toilet. He walked around to the back. It was similarly all shut up, blinds and curtains all drawn. He knocked on a patio door. Nothing. He knocked again, harder this time and with the bottom of his fist. He called Dennis's name again. Nothing.

'Come on, George,' Emma said. 'We're wasting our time.'

He walked back down the side of the house to the open window. 'Dennis! DENNIS!' He turned away to cuss. There was a big plant pot in an overgrown flowerbed, almost hidden by weeds. He had to tug it hard from nature's fingers. He turned it upside down and stood on it. His mouth was now level with the window and he tugged it further open.

'Dennis! It's George Elms! I wasn't honest with you when I came to see you a few days ago. I didn't tell you the real reason I was asking about Roberts. Now I need your help.' George paused for a reaction. He could see through to an internal door just a couple of metres away that was a few inches ajar. He reckoned his voice would be carrying right through the house. 'He has two more girls, Dennis! He's out! He escaped and he has two more! I know you can help us find him, Dennis! This is a chance to make things right! No one knows more about him than you! We need your help! Those girls, they need your help!'

The pot made a cracking noise under his weight and he dropped slightly. He stepped off and met eyes with Emma.

'We've got a lot to do, George. This is a waste of time.'

He nodded. They walked along the side of the house and back to the car. After he slid into the driver's seat he glanced back to the house. Dennis Coleman was framed in the front door. 'Emma!'

'I see him.'

'Let's go and say hello.'

Dennis Coleman was barefooted. He wore loose-fitting tracksuit bottoms that hung low under his midriff and a grey hooded top.

'Dennis! Thanks for talking to us,' George said.

'You're lying to me again!' Dennis said. 'Henry Roberts can't be out. Category A prisoners don't get out. Not these days. Not people like that.'

'I know. Listen, you can't repeat that, it's still sensitive. And I would be dubious too but it's a long story, Dennis, and one I'd rather not tell on your doorstep. We need your help.'

'You let him out! You let him out and you come up here to tell me you need my help! Why aren't you chasing him? Why are you here?' Dennis's eyes were watery and a little glazed. George caught the whiff of alcohol and Dennis leant on the doorframe as if he needed the support.

'We *are* chasing him, Dennis. Of course we are. We don't know where to start. I thought the best place to start was with the person who knows him better than anybody.'

Dennis stepped back and the door slammed shut. George hadn't seen it coming and didn't have time to wedge in a foot. He hammered on the door again.

The first response was a rhythmic thumping on the other side of the door, as if Dennis was beating a tattoo with his fist. Then he started shouting. 'You don't know! You don't know anything about him! You won't find him and you won't stop him! You don't know what he is!'

George stepped up to the door and poked open the letterbox. 'I know he kills for fun, for the feeling of power! I know he has a type — attractive blonde teenagers! I know he gets off on the fear he brings — and not just to his victims! And I know that he has two girls for a reason, Dennis! I think you know that, too! We found the missing girls, Dennis! They were both in the belly of the same bull! He made the one who went second watch the whole thing! Can you imagine how scared she was? That's what he craves — that fear, that terror! It's why he's taken another two! He was starving himself, Dennis! He managed to convince people that he was ill so they took their eye off the ball — me included! I'm part of letting this animal back out there, Dennis! I know you were a big part of putting him away. I just need a few minutes! I just need to know a bit of what you know!'

'It's all in the file! It's all in the file! It's all in the file! It's all in the file!' The shouts were hysterical — and then the rhythmic thumping started up again followed by sobbing.

'Jesus, George! We need to go. We need to leave him alone.'

George pushed his mouth back to the letterbox. 'I have your statements, your official paperwork. But I saw your notebook, too! I saw all the references to the vicar. You don't like him. You got that feeling in your gut, right? Something doesn't add up. I got it too, Dennis! I'm going to see him. Right now. I wanted to talk to you before I went!'

George stepped back. Emma was at his shoulder. Then there was the clack of a bolt. The handle dipped, the door moved in. George took a step forward. Dennis

Coleman was in his dimly lit hallway. Blood trickled from a wound just above his right eye. A lump was already forming. His eyes looked red and heavy. George waited for him to speak.

'He's something,' Dennis croaked. 'I don't know what . . .' He was out of breath and took a moment to recover himself '. . . but he's certainly something.'

'I agree, Dennis. Can we come in and talk? Five minutes. If nothing else I want to make sure you're okay before I leave. I know this is hard on you. Emma here, she told me not to come. She's worried about you, Dennis. We all are.'

'I'm so sorry, ma'am. I'm so sorry!' Dennis gasped out a sob. His head dipped, his face screwed up and he moved quickly away. George took the opportunity to follow him through into the kitchen. Dennis was tearing off a square of kitchen paper from a roll on top of the fridge and using it as a tissue.

'Let me make you a cup of tea, Dennis.'

'Fuck!' Dennis slumped onto a stool by the kitchen bench and pushed his head into his hands. The bench held a couple of supermarket bags, presumably from the van they had passed on the way up. One of them was filled with bottles — all hard liquor. George filled the kettle then opened the blinds at the kitchen window just as Emma entered. Dennis looked up and blinked in the sunlight but didn't complain. Emma rinsed a mug and filled it with cold water from the tap. As George put the kettle back on the base and flicked the ON switch, Emma took the mug, tore off more kitchen paper and sat on the stool next to Dennis. She dipped a wad of kitchen paper in the water and dabbed at Dennis's forehead. He winced a little but did nothing to stop her.

'Tea, coffee? Or something a little stronger, Dennis?' said George.

Dennis's eyes fell to the bags on the table top and he smiled faintly. 'I've been having a lot of parties, you see.'

George returned the smile. 'Yeah, this strikes me as a real party house!'

'I saw a lot of drunks. When I was in the job. We all do, don't we? I used to think that they had such sad little lives. I would screw my face up and judge them. Especially the ones that turned to it because they couldn't cope with something in their lives. And here I am, eh?'

'I did the same thing,' George said. 'I remember anyone who was anyone coming round and telling me that it didn't help. That it was the last thing I needed. You've probably had the same thing. They were wrong. I think I needed to abuse this stuff for a time to be able to move on. While reality was too painful, I needed an escape. It can be good for that. But then I got to the point where I could make a difference again. Where I was needed. I stopped there and then. I think that's when it becomes a real problem, Dennis. When you're needed and you can't switch it off. We need you now, mate. So . . . tea or coffee?'

'Coffee. Strong.'

'Same,' Emma said.

George prepared the coffees and made himself a cup of tea. 'Let me tell you what I know,' he said. 'Some of this might be news to you, most of it probably won't. John Lawrence . . . the vicar down the road from here. I spoke to him. He's upset with the police attention. He told me it was because he was concerned about the reputation of the village, about the reputation of the people in it. He didn't want us thinking his church was a breeding ground for serial killers — I think that's what he said. He wasn't telling me everything. I could understand him being upset. I could see why he might have started taking it personally.'

'He certainly did that,' Emma said.

'Okay. That on its own wasn't enough for me to get the hump with him. Yes, he was guarded. But if the police turn up to question you enough times, I can see why anyone would be guarded. I went through to the little office in his vestry. He had some CCTV rigged up to cover the nearby car park and the main entrance to the church. The car park was empty. Yet I passed his car parked back up the road a little. The vestry has its own door that leads directly outside. He can enter and leave the church any time he wants without being caught on camera. If he's done that on purpose, why?'

'CCTV? There were no cameras the last time I was there,' Dennis said.

'They were installed after you arrested Roberts. At least that's my understanding. I think the building was targeted when his name came out. I guess the link to the church was also made in the press. The local press at least.'

'So why put it up at all if it's going to cause him problems?'

'I got the impression he didn't want to. He said it was put up by the ladies who ran the church clubs. I guess he couldn't object too much. He would have been asked why.'

'Okay?' Dennis sounded like he was waiting for more.

'Okay. So, not much on its own. But the church has a charitable fund attached to it. It's received considerable sums of money. At least two hundred thousand, but almost certainly more. I could only go back a month. I will be going back further.'

'Roberts was obsessed with that place for a long time. I wouldn't be surprised if he was putting money into it.'

'I agree. But when I went to see him — John Lawrence, I mean — he gave me some sob story about raising money for river defences. They needed twenty thousand. I even gave the bloke a tenner. This was after those payments were made.'

'Maybe he didn't want to go public with the money. Maybe he was waiting for a reasonable amount of time to pass before he did. He wouldn't want it to be known that the money was from Roberts,' Emma said.

'I agree. He definitely wouldn't. But why didn't he tell *me*? I was up there snooping around, asking questions. Why even mention the river defence thing? He must have considered that I might have access to information about the church finances.'

'Maybe he didn't think it would ever be looked at,' Dennis said.

'Roberts's escape was expensive. It was only possible because he has enough money to pay off the right people.'

'You think he paid off the church? For what?' Emma said.

'No.' Dennis became suddenly animated. 'You think the church was helping him? Directing the money to where it needed to go? You think the church was involved? John Lawrence specifically?'

'And so did you. Not in the escape. That wasn't a problem then. But you thought he was involved in those girls disappearing. Didn't you? I've seen your notes. You never made anything official but you kept going back to him with questions. You're the reason John Lawrence got upset with the police attention. Either you were wrong and he was unduly harassed or you were right and you touched a nerve.'

Dennis sighed and then sipped at his coffee. 'I was never happy with him. Right from the start. And when we got Roberts I wasn't happy with the relationship between the two of them either. I considered that St Dubricius's had some strange financial dealings. But then I saw that it was a restoration project for the church they're twinned with.'

'Twinned with?'

'St Dubricius's Church is one of two on that riverbank. There's another further along called St Leonard's. It was never as well protected from the river, though. All that's left is a ruin. It's been that way for as long as anyone can remember. St Dubricius's was built a fair bit later. Maybe they knew even back then that St

Leonard's wasn't going to last. It's been abandoned for a long time. Lawrence got a bee in his bonnet about restoring it.'

'And he set up a fund?'

'He did. I don't think anyone was keen. I mean, why would you help with restoring a church that's been ruined by the river more times than enough. It's sure to happen again. That's the whole reason it was abandoned.'

'So people didn't invest?'

'Someone did. I got some information from someone working the accounts at the church that it was getting some sizeable donations. They didn't know where from. I asked Lawrence about them and he wouldn't discuss it. He just said he had to respect his donor's wish for anonymity, as he would with any donor. The accountant was sacked shortly after and I never learned any more. I put in for permission to investigate the church accounts but it was never granted. I don't blame the superintendent. On the surface it was a murder investigation and we had someone through the door who had committed the offences. So when I asked for an audit on the accounts of the church the offender had attended and I couldn't really articulate why I wanted it, I was told where to go. Fair dos.'

'But you felt there was something there, didn't you?' George said.

'Yeah. Yes, I did. But by now I was being accused of having it in for Lawrence. They thought it was personal. Sorry, Emma, but even you put a leash on me. I understand. I certainly don't blame you.'

'He was becoming a pain in the arse, Dennis. It wasn't that I didn't trust your instincts. We just needed something more concrete as a reason to be speaking to him.'

'I had the assault allegation. I wasn't allowed to talk to him about that either.'

'The what?' George leaned forward and almost spilled his tea. 'Assault?'

'Sexual assault.'

'He was spoken to about that,' Emma said. 'Our colleagues in CID took it on. The allegation was put to him and he gave a plausible denial. The victim didn't pursue her allegation and it was filed.'

'What were the circs?'

'Chloe Pope,' Dennis said, 'Roberts's first vict—'

'Chloe Pope made an allegation?' George exclaimed.

'No!' Emma cut in, clearly irritated. 'Chloe Pope did not.'

'Chloe didn't,' Dennis explained. 'But her friend in the choir did. She said that John Lawrence got her on her own and touched her inappropriately. Just on the thigh. He made some suggestive comments with it. She hinted that she wasn't the first. She dropped it all, though. Her mum was a regular at the church. Really proud of her daughter for being in the choir. I think she was pressured into not speaking to the police. We've all seen it happen, right?'

'There was no evidence. That was the issue with it,' Emma said, quickly.

'Lawrence used it. When the investigation got anywhere near his church, he brought it up every time — how he'd been "exonerated," how he'd made the police back off. I was desperate to tell him that it didn't mean he was innocent, just because we couldn't prove it.'

'You think it happened?' George said.

'I think more than that. According to Mary Pope, her daughter had become withdrawn over the few months leading up to her going missing. She refused to go to church. She had been in the choir most of her life and suddenly she wouldn't set foot in the building. It didn't take much to put two and two together for me.'

'Theories. Theories we could never prove, Dennis.' Emma was still irritated. George got the impression that Emma and Dennis had had this very same conversation before. He could see why this was such a sensitive issue for Emma.

'There's a link. Between Roberts, Chloe and Lawrence. I was certain of it — still am. I just never found what it was exactly.'

George stood up and walked to the window. When he pushed it open birdsong drifted in on a pleasant spring breeze and the kitchen seemed a little less musty. It was remarkable how much difference a bit of sunlight made.

'What are you thinking, George?' Dennis said. 'Are you going to tell me I'm a crazy old sweat too? Crazy theories?'

'Well I'm a big fan of crazy theories. Especially when they have substance to them. I have one of my own. Roberts has been planning his escape since before he even went to prison, stashing money away in a place where the Reverend John Lawrence could get access to it. Being a wealthy prisoner is one thing, but you need someone with access to the money to make sure the right people get paid. And, in this case, the right building gets built.'

'How could he trust Lawrence, though?' Emma said. 'I mean, he's a Category A prisoner and it's a hell of a lot of money. What's stopping John Lawrence just keeping the lot and living happily ever after?'

'Not trust, that's for sure. You're right, you'd never be able to trust someone that much.'

'What then?'

'Knowledge. Roberts has something on Lawrence. He knows something that's worth a lot of effort on Lawrence's part to keep it from coming out.'

'Like what?'

'I don't know. But he's just a few minutes down the road, right? Maybe we should go and see him and pretend that we do.'

Chapter 32

When George left Dennis's house this time, the door closing from behind was a lot less hurried. Dennis watched George and Emma go to their car.

'You want to head straight to St Dubricius's?' Emma said, as they drove back down the narrow and bumpy drive.

'Somewhere you'd rather go?'

'My team, George. Now Dennis is aware, I don't want any of them finding out secondhand. And we've got some leads — some work to do. We'll get a lot more done with a whole team on it.'

'I can't argue with that. I was considering turning up to see Lawrence with a search warrant anyway. We could task that out. What are the magistrates like up here? Are they pretty quick at turning them round?'

'Not as quick as a Section 18.'

'You want to arrest him!' A Section 18 search was conducted immediately after an arrest. It didn't need nearly as much red tape to obtain as a warrant.

'You sound surprised?'

'Delighted more like. If this was down in Langthorne I would be doing just that. I'm well beyond reasonable suspicion.'

'So what's different? Just because you're out of your county, the law's still the same, right?'

'It is. I'm just aware that I can be a little . . . forward, is all. I police with my size tens. I've been reminded of that recently. I can kinda get away with it in my own force. Up here I'm trying to be a little more diplomatic so I don't get told to go back to where I came from.'

'I'm pretty sure I already told you to do that once. Fat lot of good it did.'

'True. And yet here we are. I had no intention of coming back up here if that helps?'

'Of course you didn't!'

'So we go back. We speak to your team. We go and see the vicar and pull him in for assisting an offender. We're going to need more people to do a proper search of the church and his place anyway. Assisting an offender is one thing but I think there's a much bigger offence there somewhere.'

'Sounds like a plan.'

Emma seemed brighter. George felt that way, too. He felt as if they were getting somewhere. Emma's brightness dissipated the closer they got back to Hereford Police Station. She called ahead to tell one of her team that they were ten minutes away and she wanted to meet as soon as she got back. He didn't envy her having to break the news.

'You want me in there? When you tell them?'

'No. I think it's better I tell them and let them have their reaction. No offence, George, but it might be best if you aren't in front of them for that. I know this isn't your fault—'

'I understand. I don't mind being the scapegoat for now if it means they'll work for you. I'm the incompetent outsider and you can be the one who's going to fix all this. They might respond to that.'

'They'll respond anyway, George. These are good people. They care. They certainly cared about this job. We've got enough going on to keep them busy. If it's like last time, the problem comes when the activity ends. When we all have to sit down and think again about what we did. Or what Roberts did.'

'They get to make sure he doesn't do anything else.'

'Unless we're already too late.'

George didn't have a reply to that. The red brick of Hereford Police Station came up on his nearside window. He turned into the visitors' car park again. Emma was out of the car promptly. George took a deep breath to compose himself.

* * *

When Annie Cox came to, she was facing the exposed white metal on the side of the van. Her eyes were still a little blurry. The white panels all blurred into one until she was able to focus on the rivet that was holding them together. She tried to move but couldn't. Her hands were tied at her waist. She looked down to see that the rope extended around her waist too. Her wrists were painful; the rope was coarse and had severely chafed her skin. She could do nothing about it. Her movement was so restricted that she couldn't change her position at all.

She tried to think back. She tried to piece her fragmented memories together but her mind was still muzzy. She remembered being in the van with something. A solid shape that had rolled against her. The van had stopped and the boy had spoken to her. He looked young. He had come right into the back to tell her something. It was something about how she was going to be set free. She remembered how she didn't believe him. His face, the look in his eyes — it made her more terrified than ever. She knew there was something else. Something else had happened too. She was so confused, she couldn't remember. Then it came back to her: *someone* else!

Someone else had been pushed into the back of the van. She remembered now: a fleeting memory of a small girl with long blonde hair. There was another man too — older and much bigger than the first, with hair covering most of his face and terrifying eyes, dark and intense.

She jerked her body, trying to twist to see behind her, to see if the other girl was still here. She tried to speak but it came out as '*nnnng.*' She concentrated. Her mouth had a metallic taste. She smacked her lips — they were so dry. 'Can you hear?' she managed. Every word was a strain. She knew she wasn't making much sense. She heard a scuffle, it sounded like movement. She thought it was someone else. It came from behind her. She couldn't be sure. For all she knew it was her own body scuffing against the smooth, wooden floor. Her legs were numb. Her back was numb. Her eyes were heavy. She could feel sleep coming back. It came on strong. She tried to fight it; she wanted to see if anyone would answer her. She couldn't fight it any longer. Her eyes closed. Her last thought was that she could no longer hear an engine before she surrendered to the darkness.

* * *

George nursed a coffee outside the meeting room where Emma Rowe was speaking to her staff, the same meeting room he had walked into just a few days before with a cock and bull story about Henry Roberts. The truth was about to come out and he was not going to be popular when it did. George didn't care. He was used to being unpopular in his own force and it sure as hell wasn't going to bother him in someone else's. All that mattered was that the team pulled together and worked to bring Roberts back into custody.

Through the long partition windows, he watched the faces of those he could see. He reckoned he would be able to tell the exact moment when Emma dropped the news.

He turned his attention away when the phone vibrated in his pocket. It was his wife.

'Sarah?'

'You broke three of his fingers and the main bone in the back of his hand. It's so badly broken that he might have to have surgery to correct it when the swelling has gone down.'

George had almost forgotten about Ronnie's crushed hand. Had he told Sarah what had happened? He'd guessed he might. What did he care?

'Good,' he said, as his anger from that night flashed back all at once.

'No denial then.'

'Denial? No. Ronnie didn't deny it either, Sarah. And if he ever touches you again or upsets my daughter in any way I'll start breaking things right off. Things that surgery can't help. So if you just called to have a go then you should know that I don't care, that I'd do the very same—'

'I didn't.'

George was stopped in his tracks. The call wasn't unexpected. But he had fully expected her to have had a go at him. Sarah didn't approve of violence. She never had. George had always needed to be careful of what he told her about his work when they were together. And he'd always loved her principles.

'Why did you call then?' He felt calmer.

'I need somewhere to stay. *We* need somewhere to stay. I can't stay here. My mum's being . . . difficult.'

'Somewhere to stay? You're moving out? What about Ronnie?'

'I've kicked him out. That was the last straw. It's not the first time. He was always so sorry. I thought he would change. Blah, blah, blah, right? You've heard it all before I bet. I've become a cliché — battered wife!'

'Not a battered *wife*.'

'No. You would never treat me like that. I was treated like a princess compared to that. I guess . . . I guess I miss that. Any chance then? We wouldn't get in the way and it would just be until I can get somewhere sorted—'

'Yes! Fuck, yes! Of course. I'm away — I mean, I'll be back in a day or two. You can go there right now, though. There's an old lady — flat two. She makes me terrible dinners. A lot. I haven't got the heart to tell her I ditch them. She's got a key.'

'You're rambling, George.'

'I am. I don't know what to say. I mean . . . don't accept a dinner . . . This is so unexpected. Good unexpected, obviously.'

'Really? You're okay with this?'

'Yeah, I am. But what about Charley? Moving back in with me just until you get somewhere sorted, I don't want to play with her emotions. Is that not going to confuse her?'

'Well, yes. If I really *was* looking for somewhere else and if we really can't make it work then it will. But I'm always the optimist, George. I've been considering it for a while. I don't think I've had a single happy day since . . . well, since we stopped being a family. I know about your job, I know what it means to you — for us. And I still want it back. I want it all back. We can try at least.'

'I'll chuck it in. I said I would. I told you this job is nothing to me if it means I get my family back.'

'You don't need to do that. I know how important it is. It's me. I need to change my attitude towards it. I know that now.'

'I'll walk. It's been getting on top of me anyway. I said I would. This job that I'm on now is the perfect reminder — it's horrible, Sarah — what people will do to one another. I don't want to be a part of it anymore. I want to go back to being a family man and pretending that this sort of shit doesn't go on.'

Sarah actually chuckled. 'Well, don't do anything stupid. Or rash. Or rash and stupid. So when will you be home?'

George was still reeling. He couldn't think straight. 'I don't know. A couple of days, tops. There's a lot to do up here. As soon as I can.'

'I thought the job was nothing to you!' Sarah's laughter continued. George giggled too.

'This one is a little different.'

'They're all different, George. I'm not having a go. You do important work — I know that. Just like I know you can't walk away from it.'

'Not now. Not today. But tomorrow, maybe. We should make progress over the next twenty-four hours.'

'Tomorrow!' Sarah still sounded amused. 'You know what they say about tomorrow, right?'

'I do. It's the very next day!' George could see that the meeting room was emptying. The detectives were filing out. Some glanced over. Most didn't.

'Keep me informed,' Sarah said.

'I will, yeah. Go see my neighbour at number two for the key. I'll call her to let her know. Oh and there's not much food in and the bathroom's a bit rank.'

'I can hardly complain.'

'No, I just mean can you get a shop in? And you might wanna get on your hands and knees and give the floor a scrub in there! If that's not too much trouble, *princess*.'

'Cheeky shit!'

'So you're really going there now? You'll be there when I come home?'

'We will, George. It's been a while.'

George felt euphoria sweep through him. He took a rushed breath. 'Too long, Sarah. I'll be home. Soon.'

Emma got to him just as he ended the call. 'You okay, George?'

'Perfect. Everything's perfect.' He knew he was smiling broadly. He couldn't help it.

'Good to hear.'

'How did it go with the team?'

'As expected. A lot of shock and then a lot of determination. They'll do what's needed. I've already got a lot of them tasked. I see some improved CCTV has come through from a petrol station down your way. It gives a much better image.'

'Did it? When?'

'A few minutes ago. From Emily Ryker.'

'Ah. I was on the phone. I'll have a look.'

'Well I wouldn't expect you to be able to identify anyone from it. I've already forwarded it on to be put on the briefing up here for all the local officers. You never know your luck.'

'Okay. Good. Are we ready to go see our vicar then?'

'I think we are. You remember what I said about how we need to be gentle with him? Because he doesn't like our police force very much.'

'I do.'

'You can forget that, George. Let's go and piss him off.'

George laughed loudly, his spirits soaring. 'Well, if there's one thing I'm good at . . .'

Chapter 33

'Do you people not pay your road tax around here or something?' George moaned. His family hatchback was struggling over yet more ruts and bumps as he drove the last mile to St Dubricius's Church. It was just after 10 a.m. They had been reliably informed that the vicar was there from ten o'clock most days. Sure enough, his car was parked in the same passing place as last time. The road was narrow, and George needed to slow down to pass it. He noticed the bank was well worn, suggesting that Lawrence's car was always left there. George pulled up in the gravel car park. This time there was another car there, too: a small, silver Toyota. George pushed open the door to the church.

'John? John are you here?'

'Hold on, please!' It was a woman's voice, coming from the back of the church — elderly, George guessed. He walked towards it. Someone stepped out of the vestry. He had been right about her age.

'Sorry to bother you. I was hoping to speak to the vicar.'

'I see. Well I'm sorry but he isn't here. I haven't seen him today. He was here yesterday morning.'

'I see. Is that his car outside?'

'It is. I saw it this morning. He does leave it sometimes if he's going to the pub on his way home.'

George turned to Emma. 'And we know where home is, do we?' She nodded confirmation.

'Perfect. Well, thank you for your help. Once again, sorry to bother you.'

'It's no bother. I just do a bit of cleaning. Maybe some paperwork. If he comes in, who should I say was here asking after him?'

'Ah, yes. I'm Inspector George Elms. We have met before, John and I, very briefly. I said to him that if I was ever back in the area I would pop in is all. Nothing to worry about.'

'Nothing to worry about, but you're still going up to his house from here?' Her head turned sideways a little. Her lips curled. She looked like a woman who could smell a rat.

'I'm a three-hour drive away. No guarantee I'll be back up this way anytime soon. I might just bid my goodbyes is all.'

'No point going up to the house, then. He's not been there in a while. Between you and me I don't think it's very good at home.'

George was suddenly interested. 'Is that right? I'm sorry to hear that. Is it the pressure of running this place?' George gestured towards the stained window that was bleeding its colour where the sunlight was pouring through it.

'Maybe. I did wonder if it was all getting too much for him. But I don't like to pry.'

George didn't believe that for a second. 'So where would I find him? If I wanted to catch him before I left?'

The woman shrugged. 'I really don't know. I didn't think he had anywhere else to go. Maybe she's let him back in up there, but I doubt it. I thought I hadn't seen her for a while and she always used to come down, at least on a Sunday. Then she brought some of his stuff down in suitcases. He wasn't here, it was just me. She left the cases, said I should tell him not to go back. She looked furious. He must have found somewhere to be but I wouldn't fancy it was back there. Not yet.'

'Are you expecting him here today?'

'He's here every day at some point. There's an evening sermon and choir practice today too. They're both much later though.'

'Great. Thanks again for your help.'

'No problem.'

George and Emma waited until they were back in the car before they spoke.

Emma went first. 'She doesn't like him, does she?'

'No. She would appear to take a very dim view. Seems to be a running theme with our friend Lawrence.'

'So, do you think he's been messing about with another woman? That might give us a problem if no one knows who she is. We need to know where he's staying.'

'And we need to find him first. I'd rather not ask around too much either. We don't want him getting wind that we're looking for him. He can't be allowed time to ditch anything.'

'Well we're not going to find him at home and I'm not very good at waiting. I get the feeling you're not either.'

'It's not my favourite part of policing. We could still try his home address? Maybe his wife will talk to us. Tell us what we don't know already.'

'We could do that. What do you think about going to visit this other church?' Emma said.

'The ruins?' George was doubtful.

'I've not been there. I don't think anyone did as part of the initial investigation either. Why would we have done, I suppose? I don't know if it's viable as a place to hide out.'

'You think Lawrence is *hiding out*?'

'Who knows? Maybe that's where all this money has been going all along.'

'That is a fair point. And you know where it is?'

Emma was fiddling with her phone. George could see a mapping application. 'We must have passed the turning for it on the way here. There's a curve in the road, a gentle curve. It looks like if we had gone straight on there . . .'

'I don't remember seeing a road coming off it?'

'Me neither. I wasn't looking for it though.'

George turned round in the car park. As the car moved away he saw the old lady at the main entrance to the church with a broom. She was making token efforts to brush the steps as they drove past. He waved. She didn't wave back.

George was right about the road. There wasn't one. There was a track, thick with ferns. It wasn't a track that would be found if you didn't know it was there somewhere. George parked the car to get a closer look.

'Well something's been along it,' he said. 'And recently.'

Emma nodded. 'It has.'

'And they've tried to hide that fact too.' George stepped past the first layer of ferns. There were two flattened tracks leading away from the road. The ferns were tall, between four and six feet high and they had been flattened rather than broken at the stem. The layer closest to the road looked to have been stood awkwardly back up while further in they were crushed and lying down. As if someone had used the track and then made a good effort to conceal it. George held up one of the taller ferns closest to the road. He let it fall back to where it had been lying. He locked eyes with Emma.

'You don't think . . .?'

'Roberts?' George turned to peer down the track. The crushed ferns gave a clear trail to follow.

'We should call it in,' Emma said. 'Get some more patrols here before we take a look.'

'We should definitely call it in,' George said. He walked quickly to the boot of his car where he and Emma both had their grab bags. He pulled his stab vest over his head. His pepper spray, baton and handcuffs he slung over his shoulder in a covert holder. Emma did the same.

'We're not waiting, then.' Emma picked up her radio. She turned it on and waited for the beep to confirm it was joined to the network. 'I was hoping we wouldn't.'

George walked ahead. He could hear Emma on the radio. She gave their location as best she could. She requested immediate backup. She said that a 4x4 vehicle would probably manage the track. George thought his family hatchback might stand a chance, but he preferred an approach on foot. He didn't want to make a sound.

Emma caught him up. The path curved to the right, towards the river. It was close enough for George to hear it but not see it; the foliage was too thick. It sounded like they were passing a shallow section. The water hissed and gurgled as if over rocks and pebbles. They kept moving. The track now curved gently to the left, enough to limit visibility to around ten metres in front. Suddenly the terrain changed: the ferns were replaced by a wild grass underfoot. The two flattened lines were now more obvious as the exposed mud showed them to be tyre tracks with a distinctive pattern.

'There!' Emma pointed off to the right, towards the sound of the river. George now saw it too: a flint wall, old and decrepit, with no roof.

'We're here,' he whispered. He moved to the left of the ruins, staying on the track. Suddenly it opened up into a wild grass clearing with some tombstones scattered among the greenery. The ruins were scattered too, and incomplete. It wasn't clear what part of the church they were looking at. George moved into the clearing. The high flint wall they had seen to the right was long and flat with a big, rough-looking doorway cut out of the middle and tall, empty windows to both sides.

'George!' Emma was a little further forward and was staring around the end of the wall. George closed the distance between them quickly to see what she was looking at. It was a white van, side on, with its rear doors hanging open. George remained still. There was neither movement nor sound from anywhere other the chattering of the river. He moved towards the van.

'George!' Emma whispered. 'We should wait.'

'We might be too late already,' he whispered back. He ran silently over to the driver's door and peered in. The cab was empty. There were two bottles of water in the centre console and a pizza box in the passenger foot well. It looked the same as the pizza box left back in Capel and the phone number on it had Langthorne's area code.

George felt like he might burst. He moved slowly towards the back of the van. He pulled his baton and racked it. It sprung to its full length with a *thwack*. He rested the hitting end on his shoulder and gripped the handle tightly. He reached the end of the van and squatted to see under the open rear door. There was nothing on the ground — certainly no giant feet that might be holding up Henry Roberts. George didn't know what to expect. He thought he could feel the hairs rise on the back of his neck. As Emma drew up at his right shoulder, he sucked in his breath and moved swiftly round the door.

'Empty,' he said. 'But come and look at this.' George pushed his baton shut on the floor and put it back in its holder while Emma joined him at the back of the van. There were deep, fresh gouges down the middle of the van's plywood floor. Something heavy had been dragged out. Drag marks continued on the ground, too. Whatever it was had been heavy enough to churn up the turf and leave a trail that led from the ruins into dense woodland. George motioned at the radio Emma still clutched in her hand.

'How far away are they?'

'Five minutes out, I reckon.'

'Ideal.' George started walking. The drag marks were easy to follow.

'I thought that meant you were going to wait?'

'No need. They're only five minutes behind.'

Emma swore, but she fell in behind George. She spoke quietly into her radio. The path closed in almost immediately. To the right, the foliage was thicker: bushes, ferns and leafy trees. To the left was a bank made up of large rocks and mud. The going became more difficult at a couple of points, where rocks from the bank had slipped across the path. George could still hear the river to their right but it was quieter. It burbled and gurgled, but he still couldn't see it. He was certain that he wouldn't be seen from the river either.

George and Emma froze at almost the same time. There was a small clearing ahead shrouded in trees; they could only see the entrance to it. Across the entrance a rope was pulled taught at an oblique angle. George racked his baton again and edged forward.

The rope was hooked over a stout branch that, despite its thickness was bowing under the strain. One end was anchored, passing through a grey, metal hoop and then into a solid-looking ratchet device. The other end of the rope was still out of sight. George needed to move further out of the safety of the tree-lined path to see where it went. George lifted the baton so he was ready to strike. He could feel the steel resting on his shoulder. He glanced back to Emma. She was moving closely behind him. He stepped quickly into the clearing and then stopped dead.

The rope groaned and strained as it flexed. George was so tense the noise made him jump. It ran high above him and wrapped around a thick plank of wood that formed the upright of a cross that rose some fifteen feet. Its base looked to be sunk into the ground. Attached to it and facing away he could see the back of a figure in dark clothing, clinging to the wood. He couldn't see how; the legs were at an odd angle. The arms were stretched out, along the plank. George wasn't sure if it was someone or some*thing*. It looked to him like an effigy. George lowered his baton. A crucifix. Someone was playing games.

George surveyed the rest of the clearing. There was nothing else that stood out. No people. No threats. And no smoking stack of wood under an ancient torture device.

'What the hell?' Emma pushed past. She walked towards the crucifix. She had her own baton in her hand. George moved to the ground pin that was holding the other end of the rope. It had been dug out and cemented in. the concrete was still a fresh-looking grey.

'George! He's alive!' George's head snapped up. Emma was standing under the crucifix and looking up. George ran to her and saw that the figure was no effigy. John Lawrence's torso shivered from the abdomen and his breath rasped loudly at the same time. It looked to George like agonal breathing after the diaphragm and the lungs had given up. The last movements of an already dead man. Lawrence's legs hung useless and clearly deformed. His arms were smeared with a dark red. The nails that had been pushed through the centre of his wrists were wide and crude. His arms were bound tightly to the wood of the cross round his elbows, too, probably to prevent his own weight from pulling his flesh from the nail.

George searched around for something — anything — to help him reach Lawrence's legs. If he could reach, he might be able to take some of the pressure off the lungs. Lawrence was being crushed by his own weight. George readied his shoulder. He bounced off the wooden upright. It did nothing more than vibrate enough for John's shoes to shuffle against the wood above George's head. George looked down. He could see what he was up against. The bottom of the wood was dug down into another cement-filled hole. There was a small gap at the front and a steel pin at the back, the cement must have been set first. The cross rose up out of it. He could picture the cross being ratcheted against the steel pin until it was upright enough to drop into the hole. It was a clever way of getting John up there. There wasn't an obvious way to get him back down. George ran back to the ground pin. The rope was thick and strong. He had nothing that could cut it. Even if he had, he didn't think the cutting of the rope would be enough to bring the structure down.

'I can't get him down!' he shouted. Emma didn't say anything. She simply stared back and forth between George and Lawrence. George ran back to the structure. 'John! John, can you hear me?' There was no more sound or movement. Lawrence's mouth hung open. His eyes were open too. 'John! Who did this? Where's Roberts? JOHN!' There was movement at the edge of George's vision and then four uniform police officers burst into the clearing, one with a taser drawn. They were wide-eyed and breathing heavily as they took in the scene.

'We need a ladder or something!' George barked. 'We need to get him down!' The officers took a few seconds to react. Two ran back the way they had come. The other two went through the same checks as George. George let them continue, despite realising that it was hopeless. They pushed the wood base. They tried to reach up, then one linked his hands together and knelt down to give the other a boost. They made it to Lawrence's waist. The officer tried to lift him, to relieve some of the pressure on his lungs. He couldn't manage it. He couldn't reach any higher. Lawrence's shoes scuffed back against the wood. It was useless.

The ladder took another minute. It got them higher. George stepped back to watch. He knew they were wasting their time. It didn't take long for all the officers to realise the same thing. This wasn't an urgent rescue. John Lawrence was dead.

It took twenty minutes to get him down, and lay him out on the wild grass. The nails had been pushed so far in they had to be hammered out from the other side. Despite the obvious, the officers still cut off his jumper and the dog collar from around his neck and started CPR. George could see his arms. The wounds weren't bleeding. His chest was still, his skin washed out. He was gone. As was any chance of finding out what he might know about Henry Roberts.

Paramedics arrived shortly after. They were out of breath. They got to work immediately. They strapped machines to him while the CPR continued. They spent another twenty minutes doing what they could then stood up and stepped away. The uniform officers all looked at Emma, their senior officer. The paramedic must have picked up on it. They spoke directly to her.

'I'm sorry, he's gone. We're gonna call it. He's probably been gone a while to be honest, but we did all we could. I thought we might get a spark at least.'

'How long do you think he's been up there?' George spoke over a shocked-looking Emma. The paramedic turned to him and shrugged.

'That I can't tell you with any accuracy. A little while. The poor fella wouldn't have been able to breathe much at all. He might have supported himself for a little while but his legs look pretty bad and might not have worked at all.'

'His legs are broken,' Emma said, the shock clear in her voice.

'Yeah. I guess it was to stop him supporting his weight. He would have struggled to breathe. Not a nice way to go. There are some sick people out there.'

'We saw him move?' Emma was almost whispering.

'It might have been a spasm. With this sort of thing, a body will do that for a little while, after—'

'Thanks for your efforts.' George stepped in. He thought Emma might have had enough of an explanation. 'Did my colleagues get your details?' One of the uniform officers was close enough to hear and he took out his pocket book to complete the request. George turned to Emma. 'You okay?'

'Not really, George. You?'

'Same, I guess. We need to get you swapped out. Get the duty DS out here to run the scene. You and I need to get back and work out what we have here. And where we go next.'

'They're all on their way anyway. As soon as they get here . . .' She was still looking down at the lifeless vicar.

'There was nothing more we could have done, Emma,' George said.

'I know that. But he didn't deserve this. No one does, do they?'

'He was wrapped up in all this, Emma. Somehow. I'm worried that we won't ever find out precisely how. But, no, this isn't the sort of justice I believe in.'

Some of Emma's team arrived. He stepped back to let her bring them up to speed. She did well. She did what all good officers can do, she put aside all her own emotions long enough to get the scene managed and preserved for forensics. Her team of detectives would also need to start the work on finding out how it had become a scene in the first place. There were a few leads George could see. The wood making up the crucifix, the rope, the ratchet winch. Even the type of concrete. It would all be examined in an effort to try and find where it had come from, how long it had been there. There was a lot to piece together. Four of Emma's team were involved in the briefing. George was too far away to hear what was being said as he leant on a tree on the edge of the clearing, trying to find some space for his own thoughts. But he saw the same reactions from them that he had seen earlier that morning: shock, followed by determination. Then a couple of them looked over at him and he couldn't help but feel that he was seen as the man who had brought this nightmare back to them. Certainly it felt like his shoulders had carried the weight of something up that motorway. And he still couldn't shake it off.

Emma left her team and they walked back together. There were already officers in white suits buzzing around the transit van. George could remember the last three letters of the registration that Ryker had given him: POJ. The plate on this van was different. But it was a white Renault panel van. It had to be the same one.

They got back to the police station and sat down across from each other at Emma's round desk. Emma had her notebook open in front of her. They were both struggling with where to start. Emma's phone went off. She huffed. 'I'll just take this, George. I've a feeling we might not get anywhere now. I'm going to be in demand.'

George stood up to make a drink. Emma's phone conversation was a very short one. She spoke to George immediately after. 'They might want to seize our shoes. Maybe some clothes too.'

'I thought they might. I draw the line at the underpants though, they're the only ones I brought.'

Emma managed a half smile. 'I don't see the need at this point. I suggest we only worry if they come back a bit more insistent.'

'Who's running it?'

'I don't know to be honest. That was the senior forensic officer. I didn't think to ask if they were getting any direction. I'm sure someone will call me if I'm needed. It's probably better if it isn't me, seeing as I'm now a key witness.'

'I agree.'

'I could do without getting stuck out at a scene for the rest of the day. We need to be looking at the bigger picture.'

'We do. Which is proving more difficult than I anticipated. And I certainly don't think our shoes hold the key to this Emma.'

'I'm sure you're right. I just don't know what does. I've been trying to straighten it all out in my mind. It's such a mess, George.'

'Investigations like this always are. Until they're not. We need to simplify it all. Start again. Let's do a VOWS assessment from where we are. We need to get everything down that we know. The stuff we don't know is what we need to be working on.'

'Makes sense to me.'

There was a knock at the door. Emma had pushed it solidly shut, having made a point of telling the two DCs who were working at their desks that she didn't want to be disturbed.

'Yes?' Her irritation was clear. A second passed. Maybe the person the other side was having second thoughts. Then the door opened and a uniform sergeant walked in.

'Ma'am . . . sorry. They did say it was a bad time. But then I gave them a message to pass on and then they said that actually I should knock, so—'

'It's fine, Alan. Come in. This is Inspector George Elms. George, this is Alan Kemp. One of our patrol sergeants up here.'

George shook Alan's hand. He still looked a little unsure.

'It's a very quick thing. It's just that there's a slide on the briefing. I've been on rest days. I came in for late turn today and it was on there. I know who it is. At least I'm pretty certain.'

'A slide?'

'Yes. There's not much description. Just that it's come from Lennockshire, actually. It doesn't say what it's about, just that we should let you know if we recognise the person in it.'

George was suddenly animated. 'The CCTV stills from the petrol station. And you know who it is?'

'I'm pretty certain. I went to a sudden death on my last set of day shifts. It would have been Monday. There was a lad there. He found his mum dead in the morning.' The sergeant had his notebook in his hand. His finger was saving a page. He read from it. 'Liam Cooney, 14 Wilbur Way, Symonds Yat.'

'Liam Cooney,' Emma repeated. 'And you're sure?'

'I am. I know he's a bit of a distance away on the CCTV, you can just about see enough of his face for an ID. But it's his top, ma'am, that's how I know. I spent an hour with him or more, while they moved his mum out in a body bag. I took her wedding ring off before they moved her and I gave it to him. He was wearing a hooded top with writing on his chest. *Superdry*. It was off-centre. I remember him putting that ring in his hoodie pocket. I remember it well because I thought it was a bit odd at the time. Not overly. It struck me as a bit cold, I suppose. I guess he was in shock. He took a quick look at it and then stuffed it in his pocket.'

'What had happened to his mum?' George said.

'It was non-sus. She'd been ill a while. Chronic pulmonary disorder. Kept alive by constant oxygen. She was plugged into it when we found her. I guess it couldn't keep her going any longer. We found a load of medication. She did well to last as long as she did.'

Emma was looking over at George. He reckoned she was thinking the same thing. He received immediate confirmation.

'CPD? They probably wouldn't even do an autopsy. She would be written off as natural causes.'

'She would,' George said.

'I'll make a call to the coroner. We need to get that reopened and declared suspicious.' Emma was talking to George. He noticed that Sergeant Kemp was looking even less sure.

'Ma'am? Did I miss something?'

'No. You couldn't possibly have known, don't worry . . .' Emma was pacing. She bent her head.

'Sorry, ma'am. Known what?'

She lifted her head back up. 'Oh. Sorry, Alan. That CCTV slide, the person pictured is now a suspect for murder. John Lawrence was found . . . well, he's dead.'

'I heard it on the radio. I spoke briefly with the early turn sergeant. They're all tucked up at the scene. I'm going to be sending people out to take over.'

'How many are you parading with today?'

'One and seven, ma'am. Earlies have five on scene control at the moment. That leaves me with one double-crewed car to answer the calls.'

'I need an arrest and search. I'll leave your two-man car alone but can you come out with me and George? We need to get Liam Cooney in. We can worry about the search once we have him in custody. I'll have to call in resources from elsewhere.'

'Of course.'

George stood up. He picked up his car keys and spoke directly to Alan. 'What's he like? Cooney, I mean?'

The sergeant hesitated. 'I don't know the politically correct term. Learning difficulties? Is that it? He seemed a little slow to me. Like he wasn't quite sure what was going on. Not the sort of lad who could plan and execute a murder, put it that way.'

'Not on his own at least,' George said. Emma led the way out the building.

Chapter 34

The Cooney house, 14 Wilbur Way was shrouded in low-lying cloud. The street as a whole was being prodded and probed by its grey, wispy fingers. The estate looked to George like classic council stock. Social housing before it was given the posher sounding title. The exteriors were made up of weathered-looking pebble dash and number 14 was particularly drab. Brown water stains spread out from under the windows. The lawn was neat at least.

George knocked the door with Emma standing next to him. Alan Kemp was out of sight a little further down the street. Tactics around the door knock for Liam Cooney were the subject of the conversation on the way there. Alan described him as early twenties, dim witted, but quite a lump. George had his right hand gripped round the pepper spray in his jacket. He knocked again. They had been on the doorstep for a couple of minutes.

'Section 8 warrant?' Emma said.

'I was hoping it wouldn't come to that.' A Section 8 warrant would need to be granted by a magistrate. It would give the police a power to kick the door down to try and locate someone wanted for a serious offence — like the murder of John Lawrence and the abduction of two young women. He had no doubt they would be granted the warrant but it was a lot of paperwork and he didn't want to waste the time it would take to get it.

'Alan!' George called out and the sergeant appeared. 'No answer. I'm just gonna check round the back. Do you mind holding the front in case someone makes a break for it?'

Alan nodded. George and Emma moved round the side of the house. Immediately George could see that the garden was big. Long and thin. You wouldn't get a garden like that anymore with your social housing. He tried the back door. It was locked too. The top half was clear glass but with a net curtain obscuring the view. He could see into the kitchen: some of the work surfaces, including the one that housed the sink. Everything was very orderly. There was no evidence of anyone being at home. He knocked at the back door, too but there was still no movement. He stepped away and looked up at the second floor. The curtains were open. The small windows were ajar. Again, nothing stirred. He turned to look down the garden. He could see a thick conifer hedge half way down. That might have fooled him into thinking it was the end of the garden but an untidy arch was cut and he could see some outbuildings beyond. He walked down the garden. The grass was a little longer at the back, his feet dragged through it. Emma walked with him. There was fencing along both sides but the garden was on a slope so the neighbours would still have a limited view in. He made a mental note to knock a few doors either side. There were two outbuildings. The first, on the left, was a small, brick-built structure. It had a small door that looked jammed open, stuck by its own rust. The inside was covered in a layer of black. A coal shed, George reckoned. It looked like it had been out of use for some time.

The next shed was larger and made of wood. There was a padlock on the door but the clasp hung open. He twisted it and pulled the door.

'George.' Emma's tone carried a warning.

'I know. I'm just going to stick my head in.'

'There'll be a forensic search here, George. You know what they're like.'

'I do. We need to be sure it's empty, though, right? Perfectly reasonable.' George stepped in. He found a light switch. The bulb seemed hesitant and took its time to warm up to its full brightness. Everything looked very orderly, unusually so for a garden shed. Everything had its place. Saws, screwdrivers and hammers all clung to the wall and were arranged in size order. Each had a silhouette drawn round them on the wall. One tool was missing. The silhouette was the shape of a shovel.

The main workbench looked a little too high and it had sides, like a box. It looked reinforced, too, with metal struts covering every edge. A black metal object lying on top of the bench stood out as the only thing out of place. George walked to it. It was an old clothes iron. Victorian maybe? It was solid and it was heavy. It looked like it had marked the wooden bench.

'It's hinged!' George lifted the iron off the work surface and moved it to the floor. His eyes rested on a catch on the side of the bench. Another padlock was pushed through. Again it hung open. George pulled his sleeve over his hand to pull it out. He used the same technique to pull the lid up. It creaked open. It was empty.

'Shit!' Emma exhaled as she spoke. It sounded like relief.

'Were you expecting a vampire?'

'I was expecting worse than that.' George bent down to inspect the box. Something caught his eye. The box was scuffed on the inside. It was a light brown but it had grooves that were lighter still — nearer to white in colour. They were on the side that was closest to him. He had to angle his neck to be able to see it. The scuffs were letters — writing. He couldn't make it out.

'Something's written in there I think!' Emma was stood next to him. She lit up the torch function on her phone. She turned it on the box.

'Shit, George!' He was still craning. He still couldn't see.

'What? What does it say?'

'We need to get that warrant.'

'What is it?'

'P.O.P.E. It says *Pope*, George! It's from Chloe Pope. It has to be. She must have been in here!'

George could see it now. It was scratched on the surface. Not deep and barely legible. But it was definitely *POPE*. It looked about right for someone trying to write in the pitch black, digging into wood with their finger nails.

George needed some air. As he bundled out of the shed door Emma called out after him.

'We must be getting closer, George. We must be.'

'Closer's no good. Dennis Coleman was close to finding Chloe. Look how that ended! What if we can still do something for those two other girls? What if they're in a box somewhere, scratching their names into the wood so that one day someone might know what happened to them? Closer's no good.' He started walking back up the garden.

Emma called out again. 'So where do we go from here?'

'Me? I need a walk.' George kept going. He made it out into the street and walked to the end of it. There was a play park and fields directly opposite. The street was elevated, it looked down on what looked like a town and across to the other side of a valley. George couldn't recall being in this area and not being in a valley. On any other day it would have been a beautiful place to stand. He found a bench in the park that overlooked the play area. There were some parents with their children. He could hear the excited screams. It made him think of his little girl, waiting for him at home with his wife. He was struggling to comprehend just what that meant. It had been so long, he had never given up hope but had started to come to terms with never getting his family back. He knew he had messed it up the first time around. He wasn't going to mess it up this time. He watched a mother scoop up a toddler from the end of a slide and lift her to the sky. Both their faces were beaming. Pure happiness. The sort you couldn't have if your eyes were open to the world. George couldn't do anything about what he already knew, about the evil that he had been exposed to. But he could do something about his future. He was tired. He had been tired for a long time. Seeing the worst of people was making him weary. He envied the carefree parents of the world. Those that could send their kids to school without considering that there was such evil in the world and that there were no guarantees they would come back, that they could end up trapped in a box at the mercy of a man who knew none, desperately scratching their name with their fingernails. Maybe he could forget, maybe he could become carefree again, maybe his happiness could become pure. Whatever, his family were waiting for him at home. A second chance. And he had made a decision.

A car horn interrupted his thoughts. He turned to it. It was Emma. He must have been gone longer than he thought. He walked over to where her window was wound down.

'A patrol have arrived to look after the perimeter. I've requested another one up here too — in case he comes back.'

'He's long gone, Emma.'

'I know. But we might find something that gives us a clue as to where at least. The search team are going to be a couple of hours, I think. It's not ideal but we're struggling now with two scenes. Alan is staying to run it from the ground.'

George stroked his chin. 'We could do the search ourselves. I know there are contamination issues but needs must. We can worry about the evidential problems after.' George was mindful that both he and Emma had been at the St Leonard's ruins scene earlier that day. If they stepped into Cooney's house, they ran the risk of any half-decent solicitor pointing out that any DNA present linking Cooney to the other scene would have been transferred by the two police officers. They wouldn't be able to argue with it either. George considered that finding the girls alive outweighed evidential difficulties later.

'We could. But you might be needed elsewhere. I took a call. We've had someone phone in. He said he's Roberts's brother. He says he has some information that may help. But he'll only talk to you.'

'His brother? Do we know it's him for certain?'

'No. The call was traced to a payphone in London.'

'What do we know about his brother?'

'Not a lot. William Roberts. Older brother. He lived locally, but he left the area when all of this was going on. I think the family as a whole were under the spotlight. We tried to track him down, it was an obvious line of enquiry but we got nowhere. He was represented by the same solicitors as Henry and they made it clear that he would see any police contact as harassment.'

'It's hardly harassment is it, investigating a murder?'

'No, it isn't. I think his solicitors were able to scare some of the senior management enough that speaking to him wasn't deemed essential so it wasn't done. He wasn't a key witness. We were just trying to get some background.'

'So we don't know if this is him or just some crackpot wasting my time?'

'We don't. But the general public don't know much. And someone calling Herefordshire Police about Henry Roberts and asking to speak to George Elms must know an awful lot.'

'You think he might have spoken to his brother?'

'I can't think how else he would know so much.'

'Okay. Let's go and see him then.'

'I can't, George. Not with all that's going on. He's been very specific. He will meet you at Langthorne West train station, on the platform, by the payphones. Only in person. There's no number to call.'

'Langthorne?'

'Yeah, that's what he said. I've got a murder investigation, two scenes and a missing person investigation to run here, George. I can't really be driving two hundred miles away.'

'No you can't, and it's the distance that worries me. Time is something we really don't have a lot of. This might just be a way of hindering us. Sending me two hours in the wrong direction.'

'It might.'

'I have to go though, don't I?'

'I think so. The family distanced themselves from him right from the start. This was really damaging for them as you can imagine. If he's made contact and they know he's out, it's quite plausible that they would want to help make sure he was captured before he could do anything more.'

'But why me? And why Langthorne?'

Emma shrugged. 'I guess that's what you need to go and find out.'

Chapter 35

George did his best to read the information on his phone as he headed back to Langthorne. He waited until he was on the motorway where he stood a chance of diverting his eyes for just a few seconds at a time. There was no time to stop. From what he could glean, William Roberts had called Herefordshire's control room from a number that was registered to a payphone in central London. He said that he had information about his brother: Henry Roberts. He would divulge this information only if he were met personally by Inspector George Elms of Lennockshire police. This face-to-face meeting would take place at Langthorne West train station, just off the incoming platform at 14:12 hours. George was to stand by the public payphones. The log had been read and added to by a number of other persons. Someone had researched train times and put on the log that a train from London St Pancras station was due to arrive at that platform at 14:12 hours. George knew as much as he needed to know. He dialled Whittaker's number.

'George. How goes it, friend?'

'Did Emma bring you up to speed? I asked her to call.'

'She's not long off the phone. They've transferred the call details to us too. It's a strange one. What are your thoughts?'

'I don't think we have too much choice but to work on the basis that it's genuine and that William Roberts knows where his brother is and wants to help. Anything other than that we'll need to react to, I suppose.'

'We will. What do you need?'

'I need a team, Major. Foot surveillance mainly, but a car too. Whatever he tells me I want him picked up and followed when he leaves. If he's giving me a red herring he might still lead us somewhere useful. Or at least give us an address where I can politely give him his fish back.'

'No problem. How far out are you?'

'I'm struggling, Major. I'm two hours out for a ninety-minute deadline.'

'Where are you?'

'The wrong side of the M25.'

'Okay. I'll get in touch with Sussex. We'll get a marked convoy to bring you in.'

'Thanks, Major. This William, though . . . he shouldn't know who I am. Assuming he's talked to his brother he might have a description. Plan B for me not making it in time, Major . . . can you get onto HQ and have them print me another ID? If someone can bring it down to you it will be there in forty minutes. Then you just need someone who fits my description to be at that meeting.'

'Ugly and knackered, you mean? I like it, George, it works as a Plan B. But try and get here, please. I'll get those bits done. I'll pass Sussex your details so they can find you.'

'Thanks, Major.' George cut the call. Within twenty minutes he had a marked police bike in front of him. Ten minutes later and a marked BMW took its place while the bike dropped to the back. They stayed with him. He was now able to increase his speed; whenever traffic parted for the blaring police cars, he was able to slip in between them. The escort only dropped away when he turned into the road that led to Langthorne West train station. He was there with six minutes to spare. By the time he ditched the car and made it to the platform it was down to two. He was now breathing heavily and his shirt clung to the sweat on his back. He took a minute to catch his breath. He felt like he had barely breathed the whole way down here. The concentration involved in running at those speeds between two flashing cars, ducking and weaving through traffic, had taken its toll. He was shattered.

He checked his watch again. The platform was busy all of a sudden. There was already one stationary train. Another arrived, right on time. It seemed to spill out all of its passengers at the same time and they all walked past with purpose in their stride, their heads down. There were only two payphones at the station. They were both together on the wall by the exit from the platform. He stood himself directly between them, where he couldn't be missed. No one took any notice of him, although he tried to screen everyone that approached. Within a few minutes, the platform was almost empty. The only people anywhere in sight were either in high-vis railway jackets or milling around on the platform opposite, waiting for the next outbound train.

One of the payphones trilled and made him jump. He stared at it. It kept ringing. He looked around, as if it might be for someone else. There was no one close. His deadline had passed by almost ten minutes. He picked up the receiver.

'George Elms?' The voice was urgent. A man's voice. He lingered on the 's.'

'William Roberts?' George said. His throat was dry. It carried in his voice. He hadn't realised until he tried to speak.

'I don't go by that surname so much anymore. I'm sure you can appreciate why.'

'I thought we were meeting in person?'

'That wasn't what I said.'

'You have some information for me?'

'Just an anecdote, really. When we were younger, my brother and I used to visit Langthorne for our summer holidays. We used this very station. We played on the beach, went on walks — the usual stuff. There's a local beauty spot called the Warren. It's a cliff walk and we would go there every time — well, most days anyway. We met a man down there. Our mother didn't like us talking to him. Henry was fascinated by him — fixated even. He can get fixed on things. He ran away to visit him. This man lived off the land in a home he had built on the beach out of driftwood. My mother was frantic. My father not so much. I thought I knew where he was, Inspector, and I was correct. But we couldn't get him straight away. The tide down there, it used to cut this man and his home off from the rest of the world for at least three hours twice a day. I think that's what appealed to Henry. I think he liked the idea of being cut off from the rest of the world, even for just a few hours. When he ran away he timed it so we couldn't get to him. He knew he had that time alone. He told me he would live there one day. I never understood his fascination. But you get older, Inspector. You see the world. It's a beautiful spot. I suppose we all want to be cut off in a beautiful spot at some point in life, right?'

'Why are you telling me this? Is that where he is?'

'He's a gentle soul. I know who you think he is, what the world thinks he is and what he looks like, but I don't know that man. That's not my brother. He's naïve. He always wanted to fit in. Remember that about him.'

'William, I need to find him. If there's more to this, if there's more I need to know then I need to find him. Is that where he is? Has he spoken to you? William? William!' The line was dead. The call had been ended. George slammed the handset back in its cradle and turned to look around. He stayed dead still for just a minute. William was there somewhere; he was certain of it. He would have made sure George was where he needed to be and that no one else was around. George could see people in the distance. None of them stood out. It didn't matter now anyway. He walked briskly towards his car. Whittaker picked up on the first ring.

'George, did you meet?'

'No. He called the payphone. I guess he wanted to speak to the police in a situation where he could cut it off the second he wanted to.'

'He cut you off?'

'He did.'

'What did he tell you?'

'A childhood story. But combine it with what Henry told us and I think I know where he is with the girls.'

'Fantastic.'

'I'm not convinced.'

'You're not convinced what? This is good, right?'

'Are you in front of a computer?'

'Yes. Why?'

'What time is high tide in Langthorne today?'

'High tide? What the hell—'

'Please, Major, just tell me.' George was still walking fast and was breathing heavily.

'Jeez. Hang on, old boy.' There was the tapping of a keyboard in the background. `13:20 today. What the hell does that have to do with anything?'

'Do you remember a couple of years back when there was a guy who lived down the beach. Right where the cliffs turn back towards Dover? He had a place made out of driftwood. He lived there for ages. Off the grid.'

'No, George. I guess it must have been before my time here.'

'He died a couple of years ago. A dog walker found him when he had a fall. He was a bit of a local legend.

Made the papers once or twice. Henry Roberts knew him too. When they were younger he and William used to come down here. William said his brother was obsessed with the place both because of its beauty and because it's cut off by the tide for three hours a day. That's where he is, Major. He's on that beach with those girls. The tide peaked at 13:20. Slack water lasts around two hours where the tide's at its highest and then it's an hour before its low enough to get to him. Henry set the time of that phone call. He knows when I can next get to him. He's going to kill them, Major. On our beach. And he will be doing it now while he knows that I have to stand half a mile away waiting for the tide. It's another power play.'

'But we can stop him. If he thinks he has the time—'

'I think he's done what he can to make sure I can't. The 14:12 train at Langthorne and calling Herefordshire to get hold of me. Henry must have known where I was. He knew the journey would be tight to get here. And the time now? I'm leaving now and I'll get to the Warren with half a mile of beach under the sea. He wants me to sit and wait an hour until it subsides. This way I get to be the first person to see what he's done. This is all part of it, Major. This is how he fucks with me.'

'Jesus, George, it's a beach, though, old boy. The police boat—'

'Won't be able to get anywhere near. It's all rocks. When the tide's out you can see its teeth. It's impassable. We wouldn't stand a chance. The other side is a sheer cliff. There's no way you could get someone down there safely — not without Roberts being stood waiting for them with a distinct advantage. There's no room for a chopper to work either. There's just a slit of beach left.'

'So what do we do? Just let this play out like he intended? We know how that ends, right?'

'I don't know. What about snipers? We have them in the firearms teams?'

'We do. Maybe four for the county though, George, and even if we could get one there in time I can't see us finding a firearms commander who would authorise a shot from a moving boat. That needs a proper specialist. You're talking the armed forces — and an even longer wait.'

'Fine. I'm going down there, quick as I can. Maybe I will be able to see some options. I'll give you a call. Send whoever you can.'

'Okay, George.'

Chapter 36

It was the breeze that first made Annie realise that she was
alive. Then she could feel the damp, coarse ground that
was gritty against her skin. She could also feel the material
wrapped tight around her head and over her eyes. It dug
into her cheekbones and the back of her head where it was
tied off. She could feel the knot. Her head was throbbing.
Suddenly she felt a touch. Someone grabbed hold of the
blindfold and it was tugged roughly down. She slammed
her eyes shut to the bright sunlight. It took her a while to
get used to it, to be able to see clearly. Her hearing was
returning too. She realised she was lying on damp sand. It
was a small area. Rocks dominated the scenery. The sea
pushed earnestly over them, darting into rock pools,
reaching out towards her with frothy, white fingers. Just
beyond them the water looked deep. The waves retreated
quickly and with a hissing noise. She felt sick. She was
grabbed forcefully by her wrists and dragged to a crawl for
just a few metres, then pushed hard into something that
jutted out of the sand. It was damp wood. It was cold and
she could feel the roughness of a dozen splinters sticking

into her back. She realised she was in just her underwear. She didn't know where her dress was. She sobbed.

'Where am I?' she croaked as her hands were yanked roughly behind her back and tied firmly to the post. The angle was so obtuse it pulled on her shoulders and they were shot through with pain.

'It's time.' The voice was delivered right into her ear. She heard the distinctive sound of wooden logs knocking against one another, as if they were being stacked. She craned her neck towards the sound and a tall, gaunt man with broad shoulders straightened up and looked back at her. Though he was about five metres away, she could still see the intensity in his gaze. To his right a shovel was upright, dug into the sand. The logs were in a neat pile and pushed beneath what looked like a rusty, brown drum on legs. Her eyes were still a little fuzzy.

'What are you doing? What do you want with me?'

The younger man who had tied her moved from behind the post and squatted down in front of her. His face wore a big grin. 'You wait your turn! I'm going to free you, Annie. You *and* Sadie. But you're special to me. So you get to watch first. You get to share the beauty!'

He stood back up and walked away to her left. Beyond him she could see what looked like a wooden shack. It was a mix of odd colours and shapes. It was made of wood but none of the pieces quite married up. The man disappeared. When he came back out he was pushing another girl in front of him. She was very petite and her blonde hair fell untidily over a naturally pale complexion. She looked so young. Annie's mind was fuzzy, but she remembered the van journey. Another girl had been there and had been moaning. This was her! She was led past Annie, her eyes were wide in panic.

'Help me!' she muttered. It seemed like a struggle for her to speak. She fell to the ground and the man immediately scooped her up, hooking his hands beneath her shoulders. She was shaking.

'What are you doing with her? What are you doing?' Annie screamed, her head throbbing with the effort. The girl was led to where the man with the dark eyes was waiting. The drum seemed to have doubled in size. Annie squinted at it. *It had opened up!*

'Oh God! Oh God, no!' The man still held the girl under her arms as far as the drum and then her underwear was ripped from her. The two men started to bundle her to the drum. She tried to fight them off and managed to get a blow on the larger man. His head barely moved but he wiped something away from his cheek. He had been relatively still up to this point, leaving most of the effort to the younger man, but now he reached down with his huge hands and pushed her in all at once. She couldn't fight back. Not against him. The top of the drum was slammed down with a loud thud. Immediately she could hear more thuds; the girl had started hammering on it from the inside and there were faint and muted screams, too. The drum, tank — whatever it was — was clearly made of some kind of thick metal. The younger man walked back towards her.

He sighed and shook his head and hunkered down beside her again. 'She's scared because she doesn't understand. But you will, Annie. You will see and you will know. When she's free . . . ah, it's beautiful, Annie, it's so beautiful. And then it's your turn.'

'She's just a girl! She's just a girl! Let her go! Let her go, you don't need her!'

'Oh but we do! We need you both. You've earned this, Annie, with your beauty, with your grace! I mean, look at you . . .'

'Me first, then! I'll go first. I won't fight. Me first!'

'No, no. This is all for you, Annie. This is all so you can *see*!'

'No . . . please!' He was already walking away. She had seen his face: the excitement, the glee. He was hyper. It was like nothing she had seen before. His hands were shaking so bad he could barely light the kindling gathered under the logs. But he did light it. And it took almost instantly.

Chapter 37

George made it to the Warren. There were no other police personnel there yet. It was a road at its origins and it dropped away quite suddenly towards sea level past a Martello tower that had commanding views over the Channel. The road had been created to allow maintenance access to the train tracks that ran along the seafront and joined eventually with Dover. There was a campsite at the bottom too. Signs warned that it was closed for refurbishment. George took the road so fast he was praying out loud for the suspension to stay together and the tyres to stay up. The road was pitted by potholes, deep enough to cripple a car not designed for this type of punishment. He pushed on. The road levelled out. He could go straight on and run alongside the tracks or take another right. He took the right. It was a steeper gradient still and it led down to an area of hard-standing that was just above sea-level and butted up against the high tide. Now it looked like a concrete beach, but once this area had been an airstrip, a hangover from the First World War.

The front of his car scraped against it as he grounded out at the bottom. This section was only ever in danger of flooding in stormy weather. Not even a spring tide would bother it otherwise. Today there was no storm, but the breeze pushing off the sea felt stronger than it had further inland. The platform soon narrowed right down. George drove as far as he could on the concrete beach with the sea directly to his right. The train track separated him from steep cliffs to his left. He knew the train track would soon turn inland too. All that would be left would be the impregnable white of the cliff face.

He abandoned the car. A slim walkway continued. It was concrete and built at the same time as the airstrip. He ran along it. He was closer to the sea now, close enough to be caught in the spray as the waves pushed and slapped against the concrete path. He could feel his phone ringing in his pocket. He ignored it. The walkway opened up again to another platform that was almost as wide as the first. Some buildings had been here once. There were only weeds and rubble left now. He ran through them. The walkway finished and he knew this to be where path ended and the rocks started. They were completely submerged. He could just about see the pointed tops of some of them when the waves rolled over. He was standing so far left he used the cliff face as support as he leant out as far as he could to try and pick out a path. He knew this area well enough. There was a stretch of rocks, piled untidily on top of one another from ancient cliff falls and pushed tighter together by the constant tide. After that was a mile-long stretch of beach where he had walked dogs and spent lazy afternoons, but right now it was deep underwater and with no way of picking a way through the rocks to get to it while the water was this high. George was too late. Just like he was supposed to be. His phone rang again. This time he answered it. The sea skimmed the rocks to batter against the cliff face in front of him. George could see a layer of green staining on the white. The level of the sea was just under it, like it might be on its way out.

'Major.' George was out of breath.

'Tell me you made it.'

'I made it to the rocks. I can't even see the beach. From memory they're stacked at least six feet high but at low tide you can pick a path round them on the sand. I can see where the cliff turns in the distance. Henry will be just the other side of that.'

'So you can't confirm he's there?'

'No. I can't confirm anything. I can't get there. And the tide's got an hour to go. I'm as close as I can get.'

Whittaker gave out a long sigh. 'I've made all the calls. The world and his wife are on their way. It's out of my hands, George. The marine team are making their way to the area but they said the same as you. They know it — everyone seems to . . . they can't land there. They could take a RHIB in closer but it's risky and they'd be too vulnerable for the actual landing. They'll assess again though when they get there. The tide is on its way out now apparently — they might have attempted it if it was still at its highest. The risks from going over the cliff and down are unacceptable too. Those aren't my words. A command chain has been put in place. The Gold Commander is the superintendent. He's grounded us. You're the first line, George. Round those rocks is the only way we get to him.'

'Of course it is. Just like Roberts planned.'

'You'll have enough resources with you by the time you can move. I'll be monitoring the radio.'

George pushed the phone back into his pocket. He peered down at the surface of the water. It was opaque but then another large wave swept in to reveal the jagged tops of rocks. He felt the spray on his face as it bounced off the cliff face. It was just a few minutes before he was joined by other officers. He didn't speak to them. The tension tore at him. He couldn't speak. They must have known. No one spoke to him either. They hung back a few metres and talked among themselves in low tones. George paced along the edge of walkway, his eyes fixed on the cliffs in the distance. He considered leaping in. He knew it would be counterproductive. The force of the water was strong, the rocks were sharp and the currents would pull him back out to sea. George had known of a few drownings down here. The water wrapped around a corner and the current undertow would dash him repeatedly against invisible rocks. He wouldn't be able to swim it. He cussed as he dismissed the idea. He was back to walking up and down the water's edge. Now *he* was the raging bull desperate to join the fight.

Twenty minutes passed. It was the longest twenty minutes of George's life. The green staining on the cliff face was broader; the water level had dropped. He could hear radio chatter from the officers behind him. No one had moved any closer. George knew he was going to have to try soon or he was going to burst. The tops of rocks were appearing more consistently from under the surface, pushing out like they were gasping for air. They were slick with brown weed and their surfaces were covered in limpet shells suckered to the top and sides, making the surface even more treacherous. George had a point in his mind where he would move. There was a large, flat rock right in front of him. He could see it now. It was a couple of centimetres under the surface. It was becoming more and more exposed as the sea breathed in and out. Once it was all exposed, once he could see a place for his foot, he was going to go.

Ten more agonising minutes passed. George was trying not to think about what was happening just around the bend in the cliffs half a mile away. His mind played tricks on him. A couple of times he thought he could hear screams of pain, screams for help. It wasn't possible. He was too far away. All he could hear were the gulls and the flopping and hissing of the sea. He was trying to piece together what had happened, if they had missed any opportunities that might have brought him to this place earlier. He was struggling to think straight. The thoughts and doubts thrashed around in his mind like those girls would be thrashing against the sides of that bull.

The rock was exposed. The sea had retreated. It still wasn't enough but George could wait no longer. He leapt forward. His foot slipped instantly — the rock sloped away. His foot was drenched but he stayed up. He took the impact of a rolling wave to his lower leg. He had to steady himself.

'Sir?' an officer called out from behind him. George ignored him. He picked out the next place for his feet. Another rock, this time the water was deeper on its surface but it sloped towards him and it rested up against the cliff, he could use it to hold himself up. He leapt again. The cliff face was slick and slippery. He leant against it. Both his feet were ankle deep, but he was standing. He picked out his next move. One rock at a time. Painfully slow. But he was moving.

'Sir! It's too dangerous!' It was another voice from behind him. He could understand why. If he fell onto the jagged rocks it would be one of them that would have to jump it and help him out. Or maybe they wouldn't. George was past considering that.

He leapt forward. His foot landed in a sunken part of the top of a rock. He whacked his shin on the jagged edge. It was excruciating. He sucked in air to stop himself from shouting out. He lifted his trousers. A flap of white skin had been torn away, it quickly ran red. He jumped forward again. He heard a noise behind. He turned to it. One of the officers had taken his lead and jumped onto an exposed rock.

'Stay where you are! No one else needs to put themselves at risk here!' George barked.

'With respect, sir . . . If you go in, we all go in! I might as well be closer at least!'

George didn't reply. He picked out another rock. He waited for another wave to roll over his legs before moving again. It was painstaking but it gave him something to focus on. The rocks lasted for a hundred metres or so and then they stopped. George knew that the sandy beach took over from there. At the moment it still looked like a body of water but George could see a decrepit wooden groyne yawning out from under the surface. The sea was retreating.

By the time he reached the end of the rocks he could see the sand. The water was about a foot deep. He jumped in immediately and shortly afterwards heard the splashes of other officers following suit. It was too deep to run and the salt stung his shin as he pushed his feet through the water. He tripped over a sunken rock and stumbled to his knees. The water felt so heavy, his legs felt heavy; he was practically dragging himself on. His thighs burned. He pushed forward one step at a time. The beach was on a steep incline and was rising out of the water. Soon his steps got a little easier, his strides a little longer. When he was almost clear of the water, he broke into a run.

The beach was still soggy. His legs and his lungs demanded he slow down as he rounded the cliff. He could now see a bare-chested figure some hundred metres away standing on top of a rock. It was Roberts, George was certain. He could tell from his size, his confident stance. The figure turned away and stepped down out of sight. George got the impression he had been waiting.

He broke into a run again, legs powered by his desperation. Beyond the rocks he could see white smoke rising. He could smell the smoke in the air, too, mixed with the salty breeze.

The coming line of rocks had formed when a huge chunk of the cliff had fallen onto the beach leading into the sea. The cliffs were a fresh, brighter white where the weathered front had slipped. George struggled to climb up the pile of crumbling rocks. When, exhausted and breathless, he reached the top, he had an elevated view. He could see the cabin. He could see the bull. He could see the flames buffeting angrily against its belly.

'Henry Roberts!' George called out. 'This is how it ends, is it? I thought you had all that you wanted?'

Roberts moved towards him. He held a shovel across his body, raised like a weapon. George dropped down the other side of the rocks to meet him. He stopped when his feet were back on sand. Roberts was close enough now for George to see red staining on the end of the shovel. He had red across his chest too, fresh enough to still be running in drips. The officers that had been lagging behind him were now in George's peripheral vision. George held his hands out to signal for them to stay where they were. Roberts was still coming. 'Put the shovel down, Henry, or I'll have one of my mates here stick a taser up your arse.'

'You're too late, Inspector. They used me. This was their day of reckoning.'

'Where are they, Henry? Where are the girls?' George didn't wait for an answer. He could see powerful flames now, roiling around the underside of the bull. He ran past Roberts and gave him a wide berth as he did.

'Get control of him!' He shouted his instructions to the officers behind. The heat was intense, enough to stop him a metre away from the bull. It was bigger than the one he had seen in the wood. There was a catch sealing it shut. A thin metal bar was pushed through it. He grabbed it to slide it out and immediately it scorched the skin on his fingers and he jerked them back. He looked round for something to use.

'Your gloves!' he shouted to one of the officers. They were facing Henry. The taser was still pointed at him, they looked like they were frozen to the spot, as if they had forgotten what to do now they were stood in front of him. Roberts still held the shovel. 'Throw me your gloves!'

'Inspector!' Roberts called out. He had turned to face George. 'You need to listen to me. I can help.'

One of the officers pulled gloves from his trouser pocket. He threw them over. George scooped them up. They were search gloves. Needle-proof, but thin, they wouldn't make much difference. He still pulled them on. A rock pool was close. George plunged his hands into the water. He turned back to the bull. He pushed his flat palm against its body and heaved. He had to close his eyes to the smoke and turn his face from the heat. It didn't move. His feet slipped on the sand, the heat seared through the gloves almost immediately, the water turned to steam, the gloves perished and he ripped them off before they melted to his skin. He had to let go. He couldn't open it. He couldn't push it off its feet and away from the heat. He couldn't hear any noises either. No screaming, no banging to get out. No signs of life. It was a giant oven; there was no coming out of that. He turned back to Roberts. He had to fight to stay upright. He wanted to collapse onto the damp sand.

'You're a piece of scum. You didn't have to do it like this. That's what I never understood.'

'That hate you have in your heart for me. I needed that. I needed you to hate me George, so you wouldn't give up.'

'What are you talking about now? Are they both in there?' George looked back over at the bull. The metal was two different shades. The bottom half lighter than the top. But it was changing colour from the bottom up even as he watched, the lighter tone moving upwards like a shadow.

'I know you want the truth. I know you're desperate for it and you want to understand.'

'Put the shovel down.'

Roberts threw the shovel onto the sand. 'I'm not what you think I am,' he said. 'In the cabin.' George looked beyond the smoking bull to where the cabin stood. It was backed against the cliff face.

'Keep your hands where I can see them!' the officer holding the taser yelled. 'This device will shock you with 50,000 volts if you do not do what you are told!' Roberts ignored him. He was still looking over at George.

'In the cabin,' Henry said again. He stepped towards it himself.

'STAY WHERE YOU ARE!' the officer with the taser shouted.

George moved towards the cabin. 'Take him down!' he said.

The taser officer's eyes glanced from Roberts to George. 'Sir?'

'Take him down. Do it.' George kept walking towards the cabin. He heard the taser shot, followed by a fizz and a crackle as it did its work. Roberts didn't shout out, but he fell onto the sand stiff as a plank. George stumbled to the door of the cabin and hesitated. Roberts was looking up at him. George tugged open the door. It was dim inside. The light from the door lit up a clump of blonde hair. George's heart sank. He had found their bodies. Roberts had made sure it was him, just as he had predicted. Then there was movement. A girl's face turned to him, her eyes squinting against the light. She could only make a moaning noise. A rag was pulled tightly across her mouth. George moved quickly. She was trying to get up. He helped her and she bundled past him towards the door. There was more movement further in. A second girl stumbled towards him and he reached for her.

'We need some assistance here!' George shouted. Both girls burst through the door and back out into the sunlight. One wore a man's shirt over bare legs, the other was wrapped in a long jacket. They were both sobbing hard. George made it out as they grabbed hold of the uniform officers and held onto them like they would never let them go. It was Annie Cox and Sadie Edwards. They were dirty, bedraggled and sobbing but they still looked enough like the photos George had seen.

Roberts was still lying on the sand — in handcuffs now, secured behind his back. Two wires still trailed from his back to the taser device of an officer who was stood

318

over him. 'What's going on, Henry?' George demanded. 'Whose blood do you have on you? Did you hurt them?'

'They used me, Inspector.' Henry's body language was different. His voice dripped with emotion. He looked upset, agitated — even a little vulnerable.

'It's over,' George said. 'We have to take you back. And not to a sea view this time.'

Henry's head dropped. His long damp hair fell over his face, which was spotted with sand.

'Where's Liam? Liam Cooney?'

Roberts jerked his head. George looked towards the water's edge and took a few steps closer. Behind some jagged rocks he could see someone. He was lying on his front, his face fully submerged. His dark hair was tinged with blood and his hoodie was heavily stained with it. His skull had a clear dent. The waves nudged him gently as they rolled in as if they were trying to sneak him away on the ebbing tide.

'I take it he isn't going to be answering any of my questions?'

'He's already answered for what he did.' Roberts's voice was low but it still carried the same menace.

'Your turn now then, Henry. You need to answer for your sins.'

'That's all I ever wanted.'

Chapter 38

The car door clunked shut. George was in the back. Henry Roberts sat next to him in handcuffs, his hands resting on his lap. George had needed to move the restraints to the front so he could get in the car at all. Roberts's head was stooped to fit under the headliner. An officer sat in the front, he was half-turned and writing notes hurriedly. The driver's seat was still empty. The man set to occupy it was leaning on the driver's door. George could hear a muffled phone conversation.

'I'm not who you thought I was,' Roberts said. He was facing away, out of the window.

'What?'

'*Monster.* That's what you said when we first met.'

'I wouldn't promote yourself just yet, Henry.' George's attention moved to the front where an officer tapped on the window next to the one in the front seat. He gestured that he wished to speak to him.

'Are you okay for a minute, sir?' the officer in front said.

George waved him away. 'Yeah, of course.'

The officer stepped out and pushed the door back shut. Roberts was facing out of his window. The silence continued for a few minutes.

'What happened, Henry?'

'The Lord's work.'

'You're still trotting that rubbish out, are you? Why didn't you kill those girls?'

Roberts turned to George, his head still pushed to an awkward angle in the cramped car. Those dark eyes scanned him. He didn't answer straight away. 'The first time I ever killed *anyone* was today. Liam Cooney is the only person to suffer at my hands. He has only evil in his heart.'

'So Chloe Pope, Ellie Smith, her boyfriend Josh Haines, Lucy Moon . . . what are you telling me? That was all Cooney?'

'And there would have been a lot more. He told me there was nothing left for him in Symonds Yat. He was going to travel. All over. The police would have been starting from scratch. The damage he could have done . . . It doesn't matter if you believe me or not.'

'I don't.'

'I suppose I can't blame you for that. I did a good job convincing everyone I was something else.'

'Something else? They told me that when you were arrested you were wearing their bones. There's only one sort of person that does that.'

'I was. I did. I wanted to make sure I was convicted. But I had to be sure that Liam believed me too.'

'Why? What did it matter what Liam thought by that point?'

'I knew he wouldn't stop. He told me that. I made him promise that he would wait until I got out. He respected me. He looked up to me. I hoped it would be enough. I think it was. I spoke to him a lot on the phone. I could tell he was desperate to kill again. He said he was watching someone every day. I think I would have known if he had acted on it. As soon as he killed his mother he told me about it and in some detail. It made me sick. I sent my phone with that text message to my solicitor. They have instructions to present it to the police as soon as it arrives. Liam still has his phone on his person.'

'So you're helping us now?'

Roberts fixed him with a look again. 'I knew from the off that no one would believe me. I know how I look. But actually, I think you do believe me. You don't look at me the same. When you first came in to see me . . . the way you looked at me . . . it was pure hate. And I played up to that. I had to make sure you hated me. I had to make sure you would be more determined than ever to find me, so that you would come when it mattered. But you don't look at me like that anymore. I think you know there's more to the story.'

'Well, I'm sure we'll be all ears. You'll have every opportunity to tell us what went on. Be sure to include why you didn't tell us the first time around — you know, when you had the opportunity *not* to go to prison.'

'I deserve prison. I always have. I didn't stop them. I helped them even. I should have done more then. But I've stopped them now. Now I get my time to repent my sins, to make my peace. Have you any idea how exhausting it is, trying to be someone you're not, day after day?'

George didn't reply. The adrenaline was wearing off and he was realising his own exhaustion. It was creeping back in. He longed to close his eyes to this day.

'Will it be you?' Roberts said.

'What?'

'The interviews. Like last time, I guess there will be interviews. Will it be you? I don't want to have to start again.'

'No. I'm done with it. There's a lot to do before anyone sits down in front of you with a list of questions and I'll be a long way gone by then.'

'I don't want to talk to anyone else.'

'You don't have to, Henry. There's nothing you can say that's going to make a difference anyway. Talk or don't, I couldn't care less.'

'I don't believe you. You want the truth. Isn't that what all police detectives want?'

'The truth doesn't matter, Henry. That's the real truth and I learnt it a long time ago. All I wanted was you in prison, Henry. I wanted those missing girls back to their families and the two today home safe. Nothing else mattered to me.'

'Just like that. On to the next case.'

'Not for me, Henry. I'm done. I guess that's all that's left when you see the real truth.' George regretted saying it as it fell from his lips. The last thing he wanted was to reveal anything about himself to this man.

'Because of this? Because of me?'

'Don't flatter yourself, Henry. It's been a long time coming. I guess I'm tired of seeing people at their worst. I'd rather go home and see the exact opposite.' George could see movement outside of the car. An officer walked past with a blood-splattered shovel in a clear plastic bag.

'To your family?'

'To a life.'

'It sounds like the right decision. For you, I mean. I wish you all the best, Inspector. Thank you for chasing me down. I tried to make sure you would be determined. I needed you to be on time.'

'On time? You made me wait for over an hour before I could get to you. If you wanted to set those girls free, if you wanted to be arrested why not take Cooney out earlier? You could have done that anywhere. Then walked into a police station with the girls.'

'That place, Inspector. It's my favourite place on earth. For just a few hours a day it can feel like the only place left on earth. I wanted that for one last time.' Roberts looked genuine. The intensity was still in his eyes, but his expression was sad; that vulnerability was back again.

Both front doors pulled open. They made George jump. The driver settled himself and clicked on his belt.

'Sorry about that, sir. You ready?'

'Yeah, we're ready.' The engine started.

'This is it, then,' Roberts said, still staring over at George.

'This is it,' George said.

'The end of the road. For us both.'

Chapter 39

When George finally slid the key in the lock to his own front door he took a moment to compose himself. He was emotionally and physically spent. It had been a long few days. And it had been a long few years since he had needed to shake off his day at the front door to protect his family. *His family!* It made him smile just to think about it. Suddenly it flashed through his mind that it was too good to be true. That every time something looked like it was going well with Sarah and Charley, something came along and messed it up. Maybe they weren't in there at all. Maybe Sarah had changed her mind. He had sent a text with a fifteen-minute warning like she had instructed. He didn't get a reply. Maybe he was going to go into a cold flat where he would find a hurriedly scribbled note of apology on the kitchen bench. He didn't think he could cope with that.

He braced himself and pushed the door. The warmth was the first thing that hit him. Then it was the smell. Something was cooking. He stepped through. Charley saw him. She looked like she had been waiting, she was in the corridor on the other side of the door. She was on him in an instant and damned near knocked him over. He couldn't speak. The emotion hit him harder than his sprinting daughter. He swept her up and hugged her so hard she made a sound like she was struggling to breathe. But she was laughing too. She kissed his cheek. She slid down him a little and hugged him right back. She pushed her head between his neck and shoulder and clung on tight.

'Hey, George!' It was his wife's voice. She stood at the kitchen island where the room opened up. George struggled to walk. He had to crook his neck to see past his daughter.

'Alright?'

All that time. All the practicing on the way home with what he might say to her first and that was all he could manage.

'Why are you barefoot, George?' Sarah looked amused.

He had ditched his shoes and socks a little while ago. He had rolled his trousers up a little way at the same time. He was still sodden in general and he knew he smelt funny. 'I've been in the sea,' he said.

'The sea?'

'Yep. And when I came out I'd lost my shoes, cut my shin and I seem to have a small child suckered to my neck.'

'That's why I won't go in the sea. You just never know what's in there.' They both laughed. It was genuine and natural.

'You baked?' George did nothing to hide his surprise. Sarah had never baked before. There was a tray on the bench. It looked like cookies.

'We baked! I got here. I didn't know what to do. So I panicked and I baked. It seemed logical.'

'How 1950s!' George grinned.

'I know! So what, you don't like cookies?' Sarah said.

'You're kidding right? My house, my wife, my daughter and a fresh batch of cookies? This is living the dream!' George's phone was suddenly shrill in his pocket.

'Sounds like your dream is shattered.'

George ignored the phone. Charley slid down. She ran to the sofa and jumped on it. She was chattering with excitement. A children's television station played in the background. George couldn't stop grinning. It was everything he remembered. His phone vibrated. He pulled it out of his pocket. His phone announced that he had voicemail.

'I just have to play this back,' he said. He reached for one of the cookies. His wife slapped his hand playfully. His voicemail clicked in. It was John Whittaker:

'George. I got your letter, old boy. Load of old codswallop, I'm afraid. I can't make head or tail of it, man. Some rubbish about how you've lost your mojo, how you fancy yourself back in the normal world. Let me tell you, George, the normal world doesn't exist for people like you and me. Because we've seen it for what it really is. Our job is to keep it normal for the rest of them. So they don't have to see what's left of a young woman when you roast her in a box. You've a big heart, George. I know you take it all in, I know it weighs you down sometimes. It gets to us all. But this is what you are. This is what you do. The world is better because you're in it, chasing the bastards that would ruin it for everyone else. Now. I will see you Monday morning, my friend. We have a coffee machine to find and a piece of paper to shred.'

The phone announced, *end of messages*. George hung up. He threw the phone on the bench. His wife was watching him closely.

'John Whittaker,' George explained.

'What did he say?'

'That he's got my letter. And that he understands.'

Sarah reached out for his hand. She held it tight. George could feel the warmth. 'You meant it then? You don't have to do this. Not for us. I've moved past it. We managed to be a family before, we can do it again.'

'I'm not doing it for you. Not just for you. This is for me, Sarah.'

Sarah stepped in for a hug. He heard Charley jump off the sofa and run over. He felt her wrap herself round his legs. He never wanted it to end.

Chapter 40

'You sure you're ready for this?' Emma said. George looked over to the subject of her question. Dennis Coleman gripped tightly onto his coffee cup. His face looked a little washed out, his eyes were fixed. George didn't know if it was determination or fear. He guessed it was a little of both. Even under this much stress, he still looked better than he had the week before, when George had seen him last. Maybe it was just the shirt and tie.

'Let's go.' Dennis pushed the car door open at the same time as Emma. He was in the front passenger seat of the car and Emma had been driving. George pushed the rear door open and stood behind Dennis. Emma met his eyes across the car roof. Dennis was already walking towards Chloe Pope's family home. Emma looked worried.

'He'll be fine,' George muttered. They both lagged behind. Dennis was already at the door. He didn't get a chance to knock before it was opened for him. Mary and Colin Pope stood together. Colin had his arm round his wife, his grip so tight their shoulders were bunched together.

'Dennis!' Mary looked exhausted. She freed herself from her husband's grip and reached out for him. She hugged him firmly. Colin gave a tight-lipped smile. The tension was tangible.

'You'd better come in.'

The Popes stepped back into their home. Dennis lingered on the step. He took a deep breath and looked back to Emma. Then he stepped in. Emma stepped in next and George followed. The Popes were already seated in their living room. They sat on the edge of their sofa, their hands tightly entwined.

'Thank you all for coming up here today,' Mary said. 'We both appreciate it.' George noticed that she held something in her free hand. It was a well-worn photo. He could only see flashes of a young, blonde woman smiling out from its cracked surface, facing up towards her mother. 'I know you have news. Have you found her? Have you found our little girl?' Her eyes dropped to the photo. Her other hand lifted, still gripped in her husband's as if they were praying together.

'Yes,' Dennis said. The couple collapsed. The stiffness and the tension left them all at once. They both flopped forward. Tears followed quickly from both. They embraced each other in a tight hug. Neither could speak. After a minute or so George stood up.

'Does anyone mind if I put the kettle on?' Mary looked over. She shook her head. 'I don't suppose you've got any cheap and nasty biscuits do you, Mary?'

Mary snorted a laugh. Her face was a big smile. George didn't think he had ever seen one bigger. 'See what you can find!' she managed. Her husband wrapped her back up in his arms. Dennis wiped at his face too. It was the right time for George to leave the room. He was only a bit part in all this. The pain that he was witnessing dissolve just a little bit in front of him had been building up for nearly three years. He was filling the kettle when Emma

330

joined him in the kitchen. Her eyes were red too. They looked heavy with emotion.

'You don't have to fight it, Emma. These are emotional times. You and your people did some incredible work.'

'I'm not fighting it. I'm happy for them. They finally got her back. I'm happy for Dennis too. I think he needed this as much as they did.'

'You might be right. Maybe he can leave some of his demons behind now.'

'Thank you, George. I know I haven't said it.'

George smiled. 'You don't need to. I may have got in the way more than I helped at points, t—'

'You did!' Emma cut in. 'But we needed that. I think we needed someone to get in our way a bit. I know I did. I just wanted you to know . . .' She was struggling for the words.

'I do, Emma.' George carried the drinks back in. Mary and Colin had recovered enough to speak.

'On the phone. You said it wasn't as clear as you thought. About that . . . that animal. What did you mean?'

Dennis took a deep breath for a second time. He had insisted on the way over that he wanted to be the man to tell them.

'We can no longer be certain that it was Henry Roberts that killed your daughter.' George could see that Dennis had braced himself and he allowed a pause for their reaction. He got a stunned silence. 'If it were my daughter, I would want to know.'

'What . . . what do you mean?'

'He was involved. There is no doubt about that. He is now talking to officers so we are getting a much better picture. He has been interviewed a number of times this week. He wouldn't talk at all at first, but Inspector Elms came back up and was able to convince him to tell us what happened. Or at least to give us his side of the story.'

'And you believe him?'

331

Dennis licked his lips. 'I do.' He turned to George. 'We all do.' George felt both sets of eyes on him. He nodded his head. George could see that Colin's demeanour was starting to change. His breathing was becoming quicker and he let go of his wife's hand to make a fist. George stepped in.

'I know this is a shock. Dennis here can tell you the full story. There is justice at the end of it. A version of it at least. Just hear him out.'

Dennis had been dallying. He seemed to take the hint. 'Henry Roberts owned property. Or at least his family did. Some were straight rentals, some were operating as care homes. He upgraded some of his stock at the same time. He changed the heating systems and ended up with a number of old industrial-sized water tanks that he was storing at his home. He put word out that that they were for sale. They were made of copper and worth quite a bit. Liam Cooney replied to that advert. That's how Henry Roberts met Liam Cooney.'

'Water tanks and Liam Cooney? What is all this about? Who killed my daughter?' Colin's breathing was faster still. Mary grabbed his hand again. She held it tight.

'Colin, let him speak. I want every detail. That's what we've always asked for.'

Dennis wrung his hands before continuing. 'Liam Cooney was already very close to John Lawrence, who you know well. John Lawrence was accused of sexually assaulting teenage girls who were part of his choir or congregation. We know that for a fact. Just this week we have been able to identify half a dozen. None of the girls wanted to say anything, they were too scared. They knew Lawrence's place in the community. Chloe . . . she was the first person to stand up to him. She told him she was going to the police.'

'John Lawrence killed her?' It was Mary's turn to interrupt.

'No. But he may have assaulted her — indecent assault. Then he asked Liam Cooney to kill her. Henry was asked to help. If you believe Henry's story he thought he was there just to scare her. They used one of the water tanks I mentioned to conceal the evidence after.'

'Conceal the evidence? What does that mean?'

Dennis hesitated. 'They were able to change the shape somewhat. Then they set a fire under it. Extreme heat ruins any forensic opportunities.' The couple collapsed again. Dennis continued before they had a chance to come back with any more questions. Dennis seemed to have skilfully avoided the Brazen Bull.

'From what we now believe, Liam Cooney was made of evil. He made detailed drawings of torture methods, devices and kept a diary of his wishes. He stalked one of his other victims for well over eighteen months. He wrote out his plans for her, for what he would do to her. I have never seen anything like it. He was a depraved fantasist and Lawrence and Roberts were able to assist him in making his fantasies come true. So depraved was he that we now believe he was involved in the death of his own mother.'

'Oh the Lord have mercy!' Mary uttered.

'And potentially the murder of Roberts's mother to prevent her from changing her will. Roberts was used for his size. He's struggled to fit in anywhere his whole life and Lawrence saw that and sold him a very warped version of Christianity. He also convinced Roberts that silencing Chloe was right for the church. When Chloe was killed, Roberts wanted out. But Cooney wanted to hurt more. It woke something in him, a deep desire. He demanded Roberts help him. Roberts saw the only way to get out was to go to prison. He shaved his head and got a distinctive tattoo. Then he used his own van for the girl who got away. He tells us he faked it — he *let* her get away. He knew she would be able to identify him. He wanted to be caught. As you know, Roberts is a wealthy man. He hatched a plan to get himself out. He knew he was sick before he went to prison. But he paid off a doctor to fake medical notes and screening results among other things to make it appear far worse. He didn't eat either so he looked emaciated. He used Cooney and Lawrence to assist. Lawrence went along with it to be rewarded financially, Cooney so he could continue his killing. Roberts convinced him to wait until he got out of prison — then Cooney could kill and the police would blame Roberts — who had nothing to lose. Once he was out of prison he convinced Cooney that Lawrence was intending to speak to the police, to make sure Cooney went to prison too. Cooney was already mistrustful — he was paranoid. Cooney nailed Lawrence to a cross and broke both his legs with a shovel so he would suffocate under his own weight. Cooney had already kidnapped two more girls at this point. He took them to a remote spot on the coast where he was planning on torturing and killing them. Roberts bludgeoned Cooney to death using the flat side of the same shovel. He made a phone call alerting police to where he was and then he sat and waited for them to arrive.'

It was clear that Mary couldn't take it all in. Her mouth opened and closed like she was gasping for air. Colin fared a little better but he still took a few seconds to reply.

'So what — he's a hero now, is he?'

'No. He's a long way from being a hero, Mr Pope. He's a convicted criminal who will spend the rest of his days in a high-security prison. He's still a murderer. He does have cancer, but it's treatable. He will live a long and miserable life. He signed every penny of his family's wealth over to his brother after he helped the police find him. He has nothing left. Henry Roberts snatched those women, including Chloe, so that Liam could live out his sick fantasies. He will face justice for that. He said he will spend every day repenting of his sins and pleading for forgiveness. Cooney and Lawrence are already facing up to their sins. But their judgement is in the pits of hell where they will spend their eternity. I take comfort from that. I can't imagine what you might take comfort from, but I wanted to come here today to give you some closure. To give you some understanding of exactly what happened. This will be a long investigation, we're still piecing it all together but this is essentially where we are.'

Colin had noticeably backed down. Mary shook her head silently from side to side. George knew a shell-shocked couple when he saw one.

'This is a lot to take in,' George said. 'You will have questions, I'm sure of it but they will probably come later. How about we all leave you alone for a little while? Let it all sink in. When you want to speak again you just need to pick up the phone.'

'Absolutely,' Emma said. 'You have my number. Use me as your contact. I will be up to speed with the very latest but also if you have any questions at any time.'

Mary managed a rushed nod. Colin stood up. He tucked his shirt back in forcibly and offered his hand. 'Thank you. I know this has been hard. On us all. But you found her. We will always be in your debt for that.'

George stepped back out into the pleasant spring sunshine. Dennis was last out. He looked different. Maybe it was the sun hitting his face but he looked less burdened. He stood taller. He walked easier. They walked to the car.

'You want me to drop you back to your car then, George?' Emma said. 'You're sure you won't come for a coffee?'

'I'm sure. Thank you, though.'

'And this is definitely it, is it? You're out?'

'Yeah it is! I retire officially in thirty days.'

'This case has claimed a lot of good officers.'

'It wasn't just this case, Emma. I've been considering it for a long time now. It's right for me. I don't like who

335

I've become. You might not believe this, but people used to like working with me!'

'I do find that a little hard to believe! So what? You think you can just walk away from all this?'

'I think I can. My daughter sees me as a postman. She said I look good in shorts. I think I might give it a go!'

'George Elms the postman . . . I'm not sure I can picture that.'

'Well, one thing we all know, the world's full of surprises.'

'We'd better get you back to your car then. So you can get back to Langthorne.'

'Well actually, my family are up here. We thought we would get away for a few days and I happen to know this lovely little holiday home for rent. It overlooks the River Wye. It's in a beautiful little place — a million miles from serial killers and torture methods. Symonds Yat, it's called. You might have heard of it?'

THE END

Thank you for reading this book. If you enjoyed it please leave feedback on Amazon, and if there is anything we missed or you have a question about then please get in touch. The author and publishing team appreciate your feedback and time reading this book.

Our email is office@joffebooks.com

www.joffebooks.com

21558576R00203

Printed in Great Britain
by Amazon